The Contractor Stories

DAN HOLOHAN

So this is how it all started ...

In 1996, a couple of nice guys approached me about writing a monthly column for *Contractor* magazine. I asked what they wanted me to write about and they said they'd love to hear me tell some good stories about contractors and what happened to them along the way. I could even make some parts up if it helped the story along.

Who could say no to that?

Anyway, they kept me around for 67 issues until a new owner came along and had the good sense to fire us all. I complimented the new guy and left with the stories.

So here they are, together again after all these years.

I hope you enjoy meeting these folks as much as I enjoyed telling their stories. I've changed all the names, of course. You would have done the same if you had met them.

– Dan Holohan

Zack the Ripper

Zack the Ripper had no idea what he was looking at but he was not about to let that simple truth stand in his way. The device (whatever it was) was large and dark. It hung heavy from the basement ceiling, an ancient heating artifact from a time long gone. Zack the Ripper didn't have a clue, so he began to mumble to himself. This was his reaction to any unfamiliar heating device. Stare, and mumble with authority. Then rip it out. This was always an easy decision to make because Zack the Ripper figured that if he didn't know what something was, it couldn't possibly be important. And if it wasn't important, then it had no business being there. "Why mess with the unknown?" he said to the guys at the supply house. "It's better to rip it all out and start from scratch." Which is how he got his name.

"Any idea what this thing is?" David the Caretaker asked.

"Of course!" Zack the Ripper exclaimed. "I see these things all the time."

"Well, what the heck is it then?" David asked, scratching his head.

Zack the Ripper pretended that he hadn't heard David the Caretaker's follow-up question because he needed a few moments to come up with a plausible name for this unknown hunk of cast iron. He feigned intense concentration and continued to mumble to himself with great authority.

"Zack?"

"Oh, I'm sorry," Zack the Ripper said, turning his attention away from the strange device. "I was lost in concentration. I was thinking back to an earlier time – a time when men installed these devices every day of the week. Oh, what a time that must have been!"

"But what is it?" David the Caretaker again asked, his curiosity growing.

"It's a Steamencabulator," Zack the Ripper said in a matter-of-fact way. "It was patented by the Brooklyn Steam Company in 1920. Contractors used them in mansions like this one and they installed them when the building was being built because there was no way you could get them in afterwards. Look at the size of that thing. It's obvious that you have to build the house around it. This Steamencabulator is as old as this house. There's no doubt about that."

"But this house was built in 1895," David the Caretaker said. "You said the device was patented in 1920."

"Oh," Zack the Ripper said. And then, quickly recovering, he added, "Of course this particular Steamencabulator was one of the Brooklyn Steam Company's early prototypes. I mentioned that. It's obvious by the markings. I'm sure I mentioned that."

David wasn't sure if he had mentioned it. Maybe he had. Zack the Ripper was mumbling, and it was entirely possible that he had explained all of this already. David accepted that possibility. "And you've seen these before?" David asked, needing a bit of reassurance regarding Zack the Ripper's ability to deal with a Steamencabulator.

"Oh, yes. Many, many times," Zack the Ripper lied. "They're very dangerous, you know. I strongly advise that you allow me rip it out and bust it up. It can cause terrible damage to the house if it's left in, you see."

"But this Steamencabulator has been here for more than a hundred years," David the Caretaker said, concerned, but also confused. "The house has heated beautifully for all this time. We just have a little bit of knocking in the pipes now. That's the only complaint that Mr. and Mrs. Vanderpool have. Why are you saying that this Steamencabulator is dangerous?"

Zack the Ripper went back to staring intently at the device and mumbling with even greater authority.

"Zack?" David said, but Zack was staring a hole through the device and mumbling faster than ever. "Zack?" David the Caretaker tapped him on the shoulder.

"Yes?" Zack the Ripper said, turning suddenly toward David, as if coming out of a trance. "I'm sorry. I was thinking back to an earlier time – a time when men installed these devices every day of the week. Oh, what a time that must have been!"

"Zack, how do you figure it's dangerous. I mean, after all these years?"

Zack the Ripper stared at David the Caretaker. "David, there has been a recall," he said with great authority.

"Not the sort where you get a new Steamencabulator, or recompense in any way. It's too late for that. They just say that all Steamencabulators must be removed from the field. And we should waste no time in doing so." Zack the Ripper began to pace the boiler room with great urgency.

"Who says?" David the Caretaker asked, more confused than ever.

"Why, the company says," Zack the Ripper replied.

"The Brooklyn Steam Company is still in business?" David the Caretaker asked. "After all these years? They're still around?"

"Well, they're not actually in business anymore. Not directly anyway. A company that was then bought by another company was bought and then they bought them, and you know how it goes with Wall Street and whatnot. It's business. Mergers and acquisitions and mergers. Right?"

"Huh?" David the Caretaker said.

"Well, I believe I have a memo back at my office. I got it some time ago. It's an old memo, yellowed with age. I got it from my supplier. The memo clearly states that all Steamencabulators must be ripped out, busted up, carted away, and replaced with brand-new hot water heating systems. I can start ripping this stuff out first thing in the morning."

"But how does a Steamencabulator work?" David the Caretaker asked. Zack turned his total attention back to the old iron device. He stared long and hard at it. Zack the Ripper would never let on that he didn't know what he was looking at because he knew that this would indicate a serious state of technical weakness. And rich folks such as the Vanderpools, who could afford to have caretakers watch over their homes, didn't do business with tradespeople who were technically weak. So, on most days, Zack the Ripper found himself lying a lot.

"How does it work?" David the Caretaker asked again.

"Generally it works just fine!" Zack the Ripper said. "But when they're recalled they must come out. Like this one. Sixty-seven thousand five hundred dollars should do it. I can get started first thing in the morning. How does that sound?"

"I mean how does it operate?"

"It encabulates the steam, of course," Zack the Ripper said simply. "Hence the name. These old systems required constant encabulation, hence the device. But this one is obviously no longer able to perform the encabulation function, and that's why you have that banging noise that the Vanderpools are complaining about. It's also the reason for the recall. I can start ripping it all out first thing in the morning. Sixty-seven thousand five hundred dollars. Sound good?"

Now, Zack the Ripper had said all of this so simply and with such authority that David the Caretaker was beginning to feel somewhat technically ignorant. He thought that he, David, should probably know what "encabulate" meant, but he had now gotten to the point where he was afraid to ask. He was, after all, the caretaker. He was supposed to know about stuff like the encabulation of steam and such. He was supposed to be a Jack of all Trades. If word got back to the Vanderpools that he didn't fully understand the technical workings of their old home and its mechanical systems, well, then that would indicate a serious state of technical weakness. And rich folks such as the Vanderpools, who could afford to have caretakers, wouldn't want a caretaker that was as dumb as a rock.

"I see," David the Caretaker said. "Well, give me a moment to check with the Vanderpools and I'll be right back to you.

Mr. Vanderpool was reading a novel in his study. David tapped on the door and approached. Mr. Vanderpool put down his book and gave David a broad smile. "Yes, David! Come in, come in. Have you gotten to the bottom of this noise problem we're having?"

"Yes, I have, Mr. Vanderpool. The problem is with the Steamencabulator, which has been declared dangerous and must be removed immediately. The situation is quite perilous."

"Oh, my! What shall we do?" Mr. Vanderpool asked with great concern.

"I have an expert in the basement right now and he can get stared ripping it out first thing in the morning."

"By all means then, have the man do it!" Mr. Vanderpool instructed.

Before he was through, Zack the Ripper managed to squeeze another seventeen thousand bucks out of the job. He also got paid for removing a 300-gallon copper storage tank that had provided domestic hot water for five generations. "This tank is made from a very dangerous material!" Zack had explained David. "Look," he said, holding a magnet to the side of the copper tank. "It's so old that it's lost its magnetism! It could explode at any moment."

"Rip it out, Zack," David had cried. "Please!"

So Zack the Ripper did.

Total Recall

When it comes to what he perceives to be a personal screwing, Marchesi has total and absolute recall. Although he is in his late-seventies, and although he can't remember where he parks his car from time to time, Marchesi will never forget the time they sent him those circulators with the plastic couplers.

"A dozen of 'em, they send me!" he tells Anthony, who is his grandson, and who, at 20 years old, is still learning the plumbing and heating business. "Your fadda takes one look at them plastic couplas and figgas he's gotta give 'em an extra twist. Just to make sure deys tight, right? I mean, dese dings look like toys, right? They're plastic! So your fadda gives 'em a twist before he sends 'em out wit da men, and sure enough, dey break as soon as dey get on the job. I call Joe Schwartz at the wholesaler. You remember Joe? No? Well, he's dead. But back den, he calls this stinkin' rep and the rep tells Joe that he'll give us new couplas, but he ain't gonna give us no labor for changin' 'em. I tell Joe I ain't never gonna buy nothin' from dat rep again. And I ain't since. And you should do the same, Anthony. Never ever forget. And never forgive."

Anthony nods. "When did this happen, Grandpa?"

Marchesi's eyes go wide. "October seventeen, nineteen seventy-four." He slams the palm of his hand on his desk. "I remember like it was yesterday. You ask you fadda about it. He was about your age at the time. He'll remember."

Anthony met up with his father later that day. They were looking at a steam boiler replacement job and Anthony was learning how to watch out for things that could leap from the dark corners of a basement and bite an unsuspecting contractor in the wallet. Al, Anthony's father, was pointing out a pipe that dipped under the floor. "That's bad," Al said. "I remember once when we had one of those pipes and it leaked. The water in the boiler flowed right down into the floor and the lousy low-water cutoff didn't shut off the burner. That boiler cooked itself real good and broke. The rep came out to look at the mess and he told me that the homeowner didn't blow-down the low-water cutoff often enough. Then he tells me that the factory ain't responsible. He leaves me holding the bag with the homeowner. I never felt so stupid in my life, and I never bought another thing from that guy. And you know what? Even though he's retired now, I won't buy a thing from his son either."

Anthony nods. "When did this happen, Pop?"

Al doesn't even hesitate. "January twenty-seventh, nineteen eighty," he says. "I remember it like it was yesterday. You were just a baby then, but I'll never forget."

"Was that the same rep that sent Grandpa the circulators with the plastic couplers?" Anthony asked.

"No, that was a different outfit. We don't do business with them anymore either. In fact, they don't even handle that line of circulators anymore, but we still don't do business with them. I don't care what they're selling. I'm not interested in anything they've got."

"Who's got the circulator line now?" Anthony asked.

"Another rep's got it but we won't do business with them either. And that's too bad because I happen to like their other lines. The fact that they handle those circulators puts a bad taste in my mouth, though. And then there's your Grandpa to consider. It would kill him if I did business with any rep that handled that line. Your Grandpa's got a memory like an elephant when it comes to stuff like this, Anthony. And he brought me up to think the same way. The bottom line is this. You don't ever do business again with a company that screws you once. You know that old saying, Fool me once, shame on you. Fool me twice, shame on me?" Anthony nods. "Well, we believe in that, Anthony. Your Grandpa and me. We believe in that. And so should you. People don't screw us more than once and get away with it."

And Anthony makes a mental note of this.

On the other side of town, Marge Harkin stops in to check on her father, Marty, who has lived alone since his wife passed away. Marge is concerned about Marty because he has been very forgetful lately. When he stopped by to visit her last week, Marty couldn't remember where he had left his car keys. They wound up being right there in the pocket of his trousers and Marty felt silly when he realized this. Marge is now wondering if Marty, who is in his late-seventies, should still be driving a car. She doesn't know how to bring up this subject, though, so she makes him his lunch instead.

"Did you have breakfast this morning, Dad?" she asks.

"I did," Marty says, "but it was very early. I can't sleep late like I used to. I get up earlier and earlier since your mother's been gone."

"What did you fix for yourself?"

Marty starts to answer, but then he closes his mouth and turns his eyes toward the floor. He shakes his head in frustration. "Isn't that terrible?" he says. "I can't remember. I think it was cereal." He shakes his head again.

"It's okay, Dad," Marge says, the sadness creeping into her voice. "I forget things too. We all do. It's okay. There's nothing wrong with you. You just have a lot on your mind, what with Mom being gone and all." Marty shakes his head. Then shrugs. Then goes back to watching the television.

Marge walks into the kitchen and opens the cabinet door under the sink to get a pot. She notices that the trap is dripping water. "Dad," she says, "I think we're going to have to call a plumber. This pipe is leaking." Marty comes into the kitchen, bends over with a bit of effort, and looks at the spot under the sink where Marge is pointing. "See it?" she says. He nods and agrees that Marge should call a plumber.

"That's more than I can handle at my age," Marty admits. "Call someone, but whatever you do, don't call that bum that screwed us with the boiler back in January of nineteen eighty. That's when we were still in the old house. Remember? That boiler nearly burned the place down. And then that bum who had installed it shows up with this other idiot in a suit from the factory and they both try to tell me it's my fault. We're supposed to open some valve, they tell us. We're supposed to flush out some crap. Every week we're supposed to do this, they tell us. I tell him I go to work every day, and that your mother's got arthritis and she can't turn no valve handles, but they keep shaking their heads no. I wound up having to get another contractor in to replace that boiler. Remember that? That guy really screwed me good. And I ain't gonna do business with that company ever again. You call whoever you want, but don't call those stinkers, okay?"

"Okay, Dad," Marge says. "What was the name of the bad contractor?"

"Marchesi. And you keep that rotten name in mind. When I'm dead and gone you should never do business with them. Tell the kids too. Never again Marchesi. Never!"

"Okay, Dad," Marge says, and she makes a mental note of this.

A Song for Christmas

Missy's father slipped into death at the Veterans Administration hospital on a gray day when the wind blew cold from the northwest, as it so often does on Long Island. He was alone when he died. The family had stepped out for a much-needed break and he chose that exact moment to pass on, as so many veterans do.

He had taken a long time to die. He had Alzheimer's disease, which can be a bit comical at the start, but quickly develops into the most miserable sadness imaginable. During the early days, someone would say to him, "How about a beer?" and he'd screw up his face as though he was a contestant on a quiz show and answer, "Who?" Everyone in the room would chuckle and then someone would say, by way of explanation, "Not who, Pop, what. A beer. Would you like a beer?" He'd shake his head and laugh at himself, not quite sure what was happening to his mind. Then he'd accept the beer, but in a childlike way. He'd look at it for a while before taking a sip, as if he wasn't quite sure what was expected of him. Alzheimer's can turn something as simple as a cold beer into a riddle.

There was a day when he got in his car to drive his wife to work. He had retired from his job as a butcher, and he was spending most of his days looking over the racing papers and sneaking off to OTB to spend small amounts of money that he had stashed away. He didn't think his wife knew about his stash, but she did. On this particular day, he waited for her in the car out there at the curb. He pumped his foot on the gas pedal, hoping the old car wouldn't stall, as it often did on cold days. He honked the horn a few times and cursed mildly under his breath. He no longer had the patience he had once had. The Alzheimer's was stripping away his patience and replacing it with layers and layers of confusion and anger. Finally, he drove off by himself.

She came out of the house and looked down the street. He was turning the corner. She somehow knew that, from this point on, nothing would be the same. She rushed into the house and called a taxi. The driver took her to where she worked, and that's when she saw him. He was walking around and around his old car, cursing in Polish, and slapping his strong hands on the hood, the roof, the trunk. She was supposed to get out of that car and go to work. That's what she did every day. But today he couldn't find her in there.

The family took away his keys that afternoon. He wouldn't speak to any of them for a long time. And then came the months in the VA. Everyone suspected that he wasn't coming out of there, but they hoped for the best nevertheless.

Missy took her father's passing the hardest. The family had done what they could to protect her from all of this sadness while it was going on, but in her own way, she knew exactly what was happening. People with Down's Syndrome are not unaware. They know. They're like tuning forks. "My pop pass away," she said on the day that the family returned from the VA. She could tell by their expressions. She knew. No one had to say anything. "My pop in heaven," Missy said. Her pupils waggled back and forth. That's how you know when she's confused. You look at her eyes. On this day, Heaven was confusing Missy. "I miss ma Pop," she said finally, and then she waddled to her mother who was now a widow. She put her pudgy arms around her mother's shoulder and patted her mother's hair. "I miss my Pop," she said, and this made her mother sob uncontrollably. Missy looked at her family. Her pupils waggled furiously.

They buried him in a Catholic cemetery near a stand of tall pine trees that once sheltered a farmer's field in the days when there weren't as many people on Long Island as there are today. On the way to the cemetery, the hearse disturbed a flock of sparrows in a bare maple tree by the side of the road. The birds burst into the air like feathered fireworks and this made the widow smile in a way that was filled with faith and with hope. Her husband had been a bird lover and she, from inside her rented black limousine, grasped at this on that sad, gray day. "That's Pop," she said in absolute conviction as she pointed toward the soaring birds. "Look," she said. "It's Pop." And that was how she gave her man back to God.

On a cold Christmas morning, the year before, Santa Claus had left a toy violin under the tree for Missy. The violin was one of those electronic wonders that played music by itself whenever you touched it in a certain way. Missy particularly liked the way the violin played "Turkey in the Straw" when she drew the bow across it. She played this tune over and over and it could really get on your nerves if you were with her in an overcrowded house on a rainy day. Someone would eventually divert her attention while another would swipe the batteries out of the toy.

This didn't stop her, though. She'd waggle her eyes, tell you to buy her more batteries, and then she'd start singing that same old song. She didn't have enough memory to remember all the words so she'd focus on just one or two out of the entire tune and wail these over and over again while stroking the battery-less violin. "Turkeeeeeeeeeeee. Strawwwwwwww. Turkeeeeeeeee! Hayyyyyyyyyy!" And she could go on like that for quite some time.

One day she told the family that she wanted to play her violin for her father. "Your pop's in heaven," she was told. "I go cemetery!" she insisted, and then she went upstairs to practice some more. As the weeks went by, Missy grew more and more insistent about playing for her father. The family made as many excuses as they could but finally gave in as Christmas approached. After all, they had to make a visit anyway, so why not?

It was cold the day they went to the grave. The wind blew hard from the northwest, as it so often does on Long Island. There was snow on the frozen ground and it reflected a dull white light upon all of them. Missy, bundled in clothes that never seemed to fit as they should because she is so short, waddled from the car to her father's stone. She looked down and began to play. The family stood and listened to her wail the words to that old tune. Turkey in the straw. Turkey in the hay. She played with great earnestness, bundled small against the cold, a child in a tiny woman's body. This was her gift to him – the very best she could do. The wind came and picked up the notes from her toy violin. It blew them into the cold, white air, like a flock of sparrows exploding from a bare maple tree.

When she was done she turned and looked up at her family from inside her hood. The pupils of her eyes were rock steady. And for the briefest moment, by looking into those eyes, you could see straight into her perfect soul.

And there was an angel in there.

Moonlighting

Frankie and Mr. Neeley looked at each other and they could each see the larceny in the other's eyes. Frankie glanced cautiously around the boiler room, even though he and Mr. Neeley were the only people in the house. Then he lowered his voice. "You know, Mr. Neeley, my boss would fire me if he knew I was saying this." He looked over his shoulder again – just to be sure. "But between you and me, his prices are ridiculous. I mean, the guy's a real rip-off artist. He charges, like, twice the full list price for parts, and then more than anyone else in town for labor. And he pays us guys peanuts. He sits in his fancy office and collects all the money while we bust out butts out here for next to nothing."

Mr. Neeley gave Frankie a knowing nod. "How about if you come back later when you get off work and do the job yourself? I'll pay cash and no one ever has to know."

Frankie smiled at his co-conspirator and asked, "How about if I come back tomorrow? That's my day off. Would that be okay with you?"

"Sure," Mr. Neeley said. "Tomorrow's just fine. I can let you in, but then I have to go out. You don't need me to be here, do you?"

"No, I don't need you to be here. And this isn't an emergency. It can wait until tomorrow. I'll be back first thing in the morning."

"How much you gonna charge me?" Mr. Neeley asked, wanting to make sure he was getting a good deal.

"I'll charge you half," Frankie said. "But you gotta promise never to say anything to anyone at my company. And there can't be any paperwork."

"What if something goes wrong after you leave?" Mr. Neeley asked. "What sort of guarantee are you gonna give me?"

Frankie wrote his name and home phone number on the back of a company business card. You just call me at home if there's a problem and I'll straighten it out. And if I don't, you can always call my boss and get me fired. I need my job because I've got a family. I'm not gonna mess with you."

"Okay," Mr. Neeley said, pocketing the card. "Just do the job right and we won't have any problems. I'll see you tomorrow."

"Okay, Mr. Neeley," Frankie said and started to leave. But as he was going up the basement stairs he added, "And if you have any neighbors that need work done at half-price, have them call me at that number too. But before you give out my name, make sure you can trust them."

They were going through the kitchen when Mr. Neeley said, "You know, now that you mention it, Jack McNab across the street has been talking about replacing his boiler. He's retired and I know he's home right now. Let's take a walk over there and I'll introduce you." Then Mr. Neeley grabbed Frankie by the arm and added in a whisper, "And maybe you could tack a bit more onto his bill and then take some off of mine. You know, like a finder's fee?"

Frankie smiled in appreciation of Mr. Neeley's larcenous soul and nodded. "I know exactly what you mean," he said. "How does fifty bucks sound? If I get the job, I mean"

"Fifty bucks sounds very good, Frankie. Very, very good."

As they were crossing the street, Frankie said, "Give me just a second to radio in." He jogged over to his service van. "I'll tell 'em you're jerking me around on the price and that's why I'm taking so long."

"But won't they want to know what's going on when you don't bring in the business?" Mr. Neeley asked, concerned that Frankie's possible dismissal from the company might screw up his own deal.

"Nah, my boss is an idiot. When I go back to the shop I'll just tell him that you decided to wait. You're one of those people that can't make a decision. You know?"

Mr. Neeley laughed and shook his head in appreciation of Frankie's creative nature. "You got all the angles covered, that's for sure!"

And then they were on Jack McNab's stoop. Mr. Neeley knocked on the door and a moment later McNab opened it. "What's up?" he asked.

"I wanted you to meet Frankie," Mr. Neeley said, pointing at the serviceman. "He moonlights and his prices are half what his boss charges. You can't go wrong with this guy. He's gonna do my job on his day off. I knew that you were looking to get your boiler replaced so I figured I'd put you two fellas together."

Mr. McNab, who was born with an ice pick in his back pocket, reached out and yanked Frankie into the house. "C'mon in, kid. Half-price, eh?"

"Half-price," Frankie said. "But you gotta keep it quiet. If my boss knew what I was doing he'd fire me in a New York minute." Frankie looked over his shoulder, and then winked at McNab.

"He'll never hear it from me, kid," McNab said.

A half-hour later, Frankie had McNab scheduled for a boiler installation on the following Saturday.

"You gonna have enough parts with you to do the job right, kid?" McNab asked.

"Oh sure," Frankie said. "I use my boss's stuff. He lets me take the truck home at night and on the weekends." Frankie winked at McNab. "He's a real idiot, my boss. Never does inventory. He says it takes too much time to count stuff. He says he trusts us." Frankie rolled his eyes and smiled at McNab, who smiled back.

"What he don't know can't hurt him, right?" McNab said.

"That's the way I figure it," Frankie said. "And if you know anybody else who needs good work done at half-price, let me know. There's a finder's fee in it for you." Frankie handed McNab a few of his boss's business cards with Frankie's home number on the back. "Just have them call and leave a message on the machine. I'll get back to them right away."

"You know, come to think of it, I do," McNab said, mentally spending the finder's fees. "There are a couple of guys down at my lodge who have been talking about getting some work done. I'll give them your card."

"But make sure you tell them not to call the number on the front of that card. That could get me fired."

McNab put his index finger over his pursed lips. "Mum's the word, kid. See you on Saturday."

When Frankie got home that night he and his wife Sandy had a nice dinner and then they went over the work schedule for the following week. "Are you gonna be able to get to all of this," Sandy asked. "There's an awful lot here."

Frankie walked around behind where Sandy was seated and looked down at the paperwork. He put his hands on her shoulders and massaged them gently. This made her purr. "Yeah," he said, "I can get to it all. It would be different if I was working for someone, though. I honestly don't know how those moonlighters do it."

"These customers all think you're working on your day off, though. Right?"

"Right," he said, bending over to give her a peck on her cheek.

"Did you price the jobs like you always do?" Sandy asked, working the numbers into her calculator.

"Yep," he said, clearing the dishes from the table. "I just doubled our going rate and then told each of them that I'd do their job for half-price, and on my own time. I told them that my boss is an idiot. The usual routine."

"And you told them not to call the number on the front of the card, right?" Sandy asked, pushing her eyeglasses up on her nose.

"The number for the answering service? Yeah. But none of them are gonna call that number."

"You think we still need the answering service people?" Sandy asked, turning around to face him. "Hardly anyone ever calls the answering service to complain. Maybe we should dump them. That could be extra money in our pocket, you know."

Frankie considered this for a moment and then said, "Nah, let's keep them for a while longer. They may not do much for the money we pay them, but they do add spice to the conspiracy. And everyone in America loves a good conspiracy. Especially when they're in on it."

Tom and Materials

Tom drove through yellow lights, and if no one was around, he'd even pass the red ones because he fully understood the value of his time. Why, just that morning he had pitched a fit at McDonald's because his Egg McMuffin had taken longer than he thought it should have taken to get from behind the counter to his mouth. "You call this fast food?" he had shouted at the pimply manager in the McDonald's uniform. "What are they doing back there? Waiting for the chicken to lay an egg? Let's move it!" The startled manager backed up a step. So did the people on line. Most folks are willing to give way to a screamer, and when it comes to his time, Tom can scream better than most.

"It'll just be a minute, sir" the pimply kid sputtered.

"Well, let's move it!" Tom shouted. "My time is valuable, you know. If I wanted to wait, I'd go to a real restaurant!"

Tom is one of those guys who can drive a truck with his thighs as he blows the steam off the surface of McDonald's coffee with one hand, while jamming a McMuffin into his mouth with the other. He zoomed past a yellow light and leaned on his horn with an elbow. Time was money, and Tom had no time to waste.

The only thing that could slow Tom's frantic movement toward his next customer was the actual sight of that customer's house. A calm would descend upon him like quiet snow as he strolled up the front walk toward the house. This happened because, at that point, the meter was running. And when the meter was running, time became a thing to be savored, like a fine Cuban cigar or a vintage Bordeaux. No hurry. No . . . hurry. There's allllll the time in the world.

Mrs. Bender answered Tom's lazy knock with an urgency that could only be explained by the immediacy of running water. "Oh, I'm so glad you could make it here so quickly," she spurted. "Please come in." She pushed the door wide and urged Tom in with a waving hand. "Follow me," she shot back over her shoulder as she headed down the hallway.

"What's wrong, ma'am?" he asked.

"It's the sink!" she exclaimed. "There's water squirting from under the sink!"

"Which sink?" Tom asked.

"In the kitchen!" Mrs. Bender said. "Here! It's squirting. See?" She pointed at the water that was pouring from the cabinet.

"Let me take a look," Tom said. "And by they way," he casually mentioned before opening the cabinet, "I'm only going to charge you for the material I use and however long it takes to fix this. Is that okay with you?"

"That's fine with me!" Mrs. Bender shouted. "But please, please, stop it now! It's ruining my floor."

"I'll . . . get . . . right . . . to . . . it," Tom replied in a dreamy way.

He gazed under the sink and then stood up like a senior citizen getting out of a wheelchair. He turned and strolled to the basement stairs. Mrs. Bender scurried behind him. He descended the stairs with care and hunted around for the main valve. When he found it, he twisted it closed with great care. This had an immediate calming effect on Mrs. Bender. She smiled at Tom and he smiled back "That's . . . better, isn't . . .it?"

"Oh yes!" Mrs. Bender exclaimed. "Thank you!"

"You're . . . welcome," Tom said. Then he slowly climbed the stairs like a stoned rock star going on stage. "I'm . . . going . . . to . . . get . . . some . . . materials . . . from . . . my . . . truck." He gave her a dreamy smile and headed slowly out the front door.

Tom had a truck filled with material. He used the most complicated components that he could find. His favorite notation on any carton was "Assembly Required." He liked to use products that were confusing. Once, while racing down the aisles at a local trade show, he had come upon a booth where a lonely rep was trying his best to promote a boiler that looked like a nightmare with pipes. Tom took one look at that boiler and knew for certain that this was the boiler of his dreams. In order to service the circulator on this boiler you would have to remove the boiler's jacket and separate the first two sections. And that would take time. Perfect!

While at that same show, Tom had also found a line of electronic controls that required the hands of a 12-week-old fetus to service. It would take sooooo much time to wire these things. And what could be better than that?

Tom slowly unloaded most of the contents of his truck onto Mrs. Bender's driveway. He lined up his materials in neat rows, and then he leisurely began to select what he would need to repair that leaky kitchen faucet. He chose a replacement faucet that had more parts than the space shuttle Endeavor. He loved this faucet because it would go off like a mousetrap if any homeowner attempted to work on it. And it cost a lot to replace!

He began to lay out the pipe he would need for this job. He figured he would replace the hot and cold supply lines all the way back to the water meter, and he would use galvanized pipe instead of copper to do this. He reasoned, and rightly so, that once a faucet goes, there's no telling what might go wrong next in the average house. Better to be safe than sorry. Better to change it all. Besides, material was what Tom had to sell. Material, and time of course.

He took out his hand-threader. Tom didn't like those newfangled power-threaders. Power-threaders make the work go so quickly. How the heck can a T&M professional make a living with a tool like that?

He took out his lead pot and his cast-iron pipe and fittings. Those PVC drainage lines would have to go. PVC is cheap stuff. Cast-iron is heavy, and heavy is good. And besides, cast-iron takes time to install. PVC is just noisy junk. It can go at any time. Better to do a thorough job and replace it all now while there was still time.

Tom began to wonder about all the things that might break once he started to touch pipe. You could never tell with a place as old as this one was. But he had enough material on his truck to handle most problems. And what he didn't have he could always get from his supply house. Sure, his supply house was 50 miles away in the next county, and he'd have to drive there, but that didn't matter much. After all, the meter was running, and Tom was in no hurry at all. He'd take his time going for those parts. He'd be the most careful driver on the road. He'd stop at every yellow light. He'd even slow for the ripe green ones.

Mrs. Bender watched Tom from her front door. "Excuse me," she said. "Do you have any idea how long this is going to take?" She looked at her watch. "Are you going to need all of that material?"

"Well . . . some . . . of . . . it . . . but . . . you'll . . . only . . . be . . . paying . . . me . . . for . . . what . . . I . . . use," he said

"And your time?" she wondered. "How much time will it take?"

Tom took his time looking up. He gazed at his watch. He quietly burped a bit of McMuffin. And he smiled a beatific grin. He nodded. And with the most sincere expression you can imagine, he declared. "It . . . is . . . so . . . hard . . . to . . . say . . . ma'am."

And he meant every word!

Who's Better Than Bitter?

Mr. Bitter looked at Mrs. Bitter and she glared at him in that special way that makes his stomach churn. He hadn't caused this problem, but somehow (as with all things mechanical) it was his fault. Now, if there had been no toilet paper on the holder, or soap in the vanity, or coffee in the cabinet, well, that would have been Mrs. Bitter's fault. However, if something should go wrong with the car, or if the garbage cans don't make it out to the curb on Tuesday and Friday mornings, Mr. Bitter invariably took the heat – automobile maintenance and garbage both being tasks of the masculine gender.

Mrs. Bitter threw up her hands in disgust and glared at the radiator. "We need this right now?" she shouted. "Why is this happening to me! Just look at what your leak is doing to my rug (rugs, being feminine)." She looked at him in a way that suggested that he had personally taken an ice pick to the copper tubing. Mr. Bitter stared at the water that was dripping from the elbow like blood from a wound, knowing that it was his alone. "I can't stand it!" Mrs. Bitter said. "Do something!" And she stormed from the room, leaving him alone with his drip and his utter maleness.

Mr. Bitter went to the kitchen drawer and got the flashlight. He trudged back to the radiator, got down on his hands and knees, and played the light over the dripping pipe. It looked bad. There was a lot of algae-like crud on the fitting. And the rug (her rug) was getting soaked. There was no room under the leak for a bucket; the best he could do was to stuff some paper towels down there until he could figure out what to do next. He briefly considered tackling it himself, but there's immediacy to a leaking pipe, especially during the winter – and especially on a Sunday, which this was. "Better call a plumber," Mr. Bitter mumbled to himself.

Mrs. Bitter had gone upstairs to her bedroom, and he could hear her cursing both him and the leaking pipe from behind the closed door. He found the Yellow Pages, and since it was a Sunday, he picked the company with the biggest ad. "They should be able to come right away," he mumbled. "With an ad this big they should be on their way here already."

To Mr. Bitter's delight, the woman from the service company picked up the phone before the first ring had ended. She had a Sharon Stone voice that made his stomach churn, but not in the same way that Mrs. Bitter made his stomach churn. "Superior Plumbing," she purred. "We're better than you."

"Hello?" Mr. Bitter said. "Is this the plumber?"

"Yes, sir! This is Superior Plumbing. May I have your name, address, and telephone number please. We have a Hydraulic Technologist in your neighborhood right now, and I can have him at your home immediately. May I have your name?

"It's, ahh, Bitter." Mr. Bitter said.

"And your address and telephone number, Mr. Bitter?" she cooed. He gave up both of them without much hesitation. Her voice was as smooth as water running over moss. She could have talked a dog off a meat wagon with that voice.

"Mr. Bitter?" she said after clearing a few more preliminaries and chatting about his leaking pipe and wet rug.

"Yes?"

"While we've been chatting, our global-positioning satellite has repositioned one of our most qualified Hydraulic Technologists onto your driveway. He's out there . . . right now, sir." She paused and he found his heartbeat quickening. "He can be at your front door in seconds." He was starting to sweat. "With all his tools, Mr. Bitter." He was feeling very much like a schoolboy. "But first, Mr. Bitter . . . Before we can begin . . . I need you to approve our two hundred forty-nine dollar Visitation Charge."

"Huh?"

"It's for the visitation, Mr. Bitter," she explained. "May I have your checking and saving account numbers, please?"

"For what?" Mr. Bitter asked, feeling less like a schoolboy, now that she was grabbing for his wallet.

"And a major credit card, please?"

"Wait just a minute," he sputtered. "Two hundred forty-nine dollars! That sounds like an awful lot of money to fix a small leak."

"Oh, Mr. Bitter!" she giggled. "That not to fix the leak. That's for the visitation to your home and for the diagnosis.

Our Hydraulic Technologist won't be able to give you the actual charge for fixing the leak until he's able to analyze the leak. At that point, he'll be able to issue a prognosis and explain our fee schedule."

"But two hundred forty-nine bucks just to show up?" Mr. Bitter stammered. "That seem like a lot. How can you justify such high prices?"

"We don't have to justify our prices," the woman with the Sharon Stone voice explained simply, and ever so sweetly. "We're Superior Plumbing. We're better than you. I had hoped that this was clear from the start. Wasn't it?"

Mr. Bitter hung up the phone, but it rang before he could remove his hand. He jumped, as though bit by an electrical shock. "Mr. Bitter," the woman with the Sharon Stone voice said (and she said it so sweetly). "I still need your credit card information."

"How did you get this number?" he asked.

"Why, you gave it to me, silly!" she cooed. "I won't keep you. I understand that you may not want us to fix the leak. I still need your credit card information, however, so that we can bill you for the Conversation Consultation that we had."

He hung up the phone again. And it rang again. And again! He started to shake. "Answer the damn phone!" Mrs. Bitter shouted from the top of the stairs.

"I can't," he shouted back.

"Why not?"

"It's her."

"Who?"

"That Superior woman."

"Who?"

"The plumber," he shouted back.

"You hired a woman plumber?"

"Would you let me deal with this? It's my problem. It's mechanical, right? I'll take care of it." He looked again at the dripping pipe and wondered who to call next. The drip seemed to be getting worse, and the sun was getting lower in the late-autumn sky. He heard a mechanical grinding coming from somewhere in front of his house. He parted the curtains and watched in horror as this squeaky clean Superior Plumbing truck hooked up to his old Chevy sedan. He had never before seen a plumbing service truck with a full towing rig. He flung open his front door and shouted at the driver, who was wearing a white shirt, a powder-blue tie, creased trousers, a uniform jacket with the name SUPERIOR stitched across the back, and highly polished shoes. "Hey, what the hell are you doing with my car?" Mr. Bitter shouted.

The Hydraulic Technologist gave him a smile and a friendly wave. "We're holding it for lack of payment, sir," he explained. "I'm told that you refused to give our Telephoknowlogist your credit card information so that we can bill you for her Conversation Consultation."

"But you people didn't do anything!" Mr. Bitter screamed.

"But sir, our time is worth money," the HT said with a smile. Then he hopped into the driver's seat and starting towing the old Chevy down the driveway.

"Wait!" Mr. Bitter pleaded. "I'll pay." He fumbled in his wallet for his MasterCard. "Here, take it. How much did you say? Two forty-nine? Take it. Just leave my car."

"Thank you, sir!" the HT said. "I'll run your card right away. There's the two hundred forty-nine-dollar Visitation Charge. Plus eighty-eight dollars for the Conversation Consultation. And ninety-nine dollars for the towing. That's on special this week, you'll be happy to know."

"Towing charge?" Mr. Bitter said.

"Yes, sir," the Hydraulic Technologist said. "I'm afraid that once we hook up, it becomes official. It's all done by computer." He shrugged.

Mrs. Bitter was now at the front door. "What's going on here?" she shouted. "Are you people going to fix this leak? I want this leak fixed now before it ruins my rug!"

"Well, that's an official approval if ever I heard one!" the HT said, pocketing Mr. Bitter's MasterCard. "I'll just hang onto this for a while, sir. Our price for fixing a leak is seven hundred ninety-five dollars. And even if it takes me all day to get it done, you won't pay a penny more. That, of course, includes our Visitation Charge, and our Conversation Consultation charge. The towing charge, I'm afraid, is extra. But it is on sale this week!"

"How can you people get away with this?" Mr. Bitter sputtered.

The driver smiled and adjusted the Windsor knot on his red tie. "We're Superior Plumbing, sir," he said. "We're better than you. That should have been clear from the start. Was it not?"

Through the Eye of a Needle

To Johnny, the house looked like a rotting tooth in
the neighborhood's smile. This place hadn't seen a coat
of paint in generations and he groaned at the thought of
what he might find in the basement. He hated these jobs.
You had to fight your way through piles of old newspapers
and worry about rodents taking a bite out of your hand
when you reached around the furnace. But these were the
cards that life had dealt him that day, so he marched up the
broken walkway, stepped carefully onto the rotting porch,
and knocked on the scared front door. The woman who
answered his knock looked like she had seen all the misery
there is to see in this world. Two small girls clung to her
legs and stared up at Johnny with childlike curiosity. They
had hair the color of corn flakes and they were wearing
tattered jackets. Johnny glanced past the trio and into the
hallway. The plasterboard walls had holes in them, and the
rug looked like woolen vomit. "I'm here to fix the heat?" he
said simply.

"Oh, thank you so much for coming so soon!" the
woman exclaimed. "It's so cold outside tonight and I was
so worried for my babies. Please, please, come in. Can
I take your coat?" Johnny hesitated, and then shook his
head. He was concerned about where she might lay down

his coat if he offered it to her. He didn't want to leave this place with anything that he didn't arrive with. The woman, instantly understanding his hesitation, nodded in quiet embarrassment. "Let me show you where the furnace is," she said. "And thank you so much for coming." She moved off down the broken hallway. The bundled children followed, hanging onto her pant legs and glancing backward at Johnny, as if he were the most exciting thing that had happened to them in months. "It just shut off and it won't come back on for us," the woman explained, pointing to the furnace and sounding exasperated.

"Let me get in there and take a peek," Johnny said. He looked it over and sighed. This was a furnace born out of wedlock. It looked like it had been rode hard and put away wet for years. "It sure is an old one," Johnny sighed.

"I know," she answered, embarrassed by the condition of the furnace. "I hope it's not too much trouble. Can I get you something to drink?" she asked from over his shoulder. "Maybe some coffee? It's so cold outside tonight. You must be tired from having to work so hard at night. I could make some coffee. It's no trouble at all."

Johnny considered the probable condition of the cup in which that coffee would arrive, and then he shook his head. "Thank you, no. I'm fine, ma'am," he said. "Really, I just had some before I got here. I'm all set. Thanks. I'll just get to work."

"Well, okay then," she answered. "But if there's anything you need. I mean, if you need to use the bathroom or the phone or anything, please help yourself. I'm going to take the children upstairs so that they'll be out of your way." Johnny thanked her and set about his work.

He was done in just over an hour. The old furnace was up and running as best as could be expected, and the battered house was slowly getting warmer. Johnny packed up his tools, walked upstairs, and wrote up the invoice on a small, metal clipboard. The woman smiled at him. "That didn't take long," she said. "I can't tell you how happy you made us by getting here so soon. The babies, you know? I worry about them so much. They were so cold." Johnny smiled and nodded, wanting to get out of that dirty house and back into his truck in the worst way. He handed her the invoice. "Oh!" she said, scurrying toward the bedroom. "Let me get my purse."

When she returned, she had his money, but she also had something else – two drawings on red construction paper. "These are from the children," she said, handing him the drawings. "They wanted to give you something because you made our house warm again." She giggled nervously. Johnny looked at the drawings. Both were of a stick figure bent over a box. "That's you," she explained while pointing at the stick figure. "And that's the furnace." She pointed at the box and giggled again. "Kids," she said.

"That's really nice," Johnny said, truly meaning it. "Can I tell the girls how much I like their drawings?"

"Oh, they've gone to bed," the mother said, pulling nervously at the plastic straps on her purse. "But I'll tell them in the morning that you were pleased." She closed her purse and set it on a deeply scratched end table.

Johnny counted the money in front of her, and then he looked up. "You gave me five dollars too much," he said.

The woman shook her head emphatically. "No, it's not too much," she insisted. "That extra money is for you. Thank you so much for coming so soon. We really appreciate it." Johnny tried to refuse the tip. He protested and held it out to her, but she put her hands in her pockets and laughed. "No sir!" she said. "You earned it! Every cent! Thank you!"

Johnny put the five-dollar bill in his shirt pocket, thanked her sincerely, and left.

He got home very late that night. His wife had been sleeping for hours. He showered quickly and then crept into bed beside her, not wanting to wake her. He stared at the ceiling for quite a while. Their furnace, a new one, came on with a soft purr. He listened to it for a while, and he stared at the ceiling.

A few weeks later, he was on the day shift. They dispatched him to the ritzy side of town and he liked that because you get to see some incredible sights over there. There is money in America, and rich folks sure do know how to live. That's one of the things that he liked best about this business. You never knew where you'd be working from one day to the next, and there is so much to see.

He rolled up in front of this great big place. He wondered what the owner did for a living. It looked as if money poured into this house like gravel from a dump truck. He pressed the doorbell and heard chimes sound from deep inside the huge home. A well-dressed woman came to the door. "Yes?" she asked curtly, giving Johnny a look that could have froze mercury. Her cold eyes swept over him, taking in his work boots, his uniform, his cap, his toolbox. "What is it?" she snapped, clearly annoyed by his presence on her property.

"I'm here to service the heating system?" he said simply.

"Oh," she said, suddenly remembering. "The maintenance man. Yes, well, go around the back." Then she shut the door in his face.

Johnny did as he was told. When he got to the back door, the woman had the door halfway opened for him. She stood behind that door the way a cop stands behind a plastic shield during a riot. "Wipe your feet before you come in," she scolded, flipping her manicured fingernails at his work boots. Johnny did as he was told. "The heater is down there," she said, waving toward the basement. "And don't come upstairs without permission. There are valuable things in this house, and I don't allow the help to go traipsing around unsupervised." Then she held up her chin as if she was waiting for a crown to descend upon her from heaven. He started to walk past her, but then he paused. "Do you suppose I could have a drink of water before I start? My throat's very dry."

The woman rolled her eyes and said, "Use the spigot out in the yard." She gestured with annoyance in that general direction. "And make sure you don't track any mud into the house when you come back."

Johnny sighed softly, and then he did as he was told.

As the water from the spigot splashed over his face in the cold February air, Johnny thought about little girls with hair the color of corn flakes, and he thought about grace. He also thought about how very difficult it would be for a camel to pass through the eye of a needle. And then he wiped his feet on the hard stone and went back to work.

Something Fishy

When Mike walked through the door Kathy immediately knew that his day had not gone well. Married folks can sense such things. He had this broken look on his face. She flew out of her chair like a blonde cannonball and wrapped her arms around her man. "What's wrong?" she asked, placing a cool palm on his cheek. "Something bad happen to you, Mike?"

Kathy has these Christmas-morning eyes that can bring joy and hope to even the most battered soul. Mike looked deeply into his wife's eyes and drew happiness back into himself. She saw that he was going to be okay so she hugged him once more and led him to the kitchen table. "Someone refuse to pay you?" She could somehow tell.

Mike nodded. "Yep," he said, and then he shook his head. "I spent an hour bleeding radiators. I had to move most of the furniture in the house. Then the guy tells me he's not paying."

"Did he say why?" Kathy asked.

"He said that I tracked some mud on the rug and that I put a smudge on the wall. He was going to have to have the rugs shampooed and the whole place painted. I didn't do it, Kathy. I swear I didn't! He said that I should consider myself lucky that he doesn't sue me. And he told me that I could go ahead and sue him. He didn't care. He's an attorney. Like I'm going to take the time to get involved with this bum, right? I'm going to go to court over a hundred bucks? Like we have the time for that, right?" He shoved the newspaper across the table.

"How old was this guy?" Kathy asked, touching him lightly on the back of his hand.

"Early-thirties," Mike answered. "He's one of those Yuppies. He's got a BMW in the driveway that probably cost more than I make in a year. He's got leather furniture, gold-plated fixtures in the bathroom, and he won't pay me." Mike, who is as honest as an iron girder, shook his head sadly.

"Is he married?" Kathy asked.

Mike started to laugh. "Why? You interested?"

She gave him a sly look, "Nope, just curious."

Mike thought for a moment, "I'd say no. I didn't notice any pictures of a wife or kids around the place. In fact, the place looks like it could be in Playboy magazine. It's a real shag pad."

"Did you go into his bedroom?" Kathy asked.

"Yeah, I had to move this big brass bed out of the way so I could get at the air vent on the radiator. That headboard must have weighed a thousand pounds. I broke my hump for that guy and then he refuses to pay me."

The anger rose in Kathy like mental illness. "I'm going to fix this guy for you, Mike," she said.

"What are you going to do, Kath?" Mike asked.

"Something fishy," she said, and then she gave him another hug.

Now, you need to understand that when it comes to revenge Kathy is as patient as death. She waited two full months before making the phone call to Vincent Perrini, Attorney at Law. "Hello, Mr. Perrini!" she chirped into the phone. "This is Kathy from Kathy's Cleaning Service. We're calling members of the legal profession today. I'd like to offer you an absolutely free spring cleaning of your entire home."

"What's in it for you?" Vincent Perrini, Attorney at Law, asked suspiciously.

"Well, Mr. Perrini, this may sound a bit gross to you but my company specializes in cleaning the homes of crime victims. We basically mop up after someone has been murdered. It's a tough job, but someone has to do it. All of our business comes to us by word of mouth and we find that we get most of our leads through attorneys such as yourself."

"I don't practice criminal law," Vincent Perrini, Attorney at Law, said. "I'm strictly civil law."

"I understand that, sir," Kathy replied, "but you do have occasion to speak with your colleagues, right?"

"Yes."

"Then all we ask is that you mention our thoroughness when you're speaking with them. And I promise you that our spring-cleaning is absolutely free to members of the legal profession. We're here to impress you, not to charge you!"

Kathy's perkiness was irresistible, and since Vincent Perrini, Attorney at Law, could find nothing wrong with her proposal, he agreed to let Kathy into his home on the following Saturday. "I have to be there while you're working, though," he said.

"That will be great!" Kathy said. "That way you can see how thorough we are."

She arrived at his home at 9 AM and scrubbed the place for five hours. After the first two hours, Vincent Perrini, Attorney at Law, lost interest in watching Kathy and went about his business. That's when Kathy worked the big brass knob off the top of the leg of Vincent Perrini's headboard. She held the trout headfirst over the gaping hole in the brass pipe and let it ooze down. It fit perfectly! She replaced the knob and continued her work. When she was done, she left through the rear door.

Two nights later, Vincent Perrini, Attorney at Law, got lucky down at Hounds & Foxes, the club he liked to frequent. He put the key into his front door and escorted his new lady friend into his manly living room. She immediately scrunched up her pretty nose. "What's that smell?" she whined.

Vincent Perrini, Attorney at Law, sniffed the air and nearly gagged. His shag pad smelled like the inside of Jeffrey Dahmer's refrigerator.

"I'm outta here," the young woman shouted. "I'll call a taxi from my cell phone. You're a real slob!"

Vincent Perrini, Attorney at Law, slept alone and in great discomfort that night. He tossed and turned in his big brass bed, trying to imagine what could be giving off such an incredibly foul stench. He got up several times during the night and poked around under the bed and in his closets. He checked the toilets. He looked in the fridge and in the oven. He found nothing, of course.

The next morning, he tried to call Kathy's Cleaning Service but there was no listing for such a service in the telephone book. And the woman had not left a calling card. Strange, but didn't she say that she did business by word of mouth? He never had any intention of recommending her, which was why he had not asked for a business card in the first place, but still, she should have left one.

He called Fred, his next-door neighbor, and asked if he could stop by and take a whiff. Fred, who happened to be an outdoorsman, covered his mouth with a handkerchief and advised Vincent Perrini, Attorney at Law, to call an exterminator. "It smells like a couple of warthogs set up a love shack in here," Fred said.

The exterminator came, took a whiff, and demanded payment up front - to which Vincent Perrini, Attorney at Law, reluctantly agreed. Two hours later, the exterminator came up absolutely empty. "Beats me what it is. I can't find any animals in here - alive or dead. I suggest you call an exorcist." The exterminator gagged his way down Vincent Perrini's front walk and drove away.

All of this, of course, was affecting Lawyer Perrini's sex life. Nubile women no longer cared to venture any closer to Vinnie's bedroom than the sidewalk in front of his house. His most recent almost-a-conquest clicked her way down his sidewalk on her spiked heels and shouted over her shoulder. "Your house smells like a thousand buttholes, Vinnie!"

"I gotta move," Vincent Perrini, Attorney at Law, finally admitted to himself.

He found an apartment that afternoon and signed a one-year lease. He would try his best to sell the house, but he knew it was not going to be easy. Meanwhile, he checked in at the Holiday Inn.

When Allied Van Lines showed up for the furniture, the men gagged for a while and then went to work. This would not be the first slob they had moved.

The first thing they loaded onto the big truck was Vincent Perrini's big brass headboard.

Kathy waited for Mike to arrive home from work. When he walked through the door she quickly examined him for damages and then slid into his arms. "How was your day?" she asked.

"Today was good," he said. He was tired but satisfied because he had done right by people that day. He had done good work and they had all paid him promptly that day. Life can be so simple when people show respect for each other. "What's for dinner?" he asked.

"Fish," she said simply.

Rupinski's Revenge

Rupinski had to do something about the business he was losing to a severe geography problem. A big home center had just landed with a great WHUMP! two blocks north of his supply house and all that orange was making Rupinski squint. He could hardly get into his own driveway on most mornings because of all the backed-up traffic that was trying to wedge itself into the home center's parking lot.

Last Tuesday, Rupinski drove by the home center and counted 16 plumbing and heating contractor trucks in that big lot. He went around and put potatoes in every one of those tailpipes. They were big Idaho potatoes and they made a juicy squish when Rupinski shoved them deeply into the round hot metal. Then he strolled around and smeared K-Y jelly on the driver's side door handles. "That'll give 'em something to think about," he muttered. Rupinski next aimed his huge bulk at the automatic doors and set out to do bad things to as many people and products as he possibly could on what was, for him, a slow Tuesday morning.

He headed up the first aisle, which was filled with light fixtures. No one could hide in such an aisle, he thought.

Rupinski immediately spotted a guy who owed him money. "Hello, Harry," Rupinski growled at the plumber who had his hands on a big orange shopping cart. "Shopping?"

A few minutes earlier, Rupinski had put small pebbles between the caps and the Schrader valves of Harry's four truck tires. Harry would find out about this on Wednesday when it would be raining harder than it does in Brazil. For now, Harry just stared wide-eyed at Rupinski. It was the same stare you might offer your wife if she had just caught you under your desk with Monica Lewinski.

"Oh!" Harry peeped, taking a disowning step away from the big orange cart. "I didn't expect to see you here." A bit of spittle flew from Harry's mouth and landed on Rupinski's white shirt. Rupinski looked down at the spittle and then glared back at Harry.

"Shopping?" he growled.

"Oh, no!" Harry sputtered, taking another step away from the incriminating cart. "I was just . . . looking. I had some free time on my hands. Things are a bit slow today."

"This your stuff?" Rupinski roared, pointing at the heating products in the big orange cart.

"This? No! I don't know who's buying this stuff. What is this stuff anyway?" Harry peered at his selections, trying to make them as unfamiliar as possible. "I've never seen any of this stuff before! I don't know how it got here." Harry bent down and pretended to tie his shoe, did his best to avert Rupinski's glare, tired to become invisible.

"Uh, huh," Rupinski rumbled, looking down at Harry the way you might view a cigarette butt in a urinal. "Well, then I guess I'll see you around, Harry," Rupinski concluded, placing his beefy hands on Harry's orange cart. Harry stood, chuckled nervously, and scurried away, leaving Rupinski with his cart. Harry figured he could come back later for the cart. He'd hang out in his truck for a while and come back later. Yeah, that's what he'd do.

Rupinski knew this, of course. He waited for Harry to turn the corner. Then he opened the box that held the small circulator Harry had planned to install later that afternoon on Mr. McFadden's old boiler. Rupinski took a wad of Bazooka bubble gum from his mouth and jammed it deeply into the circulator's suction hole. Then he walked away, softly whistling I'm forever blowing bubbles.

Rupinski found Jimmy in the next aisle. A home center guy in an orange vest was explaining about this 80-gallon water heater and getting ready to write it up for Jimmy. Rupinski hit Jimmy with a glare that nearly set Jimmy on fire. Jimmy took one look at Rupinski and thought about how brief his young life had been. He also remembered that Rupinski had just helped him size an 80-gallon water heater – this 80-gallon water heater, in fact. Rupinski raised one bushy eyebrow, which caused Jimmy to explode down the aisle. That left the home center guy talking to himself. When he realized that Jimmy had left, the home center guy wandered off after him. Home center guys are like that. They wander quite a bit, but Jimmy was already out in the parking lot, staring in horror at the sticky yellow stuff on his right hand that had just come off his door handle. What is it?

With the home center guy now gone, Rupinski took the opportunity to give the plastic drain valve on the bottom of the water heater a fatal twist. He also bent the stem on the T&P relief valve. "Substandard crap," he muttered and then he stood back and waited - the way a spider waits.

Before long, another wandering home center guy bounded up to Rupinski like a big happy dog. "Can I help you, sir?" he said.

"Yeah," Rupinski said. "My older brother has to take sitz baths because he's got these long anal warts, ya know? They hang out about this far." Rupinski splayed his thick thumb and forefinger about that far. "You never seen nothin' like these things. They're long, and red, and ugly as sin. What size water heater do I need for warts that size?" Rupinski let his right hand stray to his rump. He dug in and scratched around furiously. He made that face that guys make while doing this.

"Uh, I'm not sure," the home center guy sputtered. He looked down at Rupinski's busy right hand and made that face guys make while watching this being done.

"Not sure, you say?" Rupinski wedged deeper into his butt and grimaced.

"Uh, no. Sorry," the home center guy replied.

"Well, thanks anyway," Rupinski concluded, slowly swinging his right hand around and offering it to the home center guy. "I really appreciate what you people do," Rupinski added. "At least you try. Here, put 'er there, pal!" He grabbed the home center guy's hand with his own, recently excavated, right hand, and pumped it up and down. After a while, he let it go and smiled. The home center guy hurried off in search of hot soapy water.

Rupinski wandered up the next aisle where he spotted a small boiler on the lower shelf. Rupinski stared at it until another home center guy bounded over with an enthusiastic offer of help. This guy was about 19 years old, but his face was still in grammar school. "Help you?" the kid squeaked.

"Yeah," Rupinski said, pointing at the label on the boiler. "You can help me. What does this here mean?"

The kid leaned in to get a better look at the fine print. "That's BTUs," he declared.

"What's that?"

"What's what?" the kid asked.

"BTUs," Rupinski said. "What's BTUs?"

"Uh, those are the British Thermal Units, I think?" the kid said.

"Where are the other types?" Rupinski demanded, turning his big head on his thick neck like a turret on a tank.

"Um . . . other types of what, sir?"

"UNITS!" Rupinski shouted. "Do I look BRITISH to you?"

"Uh, no sir," the kid sputtered, taking a step backwards.

"Why don't you carry POLISH Thermal Units? You know . . . PTU? How come all you got here is BTU? Are you prejudiced? You got something against Polish people? Hey, I'm Polish!" Rupinski roared, moving in on him.

The kid started to dribble on his shirt, which made Rupinski move in even closer. And that's when Clancy, a plumber who owed Rupinski a considerable amount of money for more than 120 days, turned the corner and went pale as he spotted Rupinski's bulk bearing down on the home center kid. Before Rupinski could turn around, Clancy ran for the safety of his unlocked van. He glanced in disgust at the K-Y jelly on his hand, but nevertheless, quickly swung his wide butt into the cab, and onto about a half-pound of fragrant dog poop. In horror and confusion, Clancy started his engine and roared from the parking lot.

And that's when his potato-stuffed tailpipe exploded.

A Bit of Advice

Rocco held the beige receipt in his mouth while he fumbled for the key to his truck. He looked like an old dog delivering a newspaper. He had a fist for a face and he glared at the truck next to his. It was parked much too close. They never left him enough room. "They don't care," he muttered through the paper receipt. He wedged himself into the driver's seat and backed into the road.

A bit earlier, while he was waiting for Tommy to bring up his stuff from the back of the supply house, that new kid Greg had asked Rocco if he could pick his brain on some problem job. Greg has the wide-shouldered rawboned look of a farm boy who digs postholes all day. Rocco, who was leaning his elbows on the counter, like a man waiting for a cold beer, glanced at Greg and considered the question. "You got a problem on some job, kid? Gee, that's too bad."

"I know," Greg said. "But I'm trying my best to do the right thing. This is an old steam system. I was hoping you'd be able to give me some advice. I'm not sure what to do and I hear you've got a lot of experience with these old systems. I figured you wouldn't mind helping me out with a little advice, you know?"

"Advice?" Rocco said. "That what you're looking for?" He took off his eyeglasses and rubbed the bridge of his nose. Then he sighed and shook his head. "You sure you want it?" Greg nodded in a friendly way. "Okay, here's some advice for you. Go see your customer. Then tell the guy that he should fire you and hire me. How's that for advice?"

Greg clenched his jaw and narrowed his eyes.

"What?" Rocco barged on. "You don't like that advice, kid? Let's go over this together. You took on a job that you can't figure out. The way I see it, you've got no business being there in the first place. Tell the guy to fire you and hire me. That's my advice for you today." Rocco turned his head and went back to staring down the aisle after Tommy.

"That's the way you help your neighbor?" Greg sputtered. "You think that's neighborly?"

"It's every man for himself around here . . . neighbor," Rocco said without turning his head. "If you don't understand that, you're in the wrong business, kid."

Tommy came up the aisle with the box of Rocco's stuff. Rocco scribbled his name on the receipt and stuffed it into his mouth. He picked up the carton, looked at Tommy with disgust, shook his head, and kicked open the door.

Greg watched Rocco go and then he gave Tommy an exasperated look. Tommy just shrugged. "Rocco ain't one to share what he knows," Tommy explained. "You asked the wrong guy."

"Where does he go for advice?" Greg said.

"He comes here sometimes," Tommy said. "Not often, but every now and then. But you gotta understand our relationship is different. I'm his wholesaler. That's just like being his bartender. Mostly, I just listen while he works out a problem in his own head. Sometimes I make a phone call to a manufacturer for him, but mostly I just listen. He likes to hold his cards close to the vest."

"But why can't he share what he knows? I mean, suppose we all treated each other that way? How the heck would guys like me ever learn? I mean, how are we supposed to learn from our elders if our elders won't teach us?"

"Rocco will never share what he knows with you," Tommy explained. "And he ain't gonna share it with any other contractor either. And he certainly ain't gonna share it with any homeowner. Rocco likes to keep what he knows locked up tight in the ol' vault." Tommy tapped an index finger on his temple. "He's funny that way."

"Well, I think guys ought to share what they know," Greg said. "That's the only way this industry can grow."

"Rocco don't think that way," Tommy said. "He's a lone wolf." He tapped his temple again. "That vault's locked tight, Greg."

Greg nodded and shrugged. "Tommy, what do you know about steam heat?"

Tommy smiled. "Pull up a seat and tell me about what's going on." He gestured toward the worn vinyl stool on Greg's side of the counter. "Talk to me."

It was right about then that Rocco was arriving at Mr. O'Toole's house. Mr. O'Toole was a guy who watched those home-and-garden shows on the cable TV. Rocco had a particular hatred for those TV contractors. Those guys were willing to give up what was in their heads for free.

They were like magicians who gave away the secrets to the tricks. Rocco believed that the cable-TV contractors were ruining his business. They were turning all of America into a do-it-yourselfer's paradise. When Mr. O'Toole had called that morning he said that he wanted to speak with Rocco about something he had seen on one of those cable-TV shows - and a proposition. Normally, Rocco would have told Mr. O'Toole to see if he could get the TV guy to stop by the house with some advice, but business had been slow lately. And that's the only reason why he was walking up the O'Toole driveway that day.

Mr. O'Toole opened the door before Rocco had a chance to knock. He smiled at Rocco but Rocco didn't smile back. "What's up?" Rocco said.

"Well, I'm hoping you can give us some advice," Mr. O'Toole chuckled.

"Don't get married," Rocco said.

"Too late!" Mr. O'Toole said.

"Then don't have kids," Rocco advised.

"Too late again!" Mr. O'Toole laughed.

"How about this? Don't waste my time." Rocco turned to leave but Mr. O'Toole reached out and touched his arm.

"I have a proposition for you," Mr. O'Toole said.

"What?" Rocco slowly turned, giving the hand on his arm a menacing look. Mr. O'Toole let go immediately.

"Two of my neighbors and I just bought new boilers from Megamax. That's the new home center out by the highway?" Rocco nodded in a dangerous way. "They were having a great sale!" Mr. O'Toole exclaimed. "So here's the proposition. We'd like you to install one of those boilers - the one that's going into my house - and we'd all like to watch and ask questions while you work. You know, sort of like TV, but . . . interactive." Rocco continued to stare at Mr. O'Toole but said nothing. "And please don't get me wrong. We don't want something for nothing. We're willing to pay you for your knowledge. But only once. We're going to split the expense three ways. We're viewing this in the same way that a student would view tuition. We'll pay you for what you know, and then we'll take it from there. Sound good?" Mr. O'Toole gave Rocco a cable-TV sort of smile.

Before climbing back into his truck, Rocco had, of course, given Mr. O'Toole some free (and very graphic) advice about steel pipe, copper tubing, and the geography of the human body.

"And don't forget the flux," Rocco yelled as he backed out of Mr. O'Toole's driveway.

The following week, Rocco and Greg found themselves back at the supply house counter. They were waiting for Tommy, who was working on Greg's stuff this time. It was an awkward moment for Greg, not so awkward for Rocco.

"Can I ask you a question?" Greg finally said.

"You looking for some more advice, kid?" Rocco said, never looking up. "You don't give up, do you?"

"I guess I don't," Greg snapped. "I'll tell you what I'm wondering, Rocco. I'm wondering if you were ever young. I'm wondering if you ever asked someone for help and they turned you down the way you turned me down the other day. Did they make you feel stupid, like you made me feel stupid? I'm wondering how you came to know what you know without anyone's help, and I'm wondering how you managed to learn anything in a business that's filled with men like you."

Rocco turned toward Greg and his face held more pain than anger. His eyes were a bit damp, like he had an allergy or something. "Kid," he said, "you want the best advice I can offer you?" There was something not right about his voice either.

"Yeah," Greg snarled. "Gimme some advice, big shot!" Greg stood up straight, like he was getting ready for a bar fight.

"Don't get old," Rocco said softly, and the emptiness bloomed inside of him, as it had been doing for some time now. "Don't get old."

The Men From The Boys

Frankie the Ferret has the size and bearing of a bantam rooster. He's a tough little fist of a man, who has no check valve between his brain and his mouth. His partner, Big Gino, is about seven feet tall, and happens to be built like a pizza oven. They've been in business together for as long as anybody can remember and they've worked out an agreement over the years that suits both of them just fine. Frankie the Ferret does the under-sink work and wriggles into all the other tight places of the plumbing and heating world. Gino tends to the big nasty stuff.

If there's a circulator with a bad coupler, and if that circulator happens to be behind the boiler and under the basement stairs (as so many of them are), then Frankie the Ferret will somehow find a way to work his way in there and fix it.

On the other hand, if there is a cast-iron bathtub that needs to get from the truck to the third floor, Big Gino will crawl under it like a tortoise on steroids, stand up with an explosion of grunts and snorts, and stomp that tub all the way up the stairs, without once complaining.

All in all, this has been a good marriage.

When they go to a tradeshow (and they always go together), Frankie the Ferret and Big Gino have about as much finesse as a train wreck. They work their way down the aisles and let the purveyors of products know that things are not as good as they used to be. Most manufacturers' reps will take at least two steps backward, or find a sudden need to go to the restroom, when Frankie and Gino turn the corner.

And it was no different the other day when Vito, their supplier, held his annual show down at the Holiday Inn. Frankie and Gino showed up mostly for the free buffet and the beer, but also to let the reps know how very unhappy they were with just about everything that had been made by all factories during the past 15 years. Frankie the Ferret and Big Gino view reps as the Doormats of Life. And this day, it just so happened, was going to be a particularly muddy one.

Frankie the Ferret liked to go first. It was a little-man thing and Gino didn't mind it at all because Frankie usually had some great stuff to say right up front. He could hit a rep between the eyes with a nasty comment in no time flat. He'd have that guy sputtering for an answer before he could even catch his breath. When they entered Vito's annual show at the Holiday Inn the other day, Frankie headed directly for the display of toilet seats, which was right next to the free buffet and beer cooler. The rep backed up and tried his best to smile. Frankie ignored him, preferring to lay his hands on a gray plastic toilet seat.

"You see this, Gino?" Frankie the Ferret said, pointing at the plastic nuts and bolts that held the toilet seat to the display rack. "This is what's wrong with our industry and with all of America." Gino nodded ominously at the plastic bolts and nuts and then turned his gaze on the rep.

He looked at him as if he were a bowl of chip-and-dip that was about to be ravaged. "Any stinkin' homeowner can get these things off," Frankie the Ferret continued, giving the seat a smack with his hard little hand.

"I could rip those things off with my bare hands," Gino said, looking hard at the rep. Looking hard at the rep's ears. The rep gulped.

Frankie reached up and tapped the rep on his shoulder, grabbing his attention back from Big Gino. "Steak knife," Frankie the Ferret said crisply. The rep didn't get it so Frankie repeated himself, a little slower this time. "Steak . . . . knife."

The rep smiled that sincere smile that all reps are born with and shrugged, all the while taking a step further away from Big Gino, and nearly tripping over a plastic trashcan along the way. "I don't get it," he nervously admitted.

"Steak knife," Frankie repeated. "That's what the homeowners use to cut though these cheap plastic bolts." Frankie fingered the bolt and glared at the rep. "They use a steak knife. And then they go down to the home center and buy a new toilet seat for next to nothing because all they sell down at the home center is this plastic crap."

Big Gino moved in on the rep like a 300-pound exclamation point. "You and your plastic bolts are going to put us out of business!" he snarled.

"That's right," Frankie the Ferret agreed, moving in alongside Big Gino. "You're killing us with this crap. You know what you're doing to us? We used to be good for, what, four or five toilets on any given Saturday? Am I right, Gino?"

"Yer right," Gino said, nodding his huge head with bitter memory. "Four or five, every single Saturday. That was our bread and butter."

"But now we don't get none of that business because of your stinkin' plastic bolts."

"And the steak knives," Gino added.

"And the steak knives," Frankie agreed.

Frankie reached up and put a hard little finger on the rep's chest. "You know what separated us from them?" Frankie tapped twice on the rep's chest. It made a hollow sound.

The rep looked down, and then up, and then down again. "Us from who?" he asked innocently.

"Us pros from the amateurs!" Frankie the Ferret boomed. "The men from the boys! You wanna know what separated us?" The rep smiled nervously, the way reps do, and nodded frenetically to show that he was indeed eager to learn. "It was the SAWSALL!" Frankie shrieked. That's what separated us from the stinkin' homeowners. We had the Sawsall and they didn't." A wistful look crept onto Frankie the Ferret's face. He turned toward Gino. "Remember, Gino? Remember those days? Those were good days, weren't they?"

"Great days," Big Gino said. "The homeowners could never get those corroded metal nuts loose from those corroded metal bolts. They'd get frustrated and go after them with a hammer and a screwdriver. One good shot was all it took. That toilet would shatter like a pane of glass and the water would be all over the place. No one wanted to talk price when that happened. They just wanted it fixed - right now."

"And they didn't want us to tell the neighbor that they were idiots," Frankie the Ferret added.

"That's right," Big Gino said. "And there'd be four or five of those idiots every Saturday. We had the Sawsall. They had the hammer. The Sawsall separated the men from the boys, and life was good then."

"But you guys went and screwed it all up with your plastic bolts and nuts," Frankie the Ferret screamed. "Shame on you! Shame, shame, shame!"

And having said that, they exited the booth, leaving behind a sweaty rep. They continued down the aisle where they next spied a fresh-faced young man who was speaking of the glories of PEX tubing and radiant floor heating. Frankie the Ferret looked up at Big Gino and said, "Gino, remember how we used to jackhammer the copper pipe out of the floor and fix it?"

"I sure do," Big Gino said.

"Those were good days, weren't they?"

"They sure were," Big Gino agreed. "Jackhammers. That's what separated the men from the boys," he said

And then they went to chat with the fresh-faced boy.

The Perfect Gift

Vicki and Brad had been married long enough to fill the house with teenagers. She worked nights as a waitress in a local pub, mostly to help pay the tuition bills. He was a plumber and in his own business, such as it was.

Vicki wanted life to be easier for her boys than it had been for Brad and her. The two of them had been working around the clock for more years than she cared to remember. She worked nights and he worked days (and often nights) and they met in passing. A good marriage can put up with that, though, and theirs was a good marriage.

Vicki was about to turn 50, although her body looked years younger than that. She was one of those women who could eat anything and not gain a pound. And she had these cobalt-blue mischievous eyes that could speak without words. "How's today's special?" a guy would ask as he looked over the menu. Vicki would make this comical grimace with the corners of her mouth and let her eyes say the rest. The guy would get the message in a hurry and retreat to the safety of a cheeseburger. And he'd leave her a good tip.

In her mind, Vicki was still 25 years old and she was as in love with Brad as she had ever been. She took the time to laugh, and she knew that they would never be wealthy. She had accepted that years ago. They were rich in their own way.

Brad, like most small businessmen, put in long days that often melted into longer nights. His customers would call at all hours and Brad would grumble quietly but go out there anyway. Mostly, he did it for the boys. Brad wanted what Vicki wanted, and this was the glue that held them together through the tough times. They were all about their kids. Two years ago, when Brad had turned 50, Vicki had bought Yankee tickets for the whole crew. They had gone to the game as a family and they had made a memory. It was the perfect gift because Brad loves his Yankees, and so do the boys. It was the sort of gift that you'll always remember.

After the game, when they were together in bed, Brad had said to her, "You know, Vic, sometimes I feel like we're shooting arrows into the future. You and me are like a couple of compound bows," he said. "We get all the tension, but the kids get to fly. They're our arrows, Vic."

She liked that. It wasn't often that Brad said anything romantic. He was more about hard work and a pat on the butt as they passed in the hallway. She knew he was this way when she had married him, but calling the boys "arrows" had been sweet, and she would remember this all the days of her life.

Now, this birthday was looming and it was a big one. She knew that she'd be getting solicitations from the AARP soon. As far as she was concerned, they could stuff their Senior Citizen discounts. Vicki wasn't ready to start thinking of herself in that way. Besides, all she had to do was add up her hours at the pub last week to convince herself that she was far from retired. She decided that 50 was just a state of mind. It didn't mean she was old. It was just a number.

And she knew that Brad saw things the same way as she did. He was two years past 50 and complaining every now and then about his aches and pains. Vicki figured that the aches and pains had more to do with the hard work that he did than the number of years he had lived, and she would tell him that all the time. "It's a milestone," she'd say, "But we're not really old." And he'd nod mischievously, and take a swat at her butt.

Mostly, she was hoping that he would remember her birthday by doing something romantic. Maybe he would make a hotel reservation for an overnight in the City. They could have dinner and see a show. They could walk in Central Park. They'd leave the business and the pub customers behind for a day. And wouldn't that be sweet?

But that wasn't to be. Brad's customers kept calling, and the pub was too busy to give her a couple of days off. Besides, the tuition payments were due, so Vicky put her hopes for a romantic night in the City on hold. Maybe they'd get to do it once the kids were out of school and on their own.

When she came home from work on the night of her birthday Brad met her at the door and he was smiling like a boy. "Happy birthday, Vic," he said, and he gave her a kiss. "How'd it go tonight?"

She hugged him and said, "It was pretty good tonight. They had a cake for me."

"That's great!" Brad said, and he took her by the hand. "C'mon, I want to show you your present. Close your eyes." She let him lead her into the house. The boys were there too and they were as excited as Brad was. "Keep 'em closed," Brad said, and she did. He led her deeper into the house, the boys following at her heels. Vicki was thinking that this gift must be something very special, something romantic to make up for the missed trip to New York City.

But she also knew her house well enough to know that, when they reached their destination, she was standing with her husband and her sons, and with her eyes closed, in her bathroom. "Ready?" Brad said. "Open them!"

And she did. But she didn't see anything other than the familiar bathroom. "What do you think!" Brad said.

"About what?" Vicki asked.

"Your present!" Brad said, and he pointed to the new single-lever faucet and the handheld shower massager. "I've been working on it all night."

A part of Vicki, the part that had lived with this man for 25 years, wanted to scream. She had dreamt of flowers, and dinner out, and satin sheets, and her plumber husband had given her a new faucet.

"Here, look," he said, reaching in to turn on the water. "It's got all these different spray patterns." Vicki felt her heart breaking with disappointment.

"Isn't it great, Mom?" her oldest son said. "Dad says it's perfect for relieving tension when you come home from work. Look at the way that water comes out. Look at the way it taps. It's like getting a massage!"

"And look, Vic," Brad said. "I also got you these fluffy white towels for when you come out of the shower." He reached out with the towel, touched its softness to her cheek. "They're the big ones, like big fluffy sheets. You can wrap yourself up in them, Vic." And then Brad wrapped Vicki in the fluffy white towel, as if she were a little girl. It covered her from her blond hair to the backs of her knees. He held her in the towel, and in his strong arms. "You deserve the best, Vic. Between the new showerhead and these towels, you're really gonna be able to relax after a hard night's work. I didn't know what to get you, and then the boys and me thought of this. It's great, isn't it?"

And Vicki thought of all the years she had spent with this hard-working man. She thought of her life, and all that they had accomplished together, and she thought of her sons. He had called them their "arrows," and she did like a nice long shower.

"Isn't it great, Mom?"

She looked up at Brad and smiled with those cobalt-blue eyes.

"It's perfect," she said. And then she kissed him.

Crackerjack Riley

It was the beer, the peanuts, and the Ruffles that had caused Crackerjack Riley's belly to spread like the Mississippi Delta in springtime. That, and the baseball on the TV. Riley wasn't nearly as busy during the summer as he was during the winter, and there are about 10,000 ballgames to watch on cable. He'd flop on the couch like a piece of melted cheese on a hoagie roll and watch and eat and watch some more. And eat. This belly of his hadn't arrived overnight. It was delivered on the installment plan, one beer at a time. It crept up on him like the years, and he hardly noticed it. It seemed normal, like a backpack on a hiker.

Riley had played baseball in his younger days, but in recent years, he has been suffering from a severe case of gravity. Officially, he still has a 34-inch waist, but that waist is now considerably lower on his legs than it was when he roamed centerfield in high school. What once buttoned at the navel now buttons much further south, sort of in South Carolina, rapidly approaching Georgia. And that button is now perched in darkness, beneath a total eclipse of the beer belly.

Like so many guys his age, Riley still thought of himself as a 34-inch-waist guy. The "official" size of the waist was whatever it read on the Levis' tag at the back of his jeans waistband. This number becomes more and more important to guys as the years roll by. It's related to man's general unwillingness to step gracefully into the Land of Lard, which arrives along with the years. Man is very good at denying the reality of both age and tonnage, and Crackerjack Riley can deny reality with the best of them. The "official" size of the waist allows man to postpone reality. As long as he can officially maintain the size worn in high school, man is not truly aging. All man has to do to confirm his youth is to glance at his label.

So as the years add up, the pants slide down, and in this, there is a certain poetic balance.

"Hey, here comes Crackerjack," Mel the counterman said to his partner Tony. Mel jerked his thumb toward the window as Riley was sliding his 34-inch waist off the seat of his van. Riley's belly hung over his waistband like a triple scoop of vanilla ice cream on a too-small sugar cone. He had no idea that his nickname was "Crackerjack" because Mel and Tony kept that to themselves. It was their private joke. They had come up with it one morning when Jack turned his back to them and bent over with a grunt to pick up a receipt he had dropped on the floor. The butt crack appeared like the San Andreas Fault and the two men nearly choked with delight. Guys are like that.

Tony walked to the window, waved at Riley and smiled. "Crackerjack's jeans are pretty low today," he said. "He's gonna lose that wallet one of these days."

"What are you talking about?" Mel chuckled. "He's gonna lose those pants one of these days. If it wasn't for his work boots, I think he'd walk right outta them."

Riley was on the pavement and hitching up the back of his jeans. "Look at that magnificent butt crack!" Mel said to Tony. "Why, you could park a mountain bike in that thing." Tony nodded and smiled. "You could drop rolls of quarters down there for a week and never fill it up," Mel continued.

"You could shout your name in there and hear it echo for hours," Tony added.

Riley walked in and they stifled a laugh. "How ya doin' fellas?" he said. Mel and Tony greeted him and Riley sidled up to the counter. He rested his belly against the metal. "You guys watch the Yankees last night?" Riley shifted his belly and grabbed at his waistband. Mel and Tony shook their heads and smiled. "Well they looked real good last night."

"Nice jeans," Mel said, trying to get something going. "Where do you buy them jeans, Jack? You go to the Kids' section for them? They're kind of small, don't you think?"

Crackerjack Riley took a proud step backward from the counter and held his arms out to his sides, palms forward. "Small? No way! They're thirty-fours. Same size as I wore in high school."

"Didn't you use to wear 'em a little higher back in those days?" Tony asked playfully.

Riley looked down at his belly. "Wadda ya mean?" he said. "A thirty-four is a thirty-four. I haven't changed a bit. Hey, numbers don't lie. Look!" Crackerjack turned, and bent, and pointed at the label on the waistband of his jeans, which was only about two feet off the floor. "See what it says?" he grunted. "Thirty-four inch waist."

"Where the heck is my Cannondale?" Mel said.

Later that day, Crackerjack Riley went to see a new customer about a boiler replacement. He got to the house, hitched up his jeans and pushed his belly up the front walk. By the time he got to the door, he was huffing and puffing. He knocked and a man opened the door. "Hi, I'm Jack Riley and I'm here about the boiler."

"I'm Jim Farley," the man said. "C'mon in."

Crackerjack looked at Farley and noticed that he had quite a corporation sticking out in front of him. They were about the same age, and together they looked like two halves of a watermelon, but Riley wasn't conscious of his own hemisphere, only Farley's. Guys are like that.

"It's this way," Farley said, waddling down the hallway and toward the basement stairs. Crackerjack followed and noticed from the rear that Farley's pants were hiked way up. In fact, they were practically up to his nipples! Who buys this guy's clothes? Riley wondered.

They got to the basement and Crackerjack bent over to read the label on the old boiler. Farley backed up a step to give him room. The view Farley got from back there was similar to what tourists see when visiting the Grand Canyon. He was a bit shocked at first by the crack, but then he noticed the label on Crackerjack's Levis. Thirty-four inches. Farley was a forty-six. This guy seemed to be about his age. How had he managed to keep himself in such great shape? They were the same age, and yet he was bigger around the middle by more than a foot!

Riley pushed himself up and turned toward Farley. "No problem," he huffed. "I'll work up a price and get back to you later today."

"Can I ask you a question?" Farley said.

"Sure," Crackerjack Riley said.

"How do you keep yourself in such great shape?"

Riley gave Farley a smile and a wink. "I guess it's the physical work I do. That's one of the benefits of being in the trades. Here look." He turned and bent and pointed. Once again, Riley Canyon came into view. "A thirty-four inch waist! Just like in high school." He straightened up and in a most sincere way said, "Can I ask you a question, Mr. Farley?"

"Sure," Farley said.

"Who buys your clothes?"

"My wife does."

"There's your problem," Riley said, snapping his fingers. "You wanna stay in shape, you gotta do your own shopping. Here look." Crackerjack Riley grabbed hold of Farley's waist band on either side. Farley gasped. "Don't get nervous," Riley said as he yanked Farley's trousers down below the ledge of his belly. "Hold them here," he said, placing Farley's hands on the waistband.

Farley looked down in amazement. Suddenly, there was all this room! "There's your problem?" Crackerjack Farley said. "Your wife's been buying your pants too big." He pointed at Farley's navel. "This is your chest. It's about a forty-six." He moved his finger below Farley's belly and pointed at the new location of the now-too-big trousers, which was about two feet off the floor. "You've got a thirty-four-inch waist. Just like me. Look." Farley did. "Start buying your own clothes, Mr. Farley and you'll feel a lot better about yourself."

"You've got the job," Farley said.

In Hot Water

"Mr. Lunk is on the board, you know. His term runs for two years. He's a lawyer, you know. He's also as red as a lobster. It happened in the shower. It was the shower water that did it. He's as red as a lobster and mad as hell."

She had a face you could use to chop wood. She was sucking on an unfiltered Camel and blowing smoke out the side of her mouth. "He's going to sue someone, but he's not sure who would be best. Can you make a recommendation?"

"A recommendation?" Vito felt queasy.

"Yes, a recommendation as to who to sue." The Camel bounced as she talked. "Mr. Lunk's not sure if he should sue the Utility for providing the gas, the plumber for putting in the water heater, the electrician for wiring it, the manufacturer of the shower head for allowing the water into the tub, or the superintendent because he lives in the basement and is supposed to watch out for us. Or maybe he should sue all of them. What do you think?"

Vito, being an honest tradesman with a seasoned respect for apartment building psychopaths, began to wonder why he had shown up. She blew smoke and spit a piece of tobacco from her upper lip. "Mr. Lunk's one of the most active members on the board. Lawyers are so necessary nowadays, don't you think?" She hacked. "There are just so many concerns in a building such as ours. Having a lawyer who is also a tenant on the board saves so much time and expense, don't you think?" Vito half-nodded, not wanting to commit. "Accountants are also good, but lawyers are the best." She turned her head and hacked again. "So, who should Lunk sue?"

"Gosh, I can't say," Vito said. "I really can't. Why don't I just try to see if I can figure out what happened here."

"Are you an engineer?" she asked.

"No, ma'am."

"That's a pity. We can sue professional engineers, you know?"

"Why don't I just see about the problem. Would that be okay with you?"

She shrugged her shoulders. "That's why you're here, isn't it?" She lit another Camel. "Go see about it."

Vito backed away and took a look around. The water heater was fairly new. "The setting is right," he said.

"Then how come Lunk's as red as a lobster? Are you telling me he didn't get burned by the water first thing this morning?"

Vito walked over to a slop sink that was next to the water heater. He checked the temperature at the tap with a digital thermometer.

"The temperature seems normal," he said. "Here, look."

84

"You trying to make excuses for somebody? You got friends at the Utility? You trying to protect them?"

"No ma'am," Vito said. "I don't know anyone at the Utility! I don't want to know anyone at the Utility. Why would I want to protect somebody at the Utility? Against what?"

"Now what, who! Against Lunk! He's the one who's as red as a lobster. He's gonna sue somebody and it might as well be the Utility. They have all the money."

"I really can't go there, ma'am. Let me just do a little more investigating, okay?"

"Oh, just get to it then!" she said. "That's what we're paying you for!"

Vito looked at the boiler. They heated this New York City building with a one-pipe steam system. The boiler had a tankless coil and he wanted to see if someone might have crossed the pipes between the coil and the water heater. Co-op boards often have that done. They figure they're getting free hot water all winter long when they use the tankless coil in the boiler and shut off their water heater. They think that the BTUs coming from the boiler don't cost anything because the boiler is already making steam. They're wrong, of course, but a lot of contractors are willing to go along with a co-op board when it comes to stuff like this. But in this case, Vito saw that they had abandoned the tankless coil, so the water that toasted Lunk couldn't have come from there.

"And while you're here," she said, "tell me why this thing is so noisy."

Vito hadn't noticed the pump before. That can happen to a contractor when he's having a conversation with a member of a co-op board. It's possible to miss a detail like a 20-horsepower pump when the conversation turns to lawsuits.

"Do you have water pressure problems in this building?" Vito asked.

"Not any more," she said. "Not since we had that thing put in. We used to lose pressure at the showers and the sinks all the time. The damn kids would open the fire hydrants out in the street to cool off and we'd run out of water."

The pump was wired to a simple on-off switch. "It looks like this pump runs all the time," Vito said.

"Of course it does. We need the pressure all the time."

"How long has this been here?"

"Not long," she said, lighting another cigarette. "Why?"

"Because pressure-booster pumps that are set up like this can make water hot," he said.

She raised an eyebrow. "Who says?"

"I've read about this," Vito said. "A pump like this is supposed to have a pneumatic tank attached to its discharge. The tank gives the pump something to pressurize. And there's supposed to be a pressure switch to turn the pump off when the system pressure goes up. This one is just hot-wired into the cold water supply to the entire building. When no one's drawing water, the pump's impeller churns in the water." Vito made a round-and-round motion with his hands. "That motion can turn into heat if the water has no place to go. The bigger and faster the pump, the more heat you'll get."

"But there's no water heater attached to that pump," she said. "It's pumping cold water, not hot water."

"But there's friction," Vito said.

"Water's wet," she shot back. "You can't get friction from wet!"

"Yes, you can," he said. "I read about it in a book."

"You think this is what burned Lunk?"

"It could be," Vito said. "I don't see anything else that could have done it. I think the water got real hot overnight from the friction. And then Mr. Lunk got in the shower and opened the valve. Believe it or not, I've read that the water can get hot enough to cause a pump like this one to explode!"

"Oh, yeah?" she said.

Vito nodded. "Did the guy who installed this pump explain that it should have a pneumatic tank and a pressure switch?"

"Yes, he said that, but his price for all that extra equipment was outrageous. We're not made of money, you know. All we needed was a pump. That guy didn't know what the hell he was talking about."

"So you had him put it in like this?" Vito asked.

"Yes. It was less expensive this way."

"And he agreed to do it?"

"Well, he argued with us at first. He was trying to get rich off of us, but we won in the end."

"He shouldn't have put it in this way," Vito said.

"But he did," she said. "And now you say it was his pump that burned Lunk?"

"Well, it's not his pump," Vito said.

"It is now! And you're going to testify in court about this."

Vito shook his head. "No court. I don't want anything to do with this."

"You're in cahoots with that other guy, aren't you? You plumbers all know each other. We'll sue you too!" She lit another Camel and blew smoke in Vito's face. "You're all a bunch of idiots!"

Lonnie's Lucky Day

Lonnie had never won a thing in his life. He had given up on the lottery and refused to set foot in a casino when he went to the big trade show in Atlantic City each year. "Those casino people see me coming," he told his mother, "they reset the machines so that they'll fill with quarters until they break. I leave, everything goes back to normal."

"You ain't lucky," his mother said.

"It would be faster to just give my money away when I go there. I'll give it to the maids who clean the rooms - a dollar here, a dollar there. I'll give it to the old people on the boardwalk. Four quarters here, four quarters there. I'll say, 'Here, go use this in the machine. Maybe you can hit the jackpot. I sure can't.'"

"Lucky you ain't, Lonnie," his mother said. "You should leave the money here for me. I can spend it just as fast as the maids and the old people can."

"Yeah, but where's the excitement in that?" Lonnie said.

If Lonnie and his mother went out for a drive and got lost Lonnie would ask her which way to turn. He knew that if he chose left then it would be right. And if he reversed himself and picked right because it felt like it should be left then it would be left and he would have guessed wrong again. So his mother would pick and be correct about half the time, which was 50 percent better than Lonnie could ever do.

When he had gone into business he asked his mother if he could open the corporation in her name because of his being such a loser. "The IRS will audit me once a week if the business is in my name," he had told her. "Please let me put it all in your name." So she did.

Lonnie liked to get the cash up front from his customers because once people got a good look at Lonnie they knew that they could jerk him around real good. He had that Cheat Me look on his face all the time and the gloom came off him like BO. That's why he insisted on cash. You can't stop payment when it's cash. He wouldn't put wrench to pipe until he had the money in his pocket because he just looked so easy to screw with.

Of course, he always had to drop his prices because of this. His customers weren't stupid. They figured that if he was demanding cash up front he was probably not paying his taxes. And if Lonnie wasn't paying his taxes, they should get a big break on the job. Most Americans enjoy this sort of fraud and don't mind paying cash - if the price is right. Lonnie knew this.

The trouble, though, was that Lonnie did pay his taxes – every nickel of them. He paid because he knew that if he were to give tax fraud a try he would lose big time on his first attempt and spend the next few years in jail, probably with some new friends he really didn't need. So he paid his taxes like an honest American and he worked for hardly any profit at all because his customers thought he was a tax cheat.

When Lonnie got to the trade show in Atlantic City, some guy in a suit handed him a raffle ticket as he walked through the main entrance. "What's this?" Lonnie asked.

"It's a raffle ticket," the salesman said. "We're raffling off a boiler every day. It's free!"

"I'm gonna lose," Lonnie said, trying to hand the ticket back to the guy. "I've never won a thing in my life. If you were raffling off herpes, that I might win, but never a boiler. Here, give it to somebody else." He held out the ticket. "Give it to one of the maids or one of the old people out on the boardwalk. At least they stand a chance of winning."

The salesman shrugged. "What would a maid or some old fool on a bench do with a boiler. C'mon you're in the trade. You can use a free boiler, right? Install it on your next job and pocket all the money. Besides, everybody who comes to the show gets a ticket. It's our way of promoting our new boiler. Maybe your luck will change." The salesman turned toward the flow of people moving through the door. Lonnie looked at the ticket again. It read KEEP THIS TICKET along with these numbers: 091270. Hey, he thought, that's my birthday. September 12, 1970. How about that? Then he stuffed the ticket into his pocket and headed for the first aisle.

A few hours later, he was in a booth by the far wall. He was telling the pump salesman about all the problems he was having with their products when the announcement came over the public address system. "May I have your attention. We're about to pick the winner of today's boiler. You must be present to win. If you have the winning ticket, come to our booth to claim your prize." There was a pause and then the voice came booming out of the loud speakers again. The winning ticket is zero, nine, one, two, seven, zero. That's zero, nine, one, two, seven, zero. If you have that ticket, please come to our booth immediately."

Lonnie took the ticket out of his pocket and looked at it in astonishment. "Did you hear that number?" he asked the pump salesman. "That's my birthday!"

"No," the guy said, "I was listening to you complain about our pumps."

Lonnie nearly knocked the guy over in his haste to get to the boiler manufacturer's booth. He hadn't stopped there earlier in the day because he had heard lots of bad things about their boilers. He had never used one and swore that he never would because of the bad stories. Why take a chance?

But hey, free was free.

He raced into the booth like a marathon runner hitting the finish line. "I won!" he said. "It's me! I won! Look! First time in my life! I won!" The Vice President of Sales smiled and checked the ticket. Then he congratulated Lonnie, had some photographs taken for the trade magazines and gave Lonnie a letter that he could use at the wholesaler of his choice. The company would deliver the boiler to that wholesaler at Lonnie's convenience. Lonnie shook hands with all the salespeople and then rushed to the phone to call his mother. He wanted to tell her that his luck was finally changing.

The following week, he was sitting with Joe and Harriet Flug at their kitchen table. "You say this is a good boiler?" Joe Flug said.

"The best there is!" Lonnie said.

"And you've used these before?" Joe Flug said.

"Thousands of times," Lonnie lied.

"But you want cash up front," Harriet Flug said, looking hard at Lonnie.

"Yes, that's the way I work," Lonnie said. "Cash up front."

"You should take something off the price then," Joe Flug said. "A lot."

Lonnie figured that he could go real low on this one because he was getting the boiler for free. "I'll take three hundred bucks off the price," he said.

"Make it five hundred," Harriet Flug said, "and you got a deal."

"Okay," Lonnie said. "Five hundred, but it has to be cash and it has to be right now." And with that, the deal was done.

Lonnie was the happiest guy in town the day the wholesaler backed that truck with his free boiler up the Flug's driveway. The cash was in the bank, and even though he was wary of this manufacturer's products, he still smiled like a kid at Christmas. Hey, free is free.

He wrestled the boiler into the basement and spent the rest of the day piping it in. When he was finished, he invited the Flugs downstairs to inspect his work. They were happy with the new boiler, happy with the great price they had gotten and happy with Lonnie.

That night, as everyone slept, the Flug's new boiler sprang more leaks than a litter of new puppies, which was actually pretty lucky because the water was helping to contain the flames that were starting to come out of the primary control box.

Tom's Thumb

Tom parked his truck down the street from the McCabe's house and eyeballed the distance between him and the front door. He figured it was somewhere between 100 or 150 feet, give or take. Close enough, he thought. He opened the truck's door and hopped out. He held his arms straight out in front of him and positioned his open palms so that his fingers obscured his view of the house. Then he closed his left eye and sighted down his arms like a rifleman. He dropped his left arm. "Don't need lefty on this one," he said to himself. "Looks like about a five-section boiler to me, give or take. Five fingers equals five sections. That's about right for this neighborhood." Tom whistled as he hopped back into his truck and drove the rest of the way to the McCabe house.

Mrs. McCabe answered Tom's knock and smiled. "I'm here to size up that boiler for you," he said.

"Oh yes, come right in!" she said. "Will you be able to give us a price today? We'd like to get this work done as soon as possible."

"No problem," Tom said. "I'll have the price for you in a few minutes." She opened the door wider and stepped back. "No, that's okay, ma'am. I don't need to come inside.

It's easier for me to do the engineering from out here. I'll knock again when I have the price. I just wanted you to know that I was here."

"Okay," Mrs. McCabe said. "You're the expert."

Tom walked to the corner, looked over his left shoulder and sighted down the edge of the house. Then he paced across the front lawn to the opposite corner of the house. He kept the line as straight as possible as he walked, stepping over the garden hose, the lawn sprinkler and the bushes alongside the front walk . "One, two, three, four, five," he mumbled as he counted his paces from one side of the house to the other. Tom knew that each of his paces was about three feet, give or take, and that his rule of thumb measurement was nearly as accurate as you would get with a tape measure, but who has time to lay a tape across a lawn nowadays? And besides, none of this is rocket science.

Tom reached the corner of the house, multiplied the number of paces it took him to get there by three, made a mental note of that, and then turned to his left and paced down the side of the house. When he got to the corner of the house, he made another mental note, and then glanced upward. "Two stories," he mumbled. "That's about twenty feet, give or take." He added that into his mental arithmetic and came up with the cubic volume of the house. The shape of the roof was a triangle, of course. Most roofs are, but he always treated them like rectangles. A rectangle is close enough to a triangle when it comes to figuring heat loss. And let's face it, it never hurts to have a little bit extra, especially with an older house.

He multiplied his cubic volume number by a factor that he uses for homes that are located south of the Long Island

Expressway and that gave him his boiler size. He walked back toward the street so that he could count the vent pipes on the roof. "Two baths," he mumbled, and then he added his rule-of-thumb load for domestic hot water. He glanced around the yard for anything that might indicate that a lot of kids lived here. He liked to throw in a bit more load if he saw swings and slides or skateboards and bikes but the McCabes didn't seem to have any children, so he went with the numbers he already had.

Adding it all together, he came up with a four-section, cast iron boiler. He clucked his tongue and made it five-section boiler, just so that it would agree with the Finger Method. It never hurts to have a little bit extra with an old house. Then he walked back to his truck and put his price together.

Tom has a rule of thumb for figuring prices. This, he has found, saves him time. He charges by the BTUH. In this case, the boiler was 175,000 Gross BTUH. For jobs south of the Long Island Expressway, Tom charges 1-1/4 cents per BTUH. That would make the price of this job $2,187.50. Jobs north of the Long Island Expressway go for 1-1/2 cents per BTUH because that's where the rich folks live, but Tom hardly ever gets to quote on those jobs. It's out of his marketing area.

He was going with Gross BTUH pricing on this job because Mr. McCabe didn't appear to be at home. When both husband and wife are home they will often beat up Tom on the price. When this happens, he usually has to drop to the boiler's Net BTUH ratings instead of the Gross ratings for the pricing. The difference between Gross BTUH and Net BTUH on a hot water job is 15 percent. On a steam job, it's 33-1/3 percent and that hurts, but what can you do? Fortunately, this was a hot water job. Or at least he thought it was. The house wasn't that old. It was probably hot water.

He knocked on the door and handed Mrs. McCabe the Gross BTUH price. He had written it in pencil on the back of his business card. She looked at the number and then at Tom. "You sure you don't you need to go downstairs and look at the old boiler?" she asked.

"Nah," Tom said. "I've seen a million houses like yours. I know what's down there. After a while, it's all rule of thumb, ya know? This is a good price I'm giving you. Trust me."

She looked at the business card again. "I have to ask you, and I hope you don't take this the wrong way, but my husband said that I have to ask."

"Ask what?"

"Can you come down on the price?"

Tom sighed and looked at his fingernails. "Well," he said, how about if I knock off about two hundred bucks, give or take. How would that be?" His rule of thumb when it's just the wife or the husband is to try dropping to the nearest round number before going all the way down to the Net BTUH number. People, for the most part, like round numbers. How about if we make it an even two grand?" Tom said. "How would that be?"

"But you said you'd come down two hundred dollars," Mrs. McCabe said. "If you bring the price to two thousand dollars that's only a discount of one hundred eighty-seven dollars and fifty cents. I'll have to check with my husband."

Tom, not being the sort of guy who lets chump change get between him and a job, said, "Okay, how about if we just call it nineteen fifty? Would that do it for you?" Tom also likes round numbers. It makes the accounting easier.

"Okay, that sounds better," Mrs. McCabe said. "I'm sure my husband will agree. Nineteen hundred and fifty dollars it is. May I have a new quote?" She handed Tom the business card. He crossed out $2,187.50 and wrote $1,950. He added his initials and handed the card back to her. She looked at it and smiled. "So when can you do the work?"

"Oh, let's figure next Monday or Thursday, more or less," Tom said. "One of those days should be okay with me. That be okay with you?"

"Okay," she said. "Do you know what time you'll be here?"

"Figure morning or afternoon. I can't say for sure at this point. This business isn't an exact science. We have to play it by ear, ya know? Ride with the tide and go with the flow. Ya know?"

"Okay," she said.

Tom walked away a happy man. He didn't have to drop to the Net BTUH level on this job. That would have cost him an extra hundred bucks, give or take. "Cash in my pocket," he mumbled as he got into his truck.

He had five more estimates to do that morning. More or less.

Louie Rheiner

Eddie had only been with the supply house a couple of days so he didn't know about Louie Rheiner yet. When Eddie needed some help getting the bundles of half-inch pipe off the truck and into the rack he shouted inside and Louie Rheiner was right there for him. Louie Rheiner is always looking for someone to help.

Louie Rheiner told Eddie he'd get the front end of the bundle and that he, Eddie, should grab the back end of the bundle as it came off the truck. This surprised young Eddie because Louie Rheiner is old, gnarled and bowlegged. He also wears glasses that are so thick they make his eyeballs look like two blowfish in a murky aquarium. Eddie did as he was told, though, because he was new to the job, and he didn't yet know about Louie Rheiner.

Louie Rheiner grabbed hold of the bundle and yanked. He has hands that look like root vegetables. He is also a lot stronger than young Eddie had figured him to be. He yanked like a pit bull and it was all Eddie could do to grab hold of the other end of the flopping 20-foot-long bundle as it slid off the truck. Louie Rheiner dragged the bundle, along with young Eddie, across the dock and toward the yawning mouth of the pipe rack.

"Here we are!" Louie Rheiner said, stopping about six inches short of the rack because his eyes don't work that well. He let go of his end of the bundle and it headed for the concrete floor at the speed of gravity. "Whoops!" Louie Rheiner said.

When young Eddie's turn in the Emergency Room finally arrived the doctor had him X-rayed and then told him he had a broken collarbone, a fractured jaw and a temporary nervous disorder that was causing his damaged head to bob like one of those ceramic dashboard dogs. Eddie was still vibrating like a tuning fork from having been on the wrong end of that floppy bundle of half-inch steel pipe as it hit the cement. "LoOOooOOeeEEee RrIIiiIIiinnNNeeEErrRR," he stammered as he bobbed his head to the inner rhythm that would stay with him for quite some time.

"Excuse me," the doctor said.

"He's saying, Louie Rheiner," Teddy the counterman said. "He didn't know about Louie Rheiner."

"Oh," the doctor said. "This Louie Rheiner, is he the man who did this to you, Eddie?" Young Eddie bobbed his head a bit faster and the doctor took that as a yes.

"Have you notified the police?" the doctor asked Teddy the counterman

"Nah," Teddy the counterman said. "He didn't do it on purpose. Eddie never should have asked Louie Rheiner for help, but he didn't know that. He's new."

"Well, I guess he knows now," the doctor said, and young Eddie bobbed faster still. "NoOOooOO LoOOooOoeeEEee," he said.

Later that week, the boss handed Frankie the shipping clerk a stack of papers. "Here are the orders that have to be pulled for tomorrow," he said. "Try not to give any of this to Louie Rheiner."

"That goes without saying," Frankie the shipping clerk said. They both knew that any order that Louie Rheiner pulled would be over or under or the opposite of what it said on the ticket. If someone ordered left, they got right. If they wanted in, they got out. "I'll have one of the other guys take care of it," Frankie the shipping clerk said.

Louie Rheiner saw Frankie with the shipping tickets and immediately asked what he could do to help. "Sweep the floor," Frankie said. Louie Rheiner nodded, grabbed a broom and headed for the last aisle.

He worked like a sled dog for the next ten minutes, sweeping the dirt and the cardboard boxes down the aisle. When he got to the end of the aisle, he gave the pile of debris a big shove with the push broom, just as Teddy the counterman came waltzing by with an armload of galvanized fittings. The metal part of the push broom, the part that holds the boom to the stick (the part with the sharp wing nuts), caught Teddy flush on his left ankle, causing him to jump in the air like Michael Flatley in *Riverdance*.

Louie Rheiner backed up a few steps, so as to give Teddy more room in which to perform his Dance of Pain. "Ooooo! That musta hurt," Louie Rheiner said. "Sorry, Teddy. I didn't see you coming."

And that was the end of Louie Rheiner's floor-sweeping duties for the day. He went and sat down near the counter, waiting to see if there were any contractors who needed help out to their trucks with their supplies. Most contractors knew enough not to ask Louie Rheiner for help because he has dropped fixtures off forklifts and he once tried to load a seven-section cast iron boiler into a guy's car trunk. No, most contractors steer clear of Louie Rheiner. In fact, most everybody steers clear of Louie Rheiner. No matter what needs doing, the first reaction most folks have (and certainly the folks who work with him) is to say, "Don't give it to Louie Rheiner!"

And so Louie Rheiner has very little to do.

The boss can't fire him, though, because Louie Rheiner has never once refused to do anything the boss (or anyone else) has ever asked him to do. He is eager to work, and how can you fire a guy for being eager?

So as the years rolled by, Louie Rheiner became a part of the supply house scenery, like an old roll-top desk - or a barrel of toxic chemicals. Since his first day as a yardbird they have tried him out at just about every job in the place and Louie Rheiner has brought disaster to each task. No one has ever thought these disasters were his fault, though, because he tries so hard and he is always so eager to please. He just doesn't seem to be any good at anything, so after a while, people have stopped giving him things to do. And there is no way to fire him.

Young Eddie came back to work after a month of convalescing. He still had the wire in his jaw but the collarbone had healed and the bobbing had slowed. The boss put him on a desk and told him to answer the phones. "Go easy, kid," he said. "And if you need any help, ask. Okay?" Eddie nodded. "But don't ask Louie Rheiner." Young Eddie bobbed.

"I'm really sorry about what happened, Eddie," Louie Rheiner said ten minutes later. "I'd like to make it up to you." He was standing at the edge of young Eddie's desk with a pot of scalding coffee. Eddie had his hands in his lap with his fingers interlaced, which is probably what made Louie Rheiner think that young Eddie was holding a tan coffee mug there in his lap. Which he wasn't.

And that's what Teddy the counterman told the doctor in the emergency room.

Plus S&H

The new steam boiler was as big as a small Dumpster and Jimmy looked at it with concern. Things weren't lining up as he had hoped they would. The old steam pipes looked like brittle bones and he wondered why he hadn't noticed that when he had flat-rated this job. An hour ago, he busted the return line off the old boiler and brown goop oozed from the pipe, like puss from a festering wound. It was still oozing now, a full hour later. It looked like rancid lentil soup and smelled like trouble. And there didn't seem to be an end to it.

He glanced over at Jay, who was just six weeks out of high school and nearly as large as the boiler. Jay was smiling down at the brown ooze. "That's cool!" he said. "Look at it! That is so cool!" Jay thought that anything that wasn't high school was cool, and he said so several hundred times a day. The expression was getting on Jimmy's nerves, but he didn't want to be critical because Jay was huge and help was hard to find. Besides, they had this boiler to move and this boiler was as heavy as a Mosler safe.

"Let's shove it back a few inches," Jimmy said. I can't make the swing with the header from this far out." Jay leaned into the big boiler like a locomotive and it slowly screeched across the floor. "That's good," Jimmy said. "Right there."

"Cool sound!" Jay said, and then he went back to looking at the ooze that was bubbling from the pipe. "What's this stuff made of?" Jay said. "It looks like the green slime on Nickelodeon, only brown. Cool!"

Jimmy looked down on it. "It's called steam goop," he said. "Just ignore it. It should stop soon. Hand me that booklet."

Jay looked at where Jimmy was pointing and picked up the installation manual. He handed it to Jimmy. "Wadda you need that for?" Jay asked. "You done boilers like this before, ain't you?"

"Never one this size," Jimmy said.

"I got this tee shirt at home says 'Real men don't need instructions.'"

"Good for you," Jimmy said as he flipped through the pages of the manual.

"Real cool shirt!" Jay said. "Real men don't need instructions. You get it? You get it? Cool!"

"Well, today we're gonna be make-believe men."

"That's cool too," Jay said.

Jimmy studied the manual and then looked from the boiler to the old header and then back to the manual. He took out a tape measure and checked the distance between the new boiler's waterline and the centerline of the old header. Then he looked at the installation manual again and then he looked at Jay who was still looking at the steam goop. And then he realized that he wasn't going to be able to do what the boiler manufacturer said he had to do in the manual. It just wouldn't fit the way they said it had to fit. He looked at Jay who had the tip of his work shoe in the goop. "Uh oh," Jimmy mumbled.

Jimmy flipped open his cell phone and put in a call to the rep, who, to Jimmy's astonishment, called back a few minutes later. They had a brief but heated discussion about spatial reasoning and the laws of physics versus the laws of economics and the rep ended the conversation by telling Jimmy that he would either have to raise the bridge or lower the river. "But I didn't figure any of that into my price!" Jimmy said. "This is a flat-rate job! What the heck am I supposed to do now?"

"I guess you'll eat it and learn," the rep said.

Jimmy was about to tell the rep that he hated him and his entire family, that he would never again buy his products, that would tell everyone he knew in the trade that the rep was a louse, and that he would pass on this hatred to his children and grandchildren in the interest of long-term vengeance. But he never got a chance to say any of that because Jay had kicked the pipe that was oozing the steam goop. It was an innocent enough kick but Jay is huge and his kick caused the return pipe to disconnect from the vertical pipe that was on the other side of the room - the one that comes down from the end of the steam main. "Whoops!" Jay said.

Jimmy went numb. He hung up on the rep and staggered over to look at the damage. On the way there he slipped in a puddle of steam goop and landed on his butt. "Whoops!" Jay repeated.

Jimmy cursed under his breath, got up off the floor and finished stumbling toward the busted elbow. He touched the vertical pipe that was coming down from the steam main. It crumbled in his hand, which is what steam return lines that are as old as Grover Cleveland are wont to do. "Wow! Looks like the rust was holding those pipes together," Jay said. "That is so cool."

"I don't have enough money in this job for all this extra work," Jimmy said. "The boiler doesn't fit and now the pipes are falling apart. What next?" And just as he said that, the end of the steam main, now unsupported because of the crumbled return line, broke free from its ancient hangers, fell about six inches and released a cloud of asbestos dust into the basement air.

"Whoa!" said Jay. "That is soooooooooo cool! Did you know that was gonna happen?"

"If I knew that was gonna happen," Jimmy said, "I wouldn't have taken this job. I wouldn't have gotten out of bed this morning. I wouldn't have hired you. I wouldn't have been born and I and I certainly wouldn't have flat-rated this one."

"Does that mean you can't charge more now?" Jay asked.

"That's exactly what it means," Jimmy said. "A flat-rate price is written in stone."

"Well, how are you gonna get the money to fix all of this?" Jay asked.

"There's no way," Jimmy said. "I'm doomed."

"Well can't you just add extra to the price now?" Jay asked. "I mean they do it all the time on TV. You know? I mean you watch this cool commercial about these video or these CDs and then they give you the price, right? But just before they're done they always say, 'Plus shipping and handling.' Why don't you just do that, Jimmy?" Jimmy looked at Jay and started to say something about him being an idiot but Jay just kept chatting away. "They always hit you with it at the last minute, you know? That's the trick. It's the very last thing you see before the commercial ends. It's right after the toll-free number. Plus shipping and handling, they say. You go to pay and then you find out that you have to pay more than you expected to pay. Sometimes the shipping and handling is almost as much as the stuff you're buying but it's okay because everybody is used to it, you know? We all watch TV so we know this is the way it goes. You know?"

Jimmy looked at Jay for a while and then he looked at the corroded pipes and the Dumpster of a boiler that wasn't going to fit unless he moved a lot of pipes and then he shrugged, "Hey, it's worth a try, I suppose," Jimmy said.

When Jimmy and Jay finished installing the boiler and replacing most of the piping in the house (because working on an old steam system is like using wrenches to work on soap bubbles), Jimmy presented Mr. and Mrs. Quaglio with the bill. "What's this?" Mr. Quaglio asked, pointing to the extra $2,456 charge at the bottom of the invoice.

"That's for slipping and handling," Jimmy said. "Slipping and handling is always extra."

"Shipping and handling?" Mrs. Quaglio said. "You mean like on the TV?"

"Yes," Jimmy said, "but it's 'slipping' not 'shipping.' It's for slipping and handling. Jay and I were slipping all over that brown steam goop that you had in your pipes. You didn't tell us you had all that goop when I gave you the flat-rate price, did you? And then there's the handling. We had to handle all those new pipes that you needed because the brown goop ate your old pipes. So it's an extra $2,356 for slipping and handling."

"Just like on TV," Jay said.

"Right," Jimmy said. "Like on TV."

"Slipping and handling," Jay said.

"Like TV," Jimmy said.

Mr. and Mrs. Quaglio looked at each other and shrugged. She wrote the check, of course. The Quaglios watch a lot of TV so they understood.

And Jimmy thought that was pretty cool.

Wally on the Web

Wally thought he should have a presence on the World Wide Web. He liked the way that sounded. Presence. If you advertised in the Penny Saver you had an ad. Same thing with the Yellow Pages. But with the World Wide Web a company got to have a presence, and that sounded so much classier to Wally, and having that feeling was how all this misery started for him.

At first, he thought he could do it on his own. He went to Borders Books and bought a copy of one of those "For Dummies" books. He read through it and then went back to Borders to see if they had a "For Total Morons" book because that's the way the Internet was making him feel. "Maybe I should hire somebody to do this for me?" he said to Gladys, the woman who ran his little office. "What do you think?"

"I think if it had a place to put a wrench you'd be in great shape, Wally. But let's face it, you ain't no Bill Gates." So Wally looked around for someone who could get him a website and give him a presence on the World Wide Web.

The first place he looked was in the classifieds on the day when the newspaper published the Business supplement. There were six ads there and they all promised the world. Wally picked the smallest ad, figuring that those folks would be the cheapest. He also liked their name. It was GetOnLineCheap.com. "That's what I want," Wally said. He showed the ad to Gladys and she nodded. "Looks good, right?" Wally said. She smiled and nodded again, so he called them that afternoon.

"Get on line cheap dot com," the woman said.

"I want to have a presence on the World Wide Web," Wally said.

"You've come to the right place. We can get you up and running and it won't cost you much. That's our specialty. Getting people up and running for cheap."

"And I'll have a presence?"

"Like you wouldn't believe," the woman said.

Wally met Amy the next morning. She came to his office. She was young and blonde and very attractive. "You seem very young to be doing this sort of work," Wally said. "I bought some books about building websites and I wasn't able to understand any of what I was reading. How did you get to know so much at your age?"

"This is a young business, filled with young people," Amy said. "We all grew up playing video games. It comes naturally to us. May I show you what we can to do for you?" Wally nodded. He had children that were older than Amy.

She gave him a proposal for the basic website and the price seemed very reasonable. "How will people find me on the World Wide Web?" he asked.

"They'll use search engines," Amy said. "We'll submit your URL and people will find you with no trouble at all."

"URL?" Wally said.

"It's like your house address. By the way, how do you like www.WallysHeating.com? Doesn't that just say it all?" She smiled. "It says your name and it tells what you do. What more could you want?" She smiled again and so he agreed.

"What do I have to do?" Wally said.

"Just give me a check and we'll get started." So he did and within two weeks Wally had a presence on the World Wide Web.

The next thing he did was to paint www.WallysHeating. com on the side of his truck. "Visit us on the World Wide Web!" it read below his URL. He also had the same thing painted on the front window of his shop, and he redesigned his Penny Saver ad so that it also touted his new presence.

"We're modern now," he said to Gladys.

"We're playing with the big boys!" Gladys said.

"The World Wide Web is our future," Wally said.

That's what Amy had told him, and as the days went by, he believed it more and more. He had paid so little to get a presence and now everyone in the world knew about Wally's Heating.

"You know what you need, Wally?" Amy said on the phone a few weeks later.

"What?"

"A bulletin board. You could answer technical questions and show everyone how smart you are."

"What's that going to cost?" he asked.

"Well, we work by the hour, as you know. I'm thinking it will take about four hours to get it up and running. Our rate is $250 per hour, so figure a thousand."

Wally gulped. "That's more than the whole website cost me to put up," he said.

"I know, but what you have is the basic package. If you want to go interactive with the public you need a bulletin board. And it's really not that much when you think about it, Wally. I mean, just think how long it would take you to do it yourself. And isn't your time valuable? And you only have to pay me once and then you'll own it forever. Forever, Wally."

So he bit the bullet and went for it and it was an immediate success. Wally began to receive technical questions from just about every civilized nation on Earth. He answered these questions as fast as he could and he tried not to get annoyed when the strangers complained that he wasn't providing this free information quickly enough.

"You look tired," Gladys said.

"I was up until three this morning, answering questions."

"Are any of these people hiring you?" she asked.

"No, most of them are in places like Pig Snot, Nebraska and Moose Breath, Maine."

"Why are you doing this to yourself?"

"I have to stand behind my presence on the World Wide Web," Wally explained. "It's our future."

A month later he called Amy. "Is there a way I can limit the people who ask questions on this bulletin board? They're taking up all of my time. I don't even have time to work any more!"

"Of course there is," Amy said, and then she went on to explain how they could reprogram www.WallysHeating.com so that it would respond only to certain Zip codes. "Of course there's a charge for this. Time is money, right?"

"How much?" Wally asked, feeling that he was now married to this young woman and her company, at least in a cyber sense.

"I'm thinking it will take about twenty hours. That would be five thousand."

"Are you serious?"

"Time is money, Wally. It's not easy to make these changes."

"But I picked you guys because you said you could get me online cheap," Wally said.

"And we did," Amy said.

"But now it's not so cheap."

"Well, you need to grow, right? Just look at it as a one-time expense, like buying a truck or a really good tool. The World Wide Web is your new tool, Wally."

"But I just want to fix the site because it's not doing what I thought it would do."

"Wally, do you work for free?"

"No."

"Then how can you expect us to work for free?" she said.

Wally wanted to tell her to go pound salt up her nose but she had him by the gigabytes. If he got her angry there was no telling what she would do with his site.

"You know what this reminds me of?" he said.

"What, Wally?"

"It's like one of those razors that you buy in a drugstore. The razor is cheap but the blades are expensive."

"Oh, Wally, I hate to have you thinking that way. I'll tell you what, how about if I knock off two hours? Then your investment will be just forty-five. How's that? I want to work with you. I want you to be happy."

"I feel like a crack addict," Wally said. "The first one was free."

"But Wally, this is your future. You said so yourself. You have to invest in the future."

"Could we just take down the bulletin board?"

"Of course we could, if that's what you really want. Is that what you really want, Wally? To give up your interactive presence, your personality, your very soul?"

"Maybe," Wally said. "How many hours would that require?

"Ummm, let's see. I'm thinking about thirty," Amy said. "But I'll have to check."

The Heating Guy

"Are you the hacksaw salesman?"

"Nope, I'm the Heating Guy," Tim said as he worked on the vandal-proof screws that held the cover on the convector. "I'm checking to see if there's air in your radiator. You're the guy complaining about no heat, right?"

"Right!" he said and then leaned in and whispered, "But I was hoping you brought a hacksaw for me." He winked at Tim.

"Back up and sit over there," the guard snarled. "Let the man do his work."

The prisoner smiled and did as he was told. "I just figured he might have something I can use there in that box of his," he said.

"Back up!"

When they were leaving the cell block, the guard asked Tim if this was the first time he had been in a prison. "Nah," Tim said. "I've been in lots of prisons. In fact, I've been just about everywhere. I get to go to places where hardly anyone ever gets to go."

"How's that?" the guard asked.

"I'm the heating guy," Tim said. "I get to go everywhere!"

Tim had learned this early on when he started in the business right out of high school. He went to work with his dad and they used to go to these fancy houses up on the North Shore where all the rich folks live. "How do you think these people get all their money?" Tim asked his dad.

"They work for it," his dad had said. "Not like you and I work for it, but they work for it, in their own way."

"What type of work do these rich people do?" Tim asked.

"It depends," his dad had said.

"Depends on what?"

"On the guy."

"What about this guy who owns this house?" Tim asked. They were in the guy's boiler room, working on one of his circulators that had been making a squeaking noise and annoying the family. "What sort of work does this guy do?"

Tim's dad straightened up from his work, looked at Tim and said, "I'm not sure, son. Why don't we go find out?"

"How we gonna do that?" Tim asked.

"You'll see," his dad said, and with that, his father grabbed a screwdriver, a vent key, a small metal can and a rag. "Follow me."

"Where we going?"

"Upstairs to the guy's office. These rich guys always have offices in their homes, and offices need to be heated, so it's okay for us to go in there and look around."

"You sure?"

"Yep, we're the heating guys. We can go anywhere we want. Always remember that, son. We can go anywhere there's heat."

And Tim never forgot that lesson. On that day in the rich guy's house, they vented the air from all his radiators (and there were radiators in every room). They also went through the files on his desk in his office while they were at it. This brief perusal established that the guy made his money on Wall Street. Tim's dad often got some pretty good stock tips this way.

While they were venting the kitchen radiators, they checked out the food in the fridge (rich folks eat better than poor folks do), and then they did the radiators in the master bedroom. Tim got to go through the dresser drawers and put some underwear on his head, as many young men are wont to do. "Is this okay for me to be doing?" Tim asked his dad.

"No problem," his father had said, as he tried on a pair of the rich guy's loafers (rich guys buy great shoes!). "Curiosity is one of the best qualities a heating guy can have. It is the very essence of troubleshooting. How are you gonna know what's going on with the job if you don't poke around?"

"You think these folks use Charmin?" Tim asked.

"Only one way to find out!" his father said. "Let's go bleed the radiators in the bathroom."

Since his father retired, Tim owns and operates the business with his own son. He takes his son to the football games every Sunday when the home team is in town. They don't have to buy tickets. All they have to do is wear their work uniforms. They carry their tools and walk right up to the turnstiles. "Tickets?" the man at the turnstile says. "Heating guys," Tim explains, pointing to his name patch and his toolbox. The turnstile guy opens the gate and lets them through and they go right to the sidelines and fiddle with those fancy torpedo heaters that the team uses to stay warm on the bench.

When they get hungry, they go up to the refreshment stand and have a couple of hot dogs and some hot chocolate. They don't have to wait on line and they don't have to pay for any of the food. They just go in the back door because there are radiators back there. They take off the radiator covers and begin to vent non-existing air from the key vents. "Boy, this hard work sure does make a guy hungry!" Tim will say, and the manager of the refreshment stand will offer Tim and his son hot dogs and hot chocolate. "Got any beers?" Tim will ask, and this, too, is never a problem. They, after all, are the heating guys.

When Eric Clapton came to town to play the big arena, Tim and his son went to the concert. They didn't have to buy tickets because they're the heating guys and the big arena is heated with hot water. Hot water systems need to be checked from time to time, and the occasion of a Clapton concert seemed to be a perfect time for Tim and his son to make some adjustments to the system's flow balance. They walked up to the Press Gate, pointed at their toolboxes and the patches on their blue uniforms. "Heating guys," Tim said. The security people let them in and Tim and his son went right backstage because there are radiators there. "Are you comfortable, Eric?" Tim asked. "I make a good living, bloke!" Eric Clapton said, and then he used a Sharpie to autograph both their toolboxes.

George W. Bush came to that same arena to make a speech not too long ago and Tim's wife, Maureen, wanted to see him. Tim put a uniform on her and together they waltzed by the Secret Service folks and chatted it up with the President of the United States of America and his lovely wife, Laura. "I like to see women entering the trades," Dubya said. "It's extraordinarium and good for the country I'm sure." Dubya smiled and so did Laura.

"Shucks," Maureen said, "I'm just a little ol' heating gal."

"Well, you keep the children of America warm," the President said. "You are one in a millenium."

Tim put the photograph of Maureen, Dubya and Laura up there on the mantle, right next to the photo of Madonna and himself.

It's good to be the heating guy!

A Good Working Knowledge of Plumbing

Andrew's father owns a gasoline station, one of those old-fashioned ones where you can get your tires rotated and your engine tuned. Andrew has grown up around men who swing hammers and turn wrenches. He never actually worked with the tools himself, but non-tool guys who are around tool guys long enough often begin to believe that they, the non-tool guys, can fix anything that's mechanical. They're usually wrong, but this doesn't stop them from trying, and Andrew is one of these guys.

He is also an architect. Not an architect in the I. M. Pei or Frank Lloyd Wright sense, but rather in the Add-an-Addition-to-Your-House sense. Five years of college, $150,000 later and he's doing dormers and extensions. He hopes that his ship may come in some day, but in the meantime, he's designing the refreshment stand along the proverbial dockside.

Now because he has never been able to get enough money in commissions from the few clients who have come his way, Andrew does things around the house himself. He believes that his background, as the son of a gasoline-station owner, qualifies him to do just about anything mechanical. His car-fixing father, on the other hand, thinks Andrew should stick to what he knows best.

"You're all thumbs, Andrew," his father says. "You're nothing more than an interior decorator with an advanced degree. Stick to drawing pretty pictures and looking for clients. Don't try to do all this mechanical stuff by yourself. You're not qualified. Believe me; I know you better than you know yourself."

"But I have a good working knowledge of mechanical things," Andrew said. "Besides, I can save a lot of money by doing it myself."

Andrew's father shook his head and smiled. "Andrew, focus on what you know. Try to make some money and then spend that money on trade professionals who know what they're doing. You're going to burn down your house and kill yourself if you keep this up."

"But I don't make enough as an architect to be able to afford to hire trade professionals," Andrew said.

"That's because the average Joe wants to design his own dormer. Those people look at your skills the same way you look at their skills. You think you can do their jobs as well as they can, and they think they can do your job as well as you do. You have to market yourself, son."

"What do you mean they think they can do what I do?" Andrew said. "It took me five years to learn what I know!"

"And it took me far longer than five years to learn how to fix cars," his father said. "That doesn't mean I can design a house or a shopping mall, does it?"

"Architects are professionals." Andrew said.

"Try spending that at the grocery store, kid," his father said.

"Are you saying that I can't work with my hands?" Andrew said. "I've been watching you and the guys in the shop all my life. I have a good working knowledge of car repair."

"Really!"

"Yes, and all other things that are mechanical. I'm an architect. I have a good working knowledge of everything that's in a building."

"Really! Remember what happened when you tried to build that deck off the back of your house?" his father said. "The blueprints looked great, but the carpentry didn't go that well, did it?" Andrew touched his shoulder. It still ached whenever it rained. "How many months did you spend in the body cast? What was it? Four months? Five months?"

"It was four," Andrew said. "But that was an accident. Anybody can cut through an extension cord. And when you get hit in the mouth with 110 volts of electricity, it's easy to back up real fast. I didn't know I was that close to the edge."

"But you're not supposed to hold the cord between your teeth, Andrew."

"Well . . ."

Andrew's father started to laugh. He held up his bent right arm, as if he were about to take an oath. "Hey, remember the body cast? You looked like you were waving to everybody. I'd take you out for a drive and the people in the other cars would wave back." His father waved and smiled like a silly idiot.

"Well, I saved money building that deck myself."

"Saved money? You didn't make any money during all that time you were laid up because you weren't able to draw. You lost whatever clients you had, and then you had to start all over again from scratch. How do you figure you saved money?"

"I didn't have to hire a carpenter," Andrew said. "You know what carpenters cost nowadays? I can work cheaper than those guys can. My time doesn't cost me anything."

"You're lucky you've still got toes, son," his father said, still laughing.

"And my disability insurance policy paid me when I was laid up."

"But how high are your monthly payments now?" his father said. "I'll bet those payments went up by a lot more than what the carpenter wanted to charge you to build the deck."

"Are you saying that I don't have a good working knowledge of mechanical things?" Andrew said.

"I'm saying that you should focus on what you do best and let others do the same. Make money and hire pros. It keeps the economy going."

"You just don't understand," Andrew said.

Andrew's toilet backed up the other day. He flushed and it all just backed up onto his white tiled floor. He looked down upon the mess and saw not a problem, but a challenge. Here before him was a simple plumbing stoppage. He should be able to fix this in no time at all. After all, what is there to plumbing? Water flows downhill, and it does so inside of pipes. All he really needed to do was to clear the clog that was inside the pipe.

Andrew prides prided himself on having a good working knowledge of plumbing. He has used plumbing all of his life. He has designed dormers and extensions that have plumbing. He hasn't actually done any of the piping layouts for the plumbing systems. He leaves that to the contractors that the homeowners hire to do the installations, but he had designed the rooms through which the plumbing passes. It's just pipes. And all it takes to clear a clog from a pipe is a wrench and a straightened-out wire coat hanger. And wrenches are easy to use. All you really have to know is clockwise and counterclockwise. He grew up around men who use wrenches.

So what was there to it?

It's just plumbing.

He walked downstairs to the basement and located the largest pipe he could find. It appeared to be made of cast iron, and there was a threaded plug at the end of a tee. This was at the low point of the pipe, and Andrew thought that this would be a fine place to insert his wire hanger. But first, he had to remove that plug.

He tried doing it with regular pliers, but that didn't work.

He tried doing it with locking pliers, but that didn't work.

He tried doing it with a monkey wrench, but that didn't work.

Remembering back to his high school science class, he decided that what was needed was heat. Heat would make the cast iron expand and that would allow him to remove the threaded plug from the end of the big tee.

He tried adding heat with a hair dryer, but that didn't work.

He tried adding heat with an iron, but that didn't work.

He tried adding heat with a propane torch, but that didn't work.

So he thought he would give the cast iron a bit of a tap with a hammer. He remembered opening the stubborn lid on a jar of salsa that way once. He heated the lid under hot water and gave it a tap with the end of a butter knife. If it works on salsa, it should work on plumbing.

So he knelt on the floor, right in front of that big cast iron tee with the threaded plug, and gently tapped the side of the cast iron pipe once, but that didn't work.

He tapped it twice, a bit harder this time, but that didn't work either.

So he got a much bigger hammer. He got a sledgehammer.

And hit it very, very hard.

That worked!

But not in the way that he had hoped.

Andrew now has a good working knowledge of massive quantities of fecal matter.

Poor Personal Planning

He now knew for certain. The words had hit him like a slap and he had been too stunned to react, so he had said nothing. He had just stood there like a big jerk. He had plenty to say now, but the man wasn't there now so he was saying it to her. But she couldn't take the sting out of the words that had been said to him. She couldn't make him feel any less foolish for having trusted the man for the past few years. All she could do was listen. So that's what she did. And now she knew too. The knowledge bloomed inside of her with a coldness that made her wonder how people could do such things to other people. She didn't know what to say to him, so she just sat there with him in the kitchen and she listened to him.

He stood up from the table and got another beer. He looked around for something to hit, but he knew that he would just have to fix whatever it was that he hit so he took out his anger on the beer, sucking it down and crushing the can in his big hand. The man had promised him a raise, or at least he had led him to believe that the money would be there, if he worked hard. And he had worked hard because he needed the money. They needed the money. The two little kids, his son and his daughter, and the one that was growing inside of her right now needed the money and they all needed him. They depended on him. He had gone into the office that afternoon to ask about the promised raise that hadn't come and the man had told him that it didn't look like it was in the cards for him this year. Maybe next year. We'll see. Keep working hard.

And that's when he tipped his hand and told the man that he needed the money because of the children. There were two children and there was another on the way, which was a blessing but an unexpected one. Children are a blessing, whenever and however they arrive. And they needed the money for a bigger apartment. There just wasn't enough room for the crib, and the man had promised more money, sort of. Hadn't he?

The man looked down at the papers on his desk. He shook his head and chuckled. Then the man looked up and asked him why he had made his wife pregnant if he didn't have enough money to afford another child. And the man's words stole the voice from his throat. He couldn't believe what the man had just said. The words hit him like a slap, and then there were more words. The man said that people who couldn't afford to have babies shouldn't be breeding. He mentioned that there were ways to reverse pregnancies. If there wasn't enough money to have the babies then the babies should not be born. Right? RIGHT?

Certainly, it was less expensive to choose this option. After all, that would be just a one-time expense and had he and his wife considered that? Had they?

He stood dumb.

The man asked what trimester she was in. Was it the first or the second? It was? Then something could be done. And had he and his wife considered that? Insurance would cover it, you know.

He wanted to go right over the desk and hit the man, but he didn't. He just stood there because he needed the job. And then the man shook his head and chuckled again and told him that he and his wife had poor personal planning. He offered this as advice, as if he had been asked for advice, as though someone had said, "What do you think caused this little problem we now have here?"

You should not make your wife pregnant if you can't afford to have all these children.

That shows poor personal planning on your part, and also on your wife's part.

There are things you can do, though.

Which trimester? It's not too late, you know.

He told her all of this at the kitchen table and her breathing slowed and she listened to the two little ones watching the TV in the living room. And the baby inside her stirred and she moved her hands to hold it. And he looked at her hands and he started to cry.

And then he again said all of the things that he might have said to the man, how he had earned the raise, how it had been promised him. Or at least he thought it had been promised. How his personal life was none of the man's business. How he loved his wife and his children and how they were of no concern to the man. And how dare he say such things! You can take this job and shove it!

And he wanted to punch his fist through the kitchen wall, but that would only upset her and the kids, and he would have to fix it. So he got another beer, and he wondered what he would do, now that he knew for certain how the man felt about him.

She told him to quit, but there was a matter of the health insurance. She said he should get another job, but he didn't know where to go. He had been at this place for a while. He didn't know if a new employer would give them health insurance. And would the Insurance Company step up and cover her, since she was already pregnant. She told him not to worry. They would get by somehow. She said that no man should have to take this sort of abuse from any other man, but he now knew that wasn't so. Some men have to take this sort of abuse from other men. They had wives. They had children. And she was having another.

This knowledge gnawed at him like hot acid.

He went in the next day, and right on time. He went about his work and when he saw the man he didn't say anything, and neither did the man. They just left it were it had been yesterday, where it would now always be. They had a new relationship now, and they each knew that for certain. He could see it in the man's eyes, and he could feel it in the pit of his stomach.

And something inside of him died.

An American Cathedral

Mike always wrote his initials on the pipes with a wax crayon. Next to his initials, he wrote the date and next to the date he drew an arrow that pointed toward heaven. He didn't write on all the pipes, just the one's that he himself had welded. It didn't matter that the other trades would soon bury his pipes behind the walls and beneath the ceilings. Mike knew what he had done, and he knew that it would be there forever.

These towers, both of them, would last. Of that, there was no doubt. You did not build something like this and then take it down a few years from now. Not even a hundred years from now. You did not build something this enormous and take it down. No, these towers would define this city and its people and they would forever change the men and women who built them. He would grow old in this city and look at his towers and know that a part of him was now a part of them, and that was good enough for Mike.

When the building was still just a deep hole in the ground and Mike had begun writing on his pipes and pointing his arrows toward the sky, his partner would laugh at him. "You're gonna need a lot more crayons," his partner would say.

"Ah, you're so young," Mike would say. "Don't you know what we're doing here, lad?"

And his partner would laugh. "Here we go," he'd say.

"The work outlives the man, lad." And Mike would nod and smile. "We're building an American cathedral here, lad. An American cathedral! It will rise to the heavens and be here forever. Long after we're dead and gone people will look at our work and admire what we built. This is a special place, this one."

His partner would shake his head and laugh. "You saw the drawings. These things are just big boxes, Mike. They're gonna be as ugly as sin. To me, they're just next week's grocery bill and next month's rent."

And Mike's eyes would gleam and he'd say, "Ah, but you're wrong, lad. This one is much more than a paycheck. This one is special. We'll never be the same after this one. Mark my words. You'll see."

"Oh, you're so friggin' deep," his partner would say.

"And you're such a young pup!"

And they'd both have a good laugh for themselves, neither taking the other too seriously, and Mike would sign another pipe and draw an arrow upward, to where they were going. And he'd smile at his partner and wink.

They were a good team, these two. They'd been together for five years, moving from job to job, always together, as it is with this trade. They knew that they'd be working on these towers for a good long time. There was no denying that at this point. The die had been cast and this was a project that no one could stop. It rose by the will of the workers, each day a bit taller. They would build these towers and they would put away some of the money for their children and for vacations and for their future. And as they arrived at work each day they would look up and up. And then they would build some more.

Sometimes they'd stop for a pint or two before riding the subways home. They'd talk about sports and politics and, of course, the work. There was always the work. It would take a good long time to finish this one.

Every day, year after year, Mike wrote on his pipes. Thousands of people rode the subways to this site and they muscled these towers upward and Mike drew his arrows and wrote his initials and the dates that marked the passing of a man's years.

And one day they were done. They finished and Mike drew his last arrow on the highest pipe in the city of New York. It was beneath a ceiling but Mike knew that it was there, and that it would always be there, and that was good enough for him. They finished and moved on and they grew old together as good partners will.

Winters came and went and so did the brutally humid summers of New York and Mike and his partner worked through some impossible situations under punishing conditions and they always got the job done. They piped between wires and ducts and beams and dealt with live steam lines and deadlines and they complained only to each other. No matter what the challenge, they got the job done, and they built this city.

One day, a man named Phillipe Petit climbed up on the roof of one of the towers and shot a line over to the other tower. He stretched the line taut and then spent a good part of that day strolling back and forth with a long balance pole. In the streets, the people craned their necks to watch.

The police arrested him when he finally came off the high wire and then they posed for photos with that funny little man.

Owen J. Quinn got up onto the roof with a parachute one day and captured everyone's imagination as well. He was arrested in the street and then he posed for his photos with the cops. Everyone was smiling because this was New York City, and absolutely anything can happen here.

And then one day George Willig climbed up the outside of the tower like a human fly and the cops spent the day with him, dangling there from a window-washer's rig, chatting it up and trying to talk him into stopping this nuttiness. And the day rolled on and they got to know each other pretty well. They arrested him up there on the top and then they all posed for pictures. And everyone smiled because this was New York City.

The towers took on a magical quality as these things happened, and later, a mythical strength when those people tried to blow it up. No one ever knew what to expect next. This was New York and anything can happen. And Mike watched it all on TV and he grew quiet. He had done good work.

And then the kids finished college and his knees gave out and Mike knew that it was time to pack it in. He and his Mary moved to a small house in Florida and he took it easy for a change. And when Mike would see New York City on the TV he would smile and remember what he had done there. He had built an American cathedral that would stand forever.

Mary found him in his chair one hot afternoon. She had gone out for groceries and when she returned he was gone. The last thing she had said to him was, "Do you need anything?" and he had smiled and shaken his head. "No, I'm fine," he had said.

They laid him to rest in the Borough of Queens where you can see the buildings of New York City standing tall just across the East River. His old partner came with flowers the other day. He looked across the river to the scar in the cityscape where a working man had once signed his initials on pipes, and left wax arrows that tried to reach all the way to heaven.

And he cried.

A Mary Christmas to All!

Mary was feeling festive as she strung the holiday cards across the front window of the little plumbing & heating shop on Harrison Street. So many cars drive by during the day and Mary wanted all the people in town to know that everyone in the company was in a fine holiday mood. "People like to do business with festive people," she said to Eileen, the woman who answers the phones and deals with the mounds of paperwork that even a small plumbing & heating shop can generate. "After all," Mary said, "'tis the season to be jolly! And besides, Christmas is my birthday. What a wonderful way to celebrate my birthday, don't you think? And I get to do it every year. On Christmas!"

Eileen, who has a face that could hammer nails and a disposition that is as sour as bad buttermilk, looked over the top of her eyeglasses and pursed her lips. "Really," she said. "How nice for you."

"I get lots of presents!" Mary said, stringing yet another row of cards across the wide window.

"I have calls backed up to Hoboken and you expect me to care about your birthday? You expect me to be jolly? I get to talk to the screamers on the phone and you get to hang the holiday cards. Nice."

"'Tis the season!" Mary chirped.

"Stuff it," Eileen said.

"Oh, come on now," Mary said. "Get into the spirit. Hey, you know what I think? I think it would be fun if the guys wore Santa hats this week. What do you think?"

"Sure, why not," Eileen said. "Most of them are fat slobs anyway. They'd look very natural with stupid hats on their heads."

"Or maybe we could have them give out candy canes to the customers," Mary said. "Wouldn't that be so much fun! It would fit right in with the season. I'll bring it up when I see them."

"Maybe you should do some work instead?" Eileen said.

"Oh, but I just need to hang the wreath first," Mary said. "And put up the Christmas tree. And hang the lights by the door."

"And anything else you can find to avoid doing any actual work?" Eileen said.

"Oh, please don't talk like that," Mary said. "C'mon, be in a good mood. 'Tis the season, you know! I have to make the place look nice."

"Yeah, nice," Eileen said.

Mary smiled at Eileen with Christmas-morning eyes. "It only comes once a year, you know," she said. "And it's also my birthday. Here, I'll hang this wreath right here. Right by your desk. It will lift your spirits." Mary stuck a push pin into the sheet rock and hung the wreath right over the printer on Eileen's side table. "There, isn't that nice?"

"That smell is enough to gag Martha Stewart," Eileen said.

"Oh but it looks so festive!" Mary said.

The wreath, which was as dry as toast, immediately began to drop pine needles into the inner workings of Eileen's printer. Eileen would find this out later that week, as she tried to get some critical year-end reports finished. But that was all in the future. Right now there were other things going on.

Mary set up the tree and strung the lights and hung the ornaments. To reach the electrical outlet, Mary used several old extension cords that had been rolled over by desk chairs for many years. The outlet was the same one that Eileen happened to be using for her computer. The short that would result from this lack of knowledge of basic electricity – the short that would fry Eileen's hard drive – would not occur until the morning of January 1. But this, too, was all in the future. Right now there were other things going on.

Tony came in through the back door of the shop. "How are you ladies doing today?" he said.

"Never better!" Mary said, a big smile on her face.

"What the hell are you doing here?" Eileen said.

"I had to stop back for some parts," Tony said.

"I've got a thousand calls backed up and you're in here restocking your truck?" Eileen said.

"I'll just be a few minutes," Tony said. "Besides, I'm on my break."

"Tony," Mary said. "I have an extra Christmas wreath. How about if we hang it on the front of your van. It will look so festive, and it won't take but a minute to do." Mary's spirit burned like a big beautiful Yule log and Tony was unable to resist its warmth.

"Okay," he said. "I can help. I got tools."

Mary grabbed her coat and scurried out the door. Tony followed. She carried another dried-out wreath and a red plastic tablecloth. "Let's put this plastic over the front of your van first. It's a pretty backdrop for the wreath. Red and green. Christmas colors!"

"Okay," Tony said, and then he used some duct tape to attach the plastic sheet across the front of his old van. He put it right over the air inlet to the old van's questionable radiator. Then he used some wire to hang the wreath over the plastic.

"Doesn't that look nice!" Mary said.

"Very cool," Tony said. "Very, very festive."

"I think so too!" Mary said.

Tony would spend a good part of that evening in a really bad neighborhood, waiting for his overheated radiator to cool down. But that was all in the future. Right now there were other things going on.

Mary looked around and then she reached into her coat pocket and came out with a two-inch diameter button. "Tony, I bought this for you. I got them for the other guys too, but don't tell Eileen. She's not in a very good mood today."

"Today?"

"Well, you know what I mean. She's having trouble getting into the holiday spirit." Mary pinned the button to Tony's jacket. It was red and green. Printed on it was a sprig of mistletoe and the words, KISS ME, I'M FESTIVE!. "Like it?" Mary said.

"Love it!" Tony said. "Hey, maybe I'll get lucky."

"And maybe you can hand out some candy canes to the customers during the week? I'll pick up some at the store."

"Yeah, whatever," Tony said.

Tony's next call was on the other side of town. It was a backed-up toilet and this was not his favorite sort of call because there are many things in this world that can back up a toilet, none of them being pleasant.

Tony parked in front of the house and walked up to the door. He knocked and a large man answered. Tony noticed right away that this man was not dressed the way you would expect a man to be dressed. No, this man gave new meaning to the familiar holiday expression, "Don we now our gay apparel." Tony looked up and down at the man's scant clothing, while the man gazed directly at the button that Mary had pinned to Tony's jacket.

"Come in, my little plunger boy," the large man said. "We'll see what we can do about that!" He pointed at the round button and smiled.

But that was all in Tony's future.

That's A Fact, Jack

Jack had developed a habit when he was a younger man that he thought would make him a lot more believable than he was at the time. Young men often have concerns about their believability. Most folks don't take the average young man seriously until that young man turns 30, and because of this, many young men try to acquire grown-up habits such cigarette smoking or they may grow a goatee or get a tattoo – all by way of appearing more believable.

Jack was never able to sprout a decent amount of chin hair, he didn't like cigarettes and he was afraid of needles, so he decided to become more believable by cultivating a habit of the verbal variety.

It went like this: Whenever he made a statement that he felt someone might question (because of his age and lack of chin hair), he would end that statement with a singe word, very emphatically expressed, and that powerful little word went like this: "FACT!"

As time went by Jack learned that if he shouted the word, "FACT!" it would usually slam the door on any potential disagreement the recipient of the mighty word might have planned. Jack preferred a world where no one ever disagreed with him. It uncomplicated his life and made him feel older, wiser and believable.

And as he grew older and more believable, he really didn't need to keep slamming the word, "FACT!" into the small space between each of his emphatically pronounced sentences, but he did it anyway because it was a habit, and habits are hard to break. FACT!

Hardly anyone argues with Jack nowadays. Most folks just listen and nod. And when they do nod, Jack nods back with the force of a rattrap springing closed. He learned early on that if you want people to respect you (especially when you are young) then you have to be firm in both your words and in your actions. You have to speak your mind – come what may – and if people don't like what you have to say, well, that's their problem. FACT!.

And this is the way that Jack has gone through life – so far.

A few weeks back, Jack went to look at a problem with a heating system. Jack sees many heating systems nowadays because he works as a consultant. He used to be a serviceman and then he was an installer, but time after time, he considered his bosses to be idiots, so he quit each job he had. There is a huge amount of idiot bosses out there, Jack will tell you.

So nowadays he works as a consultant. He doesn't have a degree in engineering or anything like that, but you really don't need a college education to be a good troubleshooter. You just need to know what you're looking at, and you need to be firm in your convictions and your conclusions. There is no room for wavering when you're a consultant. And that's a fact.

So he found himself in this basement on the other side of town. He used to work in this neighborhood when he was a serviceman and an installer, and he knew his way around. These houses are big and beautiful and most have older heating systems, which is good because it means that there will always be work for a good consultant. And Jack sees himself as a most excellent consultant. In fact, all other consultants who work in this neighborhood are idiots. Of this, Jack is certain. You can ask him.

Jack knocked on the door and Mr. Berman answered. "I'm here to solve your heating problems. FACT!," Jack said, and he bullwhipped his head in a most emphatic way, just in case there might be any doubt.

Mr. Berman smiled. "Well, where would you like to start?"

"In the basement," Jack said. "I always begin with the boiler. The boiler is the heart of the heating system. FACT!" And he whipped his head up and down, just in case there might be any doubt.

Mr. Berman smiled. "This way then," he said.

They turned left at the bottom of the stairs and entered the boiler room. Mr. Berman flipped on the light switch and Jack took a look at the boiler. "Right away I see a problem," Jack said. "This boiler is piped all wrong. FACT! It looks like it was done by a shoemaker. The pipes are the wrong size and that's why you're having problems with the heat on a very cold day such as today. The guy who put in this boiler was a real idiot. FACT!"

"We have had poor heat since we bought the place," Mr. Berman said. "The previous owner had the boiler installed some years ago. We moved in during the summer and last winter was our first one here. He never told us that there was a problem with the heat, but then, we never asked. You say that everything here is wrong?"

"Everything. Whoever did this work didn't know what he was doing. FACT!" Jack said.

Mr. Berman found himself nodding in agreement. It was difficult not to nod, what with Jack being so sure of himself.

"Have you been a consultant for a long time?" he asked.

"Long enough to know that a job like this is piped all wrong," Jack said. "I'm also a former installer. I know what's right and what's wrong. This, what we have here," Jack waved his arms around the boiler room, "Is all wrong. FACT!"

Mr. Berman leaned closer to the boiler and looked closely at the paper sticker with the company name printed on it. "There's someone's name on the sticker," he said. "Right here. Can you see it? It's hard to read. I think I need bifocals. Can you read the name? This may be the guy who put it in all wrong."

Jack leaned in. He has perfect eyesight. He's very proud of that. What he saw there on the sticker was his own name, written by a younger Jack. The date next to his name was also quite clear and Jack remembered now. It was years ago but he remembered. It was when he was working for one of the idiots.

He remembered now.

They were in a hurry that day, Jack and his helper. They were in a hurry because his boss, who was an idiot, had taken on too much work that month. The helper was new to the business and he looked up to Jack. Jack has such confidence. The helper idolized him.

"Let's get this one in fast," Jack had said to his helper. "Get me some two-inch out of the truck." The helper had gone out and come back and told Jack that they were all out of two-inch. "Then what do we have on the truck?" Jack had asked.

"We got one-inch," the helper had said.

"That's good enough," Jack said. "The boss is an idiot. He never puts the right stuff on our trucks for us. We'll just use what's there. This job has zones so it'll probably be okay. All the zones never call at the same time. Never. FACT!"

The helper had smiled at that. Jack was always so sure of himself. So he got Jack what Jack had asked for and they piped that boiler with what they had on hand. The helper admired Jack, and the way he was always so confident. Jack was never afraid to tell it like it is. And if people didn't like that, then tough. This is what you get when the boss is an idiot. Besides, Jack was already looking around for a better position. Life's too short to work for fools.

"What's the name on the label?" Mr. Berman said, leaning in. "Can you read it? Does it say who put in this boiler? I'd like to call the company and see what recourse I have. Based on what you're saying, there may even be grounds for a lawsuit. Would that be your professional opinion?"

And right about then – and for the first time in his professional life – Jack didn't quite know what to say.

Fact.

Waterboys

Dave was on the low end of the couch as he and Greg negotiated it down the tight stairwell. "Don't let it hit the wall," Dave grunted. I don't want the landlord hitting me with any charges for damages. I'm just happy to be getting out of this dump."

"No problem," Greg said. "Just watch your back. Here, let me lift it a bit higher." That got them around the turn and out the front door. They carried the heavy couch across the crabgrass and up the ramp of the U-Haul. "What's next?" Greg asked, taking a breather.

"I guess we'll stack some boxes up on top of the couch and then we'll get the recliner and the end tables," Dave said. "Let me see what Jenny's got ready to go."

Dave and Jenny were getting married. It was the first time for him, the second for her. Their wedding present to each other was a new house that they had built on the other side of town. Dave was a heating contractor, and to save a few bucks, he had acted as his own GC on the project. He had enough friends in the trades to pull it off, and although they had to rearrange their lives for the past six months, things had worked out well.

And today was moving day. Greg was there because he and Dave have been friends for years. When Greg found out that this was to be moving day, he called and offered to help with the heavy lifting. This, along with offering rides to airports in the pre-dawn hours, is the sign of a true friend.

Jenny was in the living room, kneeling down and writing on cartons with a black felt-tip marker. "What do you have that's good to go?" Dave said. "Anything in that stack over there," she said, smiling up at her man. Dave smiled back at her and then grabbed two of the heavy cartons. Greg also smiled and did the same and the two men headed for the stairs. Seeing their rough manliness pleased Jenny very much because she has not had a good track record when it comes to men.

Jenny's first husband, a guy she had gone steady with all though high school, had decided one day – and this was after five years of marriage – that he would prefer to play for the other team, so to speak.

He had come home late one night, after supposedly attending a business function, to announce that he had found his true life-mate, the one person who brought him bliss, his missing puzzle piece. And then he had said the name of this person and that name was . . . Bruce.

So Jenny tossed him out of their apartment and called a lawyer and pretty much hid from the world for a few years, until she met Dave. And Dave is a big strapping lumberjack of a man. He hunts and fishes and watches football on the TV and drinks beers with his buddies and he would never dream of playing for the other team. Not Dave. And not Greg either. These are men who stand in bars and recite Robert Service poetry – tough-guy poetry – and all from memory. They laugh loud and pound each other on the back with meaty paws and they know how to treat a woman and she knows that she and Dave will live happily ever after in their new home, which had a two-car garage, filled with manly tools, tools that Dave uses in his testosterone-stinking, manly profession.

"What's next?" Dave asked.

"Those," Jenny said, "but maybe you should think about draining the waterbed before you do anything else. That could take a while."

"Good idea," Dave said. "There must be a thousand gallons of water in that beast."

"How about if you get started on that and I'll drive over to the store and get you guys some more beer?"

"Excellent idea!" Dave said.

So she left and Dave went downstairs and returned with 100 feet of Sears-Best garden hose slung over his muscled shoulder. He was screwing the hose onto the mattress when Greg came into the bedroom. "What's up?" Greg said.

"This might take a while. I figured I'd get it started."

"How you gonna do that?" Greg said.

"I'm gonna siphon it onto the lawn," Dave said.

"You ever do that before?"

"Nope, first time," Dave said. "It should work just like a swimming pool, though. Once we get the siphon running it should flow right over the hump of the windowsill and down onto the crabgrass. Just like draining a swimming pool."

"How you gonna get the siphon started?" Greg asked. "Do you have a pump?"

"No, the pump's over in the garage and I don't feel like driving over there right now. You?" Greg shook his head. "I figure I can suck on the other end of the hose and that should get it primed." So they walked downstairs and out onto the crabgrass. Dave picked up the end of the hose, stuck it in his mouth and gave a good hard suck. Nothing happened.

"Stick your thumb in your mouth and hold it over the end of the hose when you need to take a breath," Greg said. "But don't breathe though your mouth or you'll break the vacuum. Breathe through your nose." Dave looked at Greg and gave it another try. He sucked until his eyeballs bulged like Rodney Dangerfield's and Greg started to laugh, which of course cracked Dave up and that was the end of any suction that might have been forming in the hose.

"Here, let me try," Greg said, and Dave willingly handed him the hose. Greg bent from the waist and stuck the hose in his mouth. Then he yanked himself upright, sucking for all he was worth. He moved his thumb in and out of the end of the hose, which made him look like a big kid with a serious oral fixation.

"Sigmund Freud would have had a heyday with you, pal," Dave said, and that was the end of whatever vacuum Greg might have had going as the two friends collapsed onto the crabgrass in a fit of laughter.

"Where the heck are Cheech and Chong when you need 'em?" Greg said.

"Maybe I should go for the pump?" Dave said.

"No, wait. Before you do that, I have an idea. If we can't suck the water down the hose, let try pushing it from the other end."

"What do you mean?" Dave said.

"We'll jump on the bed. Between the two of us we should be able to shove enough water out of the bed and into the hose to get a good siphon going."

"Worth a try," Dave said.

So they walked upstairs, took off their shoes and started to bounce up and down on the big waterbed, like a couple of kids at a pajama party. All they accomplished, however, was to shove the water from one side of the mattress to the other. "This isn't working," Dave said.

"You know what we're doing wrong?" Greg said.

"No, what?"

"We're not displacing enough water. We have to cover a larger area. Right now, we're just bouncing with our feet. We need to lay down and bounce with our whole bodies. We need to take full advantage of our combined size and weight."

"Okay, Mr. Wizard," Dave said. "Let's try."

And they did. They each laid on a side of the waterbed and put their big manly bodies into rocking spasms and wild pelvic thrusts that sent the water sloshing back and forth, but not one drop entered the hose.

"You know what we're doing wrong?" Greg said.

"No, what?"

"We're not working together like a team. We need to be on the same side of the bed, over here on the side that's opposite the hose connection. That way, when we bounce, the water has to go into the hose because we're both on the same side of the bed."

"You think?" Dave said.

"Can't miss!" Greg said.

So they did that. They laid right next to each other. In fact, to get the most coordinated bounce possible, they wrapped their manly arms around each other. And then they began to bounce for all they were worth.

And that's when Jenny returned with the beer. "Oh no!" she screamed. "Not again!"

Road Warriors

She had her hands at ten o'clock and two o'clock and the top of her gray head barely cleared the steering wheel of the brown Dodge Dart. She was driving 23 miles per hour in a 30-mph zone and she kept tapping her brakes and that was making Kevin nuts because he was in a hurry. He couldn't pass her because of the double yellow line and his cell phone was ringing because people were looking for him. He had the phone tucked between his ear and his left shoulder, his right hand was on the steering wheel, a ham sandwich was in his lap and a liter of Pepsi was between his knees. And she just tapped her brakes again. So he hit the horn and got a little closer to her bumper. And she tapped her brakes again. And that made him tap his brakes and the Pepsi slipped loose and spilled between his legs. He hit the horn again.

"Look, I gotta go," he said into the cell phone and snapped it closed. He inched a bit closer to her. This was getting personal. She rolled down the window and reached up and out with her left arm. She made a Back Off! gesture. and her brake lights came on again. He hit his horn again. She was the cap on a highly carbonated day and he was thinking about crossing that double yellow line when he spotted the cop with the radar up ahead, so he backed off, and she rolled up her window and put her hands back in the ten o'clock, two o'clock position, and they both drove on at a maddening 23 miles per hour.

A half-mile later, the road opened up to two lanes and the speed-limit sign now read 35 mph so he sped up and passed her, only to roll up to a red light a bit further down the road. This was the sort of light that stays red forever. He wiped at the spilled Pepsi with a napkin and glanced at his right-side mirror. She was rolling up next to him. She pulled right up to his door and looked at him the way an old librarian would look at a misbehaving schoolboy. She had a pen and a piece of paper in her hands and she was writing something down. Kevin figured she was jotting down the name of his company and the phone number. That didn't surprise him. After all, he was driving a four-wheeled billboard and there was no mystery as to the name of the company for which he worked (owned, actually).

Kevin smiled. He is a one-man shop and this is his only truck. If she was going to call to complain, he was the guy who would get the call. There was only one phone in this company and that was his cell phone. He often answered it while lying under a customer's sink. Such are the joys of being a one-man band.

He looked over at the old lady in the Dodge Dart and smiled again. "Sit low, drive slow," he mumbled to himself. Now that he was next to her, rather than behind her, it was easy to smile. He knew that she was in the wake of his day and that made him smile. He also knew that he'd be chatting with her on the phone pretty soon, so he figured he might as well begin their conversation with a smile. She scowled at him, shook her little fist, honked her horn a few times, shook her fist again. The light turned green and Kevin smiled again, and drove away.

Twenty minutes later, his cell phone rang. He flipped it open. "Anytime Plumbing and Heating," he said, a big smile in his voice.

"Yes. I'd like to report that one of your men is a very reckless driver."

"May I ask who's calling?" Kevin said.

"I'd rather not give my name but your man just ran me off the road," she said.

"He did?"

"Yes, and he was speeding and tailgating and also weaving across a double yellow line. I think he may have been drinking, or on pot. His eyes were all glassy. He was also playing very loud music on his radio and when he passed me he made an obscene gesture and I think you should know about this. That man is a disgrace to your company. He should be severely reprimanded."

"Well, we're certainly glad that you called to report this, ma'am," Kevin said. "We want to take care of this problem immediately. Did you get the truck number? We have a large fleet of trucks, you know."

"Truck number? No, but I can describe it. It's white and it has red lettering on the side with your company name and the phone number, which is how I knew where to call. I wrote it all down when we were stopped at a traffic light. Your man ran that light as well. And he nearly hit some schoolchildren who were crossing the street. He's a menace to society."

"Did you happen to get the license number of the vehicle, ma'am?" Kevin asked.

"No, but I can describe the driver for you. And I should also mention that he drove other people off the road as well. One man was towing a boat. Your driver nearly forced him into a ditch. And he ran from the police as well. I saw that with my own eyes. I think you should severely reprimand him."

"Did you get a good look at this miscreant, ma'am?" Kevin asked.

"Yes, I did," she said. "He seemed to be a large man. And I didn't like his haircut. It was very shaggy. And he had a moustache. I don't like moustaches."

"Was his hair brown, ma'am?"

"Yes, brown hair."

"Okay, ma'am, I know just who you're talking about, and I want you to know that this is the second time in the past ten years that I've received complaints about this individual."

"Well, what are you planning to do about it?" she asked.

"I'm going to fire his butt as soon as he gets back in here!" Kevin said.

"Oh my," the old woman said. "I didn't mean for you to take measures that drastic. I just thought that you would reprimand him."

"Oh no, ma'am!" Kevin said. "I've had it with this guy. Two times in ten years is enough for me. He is outta here!"

"But I hate to think that I'm the cause of him getting fired," she said.

"You're just doing your duty as a good citizen, ma'am," Kevin said. "That bum is gone. The minute he walks through this door I'm going to get his keys and tell him to call his wife to come and pick him up. I don't care if she is undergoing chemotherapy. She can leave the hospital for a while and pick him up. I want him out of here!"

"But that wasn't my intent," she said. "Oh my!"

"Don't be concerned, ma'am. You did the right thing. His children will probably have to leave high school and get jobs so that the family can keep their house. I don't care, though. Once we put him on the list, no plumbing and heating company in America will hire him."

"The list?" she said.

"Yes," Kevin said. "In our industry, we have a Bad Driver Blacklist. It is the kiss of death for an employee. Break the rules two times in ten years and you're toast. That's it! You are OUTTA here!"

"Oh my!"

"And as for his elderly mother who lives with him, she can eat dog food. That will teach them all a lesson!"

"But I really didn't want to cause this much trouble for him," she said. "I just thought . . . "

"How much trouble did you want to cause, ma'am?"

"Well, I thought just a reprimand would do."

"Okay, we'll give him one more chance," Kevin said. "And a reprimand, of course."

"Oh, thank you!" she said. "I would hate to have all of that other stuff on my conscious."

"You're a good person, ma'am," Kevin said. "I would like to leave you with one thought, though."

"What's that?" she asked.

"GAS PEDAL!" he screamed into the little cell phone.

And that felt pretty darn good.

Buddy's Beaters

It wasn't a very long list – just 25 people in all – but it nagged at Buddy in the night and robbed him of his rest. He'd toss and dream unsettling dreams of Mrs. Gibbings, that old crone who had promised to pay him for fixing her toilet, but then hadn't. "You owe me ninety-seven dollars and fifty cents," Buddy had said to her. "Sue me," she had replied.

Buddy didn't have time for lawyers or small-claims court, so he shook his head in disgust and tried to let it go. But the sour image of Mrs. Gibbings continued to visit him in the night and wake him regularly – all over a lousy $97.50. Buddy's wife would roll over and ask Buddy what was wrong. "Gibbings," he would mumble. "She won't let me sleep." Buddy's wife would utter a curse word, low and foul under her breath, and then try to go back to sleep. Buddy could never get back to sleep once the Beaters came to visit him in the night. It was all so unfair.

Mr. Jennings had called Buddy last Christmas and begged him to come over because the heat was off and he had a house filled with relatives. "We have no heat! The thermostat is all the way down to 65 degrees. You gotta get here right now."

Buddy went because he was that kind of guy. He couldn't bear to think of a family without heat on Christmas, even though this didn't seem like much of an emergency. When Buddy got to Mr. Jennings' house he saw that the problem was the setback thermostat. Mr. Jennings had mixed up the pins. It was on its night cycle. Buddy chuckled and fixed it in just a couple of minutes. Then he explained to Mr. Jennings what the problem had been. Mr. Jennings listened with rapt attention. His relatives gathered around to listen as well. Then they asked Buddy a few dozen questions about problems they were having with their own heating systems. They figured that as long as Buddy was there anyway, they were entitled to free heating consultations.

Buddy answered all their questions patiently and in the spirit of holiday giving. Then he went out to his truck and wrote up a bill for $49.95, which was his charge for a basic service call. He trudged back up the snowy walkway, stomped the snow off his shoes, and knocked on the door. Mr. Jennings answered the door, looking a bit surprised to see Buddy again so soon. "Did you forget something?" he asked.

"No, I just have the bill for you."

"What bill?" Mr. Jennings asked.

"The bill for the service call," Buddy explained. "And don't worry. I didn't charge you any extra because it's Christmas. Just think of it as my holiday gift to you and your family. I hope you'll call on me again someday."

"But you didn't fix anything," Mr. Jennings shot back. "You worked on that thing for, what, two minutes? I should pay you fifty bucks for that? What's that work out to? Fifteen hundred bucks an hour! No wonder you guys are all so rich! Hey, you know what? I could have fixed that thing myself. You sure didn't do much."

"Well, if you could have fixed it yourself," Buddy said, realizing that Mr. Jennings was a Beater, "why didn't you?"

"Look, I'm not going to stand out here in the cold and argue with you," Mr. Jennings said, "especially on Christmas. My family is here, as you can see, and now I'd like to go back to them. I thank you for your assistance, but what you did is certainly not worth what you're trying to charge me. I'm going to write a letter to Consumer Affairs about this. I think you're a stinkin' thief." And with that, Mr. Jennings stepped back into his house and slammed the front door in Buddy's face, leaving him alone on the doorstep, like an orphan in an old black-and-white movie.

Buddy rolled around in his twisted sheets and thought about Mr. Jennings. He flipped his pillow to the cool side and tried to sleep, but it was no use. His wife woke again, and again asked what was wrong. "Can't sleep," he whispered.

"The Beaters?" she asked softly.

"Yeah," he said.

"Don't worry, Buddy. I love you."

"I love you too," he muttered, and then waited alone for the dawn.

The next day, he got a call from Lonny who works for the local Penny Saver newspaper. Buddy had been running a quarter-page ad in the Penny Saver for about six months. He thought it was doing him some good, but there was no way to know for sure. Advertising is like that. Buddy had tried coupons a couple of times. They worked, but they also brought him more Beaters. He had no way of telling who they were until it was too late, though. Beaters look just like ordinary people.

He'd considered charging for his services in advance, but that just isn't the way the plumbing and heating business works. He knew that the plumbing and heating business works the way a diner works. When you go to a diner you order your food and then they cook it and bring it to you. After you've eaten the food, they ask you to pay for it. First the food, then the bill – just like the plumbing and heating business.

The opposite of this, of course, is fast food – like Burger King or McDonald's. There, you order your food, but they make you pay first before you can eat it. There's less of a chance of getting beaten if you treat your business like fast food, Buddy realized. But the trouble with plumbing and heating is that the customers don't know what they're going to order. It's not like they're going to say, "Gimme a Big Mac." They just say, "It's cold in my house." Then the professional has to figure out what they need.

No, it's definitely a diner sort of business, Buddy thought.

These thoughts were blowing through Buddy's head like a hot wind when he met with Lonny that day. "I wish I could get paid up front," he said. "Like Burger King."

"I wouldn't pay you up front," Lonny laughed.

"Neither will anyone else," Buddy admitted.

"Nope, I'm looking for a bargain," Lonny continued, hardly hearing what Buddy had said. "Gimme a bargain and I'll buy from you. That's the way it works. I'm looking for that coupon. Run the coupon, Buddy. Run it every week. That's what people want – coupons and bargains. You have to adopt the right attitude about advertising, Buddy."

And it was right then that the idea hit Buddy. It came to him like an angel from heaven and whispered in his ear. "Adopt," the angel said softly. "Open an adoption agency for the Beaters."

"Thank you, Lonny," Buddy mumbled. "You have just given me what I need – a good night's sleep."

"What'd I say?" Lonny asked.

"Come and see me again next week," Buddy answered, getting up and ushering Lonny to the door. "Run the same ad as usual this week, but come and see me again next week. I just might have something brand-new for you."

"I don't get it," Lonny said.

"You will," Buddy answered with a smile that comes only to those who have been abused, and now see a way to get even.

Buddy went home and put together this letter, which he then mailed to his list of 25 Beaters:

Dear Past Due Customer,

I have some very good news for you today. You owe me money, and I have been asking you to pay me for quite some time now, but those days are over. You no longer have to pay your debt because a local sponsor will soon assume your responsibility.

Here's how it works.

Starting next week, I will be publishing your name and address in the local Penny Saver, along with the amount you owe me, and for how long. It will be under the heading, "Adopt a Beater!"

When a local resident agrees to adopt you by paying your outstanding invoice, we will then give that kind person a coupon good for future services valued at two times the amount you have owed me for so very long. I will then publish the name of the sponsor that adopted you, right next to your name. To make sure that everyone in town knows of your new relationship with your sponsor, I will keep publishing your names on our Adopt a Beater board for one year. You won't owe us a thing, and you will have made a new friend – your sponsor.

Have a nice day.

Buddy's Plumbing & Heating

Five days later, Freddy, who has delivered the mail to Buddy's place of business for as long as anyone can remember, dropped 25 long-past-due checks into Buddy's mailbox.

And the angels watched over Buddy that night as he slept like a baby.

Fear Itself

Troubles were sprouting like pimples on prom night for Coffin. He'd gotten the okay to start the job (or at least he thought he had), but now Mrs. Murphy was having second thoughts. She called Coffin on the telephone.

"How do I know you're not going to cheat me?" Mrs. Murphy screeched. Mrs. Murphy's voice sounds like a wood file going over the end of a copper pipe. Coffin shivered, and took a moment to compose himself.

"We never cheat anyone, Mrs. Murphy," Coffin reassured her. "Not ever."

"But it seems to me you could just start the job and then add something I don't need," Mrs. Murphy rasped. "Then you'll probably try to charge me for extras. And if I don't want to pay for extras, you won't finish my job. You'll leave me high and dry and without heat. That happens, you know. I'm nobody's fool; I watch 48 Hours!"

The mention of the TV show sent another shiver through Coffin. He squirmed in his chair as if someone was holding a lit match under his butt. "We're not going to cheat you, Mrs. Murphy. Remember we discussed all of this when I came to your home? Remember?" A silence thicker than fog drifted toward Coffin from Mrs. Murphy's end of the line. He tapped his shirt pocket, making sure his nitroglycerin tablets were there. They were – right next to his pack of Marlboros. He took out one of the latter and lit it, blowing smoke away from the handset. He could hear her breathing through the fog. "Mrs. Murphy?" he said.

"And some of that technical mumbo jumbo you were talking when you were here," she continued, as though his words had not registered on the dipstick of her intelligence. "How do I know for sure you're going to do everything right? I didn't understand what you were talking about half the time, so how can I be sure you're going to do everything you're supposed to do?" Mrs. Murphy's fear was priming and foaming like filthy water in an old steam boiler.

"Well, how the hell do I know you're going to pay me when the job's done?" Coffin blurted through a cloud of blue smoke. He caught his breath, not believing he had actually given voice to the fears that had been bouncing around his brain for the past few days.

"WHAT!" Mrs. Murphy bleated. "Now you call me a thief! To think that I shouldn't pay you! From where does this thought come? Something I said to you maybe? WHAT? WHAT?" Coffin felt like he was on a sleigh ride to destitution as he watched the job slide away from him.

Maybe I won't pay him, Mrs. Murphy considered.

Maybe she will pay me, Coffin thought. He composed himself. "When I imply that you're a thief, Mrs. Murphy, I don't mean it in a bad way. It's just that sometimes people don't pay contractors when the contractor is finished. They refuse to make that final payment, you know? It's one of the perpetual fears we contractors have."

Mrs. Murphy, of course, had fully intended to hang on to that final payment for at least six months. She wanted to make sure that everything worked properly throughout the winter. She was afraid of what would happen if things didn't work properly. At least if she still had some of Coffin's money she could use it to coerce him into fixing the as-yet-to-occur but surely probable problem. "Well, I'd never do that," she lied. "Not if you do the job right."

But of course, she had already decided that Coffin was not going to do the job right. She saw that final payment as her insurance policy.

"Mrs. Murphy, let's both calm down, okay?" Coffin pleaded. He heard her breathing, low and slow. "Mrs. Murphy?"

"Okay, okay. We'll calm down," she squawked. "Both of us. But that means you too!" Coffin's hand drifted back toward his medicine. He touched the tiny bottle through the thin cloth of his shirt pocket. He had done a credit check on Mrs. Murphy, and he figured he could put a lien on her house if she didn't pay him. Coffin trusted only cash in advance; he'd do a credit check on Bill Gates if Bill Gates ever decided to call him. He figured he probably had the upper hand in this negotiation. After all, the weather was getting colder by the minute, and she needed him more than he needed her. She probably did, anyway.

But then Mrs. Murphy brayed, "You're not the only contracting company I talk to, you know."

"Huh?"

"I called them all, you know. I went through the Yellow Pages and called them all. Every blessed one of them. Your competitors will keep you in line, Mr. Coffin. I watch

48 Hours, you know." Coffin felt as though someone had just pumped up his head with a five-horsepower Sears air compressor. "So what do you have to say about that?" she demanded.

"I thought you had decided I should do this job," Coffin said finally after a long angina-filled pause. "Maybe we should just forget the whole thing, Mrs. Murphy." He didn't mean this, of course. He needed this job because he was on the verge of losing his company due to inclement business.

"Oh no!" Mrs. Murphy insisted. "I want you to do the work. I'm just protecting myself because of what goes on with all of you contractors. Let the buyer beware, right? I want you to do the work. I'm just being a wise consumer. You can't blame me for that, can you? I just have a few apprehensions to sort through."

"No, I don't blame you, but . . ."

"So," she said, cutting him off, "who will you send to do my job if I decide to use you?"

"But you said you wanted to use me!"

"I meant I may want to use you. There's a difference, you know. Now the person you send, will he be free of drugs?"

"Absolutely!" Coffin sputtered. "All my guys are clean. Absolutely clean!" He knew this to be reasonably true because he made every one of his guys go through random drug testing. Coffin was afraid of anyone who used drugs other than his drugs, which included alcohol, nicotine, nitroglycerin and Preparation H. He was mostly afraid of what some drug-crazed kid might do to one of his trucks. Coffin had seen a report on 20/20 about rising employee drug use and what these employees had done

174

to their employers' trucks. He had hired a company to do the random drug testing. The company, of course, had carefully checked Coffin's credit references before taking on the contract. They knew contracting companies could sometimes be as stable as the San Andreas Fault. They were afraid they wouldn't get paid if Coffin went belly-up.

"They do good work, your men?" Mrs. Murphy asked.

"They do very good work," Coffin said without hesitation. "We went over this when I saw you. Remember?" Coffin knew his guys were, at best, mediocre. But if he said this he knew she wouldn't give him the job. Coffin hired the unhirable because they were the only people who would work for him. Coffin, you see, sometimes had difficulty making the payroll. This was because he was often short of cash due to promises broken by others. The fact that Coffin's business was often homeport to the Three Stooges troubled him greatly, but what can you do?

"My guys are the best," Coffin lied.

"All right," Mrs. Murphy said. "You can do the job. I just have to check with a few other companies first. I'm afraid I can't tell you right now when you might be able to start the job, but I may want you to definitely do it. Soon. I think. I'll let you know."

Coffin shivered with fear, touched the tiny bottle in his shirt pocket, lit another cigarette.

How Hap Magee Gets Paid

Hap Magee is of an indiscernible age. His primary color is gray – gray hair, gray skin, gray work uniform, dusty old shoes. He has never married, and you should know from the git-go that nothing, absolutely nothing, bothers this man.

Hap is not the sort of guy that throws things away. His garage is filled with leaky car batteries, outdated license plates, bent nails in torn cardboard cartons, old motor oil in milk jugs, bald tires, hammer heads with splintered handles, and copper fittings with globs of ancient solder that cling to them like barnacles. He has a six-foot-high by 30-inch-wide wooden door with a mysterious fist-sized hole through its center. He also has a pile of two-by-fours (none longer than seven inches), 18 cast-iron boiler sections of various sizes, each with a hole through which you could hurl an alley cat, and many other items he may need some day. You can never tell.

Stacked along the side of Hap Magee's garage are many busted wooden pallets that he will someday burn in his fireplace – if he ever gets around to building a fireplace. "That's good wood from them pallets," Hap Magee tells the guys at the supply house. "A lot cheaper than cordwood, too!" The guys at the supply house think Hap Magee's house is the Rat Capital of North America, but they'd never say this to his face.

Hap Magee drives a haggard Chevy van. He'll tell anyone who will listen that he's probably put more than a quarter-million city miles on that van. The actual mileage is anyone's guess because the odometer gave up the ghost back when Gerald Ford was telling New York City to drop dead. "Plenty more miles in 'er!" Hap Magee says to anyone who will listen. The tires are only the second set to serve this vehicle – a fact Hap Magee proudly points out to anyone who has the nerve to get close enough to take a peek at these bulging pneumatic time bombs. The van's front grill, pummeled and punched for years by rocks and bugs, sneers down the road like a toothless, over-the-hill hockey player. A spider's web of cracks plays across the windshield, refracting the sunlight into a psychedelic blur, and there's a frayed red dishrag where a gas cap should be. Fluids drip from the underbelly of the van, like blood from an oozing wound, and whenever Hap Magee steps on the gas, the transmission squeals like a half-dozen river rats trapped in a barrel of ammonia.

You can still make out his catchy slogan on the side of the van. "Plumbing got you up a tree? Call Magee!" it reads in letters that have long since faded from ruby red to diarrhea brown. There's a barely discernible graphic of a huge dog lifting its hind leg against what could be a maple tree. "Gets yer attention, don't it?" Hap shouts to anyone at the supply house who will listen. When Hap Magee bumps his van out of the supply house lot it sounds like a cement mixer filled with cobblestones going by.

Hap Magee uses old copper wire to keep the van's bumpers from catching in the frayed tires. He twists the ends of the wire into eight-inch-long brown braids. Neighborhood boys regularly steal this copper wire, leaving the bumpers lying in the driveway for Hap to find in the morning. But like every other detail of life, this doesn't bother Hap Magee one stinking bit. He just gets some more copper wire from the garage and reattaches the bumpers. "Those kids know the value of scrap," Hap chuckles to the guys at the supply house. "I'm glad they don't touch my pipe and fittings, but I don't care much about the wire. I can always get more scrap wire. The world's full of scrap wire."

The neighborhood boys generally leave Hap Magee's pipe and fittings alone because that stuff is inside Hap's van and they know that also inside Hap's van is a hellhound named Chuck. Chuck is rarely seen because he hardly ever leaves the van, preferring to snooze fitfully on an old throw rug, atop a scattered pile of pipe, valves, and fittings. While he sleeps, Chuck dreams of juicy, neighborhood boys.

Chuck's lineage is muddled, but most folks who have spotted him lurking in the deep shadows of the van's interior suspect that there was at least one wolf sniffing around his family tree. No one has ever gotten close enough to confirm this, of course. Chuck's eyes, which glow like road flares through the cracked windshield, discourage prolonged investigation. Chuck is a loyal companion to Hap Magee. He's also the van's security system, as well as Armageddon waiting to happen – all wrapped up in one horrible, foul-smelling package.

What makes Chuck different from other very large dogs is that he never barks or growls, especially when the neighborhood boys come calling. He just waits. And while he waits, he runs his heavy, front paws down the inside of the van's metal walls. You can hear this from quite a distance because Chuck's claws look like the twisted 10-penny nails that Hap Magee keeps in that cardboard box out in his garage. When Chuck scratches, he does it in a patient and rhythmic way, like a convict working on a prison wall with a soup spoon. Chuck's claws, however, sound more like a backhoe than a soup spoon – a backhoe that's screeching lengthwise down a twelve-inch water main. This metallic shriek echoes dark and ominous in the night air when the boys come a-calling.

Most nights, Hap Magee lays awake and alone in his bed listening to Chuck's steady scratching and the soft, sneakered footfalls of the young scavengers. Hap speculates on the remaining thickness of the old Chevy's sheet metal, and he smiles to himself.

The boys, on the other hand, think only of glory. They've long since elevated the stealing of Hap Magee's copper wire to an extreme sport – like hang gliding into hell, or sitting in the fourth row at a Beastie Boys concert. They've never actually seen Chuck, but they have certainly heard him – and that only adds to their rush.

For his part, Chuck works patiently on the metal wall while sniffing the boys' hot adrenaline scent that wafts through the night air.

Not long ago, a certain Mr. Cully moved into town. Like Hap Magee, Mr. Cully was mostly gray and lived alone. But unlike Hap Magee, Mr. Cully was not a pleasant man. In fact, he had recently lost his wife to divorce. Mrs. Cully's last words to Mr. Cully were, "You should swallow razor blades, die a horrible death, and rot in some back alley with the garbage."

What brought on this final outburst was Mrs. Cully's frustration at spending the best years of her life with a terminal cheapskate. Mr. Cully, you see, doesn't like to part with his money, especially when he owes it to other people. He'll find any excuse to keep from having to pay his debts, and most of the time, he manages to wear down his creditors. Mrs. Cully, however, had had it up to here with the stress inflicted by countless bill collectors, so one day in October she just cut her losses and walked out.

Mr. Cully missed Mrs. Cully because he now had to do his own laundry and cook for himself. One afternoon, while trying to jam just one more empty Ginty's Beef Stew can into the overstuffed plastic garbage pail he keeps under the kitchen sink, he managed to dislodge the sink's P-trap. "Ahh nuts!" he said, as greasy water poured into the cabinet. "Now I'm going to have to call a plumber."

Hap came rattling down the street in the old van that afternoon. He whistled his way into the kitchen, diagnosed the problem, and went out to the van and found a used P-trap that would fit on Mr. Cully's sink. He installed the trap, tested it with both cold and hot water, stood back and smiled at Mr. Cully with satisfaction.

"Nothing like used parts!" Hap Magee said. "Saves us both a lot of money."

Mr. Cully jumped on the word "used" like a cat on a parakeet. "You installed used parts?" he said with disgust and incredulity. Inwardly, of course, he was delighted because he now had an easy way out of having to pay for the services rendered. Hap Magee seemed honestly hurt. "Used isn't bad," Hap said in such a beautifully simple way.

"Well, I'm not paying for used parts," Mr. Cully said. "And you can get outta my house. Used parts, my ass! Get outta here before I sue!"

Hap Magee remained unruffled. "Used parts are always my first choice," Hap said, offering a smile the way an old dog might offer its master a rubber ball. "Saves money, you know? And the sink works just fine now! Look." Hap ran the hot water again, bent over, peered under the sink at the tarnished old trap, and smiled up at Mr. Cully.

"GET OUTTA MY HOUSE!" Mr. Cully bellowed, working himself up into the hysterical frenzy that always seemed to work on the plumbing trade. He pointed a shaking finger at the front door and held his breath until he turned crimson. "GET . . . OUT!"

Hap Magee nodded. And then he gave Mr. Cully that special smile he saves for such occasions. "Hang out here for a minute, willya, Mr. Cully? I'm going out to the van to fetch my Accounts Receivable Manager. You'll find him real interesting. He has real hairy legs!" Mr. Cully just glared.

Hap Magee smiled and then strolled down the front walk toward the ancient van's rusted side door – and Chuck. Mr. Cully watched him go. And then he slammed his thin wooden front door with great, sneering satisfaction. Done with the bum, he thought. Done!

Or so he thought.

Buddy, Again

Buddy had been doing all right as far as the Beaters were concerned – at least for a while, that is. He had been collecting what was due him, and, as a result, he had been able to sleep nights. His method of collecting money from the Beaters had been a simple one. He would put the stiffs who refused to pay his invoices up for adoption by publishing their names in the local Penny Saver. He didn't do this in a mean or malicious way; he simply printed their names next to the past-due amount under the heading "Adopt a Beater." His advertisement went on to explain that if a reader chose to adopt a Beater by paying the amount of the outstanding invoice, Buddy would then provide the reader with twice that dollar amount in plumbing and heating services. Who could refuse a deal like that?

As it turned out, Buddy didn't have to actually run the ad many times because, as soon as he told the Beaters that they no longer had to pay their long-overdue invoices because they were about to be adopted (and made famous), the Beaters would quickly ante up.

All except for Mrs. Schnitz, that is. Mrs. Schnitz had a face that would have looked quite at home in a sadomasochistic massage parlor. She had not responded to the letter that Buddy had sent her explaining how his new "Adopt a Beater" program worked. Instead, Mrs. Schnitz had had her attorney respond for her. He was a scary fellow named Aaron Flick, and he took great pleasure in explaining to Buddy over the phone how he relished the chance to gnaw the flesh from Buddy's bones – financially speaking, of course. He also mentioned the possibility of a Beaters vs. Buddy class action lawsuit and this caused Buddy to rethink his position on the "Adopt a Beater" program.

"What are you thinking?" Buddy's wife asked him that night as he lay in bed and stared at the ceiling.

"I'm thinking I'd rather give myself brain surgery with a Black & Decker drill than spend another minute on the phone with Aaron Flick," Buddy said.

Buddy's wife put a cool hand on his forehead. "We don't need people like that in our lives, honey," she said. "Don't worry about the money. We'll be fine. Just let it go. We'll get by."

But Buddy couldn't let it go. It wasn't so much about the money as it was about being beaten by someone that he had trusted would pay him for services rendered. "Let it go," she said again. She kissed him softly on the cheek, and rolled over. Buddy stared at the ceiling for another hour. "If I can't get paid," he mumbled, "I should at least be able to get even." He turned his head toward her. But she had already fallen asleep.

The next morning, Buddy stopped by Charlie's Coffee Cup for a big mug of black coffee and a corn muffin. "Hey, Buddy Holly!" Charlie shouted from the grill as Buddy took his usual stool. Charlie had been calling Buddy by that name for years. Buddy didn't mind. He liked the oldies as much as the next middle-aged guy did. "The usual?" Charlie asked and Buddy nodded. "Looks like you need more than one cup this morning, Buddy. Look at those bags under your eyes." Buddy looked at his tired face in the mirror behind the counter and then back at Charlie. "What can I tell ya?" Buddy said.

Charlie laughed and went back to pushing the home fries around on the griddle and adjusting the eggs. "If you knew Peggy Sue, then you'd know why I feel blue!" Charlie sang in a bad imitation of the long-dead rock-'n-roller. He turned and pointed his spatula at Buddy. "Hey, Buddy Holly. What do you suppose ever happened to the Crickets? Those guys have gotta be older than dirt by now. You suppose they're singing in some Holiday Inn lounge somewhere?" Buddy shrugged and blew on his coffee. "Tough break for them, eh?" Charlie went on. "One day it's Buddy Holly and the Crickets; the next day it's just the Crickets. Buddy left, but the Crickets remained. Funny how we don't hear from them, though. Crickets are noisy! You'd think we'd hear from them Crickets, eh?" He laughed hysterically at his own pun.

Buddy set his coffee cup down and looked at his reflection in the mirror. "Crickets," he muttered to himself.

"Yeah!" Charlie repeated. "Crickets. You'd think we'd hear from them? Get it? Crickets? Hear from 'em?" Charlie let loose another belly laugh. He was his own best audience.

"Crickets," Buddy mumbled. He got off his stool, dropped two bucks on the counter, and walked out, as if in a trance.

"Hey," Charlie shouted after him. "You want the muffin to go?" But Buddy was already gone.

Here's how the advertisement in the Penny Saver read:

CONCERNED ABOUT THE QUALITY OF THE AIR IN YOUR HOME?

Don't be. With any plumbing and/or heating job we do, we will install an

ABSOLUTELY FREE!

MINITUBE FRESH AIR INJECTOR

in your home's heating and/or air conditioning system.

FREE, FREE, FREE!

Call for details!

BUDDY'S PLUMBING & HEATING

As you might expect, Buddy's telephone rang off the hook and business was better than it had been in years. People in Buddy's hometown are as health conscious as they are in any other American town nowadays. They wanted that Minitube Fresh Air Injector – especially since it came along absolutely free with any service Buddy performed. People figured that if they had to call someone to fix the leaky toilet, they might as well get something for nothing while they were at it.

"What exactly is the Minitube Fresh Air Injector?" Mr. Skuza asked Buddy as Buddy was putting the last screw into the new thermostat he had just installed in Mr. Skuza's hallway.

"It's actually quite simple," Buddy explained. "Have you ever heard of the venturi effect?" Mr. Skuza nodded. "Well, the Minitube Fresh Air Injector uses the principle of the venturi to draw a small amount of fresh air into your home through the duct system. As soon as I'm done here, I'm going to drill a half-inch hole in your main horizontal heating duct. I'll be installing a small plastic tube in that hole and I'll be running the Minitube, which is the heart of the system, through a second hole I'll drill into the side of your home. I'll make certain that I caulk everything before I leave, of course. I'll also install a porous cork in the end of the tube that extends outside your home. It will act as a filter, allowing only the correct amount of air to pass. When the fan in your furnace operates, the venturi effect, created by the moving air in your ducts, will draw in the proper amount of fresh air through the Minitube to keep your home's indoor air fresh and clean." Then Buddy smiled at Mr. Skuza. "And it's all absolutely free!" Mr. Skuza smiled back.

After Buddy had installed the new Minitube Fresh Air Injector he went out to his truck to write up the invoice for the new thermostat. He carried the invoice back to the front door and knocked. Mr. Skuza came to the door and told Buddy he had decided he wasn't going to pay Buddy for the thermostat because Buddy had dared to touch his white walls. "You left a smudge," Mr. Skuza said. "And now I'm going to have to hire a painter to paint all the rooms. You're lucky I don't sue you!" He narrowed his eyes at Buddy, challenging him. "You want to go to court over the price of a thermostat, Buddy? Can you afford that? You're just a . . . contractor." The last word fell from Mr. Skuza's mouth like a piece of gristle.

"Ahh, I see," Buddy sighed. "You're a Beater." Buddy nodded in disappointment. "Oh well. I never would have picked you as one, Mr. Skuza; but then again, I've never been very good at spotting Beaters under the best of circumstances. My wife keeps reminding me of that. But I keep telling her that you all look so . . . ordinary." Mr. Skuza continued to leer at Buddy with the triumph of the petty thief. "You sure you won't reconsider?" Buddy asked hopefully, but Mr. Skuza just slammed the door in Buddy's face, leaving him alone on the front steps.

Buddy walked back to his truck and retrieved the funnel and the mason jar filled with crickets. Pete's Pet Shop had plenty of crickets for sale, and Buddy was quickly becoming Pete's best customer.

Buddy walked around to the side of the house, pulled the cork out of the end of the Minitube Fresh Air Injector, stuck the narrow end of the funnel into the Minitube and poured about 50 crickets down the wide end. Then he replaced the cork and walked away.

He slept like a baby that night.

Mr. Skuza, on the other hand, stared at his ceiling in his personal Heart of Darkness and listened to the ratcheting cacophony that reverberated from his ducts and, by then . . . from everywhere.

Mrs. Santucci's Complaint

Mrs. Santucci was moving across her living room and toward Benny like a heavy cat. She was wearing the same outfit she had on the last time Benny had been to her house – that same black, widow's dress. She was also wearing those same laced, black shoes, with the black stockings rolled down around her elephantine ankles. She had the same hairnet, still holding the same gray bun tightly against the back of her head. The same knitting needle stuck through that bun, like an arrow through a dried apple. The same two black hairs protruded like tiny electrical wires from the dark mole on the right side of her chin. And she had that same unforgiving face.

The last time he had worked for her, it had taken Benny nine months to collect his money. Mrs. Santucci had told him she wanted to make sure everything worked well through at least three heating seasons. Benny wasn't quite sure why he had agreed to come back now. Maybe because her daughter had called this time? Maybe because he was afraid of a lawsuit? That wasn't rational, but there he was, nevertheless.

"Eeeeee!" Mrs. Santucci shrieked as the daughter brought Benny up close to Mrs. Santucci's squinting eyes. "Dey senda you! You da sonamabeech day senda las time!" Mrs. Santucci closed in on Benny like a dump truck approaching a landfill. Benny backed up against a red velvet couch with clear plastic slipcovers and took a shallow breath. He didn't want to take a deep breath because Mrs. Santucci consumes more garlic than all of Sicily. He thought he'd lose his cookies on her red shag, wall-to-wall carpeting if he took a deep breath.

"I own the company, Mrs. Santucci," Benny gagged. "No one sent me. I came on my own." He composed himself. "I want you to be happy, Mrs. Santucci. Your daughter, too. I don't want to have a problem with you."

"You gotta problem widda me already!" Mrs. Santucci shrieked.

"Don't get me involved in this," the daughter said, snapping her gum, and nearly knocking Benny down as she lunged for the front door. "I gotta go, Ma. I'll call you maybe next week."

"You leava me wid dis bum!" Mrs. Santucci shouted at her receding daughter. The door slammed like a bank vault. Benny looked at Mrs. Santucci.

"Whatever problem you're having with your heating system, I'm sure I can fix it, Mrs. Santucci," Benny said. "You haven't had problems up until now, have you?"

"Eeeeee! Da same sonamabeech, dey send!" Mrs. Santucci shrieked, grabbing both sides of her head with her gnarled hands. She sank slowly into the red velvet chair in the same way a 1950 Mercury would come down from a hydraulic lift. "I deserva dis?" she moaned. "Wadda I do ta deserva dis?" She looked up at the ceiling as though expecting an answer from heaven, or from her daughter who wasn't about to answer because she had had the good sense to leave while she still could.

Benny calmed himself and said, "On the phone, you said it was too cold here in your living room, Mrs. Santucci?"

"Wadda I do?" Mrs. Santucci droned on as though she was still at Mr. Santucci's wake. "Oh, wadda I do to deserva dis?" She shot a meaty arm in Benny's direction. "Dis! Dis stinker! Dis bum dat maka me freeze to det here inna ma house."

"It doesn't feel that cold to me in here," Benny said, trying his best to calm the old bag. "It feels nice. In fact, it feels . . . crisp." This ploy often worked with Benny's elderly customers. "Crisp is healthy," Benny said. "Crisp is what you had in the old country. Remember? Crisp is good!"

Mrs. Santucci let go of her gray head and shifted her attention from the ceiling to Benny. "Crispa?" she said. "Crispa! I showa you crispa!" She pushed her bulk from the chair with arms that looked like soggy cardboard cartons and scuffed to the mirrored coffee table where she grabbed a cheap plastic thermometer. She waved the thermometer up and down in the air like a four-inch paintbrush and then squinted at the temperature. "Eeeeee!" she shrieked. "Looka dis!" She jabbed the thermometer into Benny's belly and let loose another dolphin-like cry. "Eeeeee!" Benny looked at the thermometer. It read 60 degrees. He walked to the thermostat and saw that she had it set on 85 degrees. He turned and looked at Mrs. Santucci. "It's . . . crisp!" he said.

"And you a sonamabeech," she shouted back, waggling her twisted fist at him.

"Mrs. Santucci, I know I can fix this, but you can't keep cursing me like that. You'll give yourself a stroke." Mrs. Santucci spit on her index and little fingers and pointed them at Benny. She mumbled something in a language he didn't understand. "Mrs. Santucci?" Benny said.

"I fixa you," she mumbled, spitting and pointing at him again. "I fixa you good!"

Visions of Southern European voodoo pranced through Benny's head. He grasped for a diversion, something real. "Mrs. Santucci, you haven't had any problems with your heat before this winter, have you? I mean, I installed this radiation way back in 1986, right? That was a long time ago, Mrs. Santucci. Right? This problem just started now. This week? It's been very cold this week, Mrs. Santucci." Benny smiled at the old crone. "I know I can fix it, but you have to calm down and give me a chance. It shouldn't cost too much to fix either."

Mrs. Santucci padded over to the dining room table and came back with a piece of paper, which she held in her hands as though it was a note from a saint. Benny recognized the paper as one of his company's contracts. "You promisa me heat!" she shouted. "Disa no heat. Eeeeee! I gotta in writing. You see?" She shoved the paper at Benny.

Benny read through the contract and checked to see how much baseboard radiation he had specified for the room. Something had been nagging at his heating man's mind ever since he'd entered the room – and now he knew what it was. He looked around the room and realized that much of the baseboard he had installed back in 1986 was no longer there. "Mrs. Santucci, I notice that much of the baseboard I installed back in 1986 is no longer here," he said.

"Wadda you mean?" she asked, suspiciously.

Benny checked the contract again. "Well, like this sliding glass door," he said. "When did you have this installed? This wasn't here when I did the job way back in 1986, was it?"

"Dey putta dat in las July," Mrs. Santucci said. "You a sonamabeech." She spit on her two fingers again and pointed them at Benny. He cringed, and ducked, but continued.

"There used to be baseboard radiation where the door is now, Mrs. Santucci. Remember? I installed that baseboard way back in 1986. There used to be ten more feet of baseboard right over there on that wall." Benny pointed to the glass door. Mrs. Santucci scowled at him. "It's gone now."

"I wisha you was gone now," Mrs. Santucci said. "Dead likama husband."

"And this thick shag carpeting is new, isn't it, Mrs. Santucci?" Benny bent down and pushed his palm into the rug. The rug had more padding under it than a WWF wrestling ring. "Look at how your new rug comes right up under the baseboard, Mrs. Santucci. No air can get in there. See?" Benny tried to probe the space between the bottom of the radiator and the rug with his fingers. You couldn't slide a dollar bill through that space. "If the air can't get to the radiator," Benny explained, "the room can't get warm."

"I hoppa you die soon," she said.

"And I notice that you have this beautiful red velvet couch with the clear plastic slipcovers that go all the way to the floor to keep it hermetically sealed. Well, that couch is pushed right up against the rest of the baseboard I installed way back in 1986, Mrs. Santucci," Benny said. "Your furniture is blocking most of the heat, you know."

"I hoppa you fall downa da stoop ona you way out," Mrs. Santucci said, pointing her two knotty fingers at Benny again. "I hoppa you braka you neck and rot inna gutta. I hoppa da dogs eata you brains."

"Mrs. Santucci?" Benny asked, trying to salvage some sanity from the situation. "How long do you think I should be responsible for this job. I mean, especially, if you keep making all these changes to the room. You've removed radiation, added furniture and rugs that block off the air. How long can you hold me accountable for a job I did way back in 1986?"

"I holda you responsible untila you die!" Mrs. Santucci shrieked. "And I hope that comesa soon. But first you fixa dis, you sonamabeech!" Mrs. Santucci waved her fleshy arm around the room.

Benny considered his place in the universe for a few moments, and then did exactly what you would have done.

194

Ernie's Estimates

Ernie had been building his business like a man laying bricks. He believed in being methodical, and he believed in doing things right. You advertise. You return calls promptly. You give estimates. You follow-up. You get the signed contract. You do the job the right way. You get paid. You advertise some more. And so on. Ernie believed in the Wheel of Business. Get that big wheel turning and things will be just fine. Deliver a good system for a fair price and your business will grow like corn. All you have to do is keep that wheel turning.

The trouble Ernie was having, though, was that his Wheel of Business had a big bulge in it. The bulge was right at the "You give estimates" part. Ernie's estimates, like the estimates of just about every other contractor in North America were as free as oxygen. It said so right there in his newspaper advertisement. "Free Estimates!" the ad read.

"There's no getting around it that I can see," Ernie told Kevin down at the supply house. "People in this town want to know up front how much the job's gonna cost. There's no way you can get the job without an estimate. And you can't charge for an estimate when everyone else is doing them for free."

Kevin nodded his head in agreement. "Yer right," he said.

"Trouble is," Ernie continued, "before I can give them an estimate, I gotta go through the trouble of sizing the whole job. I gotta do the heat loss calculation. I gotta size the pipes, the pumps, the valves, the radiation, the boiler. Everything! I gotta figure my prices on all the equipment. I gotta put it all down on paper. I gotta go see them again and go over the whole thing with them. And then eight out of ten customers take my design and shop my price. And there's always gonna be guys who are cheaper than me because they don't do the sizing like I do. They just use my design and undercut my price."

"Yer right," Kevin said, having heard this sad story many times.

"But there's no getting around giving free estimates," Ernie said. "If other guys give 'em, I gotta give 'em too."

And Kevin nodded. "Yer right," he agreed once again.

Ernie got beat again later that day. He had given a free estimate to a homeowner the week before. This one hurt Ernie more than usual because he really thought he would get this one. The homeowner had an ancient boiler that had originally run on coal. Someone had converted it to oil years ago. The oil burner had a long gray beard. The boiler was about the size of a minivan. You could see tongues of flame lapping at the ancient metal through the spaces between the sections. The homeowner told Ernie he thought it might be time for a new boiler and that he thought the new one should be the same size as the old one so that his family would have enough heat.

Ernie was very patient with this homeowner. He explained that new boilers were much smaller than old boilers. He also explained about how houses change over time. Old windows get replaced with new. Insulation gets added. The homeowner understood and was delighted when Ernie proved, by doing an accurate heat-loss calculation on the place, that the new boiler could be considerably smaller than the old boiler, and still get the job done. Ernie then went on to explain his method of piping and how he was going to control the system. The homeowner took a lot of notes while Ernie rhapsodized about what he would do once he got the job. "Whose boiler did you say you were going to use?" the homeowner asked, and Ernie repeated the name of the manufacturer. "What was that model number again?" the homeowner queried, and Ernie, now fully in the spirit of sharing what he knew with this layman, willingly gave it up.

A week later, when Ernie called the guy to follow up on his free estimate, he learned that his stinking competitor was doing the job. "He was ten percent cheaper than you were," the homeowner said. "And when I explained your design and told him what boiler to use, he was in total agreement. Too bad your price was so high. I thought you were very smart. Goodbye."

Ernie wanted to bang himself on the head with the telephone.

"I must be out of my mind," Ernie concluded the next time he saw Kevin. "I'm doing all this engineering for free and then some bum who does nothing gets the job. I gotta find a way around this free-estimate thing."

"Yer right," Kevin said, in total agreement, but without a suggestion.

The phone rang and Kevin picked it up. Ernie walked down to the end of the counter and poured himself a cup of coffee. "Yeah, sure, but be careful. Some of those old pipes break pretty easily," Kevin said into the phone after listening for a few minutes. "Lots can go wrong with those jobs." Kevin listened a bit more and then said, "Just give 'em a high number and tell 'em it will probably be less, but they gotta let you do the job the way you know it needs to be done." He listened again, and then said, "Yeah. You bet. Good luck."

"What was that all about?" Ernie asked.

"Oh, that was Freddy. You know Freddy, don't you?" Ernie nodded and sipped his coffee. "Freddy's quoting a job that's got steam heat. The owner wants Freddy to give him an estimate on changing the steam traps and some other stuff, but he wants the number to be exact. Freddy wasn't sure what to tell the guy. I told Freddy to give the guy a high price and, well, you heard the rest."

Ernie felt as though he had just heard the Voice of the Prophet. "Thank you, Kevin," he said, grabbing Kevin's hand and pumping it up and down.

"You're welcome," Kevin said. "For whatever." But Ernie was already out the door.

That afternoon, Ernie was looking at a boiler that was older than meatloaf. It was sitting in the basement of a Victorian house. "Well," the homeowner said, pen poised over notebook, "what do you think? What's your estimate?"

"Well, it depends on what you're trying to achieve here," Ernie said. "Do you want me to just replace this old boiler with one that's the exact same size of what you've got here? Or are you interested in saving the maximum amount of fuel from now on, while enjoying the most comfortable home this side of heaven. I can go either way – or anywhere in between."

"Well right now, I'm just interested in a free estimate," the homeowner said.

"Okay," Ernie said. "I estimate it will be somewhere between a thousand dollars and twenty thousand dollars. It all depends on what you'd like me to do." The homeowner started to gag, but Ernie just kept laying it all out for him. "For one thousand dollars," Ernie forged on, "I can do a complete heat loss calculation on your home, and engineer a system that will save you lots of fuel while providing unsurpassed comfort. Of course, it will cost more for me to actually install that system. Anywhere up to twenty thousand dollars, I'd say, but that's the very high end. I'm sure the actual price will be much less than that, but there's no way of knowing for certain unless I first do the engineering. Then, I'll be able to tell you for sure. And as I said, your investment in the engineering will be a thousand dollars. But I'll tell you what. I'll deduct that thousand bucks from your total investment in your home once you give me the go-ahead to do the work. Imagine that! A one-thousand-dollar discount! Hey, you can't lose!"

"But your competitors are willing to give me free estimates," the homeowner sputtered.

"So am I," Ernie cheerfully replied. "In fact, I just did. You can choose between my engineering service or my engineering-and-installation service. If you choose the latter, the engineering service will be absolutely free, and I'll guarantee the results of my work – in writing. If you'd like only my engineering service, I'm afraid I won't be able to guarantee the results, however. Other contractors are simply not as good as I am. And I have no control over their slipshod way of cutting corners." And then Ernie gave the homeowner a smile you could pour on a pancake. "Like to see some references?" he asked.

"But," the homeowner said, "I thought you were going to give me an exact price. Can't you give me an exact price?"

"Sure!" Ernie said, "But that's not an Estimate, that's an Exact. Exacts aren't free. Exacts cost a thousand dollars, but I'll deduct the price of the Exact from the total price of the Done. As soon as I am done, that is.

"You don't work like other contractors," the homeowner said.

"I know," Ernie replied. "I'm much better! But we do still have free Estimates, You can't be in business around here without free Estimates. We charge only for the Exacts and the Dones. That's fair, isn't it? Now, how about those references? Like to see 'em?"

He got the job, of course. And ever since he made this minor adjustment to his day-to-day life, Ernie's Wheel of Business has been spinning in perfect alignment.

A Decent Living Wage

Dave had a queasy feeling. He wasn't going to get this one. He could see defeat forming like mold on wet bread. There was something about the way the guy was looking at his hands and then back at Dave. Tough to put your finger on stuff like that, but when you do enough selling, you can smell it coming. Defeat smells sour.

"That's your best price?" Mr. Kromker asked, laying his open palms on the kitchen table like two raw steaks.

"Yes," Dave said. "For what you're asking me to do, that is my best price."

Mr. Kromker had a head like an artillery shell – shaved clean, like a TV wrestler's. It was as shiny as a brand new nickel. "Well, I think you can do better," he said. "Everything's negotiable in this life, Dave. Everything. Reasonable men can always come to a reasonable agreement. You can't always get everything that you'd like to get, Dave, but you can get a reasonable agreement if you're willing to bend a little. Are you willing to bend a little, Dave?"

Dave took a deep breath and let it out slowly. You would think he was negotiating the release of hostages here instead of a simple boiler job. "Mr. Kromker, eh, may I call you Fred?"

"You may call me Mr. Kromker, Dave," Mr. Kromker said.

"All right," Dave continued. "Mr. Kromker, then. Mr. Kromker, we are going to install a boiler in your home and a number of new, state-of-the-art controls that will save you money on fuel while bringing you a much greater level of comfort. We also have quite a bit of piping to do. The price I've worked out is $5,200 for the entire job. I won't come to you at the end with any hidden extras. That's the price for the delivered job. I guarantee that everything will work to your satisfaction. This is the price I need to do the work and make a reasonable profit. If you would like me to do the work for less, please let me know which part of the system you would like me to remove." Dave sat back and watched as Mr. Kromker clenched and unclenched his fists.

"Well, Dave, let's talk about that," Mr. Kromker said, squinting at Dave, the way you might sight down the barrel of a rifle. "I've been doing my homework. What are you paying for three-quarter-inch copper elbows? I priced those at the home center over the weekend. They were on sale. What do you pay?"

Dave could smell the mold forming on this one. "I can't break down the price of the job, Mr. Kromker. That's not reasonable. That's not how we work. I gave you a flat price for the whole works."

"Can you tell me your price on the boiler? I also looked at boilers when I was at the home center. They had no problem giving me a price for a boiler. Why can't you?"

"I'm giving you a price, Mr. Kromker. It's $5,200. That's for the whole job. I can't start telling you my costs on individual items. I'm sorry."

"But, Dave, you just asked me to tell you which part of the system I'd like removed so that you might be able to lower the price. How can I make that determination if you're not willing to cooperate with me and tell me how much each part of the system costs? Now, what about the circulator? What brand are you going to use? I priced a few that seemed reasonable. Let's talk about that."

Dave felt like he was being pecked to death by a duck. He thought he'd try a different tactic. He knew that most people like to talk about themselves. He had learned that when he took a sales course a bunch of years ago. Maybe he could get Mr. Kromker talking about something other than the price of components. Maybe he could find an analogy in Mr. Kromker's business that he could use to show the foolishness of this conversation they were having. Maybe Mr. Kromker was a surgeon or something like that. Yeah, the guy looked like a surgeon. He had really clean hands and he talked like a general in the Army. Surgeons were like that. He'd seen them on TV. That would be great if Mr. Kromker was actually Dr. Kromker. He could ask him if he ever broke down the cost of an operation for his patients. You know, how much for the incision? How much for the removal of the bad part? How much for the bandage? And couldn't he get a better deal on the bandages? I mean, they sell bandages at the discount drug store, right? Does he have to get his bandages from the medical supply house? Can he break out the cost of the aspirin he gives his patients when they suffer pain after the operation? Gosh! That sure seems like a lot for an aspirin, Dr. Kromker. Dave smiled.

"You know, I never asked you, Mr. Kromker, but what is your occupation?"

"Why do you ask?"

"Just curious!" Dave said with a big, friendly grin. "I meet the most fascinating people in this line of work. Why, just the other day I did a boiler job that was very similar to yours. The fellow was a surgeon! That's got to be the most important profession there is."

"A surgeon!" Mr. Kromker guffawed. "That's not the most important profession. Not by a long shot. Surgeons are a dime a dozen. A bunch of fat cats, if you ask me."

Dave's mind whirled. Maybe he's a corporation president. Clean hands. Talking like he owns me. Yeah, a corporation president. That's it!

"I did another boiler job that was similar to this one," Dave continued. "It was for the president of a big corporation. I'm trying to remember the name of the company. Boy, he was an interesting guy! Just like you. What is your profession, Mr. Kromker?"

Mr. Kromker chuckled and shook his big, shiny head. "Well, Dave, I certainly don't run a corporation. Those guys are a bunch of stinking thieves. I work for the working men and women, Dave. I work for the union. I'm a union official. The working men and women duly elected me to do what's right for them. It's my job to make sure that thousands of working men and women are able to take home a decent living wage to support their families."

"You don't say," said Dave. "That's fascinating! Tell me more."

"Well, Dave," Mr. Kromker went on, "In union there is strength. Have you ever heard that expression?" Dave nodded. "Well, if you understand that expression then you understand why men like me are so important. I work hard to make sure that regular people get what's coming to them. If there's one thing I hate it's a company that tries to screw its workers by pressuring them to work for less than a decent day's wages. I will not stand for that. Are you in a union, Dave?" Dave shook his head. "Well, that's a shame, Dave. A union can get you what you deserve. You should give that some thought."

"I will," Dave said.

"Now, enough about me," Mr. Kromker said, with a dismissive wave of his beefy hand. "We were talking about the price of this heating job. Have you considered what I've said? Are you ready to reconsider your price?"

"Yes, sir," Dave said.

"So what's it going to be?" Mr. Kromker said with that big, self-satisfied smile of his. "It was $5,200, but what's it really going to be, Dave?"

"Well, in consideration of all that you've said about the working man deserving a decent living wage, the new price is gonna be eight thousand bucks, Mr. Kromker. And not a penny less."

The Neighborly Thing

The Duke has a regal way about him that practically screams confidence. He can fill any garage, backyard, or basement he enters with a truckload of white-haired, jaw-jutting, foot-stomping conviction. Why, he's so sure of himself that even when he offers advice that's dead wrong, folks still believe him. Needless to say, everyone in the neighborhood consults The Duke before taking the smallest step toward home improvement or repair.

Take Fred, for instance. One time he had a leak in his vinyl swimming pool liner. He consulted The Duke who immediately told him to pour three pounds of oatmeal into the water. "I've seen it work thousands of times," The Duke said, waving his cane confidently in the air. "Oatmeal goes right for the leak, swells up and seals it. It's just like the stuff you pour into your car radiator, only it's organic." He whacked his metal cane against Fred's redwood the way a judge might rap a gavel. "You'll never have to worry about that pool again," The Duke assured him. "Believe me."

Fred wanted to believe The Duke. Everyone did. After all, The Duke had lived in the neighborhood longer than anyone, and everyone acknowledged his superior knowledge of just about anything you could install in or on a house.

Fred went to the supermarket that same day and bought the three pounds of oatmeal. He sprinkled it on the surface of the water and stood back. Then he watched it all afternoon. Unfortunately, all he got for his efforts was dirty pool water.

"What brand of oatmeal did you use?" The Duke asked Fred as the two stared into the murky water.

"The store brand," Fred said. "I figured, what's the difference? It's just going into a swimming pool.'

The Duke shook his head sadly, as though Fred was as dumb as a cork. "Heh, heh, heh," The Duke slowly and sarcastically chuckled. Fred looked at The Duke the way a child looks at a beloved grandfather. "You have to use Quaker Oats, Fred," The Duke said finally, never looking up from the water. "Didn't you know that?" The Duke shook his head again.

"You didn't tell me that, Duke."

"Fred, Fred, Fred," The Duke continued, sadly shaking his head from side to side. "Must I tell you everything?"

Fred's shoulders sank a full inch. "Gosh, Duke, I just didn't know. Can I put the Quaker Oats in now? I can go back to the store right now. They're still open."

Once again, The Duke shook his head slowly and sadly. "Nooo, not now, Freddy my boy. The water's contaminated now. Look!" The Duke stuck his cane in the water and stirred the oatmeal. "It's toooo late, Freddy. Now you're going to have to drain the pool and put a patch on that liner."

Fred did just that the following weekend. When he saw how well The Duke's solution worked, he took a walk through the neighborhood, singing The Duke's praises. "Oatmeal!" he said. "Just some oatmeal and a patch! I tell you, The Duke has more tricks up his sleeve than a magician."

"The Duke knows everything," Mel from across the street agreed.

Now, it came to pass that Ida the Widow needed something done about her boiler, which had been acting up. She had meant to do something about it in the spring, but then the weather had gotten so nice. Summer followed with heat that could rival a pizza oven's, and the last thing on Ida the Widow's mind was her old boiler. So, once again, she put it off.

But now it was late September, and she figured it was time to get moving, and that's why she was leafing through the Yellow Pages on that Tuesday.

Ida the Widow wound up picking three companies from the dozens of Yellow Pages advertisers. The first company had a large ad, which to Ida the Widow meant they had lots of people on staff, and that their prices would be high. The second company used a medium-sized ad to tell their story. Ida the Widow reasoned that this company had fewer good people, but their prices would be more reasonable because they didn't waste a lot of money on big ads. The third company had a listing, but no ad. Ida the Widow figured this company wouldn't be any good at all. After all, if they were any good, they would take an ad, right? Be that as it may, she would use this company as a bludgeon to beat up the other two companies on price.

Ida the Widow always picked service companies this way, regardless of the trade. "That's the way my Harry did it," she explained to the Card Club ladies. "And Harry never got screwed." She smiled at Alice, and shifted the playing cards around in her hand.

"My Larry, may he rest in peace, did the same," Alice said. The other Card Club ladies agreed that this seemed like the best way to deal with a contractor – heating, or otherwise.

"Let them kill each other over my business," Alice said. "I work too hard for my money to give it away."

Ida the Widow smiled, and called the three heating contractors the very next morning.

The Big Ad company sent a Mr. Klinger who wore a three-piece suit. He looked around, and then explained to Ida the Widow that her boiler was older than she was, that it was leaking, and that it deserved retirement. He gave her a price, and told her that his company could start the work on Monday morning. Ida the Widow thanked him, walked him to the door, and told him she'd get back to him.

The Medium Ad company sent a guy in a blue uniform. "Jake" was embroidered over his shirt pocket in gold thread. Jake told Ida the Widow the same thing Mr. Klinger had told her, which was that her boiler was hanging onto life by a thread. "I'd rather look for a hot date in a convent than try to find replacement parts for that burner," he said. "Besides, it's leaking like a spaghetti colander. Look!" Jake pointed to the wet spot on the floor, and then gave her a price for a replacement.

Jake's price was, as expected, lower than Mr. Klinger's.

"I'll let you know," Ida the Widow said.

"I can start the job in about three weeks," Jake said on his way out the door. "But don't wait too long because I get real busy when the weather gets real cold. Lots of people like you wait too long, you know. And if you snooze, you lose."

"I'll let you know," Ida the Widow said, closing the door in Jake's face.

The guy who had just a listing in the Yellow Pages also had just an answering machine. Ida the Widow left a message, waited four days, and finally received a return call at 10:45 PM. "Yeah, it's the plumber? I'm returning your call?" the voice said.

"I need a price on a new boiler," Ida the Widow told him. "Can you stop by and look?"

"I'm too busy to stop by and look," he said "And besides, I don't need to look. Just give me the best price you got, and I'll beat it by ten percent. Guaranteed. That's the way we work, lady. Ask around your neighborhood. Everyone knows us. Ask around."

Having gotten exactly what she was looking for from Mr. Lowball, Ida the Widow said, "I'll let you know." And then she hung up on him.

Her next step, of course, was to call The Duke. No one in the neighborhood made a move, especially a move of this magnitude, without first checking with The Duke.

Now, at this point, you need to know that what The Duke knows about heating systems, he can write on the back of a postage stamp using a Magic Marker. But this didn't stop him from offering Ida the Widow his sage advice.

He sat at her kitchen table and stared through his bifocals at the three contractors' proposals. "I think they're all full of crap," he said finally. This made Ida the Widow smile because The Duke reminded her so much of her dear deceased Harry.

"Harry would have said the same thing," she sighed.

"Damn right," The Duke said. "Harry was a good man. These guys are bums. They're trying to sell you something you don't need. Why, that old boiler has served your family well for all the years you've lived here. And it served the Johnsons before you, and the McCarthys before them just as well."

"But what about the way it broke down last winter?" Ida the Widow asked with concern.

The Duke placed both of his palms on the curved top of his cane and leaned toward Ida the Widow. "You tell 'em to fix it!" he said, lifting, and then slamming the cane's rubber tip into the linoleum. "You can get plenty more good years out of that old boiler. Those bums are just trying to sell you a bill of goods."

"But they said it was leaking," Ida the Widow said, remembering the puddle she always seemed to be mopping up around the boiler.

"Leaking, eh?" The Duke asked. He pursed his lips and narrowed his eyes. "Did you ask them about Quaker Oats?" he said.

"What about Quaker Oats?"

The Duke slapped the Formica table with his gnarled hand, and let loose a hearty laugh. "Why, that's the way you fix a boiler that's leaking, Ida!" he shouted. "You ask any heating contractor worth his salt and he'll tell you it's true. Good ol' Quaker Oats. These guys just want to sell you a bill of goods. They're bums!"

"You really think so?" Ida the Widow asked.

"Here," The Duke said, standing and pointing toward the kitchen window and Fred's back yard. "Look at what oatmeal did for Fred's swimming pool! And Fred's pool has a lot more water in it than your boiler does," he said.

The logic was undeniable.

Mr. Klinger and Jake each called Ida the Widow a few days later to follow up on their visits. "I haven't decided yet," she told them both. "And I think I'll wait until the weather gets a bit colder. The boiler seems to be working fine right now."

And then she went shopping for Quaker Oats.

School Daze

A boiler room was his natural habitat. He knew that, but still, he had to be in this class two nights a week because his boss had insisted upon it. "You'll go on your own time," his boss had said. "You'll go at night, and you'll learn as much as you can. I'll pay for the course, but you'll go on your own time." He much preferred boiler rooms. Boiler rooms were real. This place was about theory, and the instructor, Mr. Persinger, was the sort of guy that would look bored during an earthquake.

Her name was Zoe. He remembered that from the first night's roll call. He went home that night and looked it up. Her name meant, "Life." He liked that because she was sort of plain.

She didn't know his name. It was too ordinary a name to flop out of a roll call the way Zoe's had, and, as it turned out, that first roll call had also been the last – a one-shot deal.

Mr. Persinger was in this for the extra money, pure and simple. He didn't care about the students. They were a bunch of wrench jockeys; he was an engineer. To him, the students were no more significant than the chairs upon which they sat. He didn't even know their names.

He believed that when given a dozen eggs, one should check once to make sure the eggs were all there, and that none were cracked. One should not try to differentiate between the eggs, let alone name them, or, heaven forbid, try to remember their names. The highest level to which one could expect to rise in this class was to be "the man in the blue shirt," or "the woman near the radiator." He returned test papers by placing them in a pile on his desk and instructing the eggs to come and get them. No one ever questioned his objectivity in grading. He simply didn't care.

So Zoe never heard his name or asked him what it was. By the fourth week, it was too late to ask. Both would have been embarrassed. Nevertheless, a friendship was forming between them. They chatted about their day jobs and their families. She addressed him simply as, "Hi!" and there was a certain purity to that. After all, what's in a name? He couldn't help but think about the way new dogs sniff each other and wag their tails. We really don't need names, do we?

He realized after the first session that the course would be empty of usable substance. It wasn't at all what the brochure had promised. He thought about those phony cakes in the bakery window – nothing but sun-yellowed icing over a cardboard box. "Cakes for all occasions." All show, but no substance. He was glad he wasn't paying the tuition.

In spite of his disappointment, though, he listened intently. He was like that. He would try his best, even though he would rather be in a boiler room where things were real. Mr. Persinger spoke a language from some other world, yet he still tried to follow along.

But something was wrong. No matter how hard he tried to concentrate on Mr. Persinger's lecture, his mind would always slip into a fuzzy state of near-total numbness. Mr. Persinger did it to him every time. He'd enter the room, perch himself atop his desk, begin his lecture and slide gently into a sort of hypnotic buzz. Occasionally, Mr. Persinger's hand would slowly sweep through the air as he made a point. He watched the hand move, like clouds going by on a humid day. He couldn't concentrate. He tried so hard, but the buzzing was mesmerizing. Fighting for alertness, he'd grasp at syllables and try to coax meaning from them, but it was no good. Night after night, the words enveloped him like a blizzard of cotton balls.

And then one night he figured it out. The realization fell on him like a flowerpot dropping from a ledge. By an intense effort of concentration, he heard quite clearly the words, "if you will." Like a beacon of light through a soupy fog it came to him. "If you will." "That's how he does it," he mumbled to himself. He listened, and heard it again. "If you will." And again. "If you will."

"The equations, if you will, for evaluating radiant-energy transfer in the heat-balance analysis of a panel heating or cooling system, if you will, are modified forms of the basic rational equations for radiant exchange, if you will. This should be clear to you all, I would hope."

From this hive of technical mumbo-jumbo, the buzzing just kept coming. It stomped on commas, periods, and semicolons. It filled dead air and connected the words like beads on a rosary. It slammed nouns into verbs, adjectives into prepositions, mashing them all together in one monotonous blur. Ifyouwillifyouwillifyouwill."

"Corresponding to a given value of the outside-air temperature, if you will, and for a room in which the panel area, total energy input, and ventilation rate are fixed, if you will, the inside air and each point of every inside surface will reach equilibrium temperatures, if you will, which will be fixed with respect to time at values determined by the heat-transfer characteristics of the room, if you will."

He shook his head, trying to clear it. The words were harder to follow than a Mafia hit man, but at least he had discovered the key! It was, simply, If you will. He leaned forward, fascinated. "If you will." Again, Persinger had said it. "There," he mumbled to himself. His head was beginning to clear. "If you will." He smiled and nodded. "There."

"Read, if you will, the next chapter for our next session, if you will."

An involuntary shiver shook him. The bell rang and people stumbled from the room. He stood, stuffed an arm into a coat sleeve and staggered into the hallway after Zoe.

"Hi!" she said.

"Hi. I know how he does it."

"Does what?" Zoe asked.

"The buzzing. I know how he does it!"

She rolled her eyes. "Tell me," she begged.

"He has a mantra. It's, 'If you will, if you will, if you will'."

Zoe stopped in mid-step. "You're right!" she said. "I wasn't hearing it until you mentioned it. Now it's going to drive me crazy."

"No, it won't," he said. "That's just it. Once you realize how he's doing it, you're free from it once and for all! He can't control you anymore." He looked at Zoe for a long moment. "He can't," he said.

The following Monday, he began to keep score.

"Hi!" Zoe said after the class.

"He said it two hundred thirty-four times," he reported.

On Wednesday, they both kept count. "What did you get?" he asked her after the class.

"Three hundred-twenty-five?"

"I got more. Three hundred twenty-nine," he said.

"It's easy to miss a few," Zoe admitted. "What the heck, you got more than I did. C'mon, I'll buy the coffee."

At the diner, they ran into three of their groggy classmates. Feeling compassion, they let the poor souls in on the Persinger's mantra. Eyes began to clear.

Three weeks later, the students strolled into the class. One by one, they passed Zoe's desk. Each dropped a small slip of paper containing a name and a number into her empty paper coffee cup. Each also handed Zoe a single dollar bill, which she pocketed.

Persinger walked in and perched on his desk. He was right on time. "Tonight, if you will, I will discuss the substance of Chapter Seventeen. Please turn to page two hundred twenty-seven in your texts, if you will." The three members of the Scoring Committee discreetly scratched two hash marks in their notebooks. Someone coughed, bit a knuckle, and choked back laughter. They all wondered who would win tonight's lottery. Zoe was holding 26 bucks tonight.

He turned and smiled at her. She smiled back. This was the best class he had ever taken.

The Hinge Principle

It took Wayne a half hour to realize the homeowner hadn't understood a word he had said. "It was like explaining clouds to fish," he told his partner, Walter. "But I got all the way up to the part about the reset control before I realized that," he said. "And even at that point, the guy was still nodding. A real fast nod, too. I thought I was doing okay because of the smile and the nod, you know?" Wayne bobbed his head like one of those plastic dogs people put by the rear windows of their cars. Walter bobbed in response. Watching Wayne, he couldn't help but bob.

"He didn't understand anything you told him?" Walter asked incredulously, his head continuing to rock.

"Seems so!" Wayne said, "But I didn't find out until the end. I hate that." Wayne rubbed the back of his neck. "It was a total waste of time."

"What made you think he understood you in the first place?" Walter asked, upset that Wayne had once again failed to ring the bell on what would have been a really nice job.

"Well, he told me I was the fifth heating contractor he was interviewing. I hate when they put it that way –

interviewing. It makes it sound like I'm there looking for a job."

"You were there looking for a job," Walter reminded him.

"Yeah, but it's not like I was looking for a job job. I just wanted to sell him a heating system. I wasn't planning to make a career out of the thing. And besides, I figured since I was the fifth guy in there, he probably knew what he was looking for. I mean, the guy's building a heck of a big house. I figured he should know what he wants."

"I would have felt the same way," Walter said. "So tell me, how did you explain what we were going to do for him?"

"Well, first I showed him the specifications on the boiler we were going to use, and I explained that this boiler gives great AFUE."

"And what did he say to that?"

"He smiled and he nodded," Wayne said. "Just like I told you."

"Did you tell him what AFUE stood for?"

"I figured he knew!" Wayne said, shaking his head in frustration. "I was the fifth guy in there, for Pete's sake! And besides, he kept nodding and smiling, you know?"

"Uh huh," Walter said. "I would have figured the same thing. What happened then?"

"Well, I showed him a picture of the radiant tubing we were planning on using, and I told him how our system was going to balance out the MRT in his new home."

222

"What did he say?"

"He just nodded. It was like he had a hinge in the back of his neck. His head just kept going up and down, and he kept smiling like a happy idiot."

"And then?"

"I showed him the DIN standard for the tubing, and I told him how the manufacturer we use meets that standard, and that everything was going to be just fine."

"Did he know what the DIN standard was?"

"He seemed to," Wayne said. "I mean, I didn't tell him or anything. I figured he must have known because of the way he was nodding and all. And besides, he had talked to all those other guys before me, right?"

Walter nodded. "You're right. So what happened next?"

"I looked at the plans and explained about the available emissive surfaces in the rooms. I explained how we might have to supplement with a water-to-air heat exchanger on a separate zone because of the R-value of all the glass he was planning to use, and how we had to get the CFM just right. He kept nodding and smiling. The more I talked, the faster he nodded."

"Did you explain about how we install bimetal thermometers to monitor the delta-T?"

"I sure did! And I told him about the variable delta-P as well, and how we were going to handle that with a DPR. He nodded at that too. I asked if any of the other four contractors were going to do it that way."

"What did he say?"

"He just nodded and smiled."

"Did you tell him how we were going to control the heat in the kids' bedrooms?" Walter asked.

"With the TRVs? Yeah, I told him all about the TRVs, and how the ones we use respond with just a four-degree P-deviation. Can't do better than a four-degree P-deviation."

"And?"

"And he nodded. I thought he was impressed by the four-degree P-deviation. Hey, it impressed the hell out of me!"

"So when did you tell him about the reset control?"

"Right after I explained about the microbubbles. How you can't see them, but that we were going to get rid of them anyway?"

"That's great," Walter said. "But what about the reset? What went wrong?"

"Well, as soon as I mentioned the reset control I realized the guy hadn't understood a word I had said to him. I'd been talking to a total dummy! When I started to tell him how the water temperature would get colder as it got warmer outside, he nodded faster than ever, but he also put his hands up. He told me he doesn't like to take cold showers, no matter how warm it is outside. Can you believe it?"

"It is hard to believe," Walter said. "Did you try to explain?"

"I tried to tell him about proportional plus integral plus derivative and all, but he wouldn't listen to me anymore. He thanked me for coming, and walked me to the door, nodding all the way. I mean, the guy was just so unbelievably stupid, you know?" Wayne shook his head. "I don't think he understood a word I had said, but you'd never know that by the way he was nodding. It was like he had a hinge in his neck. A regular hinge!"

"You think maybe you were too technical with him? Maybe he didn't understand, but he just didn't want you to know that, so he nodded instead?"

Wayne considered this for a moment and then said, "Hey, I was the fifth guy in there. That bozo shoulda done his homework. The way I figure it, if you're gonna buy a heating system, you oughta learn to speak the language. I got no sympathy for that loser, none whatsoever."

Walter paused a moment, considering this, and then he nodded in agreement.

Phelan On The Phone

Phelan looked at his wristwatch before placing the call. He wanted to give Gitzkey at least ten minutes to get out of his office before he punched in the numbers. Phelan liked to leave a bit of a margin during lunchtime. He waited another full minute and then made the call. The phone warbled three times in Phelan's ear before Gitzkey's receptionist answered. "It's a great day at Gitzkey Mechanical Contracting!" she said, a pleasant chirp in her voice. "How may I help you?"

"Yes, is Mr. Gitzkey out to lunch right now?" Phelan asked.

"I'm sorry, sir. He is. May I take a message?"

"Yes, please tell him that Mr. Phelan from Phelan Engineering returned his call."

"Oh, Mr. Phelan!" she said with obvious disappointment. "I'm so sorry. You just missed him. He was waiting all morning for your call. Is there a number where he can reach you this afternoon? He said it was very important that he speak with you today."

Phelan had known that she would ask for a number where he could be reached and he was ready with his answer. "Oh gosh, I am sorry," he said. "I'm going to be in a deep basement for the rest of today. I have to go to a site to help straighten out a problem that another mechanical contractor caused, you see. Cellular phone reception is impossible in those deep basements. There's really no way I can call him today, and I am sorry, but he won't be able to reach me at all this afternoon. The basement is so very deep, you see. Would you please tell him that I called, though? Thank you so much."

She began to ask if there was a number where he could perhaps be reached that evening, but by the time her lips formed the first words, Phelan had already hung up. Phelan knew just when to hang up to avoid questions such as that one. His timing was impeccable in this regard. This receptionist had been almost too easy. Others (mostly the older ones) were far more difficult, but Phelan was a whiz when it came to the telephone aspects of the engineering business. Rarely, if ever, did he get snagged by a mere contractor.

It had been 10 years since he had started his little firm and he prided himself on having returned every call a contractor had ever made to him. He had done this without actually having to speak to any of the contractors, mind you, but he had returned their calls. No one could ever accuse Phelan of not getting back. It's just that he got back when they weren't there. At this, no one in the industry was better than Phelan. He knew when every contractor in America started and finished their work day, when they went to lunch, when they were occupied with bodily functions, when they took vacations, and when they had to be on the site. He always returned their phone calls when they weren't around to answer them, and there was a simple reason why he did this.

Phelan had learned early on that contractors call engineers because they, the contractors, have complaints about the plans, the specs, or the building itself. The only other reason why a contractor would ever call an engineer was because the contractor was looking for an extra.

Phelan could not think of a reason why he would want to discuss any of those four subjects with a contractor. Contractors were like mosquitoes to him – annoying, but, with proper planning, generally avoidable. Phelan would draw a boiler room on a blueprint, only to hear from some mechanical contractor that the equipment Phelan had specified wouldn't fit within the allotted space. Phelan wouldn't actually talk to the contractor, of course. The message would come to him by way of his receptionist. He would then look at the plans and see that all the tiny blue shapes he had drawn fit neatly within the confines of the tiny blue walls he had drawn around the shapes. "No problem," he'd mumble, preferring the blueness of a plan to the reality of a job site.

This, in fact, had been Gitzkey's lament. He had called Phelan earlier that day. "Would you please tell Mr. Phelan," Gitzkey had said to Phelan's receptionist, "that I cannot get ten pounds in a five-pound bag? What would he like me to do? I have men waiting on the job. The equipment he specified won't fit. I'm losing my shirt. I need to speak with him as soon as possible."

"I'll have Mr. Phelan call you as soon as possible, Mr. Gitzkey," Phelan's receptionist replied. "What time do you go to lunch?"

"I generally go to lunch at noon," Gitzkey had said.

"Thank you, Mr. Gitzkey. I'll have Mr. Phelan return your call."

Which Phelan had done – at precisely 12:10 PM.

Later that afternoon, Phelan's receptionist told Phelan that Mr. Gitzkey of Gitzkey Contracting had called six times since 1:00 PM. "Call back and find out what time he gets to his office in the morning," Phelan instructed his receptionist. "Tell 'em I'm in a deep basement and can't be reached, but that you'll get hold of me at home tonight and that I'll call his office first thing in the morning. But whatever you do, don't give him my home number."

"That goes without saying," Phelan's receptionist said with a wink and an evil grin. She enjoyed these phone games nearly as much as Phelan did. She liked to hear the contractors slobber in near apoplexy when they called back to find Phelan not in. She smiled again, this time to herself, and made the call to Gitzkey. A few moments later, she tapped on Phelan's office door and informed him that Gitzkey would be at his desk at precisely 7:30 AM, anxiously awaiting the call.

Which is why Phelan called at precisely 6:45 AM the next morning and left a message on Gitzkey's voice mail. "This is Mr. Phelan of Phelan Engineering. I'm returning your call. So sorry I missed you. I thought I'd call early because I'll be out in the field all day. You won't be able to reach me because I'll be in a lead-lined mechanical equipment room deep beneath the river. If you'd like, please call my receptionist and give her a time when you can be reached."

And then Phelan hung up. Gitzkey called 19 times that day, much to the delight of Phelan's receptionist.

Phelan had a similar way of dealing with clients, but it was far more creative. If there was a problem on a job (as there usually was), Phelan liked to have all his ducks in a row before discussing that problem with a client. Sometimes the client would call at an unexpected time and get through to him with the suddenness of a mortar round. Phelan's receptionist, you see, was under strict orders to put them through because they paid the bills. She'd just give him a "Code Red" hand signal they had worked out and Phelan would pick up with a cheery How's-the-wife-and-kids greeting. The client would ask a blunt question about the job, one which Phelan was not able to answer because his ducks were not quite lined up in that all-important row.

"I'm so glad you asked me that," Phelan would say. "I have the information you need right here. I was anticipating your call. Okay, do you have a pencil? Here's how it is going to . . ." And that would be the end of the conversation because Phelan would hang up the phone. He'd just put his finger down on the button while in the middle of his very own sentence and it worked every time because no one on this planet will ever suspect you of foul play if you hang up on yourself.

Naturally, the client would call right back. "I was cut off," he'd say to Phelan's receptionist. She would chat with him for a moment about the state of modern technology, and then she'd apologize because she had just given Phelan another call. And it was from Europe. Or better yet, New Zealand!

Phelan's receptionist would then promise the client a return call as quickly as possible, and ask the client if he was going to be at his desk, and what time he was planning on going to lunch. This would give Phelan ample time to get his ducks in a row, and he would, of course, return the call as soon as possible.

Which usually meant around 12:15 PM.

The Power of
Negative Thinking

In a basement flooded with mechanical sin, Grover sat
on his haunches and considered his options. He could make
a list of all the things that he found wrong with this job
and then go home and spend time figuring it all out tonight
while other guys were watching the ballgame on TV. Then
he could write it all up and come back tomorrow to face
what he was sure would be certain failure. Or he could just
walk away and forget the whole dirty business.

He was working in light fit for a cat because he didn't
bring along a flashlight. Grover figured the homeowner was
upstairs laughing at how long it was taking him to come up
with a proposal. He squinted at the boiler nameplate. He
never brought a flashlight on jobs such as these because he
knew he didn't stand a chance of getting the work anyway.
Why his boss had sent him here was beyond Grover's level
of reasoning. This system needed too much attention, and
Grover knew his price would be too high for any consumer
to consider. He figured that this woman upstairs, like most
women he had met, was just a stinking cheapskate. He
could tell this from the look she had shot him as he passed
her on his way to the basement. He had a sense for such
things. "She can't afford this work," Grover mumbled. "I
know she can't."

He squinted at the nameplate again, and considered his options one more time. His eyeballs felt like they'd been rolled in sand and dropped into a wool pocket. He hadn't felt this lousy since last week when that old crone on Cassandra Street had thrown him out of her house. He supposed he may have taken the wrong approach with that 20-year warranty business, but he had told the truth. And some people just needed to hear the truth, right? He could tell that just by looking at them. "That 20-year warranty is a good deal, ma'am," he had told the old hag, "but that probably doesn't make much of a difference to you, does it? I mean, from the looks of you, you won't be around much longer anyway. Have you made your funeral arrangements? Or are you planning to stick your family with the expense? I'm sure you don't have any money of your own. Look at this crappy furniture." The next thing he knew, he was out on the sidewalk. "But it's true!" he shouted at the closed door. "You're old! And your couch is threadbare!"

Grover stared again at the nameplate, trying to arrive at a decision. His eyebrows came together as if he were in the middle of the medical boards. I should be able to get some of these jobs, he thought. After all, in this town, you could fit all the good heating contractors on one barstool. My company stinks, I know that. But the good guys are so busy. They can't possibly do it all. I should be able to get at least one of these jobs. He considered the prospect of success on this particular job for a moment and then shook his head. "Nah," he said. "People are just too cheap. All they're interested in nowadays is a low price," Grover looked through the gloom at the dirt on his hands. He wiped them on his trousers. "It doesn't pay to bring up anything else nowadays. When you come right down to it, no one cares about anything nowadays except price." Grover wasn't old enough to work up a good case of sentimentality about anything, but he felt confident about this price issue. There were no good old days for Grover. For Grover, it was all just nowadays, and nowadays was as bad as it gets.

He stood and stretched his back. He'd be crippled before long if he kept doing this sort of work. He just knew it. He had a sense for such things. "I'm not quoting this one," he said aloud to the basement's gloom. "It makes no sense. Too much needs to be done here. I'll never have time to figure it all out. And what if I make a mistake? That witch upstairs looks like she'd screw me over really good if I made a mistake. Sid wouldn't understand. He's a rat to begin with. The worst guy I ever worked for. What's the use in trying? This one upstairs is too cheap anyway. The stuffing was coming right out of the arm of that easy chair and her rugs are filthy." He shook his head and trudged up the stairs.

"So?" Mrs. Connor grumped. "You have a price for me?" Mrs. Connor had the sort of face you see on long lines at the supermarket. She looked like she was willing to walk all the way to Saint Louis and punch some stranger in the face. She wouldn't even think twice about it. She thought all heating contractors were slime. She knew that they were a bunch of crooks who were just out to rip her off. She was an avid watcher of 48 Hours. "That price had better be a good one," she threatened.

Grover looked down at his shoes. "I'm not going to give you a price on this job because there's too much wrong down there," he said to his broken laces. "It looks like a bomb went off in a scrap yard down there." He glanced up at Mrs. Connor for the first time. "Don't you know how to take care of anything, ma'am? What's your husband do? Sit around and watch TV? Drink beer all day? But then again, you're probably not married, right? I mean, who would, right?" He made a lemon-eating face. Mrs. Connor worked her fists into hard little balls and started to quake. Grover continued, unable to stop now that he had opened what he thought of as the Honesty Box. "Any price I gave you would be too high, ma'am. I can tell that's true because you have all this old furniture." He waved his thin right arm around the room and shook his head sadly. "And you probably buy your food in one of those warehouses where they sell stuff in bulk. My guess is you probably buy only the cheap generic stuff. Look at that end table. It's all scratched! If there were a trailer park nearby, you'd move in tomorrow, wouldn't you? I can tell these things. It makes no sense at all for me to give you a price on anything because you would only say no." Grover stared at Mrs. Connor, knowing that all he had said was true. He believed that she knew it too.

Mrs. Connor looked at Grover the way an exterminator looks at a cockroach. "Get out of my house, you dog turd," she said through clenched teeth and moved on him quickly, like a crab on the beach. And so it was that Grover found himself once again out on the sidewalk, this time rubbing a welt on his cheek. "Another cheapskate," he mumbled. "What's the use? All they're interested in nowadays is the bottom line. Price, price, price."

When Grover got back to his office Sid casually asked him how he had made out with Mrs. Connor. "Your price was too high," Grover reported. "You really should do something about lowering it. Nobody wants to buy from you because your prices are outrageous. I'm wasting my time out there. The public won't stand for this, you know. You can only charge what the market will bear." Grover stood there, looking as resigned as a melting snowman. Sid began to sweat. He had been suspecting that his prices were still too high. He'd have to make a few calls to his competitors. Pretend he was a potential customer and ask them for their prices. They'd tell him. They always did. And then he'd drop his prices below theirs. After all, that's all that anyone is interested in nowadays, right? Price.

"I'm sorry it's been so hard for you, Grover," Sid said. "Things will go better on your next call. I promise."

"Yeah?" Grover sulked. "Well, I seriously doubt it."

So Thorough. So Quiet!

Howie had left his meter in the truck. He didn't think he'd need it because he didn't know how to use it. In the past, whenever he had carried the meter into a basement it just sat there in his bucket like a dead fish. No one had ever taught him how to use the thing, and he wasn't about to start learning anything new at the ripe old age of twenty-two. Besides, he figured he didn't need to be carrying around anything so exotically electronic. Electronics scared the hell out of Howie. He preferred wrenches and hammers to computers and meters. He had found a place for the meter deep under the seat in his truck, which is where it was when he touched the hot wires.

Howie had seen an old-timer do the trick once. The old guy had wet his thumb and index finger and then carefully reached toward the wires, as though they were the business end of a loaded rattrap. The old guy had jerked his hand reflexively when the voltage bit him. He had winced, shook his head, and smiled at Howie. "She's hot all right!" he had said. Howie had nodded and smiled. That's the way a real man did things, he thought.

On the morning that Howie managed to weld his arms to the Kritzer's electrical panel, Cajun-cook his brain, and stop his heart for all time, he had been feeling adventurous. He had decided to try the old-timer's trick, but with a "Howie twist." Instead of checking the circuit by wetting the thumb and index finger of one hand, Howie would try two. He sucked deeply on the middle finger of his right hand, and then on the middle finger of his left hand. He held them both up, all shiny with saliva, and he smiled. This would be, he reasoned during the final moments of his short life, not only a test of high voltage, but also a testament to the way he felt about his job. He pointed his two wet middle digits at the panel in an obscene salute, reached in to test the circuit, and much to his astonishment, plugged himself into Eternity. The last thing Howie the Serviceman saw was a brilliant flash of blue light. His last thought (and it was a very brief one) was of the meter tucked safely under his truck seat.

Mrs. Kritzer turned to Mr. Kritzer who was watching Judge Judy shout at some guy on the TV. "That serviceman has been downstairs for a long time, don't you think?"

"He's thorough," Mr. Kritzer mumbled, not turning his attention from the old console. "It's good to be thorough." On the TV, Judge Judy was berating this guy who had damaged an old vacuum cleaner the plaintiff said she had brought to him for repair. "I like this Judge Judy," Mr. Kritzer said. "She tells it like it is! Too many of these service companies don't do a good job. You pay them good money and they let some moron screw around with your stuff. Judy knows how to handle those bums."

"But that serviceman got here at eight o'clock this morning," Mrs. Kritzer continued, "and now it's after four o'clock in the afternoon. That's a long time, don't you think?"

"All workmen should be as thorough as that guy," Mr. Kritzer said, lighting an unfiltered Lucky Strike. "It's good when they take their time. That way they're thorough. They don't make as many mistakes. Look at this bum on the TV. He wasn't thorough." Mr. Kritzer stabbed his cigarette at the defendant. "Besides, we have a service contract, you know. The more time that serviceman spends in our basement, the more we're getting for our money. Don't complain!" He sucked deeply on his Lucky and exhaled a blue cloud. He hacked and leaned in on the TV. "You tell 'em, Judy!" He laughed and turned to Mrs. Kritzer. "She's a pistol, ain't she?"

"He's very quiet, don't you think?" Mrs. Kritzer said during the next commercial.

"Who?"

"The man in the basement. I haven't heard him working at all. There's no banging. You usually hear some banging. He didn't come up for lunch, or ask to use the bathroom, or go out for a smoke, or anything. I haven't heard a peep out of him all day long."

"Quiet is good," Mr. Kritzer said, turning his attention back to Judge Judy, who had just returned with her decision. "If he was noisy like some of the other bums we've had working in this house we wouldn't be able to hear ourselves think. Besides, he's not disturbing my show. You are! You should be as quiet as that guy is. You should be as quiet and as thorough. Everybody's in too much of a hurry nowadays. Now shut up and let me hear this." Mr. Kritzer stubbed out his cigarette and lit another.

Back at the shop, Eli was wondering why Howie hadn't called in. It was now after five o'clock. Eli had told Howie to call in after every job, but not to use the customer's telephone. "Find a pay phone," Eli had said. "We can't afford no stinkin' car phones or radios. Use the pay phones. That's why they're out there on the street. Use 'em!" Eli believed in doing business the old-fashioned way.

Six o'clock rolled around and Howie still hadn't checked in. Eli wanted to go home. "You hear from Howie?" Eli asked his son, Gene.

"No, Pop, you hear from him?"

"Not a peep!" Eli said. "He must have finished up at Kritzer's place by now. Maybe he went home?"

"Howie just might do that," Gene said.

"You got Kritzer's phone number?" Eli asked. Gene dug though the tickets and read the number. "Slow down!" Eli said as he punched the numbers into the phone. Mr. Kritzer picked up on the fifth ring.

"Hello?"

"Mr. Kritzer?"

"Who's this? Some salesman? You bums are always calling during the news or when I'm having my dinner. Whatever the hell you're selling I don't want any!" Mr. Kritzer started to hang up, but Eli caught him. "It's the heating company, Mr. Kritzer," Eli said. "I'm looking for my man. He was at your house today, wasn't he?"

"Yeah, and he's still here. That's a thorough man you have there. And quiet! I'll tell you, I'm impressed with this guy. He's been working like a dog all day long. I can't believe the service I'm getting from you people. So thorough. So quiet!"

"Who's that?" Mrs. Kritzer asked from the kitchen.

"It's the heating company," Mr. Kritzer said, not bothering to cover the phone. "He's asking about his guy. I told him we're very happy with the service we're getting."

"Can I speak to my man?" Eli asked.

"No. I don't want to bother him," Mr. Kritzer said. "He's hard at work and he's being thorough." Mr. Kritzer wanted to suck every ounce of service he could out of his service contract, and he figured if he called Howie out of his basement this bum on the phone would send the guy to another job. "I don't want to stop your man from working. He's doing a great job in my basement! Every company should have people like this. I'm going to tell all my neighbors about how good you people are. My neighbors will all want to do business with you too. You'll see. Now I have to go because I'm watching the news. Don't call here anymore. Your man will be done when he's done." Mr. Kritzer hung up the phone.

Eli let the prospect of new business wash over him as he stood there holding the dial tone in his hand. He could use new business. "You find Howie?" Gene asked. "Yeah," Eli said. "He's still there. Kritzer says he's being thorough. He says other companies should be as thorough as we are. He says he's gonna recommend us to the whole neighborhood."

"You sure this guy's talking about Howie, Pop?"

"That's what he said. Kritzer said Howie was thorough. And quiet. I never thought of Howie in that way." Eli shrugged his shoulders. "Guess you can never tell, eh? Maybe he's finally growing up. I suppose we'll hear from him when we hear from him."

The next morning, Mrs. Kritzer wondered if she should offer the serviceman a cup of coffee. He had been working quietly through the night without a break. He'd probably welcome a nice hot cup of coffee right about now. And maybe an English muffin?

Mr. Kritzer, who was watching the last minutes of the Jerry Springer Show, told her to leave Howie alone. "Don't offer him anything. Leave him alone. He'll come upstairs when he's through."

Mr. Kritzer had never seen such fine service!

Katie Delaney's Marshmallow Roast

When Murray looked up from his work and saw five-year-old Katie Delaney's blue eyes he could think of just one thing: Trouble.

"Does your mother know you're down here in the basement?" Murray asked. Katie gave Murray an impish grin and dragged the toe of her sneaker against the concrete floor. "I know what that is," she said, pointing to the bicycle pump.

"What? This?" Murray asked.

"That's a pump," Katie Delaney said. "You use it to pump up a bicycle, and that!" She pointed toward the compression tank.

"That's right. We do have to pump these up sometimes," Murray agreed, going about his business. "That's part of our job. Say, does your mother know you're down here?"

"I'm six years old," Katie Delaney said, reaching down to touch Murray's box wrench. "How old are you?"

"I'm a lot older than six," Murray said, snatching the wrench from the girl's reach before she could touch it. "Don't do that," he said. "You could get hurt."

"You're fat," Katie Delaney said, which was true.

Murray bit his upper lip. "You should go upstairs now," he said.

"Well, it's true!" Katie said as she scampered up the steps.

Ten minutes after Murray had finished installing the new compression tank and had gone, Katie Delaney skipped back downstairs to continue doing what she had been doing all week, which was to use the air in the compression tank to inflate a red balloon. She then held the neck of the balloon and let it scream as it released its air. Katie Delaney liked the sound it made.

The boiler's relief valve popped later that afternoon, of course, just as it had for the past five afternoons. Neither Katie nor her mother, Anne, made the connection between the relief valve's popping and Katie's new pastime, however. Anne just called the Service Company again, forcing Murray to return.

Murray cursed the tank manufacturer for his misery as he drove back to the Delaney's. "Crap, they make nowadays. Crap!" he said.

"Hi, Fatso!" Katie Delaney said as Murray slogged down the basement.

"Go upstairs!" Murray growled at the child.

"It's my house," Katie Delaney said. "Not yours!"

Murray installed yet another compression tank and left as quickly as he could.

Now, by watching Murray work during the last several days, Katie Delaney had decided that she could toast marshmallows over the new boiler's atmospheric gas burner. In the days before Murray began to hate the little girl, he had done his best to answer her questions. "What's that?" she had asked, on the first day, pointing to the flaming gas burners. "That's where the fire comes from," Murray said. "Don't touch it. It's very hot."

Katie Delaney began roasting marshmallows over the fire that very same afternoon.

She used a long fork, which her father Ron stored in the basement once the barbecue season ended in early October. She had found the marshmallows in the cabinet next to the refrigerator. There were plenty of them.

When she first got down on her belly and stuck the fork with the marshmallow into the combustion chamber, she couldn't believe how quickly the thing had flared up. She had blown out the first few marshmallows and ate them right off the end of the long fork, but after a while, she began to enjoy the sight of the flaming marshmallows as they blackened and dripped into the burners. "It's gooey!" she said to herself.

She told her friends at school about what she was doing, of course. She made the experience sound so appealing that they began doing the same thing the very next day. Before long, there was a regular marshmallow roast going on throughout Katie Delaney's neighborhood. The cold winter air smelled just like summer camp.

Murray, you should know, serviced all the homes in Katie Delaney's neighborhood. His first reaction at seeing the goo stuck to the burners was that the manufacturer had screwed up. This is the normal reaction of most American contractors when there is a problem with heating equipment. "Look at this!" Murray cried as he scraped the gooey foreign matter from the burners. "The gaskets are melting! I knew this would happen! This is what I get for listening to those bums!"

Before another hour passed, Murray was called to service every single boiler in the neighborhood. In each case, the compression tank appeared to have failed, causing the relief valve to pop. And the boiler gaskets had apparently melted and leaked all over the gas burners.

The parents of Katie Delaney's schoolmates were calling Murray because he was the guy who had installed all of the boilers in the neighborhood. You see, Murray had worked a deal with the Gas Company to install the boilers they were giving away through a special promotion. The deal was that if you switched from fuel oil to natural gas, you got a free boiler from the Gas Company. Murray put the boilers in for next to nothing, but he figured if he did enough of these conversions he was bound to make a profit somewhere along the line. He wasn't sure where the profit would come from, but he figured if he stayed really busy, he'd eventually make money.

Although he wouldn't say it to the homeowners, Murray hated the boiler the Gas Company was giving away because it had those rubber gaskets between each cast-iron section. "Those things are crap!" he barked at his wife. And now his worst fears were confirmed as he scraped away at the congealed marshmallow. "I knew this would happen!"

he shouted at her. She just waved a hand in his direction and walked away.

When Murray got back to his office, he called the representative from the Gas Company. "I'm not going to be responsible for all of this!" he screamed. The guy from the Gas Company told Murray to stay calm, and that he would get back to him. The Gas Company guy then panicked and called the manufacturer. "We're not going to be responsible for all of this!" he screamed. The manufacturer panicked as well and said he would send an investigator immediately.

The investigator was the local rep, of course – a young man named Kenny. Kenny wasn't going to be responsible either.

As Kenny bent down to look at the burners, Katie Delaney and her mom watched from the doorway. Kenny scraped some of the marshmallow residue into a plastic sandwich bag. He smiled at Katie and Anne as he was leaving. He didn't want to speak because he was afraid that anything he said might be used against him in a court of law.

"Eeewww. You smell bad," Katie Delaney said as Kenny was leaving. He didn't answer her. He just smiled nervously and scurried away.

It didn't take the chief technician more than a few minutes to determine that the foreign matter collected from Katie Delaney's boiler and the rest of the boilers in the neighborhood was marshmallow. At a loss to explain the phenomenon, the technician notified the president of the boiler company, "This must be a conspiracy," the chief technician said. "Someone on the factory floor is putting marshmallows inside our boilers. I surmise that it's someone in the employ of the fuel oil industry. They're obviously trying to sabotage our products because we're selling all these boilers for gas conversions."

"Are you absolutely sure?" the president of the boiler company asked.

"It's the only possible explanation." the chief technician said.

This, of course, led to the firing of all the boiler manufacturers' short-term employees. Anyone who had been on the job for less than one year got canned. "Our long-term employees would never do such a thing," the president concluded.

The union called a strike over this issue, which would eventually put the boiler company into Chapter 11 bankruptcy. But this would take some time.

In the meantime, Katie Delaney's parents along with all the neighbors banded together and contacted the county's Office of Consumer Affairs. Consumer Affairs went to work on Murray who eventually wound up broke and divorced. He died a horrible death while sleeping in a storm drain. But this, too, would take some time.

Katie Delaney's parents, dissatisfied with the inability of Consumer Affairs to go after the Big Fish, contacted Mike Wallace. He and a crew from 60 Minutes looked into the matter. They had their own investigators analyze the material. These experts concluded that the material was marshmallow. The show's producers were not aware of the competitive battle between the fuel oil and natural gas industries, so they never suspected marshmallow sabotage on the factory floor. They decided to conclude, instead, that the boilers were somehow producing marshmallow as a byproduct of combustion. This marshmallow residue, they reasoned, coated the boiler and led to excessive temperatures and pressures which eventually popped the relief valves.

It goes without saying that the sudden discharge of hot water under any circumstances poses a serious health hazard. And since no one could be sure what chemicals spewed from the heated water and entered the atmosphere during discharge, the show's producers reasoned that these unknown chemical compounds were most likely recycling back through the combustion chamber, creating the Marshmallow Effect.

These compounds could very well be generating a chain reaction – the consequences of which no one could predict.

The Sierra Club got involved.

The Delaneys, fearful of living in a neighborhood that had become so incredibly toxic, sold their home to the insurance company and moved to New Jersey where they now live normal lives.

Katie Delaney has made many new friends.

Muller From Fuller

Muller wasn't sure he could do this again. He had done it before, twice, and had barely pulled it off the second time around, but three times? What credibility he had left was hanging around his ankles like a pair of old brown socks. But, he remembered, you can't be holier than the church, right? He was just going to have to do the best he could.

"Jack Thompson, please," Muller grumped into the phone.

"May I tell him who's calling?" the receptionist asked.

"Muller from Fuller Sales," Muller said. He waited a few minutes before she came back on the line.

"I'm sorry, sir. Mr. Thompson is gone for the day," she said.

"Is Harry Swenson there?" Muller asked.

"Please hold and I'll check," she said. After another few minutes she was back. "Mr. Swenson's not here either," she said, a bit shorter this time, a tad nasty.

"Well, I'll speak to anybody other than you then," Muller said. "Are any of the buyers in?"

"Please hold."

Muller shook his head and sighed. He looked through the pages of the new catalog while he waited. He tried to make sense of this new boiler line but it was like being forced to change your religion. "This stinks," he mumbled to himself.

"Sir?" the receptionist was back.

"Yes!" Muller pulled his bulk up a bit in the chair.

"There's no one here right now."

"It took you that long to figure this out?" Muller said. "You're there alone? Got the whole place to yourself? You couldn't just tell me that up front?"

"I'm sorry," the receptionist said, acid in her voice now. "Would you like to leave a message?"

"Yes, I would. Please tell Jack Thompson that Muller from Fuller called. Tell him that we now have a new boiler line. This is the best boiler line I personally have ever seen in my long life and I would like to make an appointment with him so that I can tell him of its glories."

"Will he know who you are?"

"I sure hope so," Muller sighed, rubbing his aching temples with a thumb and forefinger. "I've been marching through your place since before you were born. Just say it's Muller from Fuller. He'll know. He's met me many, many times. So have you, although not in a way so that you would remember. I'm sure you meet hundreds of fascinating men like me. I remember you well, however. You are the woman who likes to file her nails. I have enjoyed the hospitality of your lobby for many long, anxiety-producing hours while waiting to meet with your bosses for a few brief moments. I would now like to meet with them again. If you would please convey to them that message, I will be most grateful."

"I'll do that," she said icily and hung up.

Muller put the phone down gingerly and turned another page in the brand-new catalog. He tried his best to take in the majesty of the product he was about to declare the heavyweight champion of the heating world. These boilers happened to be the engineering opposite of the boilers he had been selling for the past three years, and those were off by at least 90 degrees from the boiler line he had sold just prior to that. "You can't be holier than the church," he mumbled to no one in particular and flipped the page.

Fred Fuller, who had inherited Fuller Sales from his father, maneuvered the red Cadillac into his private spot by the front door of the squat, brick building in the industrial park. He hopped from the car and breezed into the office. He smiled at everyone and picked a tiny thread from the sleeve of his plaid suit. He smiled especially hard at Muller, his oldest employee. "How's it going, big guy?" he asked.

"Lousy," Muller said, looking up from his gloom. Muller used to give Fred Fuller nickels for ice cream, but that was a long time ago.

"What's wrong?" Fred Fuller asked, sounding genuinely concerned, although Muller knew better.

"Ah, it's this new line of boilers you took on. How the hell am I supposed to go back to the people I've been calling on and convince them that these boilers are better than the ones I've been telling them about for the past three years? I've been knocking this line for as long as I can remember. And now you're making me sell it? I lose credibility when I have to do things like this. People look at me like I'm a no-good liar."

"I really wish you didn't feel that way," Fred said sincerely, although Muller knew better.

"I wish I didn't feel that way, too," Muller moped. "But what you do to me makes me feel that way. You give me pains in my head and my stomach and I'm getting too old for this. Why couldn't you just keep the old line? I liked the old line. I knew the old line. I had the customers convinced that the old line was the best line. And now I have to go out there and tell them that's not so? I have to go out there and compete against myself? How can I possibly do that?"

"You shouldn't look at it that way," Fred Fuller said. "That's negative thinking." He reached over and squeezed Muller's shoulder in a fatherly sort of way, which made Muller want to put him through the wall. "I like positive thinkers on my team," Fred Fuller said, giving Muller a sincere smile, although Muller knew better. "You're a positive thinker, aren't you? Dad always said you were. I'd like to agree with him. Will you allow me agree with him?"

"This is so easy for you to say," Muller shot back. "You don't have to go out there and talk to the customers."

Fred Fuller fixed Muller with a warm smile, although Muller knew better. "Now, is that fair? I came up through sales, you know," he said. "My father used to take me with him on his sales calls. I've been out there at least a dozen times. I know what it's like to be in the trenches. I may not be there all the time, but I try to live vicariously through your experiences. And that's why I enjoy these conversations so much." Fred Fuller poured another smile over the older man. "Now, just try to keep your sunny side up . . ."

"Your father kept the same line for thirty years," Muller spat out. "You lost your father's line. You change lines like other reps change underwear!"

"Ah, that's where you're wrong," Fred Fuller said, shaking his head sadly. "I change lines because of opportunity. Each line we take on is better than the previous line. Much, much better! Here, look at that catalog! Have you ever seen such high-quality paper?" Fred Fuller smiled and fingered the glossy page as if it was a lapel on a three thousand-dollar suit.

"If this line is better than the last line, how come you didn't take it on sooner?" Muller asked. "Does that make sense to you? I have to keep going back to these same people. You make me feed them a line of crap about how this boiler – the one we have now – is great but the boiler that I was selling them last month is now lousy?"

"That other boiler is the competitor now," Fred Fuller countered.

"Maybe so," Fuller said, "But then they ask me why I didn't tell them the old boiler was lousy when I visited last month. How can I answer that? I'm losing all my credibility."

"Last month that boiler was fine! It's just not anymore." Fred Fuller said, and then smiled in a knowing way. "Listen, if you honestly feel this way, if this is really bothering you that much, if you just can't get in touch with our mission, then perhaps it's time for you to move on."

Fuller knew Muller wasn't going anywhere. Muller had started with Fred's father and was now embroiled in those later years that tend to make a man very careful, but also sometimes a bit suicidal. "Think of it as a bright new opportunity!" Fred Fuller continued, walking toward his office. "You can do it!"

"You change lines because you lose lines," Muller shot after him, and this stopped Fred Fuller in his tracks. "You lose lines because you don't meet your quotas. You don't meet your quotas because you don't work as hard as your father did. You play golf. You're a stinking playboy!"

All of this, of course, was true.

Fred Fuller turned and glanced down at a manicured nail, deflecting the glare from Muller's blazing eyes. "I'm not just playing golf, you know. I'm staying in shape. Strong body, strong mind, you know!" He looked up and smiled. "C'mon, big guy!" he said. "Let's just sell what we have to sell today, okay? I'm sure you can find plenty of good things to say about this new boiler line. The manufacturer sent us the literature, right? It's great-looking stuff! Spend some more time reading it. Feel that paper! C'mon, you can do it! Besides, you can't be holier than the church, you know."

"But this line is entirely different," Muller pleaded. "It goes against everything I have preached for years. It goes counter to what I've stood for. Who's going to believe me?"

Fuller gave Muller a most sincere smile, although Muller knew better. "We're manufacturers' reps," Fuller said. "Let's buck up and act like reps."

"And how exactly are reps supposed to act?" Muller answered.

Fred Fuller considered this for a moment. "We . . . adapt," he said finally and lit up the room with the brightest smile Muller had ever seen.

Bailey's Great Experiment

It was the spike in the cost of paper that eventually led to Bailey's Great Experiment. The printer blamed the 50 percent increase on El Niño and lousy weather in the Pacific Northwest, or some such crap. Bailey thought the printer was a stinking thief, but he couldn't get relief from any other printer in the United States of America because those bums had a trade association. "They plan this," he mumbled at the invoice. "They get together in big rooms at their conventions and plan this."

Bailey was the president of Bailey Boilers. He was getting his brains kicked in by a dozen competitors, two unions, a nagging wife, three ungrateful kids, and this stinking printing company. The only one he thought he might be able to get back at was the printer. He initialed the invoice for the 5,000 installation-and-operation manuals and tossed it in the "Hold for as long as possible" bin. His bookkeeper would now pay that invoice when the printer's lawyers showed up with the sheriff and a warrant for Bailey's arrest, but not a day sooner. "Gosh, I'm so sorry for the delay," Bailey would tell the printer when that day arrived. "It's that El Niño, you know? It really slows things down at this time of the year. We sell fewer boilers because it just doesn't get that cold anymore. What can you do?" Bailey would shrug his shoulders and look exasperated.

The thing that got to Bailey most about the printing bills was that he was starting to believe that no contractor had ever read the expensive installation-and-operation manual he included with each boiler. He suspected that contractors used the manuals to prop open basement windows and light gas pilots. He suspected this because the engineer he had hired to write the thing spoke only Martian. Bailey himself couldn't understand what the heck the guy was saying most of the time. And to make matters worse, when the engineer had finished writing that manual a few years back he had passed it on to the Legal Department. Those people spoke the language of the planet Uranus. Bailey was positive that the installation-and-operation manual was both technically and legally correct, but it was also incomprehensible. And it was thick – 542 pages! There was even a clause in there stating that if any contractor should trip over the manual and get hurt, Bailey Boilers could not be held liable for damages.

"You think we have to keep publishing this thing?" Bailey asked Schtunk, his marketing manager.

"Of course we do!" Schtunk exclaimed. "That's our installation-and-operation manual. You can't sell a boiler without an installation-and-operation manual." Schtunk chuckled, as if Bailey's question had been the joke of the day.

"But I don't think a single one of our customers has ever read this thing." Bailey hefted the volume and dropped it with a Whomp! onto the top of his desk. "Do you seriously think anybody reads that thing? I can't understand it and I own the company. Can you understand it?"

Schtunk looked at the tome and shook his head. "No. I'm Marketing, not Engineering. I've never even tried to read it. Marketing people don't have to be technical. I have no idea if our customers read it. But we do have to furnish one with the boiler. I know that for sure."

"But isn't it a function of Marketing to learn what our customers want?" Bailey persisted.

"No," Schtunk said. "That would be Research. And we outsource that sort of work. I can have that done, if that's what you'd like, Mr. Bailey."

Bailey took off his glasses and rubbed his eyes. "No," he sighed, "the last thing I need right now is more expense." He looked down at the volume and nudged it with his index finger. It barely moved. "Why are we printing this?" Bailey asked rhetorically. "Do you have any idea what it costs to print this stuff nowadays?"

Schtunk shook his head. "That's Advertising," he said.

"You really think we need to print it if no one reads it?" Bailey asked again.

"Absolutely!" Schtunk said emphatically.

"Why?" Bailey asked, yearning to know.

Schtunk opened his eyes wide, as if he was about to reveal one of the Great Truths. "Because our competitors print them," he said.

"Are theirs any better than ours?" Bailey asked. "Does anyone read theirs?"

"Again," Schtunk said, "that would be Engineering and/ or Research. Would you like me to look into it?" Schtunk gave Bailey one of those flashy, Marketing Guy smiles. Bailey shook his head, rubbed his eyes again, and sighed.

It was later that same day that Bailey came up with the idea for his Great Experiment. He took a ride down to Sir Speedy, which was the cheapest and quickest printer he could find, and had the guy behind the counter make up 50 index cards containing the following message:

If you find this card, please call our toll-free number and ask for Mr. Bailey. You will receive a prize.

He figured he'd go out onto the factory floor and slip these 50 cards into the next 50 installation-and-operation manuals that went out with the next 50 Bailey Boilers. If anyone opened the manual, the card would fall out. When they called Bailey for the prize, he would send them a ballpoint pen with the company's logo. That would be his way of saying thanks for their participation in his Great Experiment. It would also let him know if anyone ever peeked inside the massive and way-too-expensive manuals.

Several weeks passed but no one called for a ballpoint pen. Bailey began to suspect the worst. He wandered by Technical Support one afternoon. The five Tech Support people were busy on the phones, answering hundreds of contractor questions. Bailey knew that everything the contractors needed to know was contained in the thick installation-and-operating manual, but the contractors called nevertheless. "They don't read," Bailey mumbled to himself. "I just know it!"

He walked back to his office. His bookkeeper handed him a message from the anxious printer. "He's still looking for payment," she said. "Do you want him to stay in the When Pigs Fly bin?"

"Yes, and explain to him that there's an unexpected cold front on the way with possible thunderstorms predicted. Highly unusual for this time of the year, but with El Niño you can never tell. We can't possibly pay bills when there's a thunderstorm in the area. It wouldn't be safe." Bailey shrugged his shoulders. "Explain to him that it's quite warm in the Pacific right now. He'll understand."

Bailey took another ride down to Sir Speedy at lunchtime. "Print me up another 50 index cards," he said.

"You want the same message as the last time?" the guy behind the counter asked.

"No. This time have it read this way." Bailey handed the guy a piece of paper. Later that day he picked up the cards. This was the message he had chosen:

If you call this special toll-free number right now,

I will give you $50 and a case of cold beer.

1-800-BREWSKI

"This ought to do it," Bailey said to himself as he slipped the cards into the manuals. "No contractor in America can refuse free money and beer."

Two weeks later, Bailey had Schtunk back in his office. "No one's reading our manuals," Bailey declared.

"How can you tell?" Schtunk asked.

"I've been doing some experimenting on my own," Bailey said, and then he told Schtunk about his Great Experiment. Schtunk squirmed in his seat because he thought the Great Experiment came uncomfortably close to Marketing, which is what Schtunk was supposed to be doing. Sure, it might be considered Research in some circles, but when you start giving away free beer and money, well, that's Marketing. Schtunk was worried that he was going to get downsized if he didn't do something – and fast!

"I can look into this a bit deeper if you'd like," Schtunk said. "Just to be positive."

"I sure wish you would," Bailey said. "I think that's part of what you're supposed to be doing, isn't it?"

"I'll take care of it, Mr. Bailey," Schtunk said, leaping from the leather chair and scurrying out of the office.

At lunchtime, Schtunk went to Kinko's and had 5,000, 8-1/2" × 11", neon-red handbills made up. The copy read:

CALL TOLL-FREE (1-800-BREWSKI)

YOU WILL RECEIVE $5,000 CASH,

12 TICKETS TO THE SUPER BOWL,

YOUR VERY OWN BEER DISTRIBUTORSHIP,

AND A HOT DATE WITH MISS JULY!

THERE IS NO LIMIT TO THE NUMBER OF CONTRACTORS WHO CAN PARTICIPATE IN THIS GREAT EXPERIMENT.

AND THERE IS NO PURCHASE NECESSARY.

GET TO THE PHONE NOW!

"This will prove, beyond a shadow of a doubt, that no one in the world reads our installation-and-operation manuals," Schtunk said to the Kinko's guy. "Mr. Bailey is going to be so proud of me!"

Three weeks later, Benny Steinberg of Brooklyn, New York dropped a Bailey Boiler off the tines of his forklift truck at the wholesale house where he had worked for 22 years. "Oops!" he said. The boiler crashed down into the loading bay and split into pieces. A thick book flew from the rubble and a neon-red handbill fluttered onto the greasy pavement.

A few minutes later, Benny Steinberg walked into the counter area where there were no less than a dozen burly, New York City contractors waiting for supplies. "Fellas," Benny Steinberg said, "I am about to make you all very, very happy,"

Thirty-six hours later, Bailey Boilers went belly-up.

Flott's Bold Move

Flott has that special quality of fixation often associated with dim farm animals. It can be pretty unsettling if you don't know the man. You can stand at Flott's desk for a full five minutes before he notices you. And even after he does, it often takes another minute or so before he's able to shift his attention fully and ask what you want.

Had Flott taken the police test, as his father had suggested when he was a young man ("There's nothing as secure as civil service, son."), he would surely have been killed years ago by minor street criminals. They could have walked up behind Flott, banging galvanized steel garbage can lids, and pushed him in front of a bus. Flott never would have known what hit him. Such is the way of a totally focused man.

Flott is able to achieve this trance-like state because he is a Deep Thinker. His official title in his company is New-Products Development Manager, which means the company pays him to think Bold Thoughts about their future.

A manager might suggest to Flott that the company should head in a direction that would make them more profitable. "We're not making enough money," the manager might say. "Find us a product that will make more money for the company." Flott would then set to work on a Bold Plan of Development for the company.

In the past, these Bold Plans usually involved making a deal with another company that was willing to brand name their existing products for Flott's company. This required very little effort, and even less capital expense on the part of Flott's company. Flott would make the deal, and then take credit for the New-Product Development.

Schnick, the Advertising Manager, would then launch an advertising campaign that stated, in essence, "We Make One of Those Too! And Ours Is Just As Good!"

The supplier to Flott's company would then proceed to beat the snot out of them on price, and, after a year or so, Flott's company would decide there wasn't enough money to be made with this particular product. So they'd bail out.

The Bail Out Procedure was an interesting one. Phlegm the Manager of Old-Product Dispersal would send a fax to the distributors, announcing their withdrawal from this particular market. This, of course, would leave the distributors with tons of unsold inventory, but such was the nature of a free-market economy.

One spring day, Flott was staring holes in his Lucite paperweight when he fixed on a Bold Plan. Why not actually make a new product? That would eliminate the probability of the competitor (who was also the supplier) beating them up on price, and ultimately driving them out of the market. Why, if they played their cards right, and made the right stuff, they might even be able to declare themselves Market Leaders for a change.

Flott immediately set out to think of a new product that his company could actually produce in a factory rather than in a conference room. He stared out the window for 45 minutes, fixating like a madman on the telephone wires. The wires, unfortunately, provided no inspiration, so Flott shifted his gaze to the pulsating lawn sprinkler. He watched the sprinkler for over an hour as it machine-gunned its way in a circular pattern, spraying the lawn, the cars driving by, and the employees returning from lunch.

Suddenly it hit him. He jumped from his desk and ran down the corridor to the president's office. He burst past Millie, the president's elderly secretary, and crashed into the Big Guy's office. "THERE'S TOO MUCH PRESSURE!" Flott screamed, causing the president to spill his coffee and dive under his mahogany desk. The president had developed a healthy fear of disgruntled employees.

"I know there's pressure," the president pleaded, "but please let me go and I'll give you as much paid vacation as you want!"

Flott fixated on this development for a moment, and then shook it off. "No, it's not me, sir, it's the water. There's too much water pressure. We should make our own water pressure reducing valves and sell them to people. We won't buy someone else's. We'll make our own!"

The president peeped around the end of his desk, and seeing that Flott was still in possession of his senses, said, "You think people will buy them from us?"

"I know they will, sir!" Flott shouted.

"What sort should we make?" the president asked, standing and getting caught up in Flott's unbridled enthusiasm.

"Oh, I don't know," Flott said, "At this point, it really doesn't matter, does it? What's important is that there's just too damn much pressure."

"How many can we sell in the first year?" the president asked, "And how much will we make on each one?"

"I don't know," Flott said.

"Well, let's find out!" the president said, giving Flott a smile that lit up the office like a 500-watt incandescent bulb.

Flott set to work figuring out what sort of reducing valve they should make, how many they could sell in the first year, and how much money they'd make on each one. He began by finding out who the serious manufacturers of reducing valves were by looking in a six-month-old trade magazine he found on an end table in the lobby. He figured that if a manufacturer was serious about the business of selling something, they would have to advertise in a magazine. If they weren't serious, they wouldn't advertise, so Flott knew he could discount as serious competitors the people he didn't know about.

After paging through the magazine, he came up with a list of two potential competitors. He decided to focus on the one with the larger ad, figuring they were the most serious.

Next, he set out to learn the yearly sales of this serious potential competitor. He figured that once he knew their yearly sales, he could decide how much of that business his company would be able to swipe within the first year. That would give him two-thirds of the information the president needed to make a decision on whether they should enter this lucrative market. The missing third of the equation (what they should actually make) would follow easily.

Learning the serious competitor's annual revenues was difficult, though, because they weren't publicly owned. Flott solved this problem by sending one of his assistants to the serious competitor's factory to count the cars in their parking lot. He then assigned an arbitrary sales-dollar amount to each car, figuring each car belonged to one employee, and that for a company to have X employees, it must have Y dollars in sales.

"Suppose some of them carpool?" Flott's assistant asked, before leaving on his mission.

"Don't think like that," Flott said. "It only complicates the equation. Focus on the problem!"

The assistant returned a day later with the exact number of cars found in the lot. Flott assigned his arbitrary number of sales dollars to the cars, came up with a total, and then arbitrarily selected a percentage of the total his company would be able to filch from the competitor within the first year.

The numbers, unfortunately, didn't justify the start-up costs Flott's company would incur by going into the water pressure reducing valve manufacturing business. But Flott was a man who knew how to FOCUS. He wasn't about to let a column of numbers stand in the way of his Bold Plan.

He decided to arbitrarily adjust his arbitrary numbers until they came out the way they were supposed to come out.

As he walked down the corridor to the president's office, he felt the sense of pride that comes easily to Bold Thinkers. He had assembled all his facts and figures into a thick, laser-printed report with a baby-blue plastic cover. It looked so fine. And it was all in there – what they would manufacture, how many they'd sell within the first year, how much money they'd make on each one. The report made an irresistible case, and the president decided that, yes, they should proceed to the next step in the manufacturing of water pressure reducing valves.

That next step was a simple one. They had one of their contractor friends buy all of the serious competitor's products from a local plumbing and heating wholesaler. Flott then had the company engineer take the products apart, examine them, analyze how they worked, and then figure out how to make the same thing, with just enough of a change to avoid a patent-infringement lawsuit.

After great deliberation, the engineer decided to change the color. And the box.

Flott's marketing people introduced the new product by pricing it below the serious competitor's product. "We have to buy our way into the market," said Spicer, the Director of Marketing.

Schnick, the Advertising Manager, launched an advertising campaign that stated, in essence, "We Make One of Those Too! And Ours Is Just As Good!"

Two weeks after the new product introduction, the serious competitor responded by suing Flott's company for patent infringement.

"How can they do this?" Flott screamed at the company engineer. "We changed the color and the damn box, didn't we?"

"Anybody can sue anybody in America," the company engineer said with a shrug of his shoulders.

Word got out on the street that Flott's company was in serious legal trouble, and no contractor in America wanted to buy the new product from the distributors because they couldn't be sure if Flott's company would still be around next month – or even next week.

In a brilliant move, Director of Marketing Spicer lowered the price again, but that didn't seem to make much of a difference (except to a select group of contractors who would buy nuclear waste if the price was right).

In the end, Flott's company decided to go out of the water pressure reducing valve business once and for all. They hadn't achieved their sales goals for the first six months, and it didn't look like they were going to do much better in the second six months.

Phlegm the Manager of Old-Product Dispersal immediately drafted a fax to the distributors. The fax explained that the company was no longer in the reducing valve business, and that they, the distributors, could do whatever they wanted to do with their tons of inventories – as long as they were current with Accounts Receivable.

Flott, of course, blamed the company engineer, who, of course, was downsized.

There was no reason to downsize Flott, however. After all, none of this had been his fault.

Doc Feeney and the Trickle-Down Principle

Doc Feeney's left eye wanders, giving him the appearance of medieval insanity. He is bent over like a gnarled tree from years of tinkering with things that are closer to the ground than he is. Most people stay out of his lab while he's working (which is always) because his high-octane enthusiasm often has him scuffing shards of metal from between his legs like an old dog digging for a lost bone. He hunkers over his contraptions, probing their orifices with his bony fingers as though looking for lost coins in pay phones. While doing this, he stares simultaneously at the floor and the ceiling and mumbles to himself nonstop. Every few minutes he stops to scratch his ribs furiously with all ten fingers. "Gotta tell about it!" he'll say. "Really tell about it!" If you ask, What do you have to tell about, Doc? he'll just shake his head as though he has a bee stuck in his hair. His left eye will spin around like a cork in a blender. Then he'll bend over and continue working at a furious pace. "Gotta tell about it!" he'll repeat, as though in prayer.

Doc Feeney is in charge of all of heating. Both knowingly and unknowingly, he has developed every new product and conjured every breakthrough idea in the world of heating since 1930. Other companies like to think they developed some of these things, but the truth is everything has come, either directly or indirectly, from the mind of Doc Feeney. In the early years – between 1930 and 1964 – he regularly gave away his company's secrets by mumbling incessantly while attending industry functions and trade shows. His wandering eye would meander up and down two aisles and across the ceiling and floor at the same time while he gave up secrets that were worth millions of bucks. Competitors just had to stand next to Doc Feeney and pay attention as new-product ideas and technological breakthroughs tumbled from his quivering lips like coins from a slot machine. He never realized anyone was listening because Doc's wandering eye denies him stereoscopic vision. To Doc Feeney, the world is a cardboard forest. His thoughts, however, are four-dimensional.

His company stopped sending him to trade shows and industry events during the summer of 1964 when they realized Doc was spilling more beans than the night shift at a Mexican restaurant. It took Doc's company 34 years to figure out that he had been giving it all away because no one at Doc Feeney's company feels comfortable speaking with him. "It's like having a conversation with a high-tech Quasimodo," the president said. "Too creepy for me." Management has always preferred written reports from Doc Feeney, which he sends in whenever he has the time, that being hardly ever.

When his company stopped bringing him along to trade shows and other industry events, the competitors simply began following Doc Feeney on his weekly trips to the supermarket. Doc spilled as many beans there as he did anywhere else, and unlike industry events it didn't cost anything to go to the supermarket and walk behind the great man who is in charge of all of heating. So they did.

One day, Doc walked down the cereal aisle and gave up an idea for a new type of water pump. Another day (it was in August), he mumbled a solution to a nagging problem with boilers while reaching for a frozen lasagna. The produce section inspired him on a pleasant March morning to reveal a brand-new way to control multiple-boiler systems. You never know what you'll get when Doc scurries down the chip-and-dip aisle. The competitors continue to follow Doc to this day. They ram each other's ankles with their empty grocery carts, trying to get as close as possible to the great man. Once they hear something, the competitors race back to their factories and try to be the first to turn Doc's mumblings into new products. Here's how it all works.

A product first gets produced by someone who overhears Doc Feeney's mumblings. This person's company then introduces the product with nearly as high a level of enthusiasm as Doc's. The company then presents the product to their manufacturers' rep, but this is where a serious dilution of enthusiasm begins. The rep, you see, has more than one line to represent. This is because reps don't like to put all their eggs in one basket. What if they lose the line?

Anyway, when the rep receives the new product from the manufacturer, he will grant it about 1/100th the dose of enthusiasm applied by the manufacturer. Reps never get to meet Doc Feeney because his level of enthusiasm would set them on fire. Doc Feeney burns white hot; reps merely glow. "Hey, nice product!" the rep will say. "I'll bet we could sell some of these if we really tried." This pleases the manufacturer who then allows the rep to keep the line for another 30 days.

The rep takes the new product to the wholesaler who stocks thousands of other products. "Here's something new," the rep says. "Isn't it great? A real breakthrough! You can make lots of money with this."

The mention of money gets the wholesaler's full attention, of course. "How much money?" the wholesaler asks. "And what's your best discount?" The rep goes though his routine and the wholesaler gets somewhat enthusiastic about the product, but only about 1/1000th as much as the manufacturer. "Leave me some literature," the wholesaler says, "and I'll see if any contractors bite." The rep complies, and as soon as he's out the door, another rep shows up with even more heating-product literature for the wholesaler to read and consider. This is because Doc Feeney is forever inventing new things in the world of heating, and he goes shopping at the supermarket every week. "Who's got time to read all this stuff?" the wholesaler finally says as the tall pile of literature topples from his desk.

Which brings us to the next link in the chain of distribution – the contractor. Now contractors are enthusiastic people, too, but since they have the entire spectrum of heating to consider, they're not likely to get wildly enthusiastic over any single product or idea. They don't even know Doc Feeney exists, and that's a good thing because if they ever stood too near his passionate inventiveness, they would explode.

Most contractors will apply 1/10,000th of the enthusiasm for a new product that the manufacturer has applied. This is because that's all that has trickled down to them. Contractors have just so much enthusiasm to spare, and what they do have they spend in the pursuit of new jobs and old invoices.

Which brings us to the consumer.

The consumer sits and surfs TV channels, stopping very often on some home improvement show or another. Consumers like to watch these shows because they believe contractors are thieves. Consumers want to learn how to do it themselves, and as quickly as possible so they won't have to deal with contractors anymore.

When they see new heating products on those home improvement shows, however, they immediately stop thinking about doing it themselves. This is because, to the average consumer, a well-thought-out heating system looks like a hot date with RuPaul – simple in concept, difficult to consummate. "That sounds like a wonderful way to heat a home," the consumer will say. "Let's go to the Big Home Center and ask if they do this." The guy in the aisle at the Big Home Center smiles at them like Gomer Pyle, which makes the consumer say, "We'd better go ask a heating contractor."

Which is what the consumer does. "Tell me about it!" he says. But at this point, the enthusiasm for the new product has trickled to a point where it's about as potent as a lukewarm O'Doul's.

"You don't want that," the contractor tells the consumer. "It's way too expensive."

"Oh," the consumer says.

And while all this is going on, Doc Feeney continues to work furiously in his lab. He rolls his crazy eye across the universe, burns white-hot with excitement, and invents more and more good stuff.

"Gotta tell about it!"

Don't Assume

Fat Tony was sweating like a cheap beer cooler in July.
His breath came in labored huffs as he lit another unfiltered
Camel and sucked hungrily. He hitched the side of his pants
up with his pudgy left hand, and mopped his brow with the
dish towel he always carries in his right hand. He turned
toward Joey, squinted through the smoke, and asked. "So
wadda you think, kid?" He leaned forward and planted the
palms of his hands on his knees, as really round men will
do. He nodded toward the small circulator, and asked. "Is it
the right size or not, kid?"

Joey stared at the circulator and, almost imperceptibly,
started to shake. He scratched at a zit on his chin and
another behind his ear. He looked at his scuffed shoes,
and then around the room. He stole a glance at Fat Tony,
who, of course, was glowering, and then he looked back at
the circulator. He took a shallow breath and mumbled, "I
assume it's the right size. After all, it's here, right?"

Fat Tony was on Joey like cheese on a pizza. He
snatched the cigarette from between his lips and pointed
it like a weapon at the younger man. Joey almost tripped
as he backed up two full steps. Fat Tony waddled in on
him, closing the gap. "YOU ASSUMED!" he bleated with

glee, his lips curling into an evil grin. Fat Tony's lips look like two thick slices of liverwurst. When he cranks up his Stinging Reprimand, as he was now doing, his jowls waggle like raw chicken cutlets, and his ears twitch like tortellinis in boiling water. Fat Tony turns into a regular deli case when he gets going, and Joey had just flipped the GO switch.

"JOEY, WHEN YOU ASSUME . . . YOU MAKE AN ASS OUTTA YOU AND ME." He traced the letter U in the air with the cigarette when he got to that part, and when he said the word, ME, he pointed his thumb at his heaving sternum, and laughed a wicked laugh. Fat Tony's thumb is as big as a fried chicken leg, and his laugh sounds like a key turning in an already-started car's ignition.

"Get it, Joey? It's all dere in the woid. A.S.S. Dat's ass, right?" Joey nodded, having heard this lecture several times before. "And den dere's U." He pointed at Joey. "And next dere's M.E. Dat's me, right?" He pointed at himself. Joey nodded. "SO DON'T ASSUME, JOEY! 'CAUSE WHEN YOU DO, YOU MAKE AN ASS OUTTA YOU AND ME." Fat Tony stomped his foot on the cement floor. Joey jumped back because Fat Tony's white sneakered foot looks like second base, and Fat Tony weighs about as much as the starting line-up.

Fat Tony placed the Camel back between his lips and took a deep drag. He held the smoke for an impossibly long time, and finally let loose a blue cloud that enveloped the boiler, the circulator, and Joey.

"You check stuff out, ya unnerstan, Joey? You don't assume nothin'." Fat Tony spit a big glob of phlegm onto the floor. "When you ain't sure, you check." He stabbed the air with his index finger. Fat Tony's index finger looks like a knockwurst. "I didn't hire you to go assumin' stuff. Ya unnerstan'?"

Joey nodded, furiously.

"It's important, kid, 'cause WHEN YOU ASSUME . . .YOU MAKE AN ASS OUTTA YOU AND ME!" Fat Tony started a laugh that turned into a cough, which wracked his huge body and turned his face crimson. The cough went on for a full minute. It sounded like very bad things were happening inside there.

Fat Tony had learned the lesson about Not Assuming from his father, Big Tony, who had pounded it into Fat Tony's head for the past thirty years or so. When Big Tony decided to slow down and give Fat Tony a shot at running the company, Fat Tony's idea of good management was to pound the same lesson into the heads of his young employees. Fat Tony hired only the Young, Inexperienced and Impressionable because he couldn't stand the thought of hiring anyone who might know more than he knew. "I'm the smartest guy around dis place," he'd say to his young employees. And he, of course, was right.

Fat Tony loved to trip up his guys at every possible opportunity. He deliberately confused them, just so he could correct them. And the Don't Assume line was his favorite in the entire world. "Ay," he said one day as he entered the shop on a cloudy morning. "The guy on TV says it's gonna rain. Wadda you guys think?" One of the newer kids got sucked in right away. He shrugged and said, "Looks like rain to me, Tony."

"AY! DON'T ASSUME, KID! 'CAUSE WHEN YOU ASSUME . . . YOU MAKE AN ASS OUTTA YOU AND ME!" Fat Tony's Jack-O-Lantern face lit up as he waddled like a 350-pound duck to the Dunkin' Donuts box. The youngsters looked at each other, not believing that he'd managed to get them again.

"Ay, which of these you figure has the least calories in it?" Fat Tony shouted as he rifled through the donuts in the box, grabbing two.

Marv, the apprentice who had been there the longest, mumbled, "The one you don't eat, you fat bastard."

"Whasat, Marv? You say sumptin'? HUH?" Marv smiled weakly, thought of the long lines down at the Unemployment Office, and shook his head. "I didn't think so," Fat Tony spat out. "Ay, Joey! Which one you think has the least calories?" Fat Tony held up two donuts and nailed Joey to the wall with eyes that looked like lit cigars.

"Uh, the one without the cream and the chocolate icing, I suppose?" Joey said.

"YOU SUPPOSE?" Fat Tony shouted. "Ain't that just like ASSUMIN', Joey? Didn't I tell you not to ASSUME, Joey?" Joey picked at a zit and looked at the floor. Fat Tony laughed and scarfed down both donuts. He chewed with his mouth open, and shook his head in wonder at how stupid his employees could be.

After a while, the apprentices got so gun-shy they were afraid to assume anything. As a result, their troubleshooting skills, which were rudimentary to begin with, began to suffer. For instance, they'd want to use an ammeter to check out a circulator or a control because they didn't want to assume the circulator or control wasn't working. But then, what if the ammeter wasn't working? They couldn't just assume that it was, could they?

And if it wasn't, how could they check out the ammeter? Could they use another ammeter? And if so, how could they be sure that ammeter was working? This situation alone provided hours of indecisive inactivity during which the apprentices would stare at controls and circulators, wondering what to do next.

Any of the apprentices would accept a service call and drive to the customer's house. But once they'd arrived, they would wonder if they had the correct address. Maybe Fat Tony had made a mistake and given them the wrong address. Could they assume he hadn't? Maybe it was a test.

And how could they be sure the customer was even at home? What if he wasn't? And if they rang the bell, would the customer hear it? Could they assume the bell was working? Maybe they should knock instead?

As it turned out, most of the apprentices sat in their trucks for at least a half-hour pondering this conundrum, never quite sure what action to take. Whatever they decided, they stood a chance of being wrong. And they certainly didn't want to make an ASS OUT OF YOU AND ME.

As the apprentices continued to fear the Laws of Probability, the Laws of Profitability kicked in, and profit, such as it was, withered. Big Tony questioned Fat Tony about this.

"These kids are stupid, Pop," Fat Tony explained. "Nowadays, no one's as smart as me and you. You just can't get good help nowadays, ya know?"

Big Tony, not wanting to feel stupid about having handed the reins of power over to his son, willingly accepted this explanation – so the situation worsened.

When and if an apprentice ever finished tuning a burner or cleaning a boiler, the customer might ask if everything was going to be all right now. The apprentice was, of course, afraid to say yes for fear that it might not be all right now. Who were they to assume their work was good enough to last through a harsh winter? What if it didn't?

And what if the winter wasn't harsh? They couldn't assume that it would be harsh, could they? But neither could they assume it wouldn't be harsh. There was just no way to know for sure. And they certainly didn't want to assume. So they didn't answer the customer's question. They just stood in the doorways and smiled like charter members of the Lobotomy Club.

Joey even stopped brushing his teeth because he couldn't assume the toothpaste wasn't poisoned by some crazed dental terrorist. Hey, look at those people who ate that Tylenol back in the Seventies and then died. They assumed that medicine was okay, but it wasn't, right? The thought haunted Joey as he stared at the tube of Crest each morning and evening. Day after day, he'd take it out of the medicine cabinet, look at it, smell it, and then put it back.

"Whew!" Big Tony said to Fat Tony one afternoon. "You get a whiff of Joey lately? He smells like a ferret crawled down his throat and died. Doesn't that guy ever brush his teeth?"

"I don't know," Fat Tony said, taking another bite of pepperoni pizza while simultaneously lighting his forty-fifth Camel of the day. "I can't assume that he does, Pop. I just don't know."

It Ain't Easy Being Sleazy

Randy had had it up to here on the afternoon he decided to swing Jake the Snake's service van into the Platinum Banana's parking lot. Randy had been working like a sled dog for two years, but Jake the Snake never said thanks, and he never came across with any of that cash Randy had been picking up for him from the customers. "The hell with him," Randy mumbled to himself as he edged the company truck into a space between a blue Dodge pick-up and a tan Taurus. "Everyone's entitled to a little fun every now and then, right?"

An old Chevy sedan stuffed with teenage boys from the High School rumbled by. They hooted at Randy as he hopped from the van. "Hey!" a pimply kid screamed from the passenger seat as he pointed to the side of Jake the Snake's service van. "You gonna show the babes your snake?" The kid let loose an explosive laugh, and shouted, "Snakeman!" Randy turned toward the van and immediately spotted the irony. The bright red plumber's snake painted on the side of Jake the Snake's van stood at the same phallic angle as the neon Platinum Banana on top of the squat building. Randy smiled slyly, gave the lads in the receding car a triumphant wave with his closed fist, and then he headed for the pink door.

But on his way to that door, Randy had one of his occasional brilliant ideas. As long as he was going to park here anyway, why not give Jake some free advertising? The cheapskate could probably use some free advertising, right? And those schoolboys sure enjoyed the joke. Hey, maybe they'll come back with their friends!

Randy nodded to himself, and headed back toward the van. He hopped in, and, smiling in a self-satisfied way, positioned the van perpendicular to the busy road. Jake the Snake's van was now as noticeable as a half-acre billboard for hemorrhoid medicine. "Now, that's what I call advertising," Randy said to the nearly empty parking lot as he stood back to admire his work. "No parking in the rear for Randy!"

Cars flowed like river water on the main artery, and Randy smiled at them for a while. Jake never comes to this side of town, he thought. He smiled up at the Platinum Banana. About a billion people should pass by while I'm in there. And won't that be great for Jake's business! People will really want Jake in their homes when they learn he hangs out at the Platinum Banana. Randy figured that if he couldn't get the cash, at least he could get even. He chuckled and hitched his belt up over his ample belly. "It's Miller time!" he said to the parked cars as he headed for the pink door.

When Randy entered the Platinum Banana, it took a moment for his eyes to adjust to the dull, smoky light. You can imagine his surprise when he spotted his boss, Jake the Snake, sitting at a table, sipping a long-neck Bud. Jake didn't notice Randy right away. Jake's eyes were riveted on a table dancer named Moaner Lisa. Moaner Lisa was wearing high heels, pearls, dental floss, and five dollars bills. Jake the Snake had been hanging the fivers on Moaner Lisa's floss with lusty enthusiasm for the past two hours. The sight of his boss hit Randy's brain like a 220-volt jolt in a copper bathtub. Survival instincts, garnered from a million years of male evolution, kicked in. These instincts were joined by about a gallon of adrenaline as Randy emphatically shouted, "Somebody called about a clogged sink!"

Jake the Snake and Moaner Lisa, along with everyone else in the shadowy bar, turned to look at Randy. Moaner Lisa mentally counted the potential cash in Randy's pockets, and then aimed her electric-blue gaze back at Jake, who looked like death had just kissed him on the lips. "Ohhhh noooo," Jake moaned.

"I'm going outside to get my tools now," Randy proclaimed to the confused barmaid, the half-dozen men at the bar, the nearly nude dancers, and everyone else. "My wrenches, and my snake, and my bucket. Those are the things I will need from my truck, which is parked at the edge of your parking lot, and I'm going out there to get them now. I'll need them all. My wrenches. My snake. And my bucket." Randy pointed back at the pink door with his thumb. "I'll be back soon, and then I'll fix that clogged sink in your men's room in no time at all. Yes, indeed, I will!" Randy turned and scurried from the bar, trying his best to be blind. Jake the Snake, at that same moment, was trying his best to be invisible.

"Did somebody call the plumber?" the scantily clad barmaid asked the men at the bar. They shrugged. "Girls, did any of you call the plumber?" The two young women who were dancing on the stage to an old Joe Cocker song shook their heads in a dreamy way.

"I'm the plumber!" Jake the Snake suddenly shouted as he jumped from his chair, nearly knocking Moaner Lisa to the floor.

"I know you are, honey," Moaner Lisa cooed, reaching for Jake's wallet, but Jake the Snake didn't hear her. He was already on his way to the men's room. He heard nothing but an inner voice that roared BLACKMAIL! and ALIMONY!

"I'm here to fix that clogged sink!" he yelled to the sparse group at the bar.

"Good for you," a man in a business suit mumbled into the neck of his beer bottle.

Jake crashed through the men's room door, and just had time to get down on his back under the sink in the beer and the urine before Randy, who had visions of unemployment dancing through his head, entered sheepishly. "Oh, Randy! I'm glad you're here!" Jake said. "Hand me that adjustable, will you?" Randy did as he was told. "Gee, I told the answering service that I'd take this call, but I guess they called you too, eh?" Jake continued.

"Yeah, boss," Randy said, his muddled mind struggling to find equilibrium.

"But you know how that answering service keeps screwing up calls," Jake said. "Maybe it's time we get another answering service, eh, Randy?" Randy felt as though he had astral projected into another time, taking a totally innocent Jake the Snake with him. Randy was more than willing to be there in that far, far better place.

"Yeah, I think that's what we're going to have to do, Randy," Jake the Snake said as he worked feverishly in his puddle of beer and urine to free a clog that wasn't there.

"We'll just have to get another answering service. And you know what, buddy, I think we should also discuss a raise for you. How long you been with me now?"

"Uh, two years, boss."

"Well, I think it's time for a raise, don't you, Randy-me-boy?"

"If you think so, boss, that would be fine with me. Sure." Randy rattled his head up and down.

"Yeah, I think you deserve a big raise. Say maybe, oh, I don't know – double? How's that sound, pal?"

"That would be great, boss," Randy said, pondering the mysteries of life, and fate, and circumstances. He rattled his head again.

"Yeah, you and me, pal. We need to stick together. You know what I mean, Randy?"

"Uh, yeah. I think so."

"So let's get this job done, and then let's get out of here. Places like this make me uncomfortable. Don't they make you uncomfortable?"

"Uh, yeah, boss. They sure do."

But They Got a Good Price

Ray set the boom box down gingerly on the basement floor, as if it were an overstuffed suitcase with an old zipper. He looked around for an outlet and spotted one next to the freezer. He yanked the freezer's plug the same way he would have pulled the tail of the family cat, had one been creeping around "his" boiler room. He tossed the plug behind the freezer so it wouldn't be in his way. "Hey, remind me I did that, okay?" he said to Billy, the giant who had been his helper for several months now. "I forget to plug that back in and this place is going to smell like a multiple homicide in a couple of days."

Billy looked at Ray through five-watt eyes. "Huh?" he said.

Ray laughed, and shook his head. "Never mind, Billy Boy. I'll remind myself, if I remember to. Now boogie on upstairs and grab the rest of the stuff, willya? We gotta get outta here as fast as we can. Got two more boiler jobs to do today, ya know?"

"I gotta take a dump," Billy said, squirming like a three-year-old.

"Just get movin', and bring those fittings down here right away. I'll start ripping out this mother." Ray looked the boiler up and down as if it were some old man who had challenged him to a bar fight.

Billy took the steps two at a time as Ray plugged in the big stereo. He hit the On button and the boiler room light dimmed. Cream's "Sunshine of Your Love" exploded from the thick speakers. "Da-Da-Da-DUN! DUN-DUN-DUN-DA-DA-DA!" Ray screamed. He reached down for the volume knob, which was about the size of a small steering wheel. He twisted it as far as it would go to the right. It sounded like the woofers were going to spit up blood. "I'll be with you darlin' sooooon," Ray crooned. "I'll be with you 'til my seeds are driiiiiied OP!" He hit the top of the boiler with a crowbar, just to let it know that The Ray Man was in the house. He opened the boiler drain and let the brackish water spurt across the basement floor like blood from a slaughtered animal. He rocked his head to the pounding pulse of the music and dumped the contents of his heavy toolbox onto the concrete floor. He kicked the stuff away from the gathering water, never missing the beat that was pummeling the walls of the house. "Clapton is GOD, man!" he cried to the gloomy basement. "GOD!"

Upstairs in the living room, Mrs. McDougal gaped at Mr. McDougal. She had gone wide-eyed and started to quiver when the music set the walls to quaking. "Is that coming from our basement?" she asked. But before Mr. McDougal could consider his wife's question, Billy stomped into the room. The McDougals looked up at this man-child who was built like a tow truck. His jacket was so coated with grease you could have fried a pancake on either sleeve. His work boots looked like they had just lost a battle with a cow pasture. He held a greasy, 5-gallon, plastic bucket filled with steel fittings. His head was snapping around like a dog seeing rabbits. "Ay!" he shouted over the music. "Where the hell's the crapper at?"

"Excuse me?" Mrs. McDougal said, staring at the young ruffian in disbelief.

"The bathroom. Where's it at? I gotta take a monster dump, ya know?" Billy said, setting the greasy pail down on the McDougal's shag carpeting while tugging at his belt. "I mean like right now, ya know? Where's it at? C'mon!" He had his belt open and was working on the button that was buried deep in his enormous belly. Mr. McDougal pointed down the hall. "There!" he said. "It's there. Just down the hall. Our bathroom is down that hall. Go!"

"Thanks, dude," Billy said, stomping off in a huge, hairy hurry and lighting a cigarette on the way. Mr. McDougal looked at Mrs. McDougal. Ginger Baker hammered his drums in the basement and shook the china in the kitchen cabinets. "LU-UH-UH-UH-UH-UH-UH-UH- UVVVVVE!" Ray shrieked from the basement as the song reached the top of its next hill.

"Did you know it was going to be like this?" Mrs. McDougal asked her husband.

"No . . . but we got a good price," he said sheepishly.

"I suppose, but did you know they were going to be so noisy? And so . . . large?"

"I wasn't really thinking about that," Mr. McDougal said. "Their price was so low. It just seemed like such a good deal. I didn't know it would be like this, though."

"BILLY!" Ray screamed from the basement. "WHAT THE HELL YOU DOING UP THERE? YOU TAKIN'

A CRAP? I HOPE YOU AIN'T GOT THOSE NASTY
MAGAZINES IN THERE WICHCHEW!"

Billy eventually came stomping out of the bathroom.
"ALL RIGHT, MAN! I'M COMIN'!" he screamed toward
the basement stairs as he pounded toward the McDougals,
who stared in horror. Billy struggled with his fly. "Stay
outta there for a while, man," he said to them as he went
by. "Stinks like hell. Don't say I didn't warn ya." He picked
up the greasy fitting bucket. "YO, RAY! CATCH!" Billy
shouted from the top of the stairs as he let the fitting bucket
go with the gracefulness of a softball pitcher. "Whoa! You
missed, dude," Billy mumbled as he clomped back to the
truck to get the boiler.

"YA ALMOST NAILED ME, YA FRIGGIN'
MORON!" Ray screamed over Iron Butterfly's
"Inagoddadavida." He kicked the fittings aside and laughed,
shaking his head. "Kids!" he said to himself. Ray wasn't
so much concerned with Billy's method of delivery as he
was with his aim. He had taught Billy that gravity could
be a heating contractor's best friend on a quick boiler
replacement job. Ray liked to approach each job as if it
were an extreme-skiing competition. "Get down fast!" he
always told Billy. "But don't hit the boss. That's me." The
two moved through boiler rooms like they were playing
one-on-one basketball in a concrete park. Cut, fake, shoot.
In and out real fast. Get it done, and keep the price down.
That's what the public wants. Low prices. That's how you
stay in business.

Billy, being the sort of behemoth who could move
a four-section, cast-iron boiler all by himself, returned
with said object a few minutes later. The boiler was bare,
with no jacket, insulation or controls. Ray sold boilers
this way because it gave him an advantage over his more

expensive competitors. "With our boilers," he would tell a prospective customer, "you get a free zone of basement heating. It makes no sense to keep all that heat bottled up inside insulation when you can use it to heat your basement for free." And since few homeowners understand the subtleties of boilers, this was, more often than not, quite appealing. "And other companies are gonna try to force you into buying new boiler controls and a new circulator," Ray would continue. "That's a rip-off because there ain't nothin' wrong with the stuff you got now, right? That stuff's worked for years, right?" He'd wait for the prospective customer to nod and then he'd move in with the closer. "Yeah, them shysters are just trying to rip you off by forcin' you to buy stuff you already got! Not us, though. We recycle all the stuff that's already on your old boiler. We believe in saving the environment. We've been saving environments for years." And since few homeowners understand the subtleties of environmentalism, this made perfect sense.

"YO! YOU READY?" Billy screamed from the top of the stairs. "MOVE OUTTA THE WAY!" And with that, he let gravity launch the boiler into its new home. It slid down the stairs like a guillotine's blade. This part of the job always delighted Ray because the boiler often served to clear its own path to the boiler room. In this case, there was a thin wall in the way, but they would have had to move that wall anyway to accommodate the new boiler. The boiler was just helping to speed its own installation, and what could be sweeter than that?

"PERFECT, MY MAN! JUST PERFECT!" Ray shouted as the boiler skidded to a stop on the proper side of the now-gone wall.

The McDougals, who had witnessed this from their perch on the living-room couch, carefully approached Billy who was hulking at the top of the stairs, admiring his aim. "Won't that hurt our new boiler?" Mrs. McDougal asked sheepishly. Billy, dug a wad of snot from his nose and said, "Nah, cast-iron's tough. Can't hurt it." He looked around, and then wiped the snot on the underside of the banister.

Ray spotted the McDougals and asked, "Hey! Which side of the basement you want me to leave the old boiler? I can shove it over either way. It don't matter to me."

The McDougals looked at each other. "But don't you take the old boiler with you?" Mrs. McDougal asked. "We assumed . . ."

Ray laughed. "No effin' way! That thing's loaded with asbestos. We ain't got no license to dispose of that stuff. You can do whatever you want with it. That's your problem. Just let me know which side of the basement you want it to go on. And make it snappy. We ain't got all day."

"But . . . we thought the removal of the trash was included in your price," Mr. McDougal said.

From the bottom of the stairs, Ray gave the McDougals a heavy-lidded stare, like a snake about to doze off – or strike. It was hard to tell. "You got a good price, didn't you?" Ray menaced. The McDougals nodded immediately and took a step back toward the couch. "Then what the hell did you expect? Everything?" Ray started to head up the stairs – right at them.

The McDougals looked at Billy, as if for help. He was busy working on his other nostril.

It's About Time

The association was paying this guy the big bucks for this speech. He was the hottest thing on the lecture circuit this year. They had to fly him in from LA (first class, mind you) along with his two secretaries, who now sat all blonde and willowy in the rear of the room. They were doing their job, which seemed to be to stare adoringly at the speaker. The contractors were lucky to have been able to get this guy for their convention. He was in such great demand right now. He probably could have spoken at the UN if he felt like it. This guy was hot!

Fulcrum's phone rang for the first time when the speaker was about ten minutes into his three-hour presentation on Time Management (a subject that's on the minds of nearly all contractors nowadays, time being money and all). The phone went off with an electronic warble that stopped the speaker in mid-sentence. He glared at Fulcrum, and then continued his lecture. Fulcrum answered the call without moving from his seat. "Yeah, what?" he said into the little mouthpiece. "WHAT! Tell 'em that's the best price he's gonna get outta us. That's it. If he don't like it, tell him we don't want the job. Yeah, okay. Right." Fulcrum snapped the phone closed as the speaker continued to glare at him. Fulcrum remembered the guy had been saying something about the importance of having a schedule and then sticking to it.

"It's most important," the speaker continued, believing his stare had welded Fulcrum to his seat and recaptured the group's full attention, "to have a plan, and that plan should be in writing. Every day you must plan! A plan for every day is most important."

Fulcrum switched the tiny phone to its vibrate setting. He figured that way, the guy wouldn't give him any more dirty looks. Besides, Fulcrum liked the way the phone felt when it vibrated in his pocket. He wasn't really all that worried about disturbing anyone. He knew all these guys. They were all in business, just like him, and besides, he had paid good money to be here. This jerk was working for him, right? He needed his phone, and if anyone objected to him using it, well, the hell with them. This is America, right? A man's gotta have his cell phone.

"And so it is that you must spend a part of your time making a plan for the following day. Every day!" The speaker smiled. The blondes swooned. The contractors looked at each other, and at their watches.

Fulcrum's phone went into its tiny electronic seizure for the second time a moment later. It hit him right on his left nipple like an electrical shock. He liked that. He fumbled the phone out of his shirt pocket and flipped it open. He was proud of how very little his phone was. The smaller the phone, the more successful the man. This one wasn't much larger than a deck of playing cards. Fulcrum smiled at the guy next to him. "I just gotta take this call," he said. "Hello?" Fulcrum whispered into the tiny electronic marvel and then, "Hello?" but louder this time. He stuck his right index finger into his other ear and said it again, louder still. "HELLO!"

The speaker stopped speaking and looked at Fulcrum the way Queen Elizabeth might gaze into a cesspool. "Excuse me," the speaker said into his microphone, "Is that call for me? Would you like to share any news with the group? Is that call relevant to this seminar? Must you take it right here? Would it not be better if you stepped outside?" Everyone in the room turned their attention toward Fulcrum. The speaker waited, fully believing that the collective attention of the crowd would cause Fulcrum to become embarrassed and put away his phone. The speaker waited. So did everyone else.

But they didn't know Fulcrum. A five-dollar hooker with photographs couldn't embarrass this guy. And besides, the speaker had never been to a contractors' association convention before.

"What do they mean they can't deliver the pipe to the job first thing in the morning?" Fulcrum shouted into the phone. "You tell those idiots they had better have my stuff on that job or else! I want it there by seven AM! Got that?"

The speaker cleared his throat. "Speaking of time management," he said. "Here's a good example of how our collective time is being wasted by one inconsiderate person with a cellular telephone. Excuse me," he said to Fulcrum. "Are we disturbing you?"

Fulcrum looked up, and then told the person on the phone to hang on for a second. "No, I'm okay," he said to the speaker. "I just gotta take this call. You keep talking. You're doing fine. I'll catch up. Don't mind me. I gotta make sure that friggin' pipe gets to the job site tomorrow."

And then he went back to screaming at the person on the other end of the line.

Coincidentally, it was at that moment that Ballbricker's beeper began to chirp hysterically. Ballbricker, who weighs in at a good 325 pounds, was having a tough time digging the beeper out from his massive belly flesh. The beeper was hanging down there on Ballbricker's belt somewhere. It's just that, in a seated position, Ballbricker's body takes on the shape of risen dough and it's not that easy to find things in there.

The speaker turned his glare away from Fulcrum and leveled it at Ballbricker. "Sorry," Ballbricker grunted as he finally came up with the beeper. He shut it off. The willowy blondes in the back of the room looked at each other and then at the speaker. They weren't quite sure what to do. This was also their first contractors' association convention. The speaker gestured at the young women with a manicured hand, letting them know all was well and that he was in total control. They could relax. "Is that also an important call?" the speaker asked Ballbricker. "Uh, huh," Ballbricker said as he dug a tiny phone from the pocket of his sport coat. "I won't be long. Just keep going. You're doin' pretty good so far."

"Would you mind making that call from outside the room?" the speaker asked.

"Yeah, I would mind," Ballbricker said, as he dialed the number. "It ain't convenient for me to be moving around, ya know?"

"CAN YOU KEEP IT DOWN?" Fulcrum shouted from his side of the room. "The reception in here sucks! I can barely hear!" The speaker looked at his secretaries, his magnificent confidence slipping a notch. He had never spoken at a contractors' association convention before. These people weren't obeying him!

Nutbuster's portable fax machine sprang to life just then with its own particular brand of electronic barnyard sounds. It began grinding paper over the edge of the table. Nutbuster got all excited and poked his partner, Chopstomper, in the ribs. "Here she comes!" he said.

"Does everything look right?" Chopstomper asked, turning his full attention toward the machine and the contract that was oozing out of it like a long flat sausage.

While this was taking place, the battery on Nadcrusher's laptop computer began to squawk and threaten to quit, as it had so many times in the past. Nadcrusher, who was every bit as big as Ballbricker, and who was now in fear of losing his unsaved data, leapt to his feet. In doing so, his ample butt tipped a pitcher of ice water into Fulcrum's fully exposed lap.

The speaker, not used to what goes on at a contractors' association convention, no longer knew what to do. Other phones began to warble. Electronic organizers chirped to life, reminding the busy contractors that it was time to take their TUMS. The speaker tried his best to return to the subject of time management by asking the rhetorical question, "Ladies and gentlemen, do modern machines really save time?"

"CAN YOU TURN DOWN THAT DAMN AMPLIFIER!" Fulcrum shouted as he tried to brush the flood of ice water from his lap while continuing his tirade against the poor soul on the other end of the line. "I CAN'T HEAR A THING!"

Dancing Mary

Mary stood flat against the wall, very still and very straight. She held her arms tightly at her sides, as if she were about to be fired from a cannon. No one really noticed her. She wore a shapeless dress that drooped around her shins. The dress was beige, just like the wall behind her. The DJ was playing some Kenny G. cocktail hour music and the employees were drinking as much free booze as they could get their hands on. Every now and then she would take a nibble on her left thumb's cuticle. In a room filled with loud people, Mary stood alone, like a tiny, deserted island. No one spoke to her. She glanced at her Timex at one point. Kenny G. played on and on in that monotonous way of his.

On the other side of the room Pete took a long pull on his beer. He wiped his mouth with the back of his hairy hand and pointed the half-empty bottle at Terry. "You get that job?" Terry shook his head. "You didn't?" Pete was incredulous. "Hey, they should have sent a real man. They should have sent me!" Terry answered the comment with an obscene gesture and they both laughed. Pete and Terry were good friends, even though they had very little in common.

Pete was middle-aged paunchy. He had a bald spot the size of a tea saucer on the back of his head. He had grown a short ponytail to compensate for what was missing on top. He had also gotten his left ear pierced and he now wore a small diamond in the lobe. He was considering a tattoo, but he wasn't sure what he would get, and where he would have it placed. It was important to Pete that the tattoo he chose not look silly in some nursing home years from now. He didn't want the nurses laughing at him while they drank their coffee in the canteen after his sponge bath. A tattoo was a big decision. Maybe he'd grow a goatee instead.

Terry wasn't into all of that. He was crewcut-conservative. He owned three gray suits, which he alternated like standby boilers from day to day. Terry looked like a high-school algebra teacher from the 1950s and it troubled him that Pete's sales figures were better than his were. He thought Pete looked ridiculous, and he could never figure what the customers saw in him. Pete, however, could sell poison ivy for toilet paper. This was mainly because Pete suffered from a severe honesty deficit. He would promise things the company couldn't possibly deliver. But since the fulfillment of promises fell to the other people in the company, and since they rarely did work for the same customers more than once, Pete didn't concern himself too much with all of that. And this was mostly why he was always ahead of everyone else in the company.

"Some party, eh?" Terry said, taking a sip of his Jim Beam.

Pete rolled his eyes toward the ceiling. "About the same as last year, and the year before that, and the year before that. Nothing to write home about. At least the beer's cold." He raised his bottle as though he was saluting the room with a rapier, and then he took another long swig. He glanced around the room. "Same crowd as last year. Except for Mary," he said, pointing toward her with the Budweiser. "What's the deal with her?" he asked. "She come to us from Kelly's Funeral Home, or what? Look at her standing over there, holding up the wall."

Terry shrugged. "All I know is she does an okay job on the phones. I mean, she's with us, what, six months now? None of the customers have complained about her. She never cuts anyone off. She moves the calls through the switchboard pretty efficiently. She gets the messages right most of the time. What more could you want?" He looked over at Mary. She blended into the wall like a pencil mark on gray paper. Her dress had a high collar and she wore a cameo brooch at her neck. Her hair, which was the color of bran flakes, clung to the top of her head in a tight bun. She wore sensible shoes. And she didn't make eye contact with Pete, Terry, or anyone else in the room. She didn't even seem to be aware that the two men were watching her. She stood there listening to Kenny G. with that thousand-yard stare piercing a hole in the opposite wall. She got the same look whenever she was at her switchboard and not speaking to a customer on the phone. Jean, who worked in Accounting, said she thought Mary was listening to the "on-hold" music. It was hard to tell because Mary wore one of those operator's headsets. You never knew whether she had someone on the phone or not. And because of this, no one ever really spoke with her. Just a hello in the morning and a goodbye at night. Most of the time, Mary just stared . . . out there somewhere. It was as though she were waiting for a bus that never came.

"She's a knucklehead, all right," Pete said as he turned his attention toward another bottle of Bud. "A prim little mouse. No personality whatsoever. She'd never make it in sales."

And it was at that moment that the DJ decided to liven up the party. He segued from Kenny G. into some old Donna Summer tune that everyone in the world has heard a thousand times. And that's when Mary, without saying a word, and without benefit of a dancing partner, walked from the wall and into the center of the dance floor. She reached up with both hands, stretching her lithe body in a way no one at the holiday party imagined was possible. She closed her eyes and pursed her lips. She moved her fingers and hips in tiny, jerking motions that were most definitely not what you would expect to see at a construction company's holiday party. She reached down momentarily with her left hand and pulled a pin that caused her hair to tumble and cascade down her back and onto her face, which at that point, looked as if it were gazing straight into heaven.

"What's this?" Pete said. Terry's mouth had dropped open. Two drunken workers who had been arguing over something that had happened on a job last July stopped in mid-insult and directed their total attention toward Mary. She was hardly moving but there was definitely something happening here that was positively primal. The women from the Accounting Department dropped their hors d'oeuvres and stared in disbelief. Every part of Mary's body seemed to quiver to the beat of the music, but her movements were almost imperceptible. It was the most erotic thing any of them had ever witnessed. The rest of the employees moved quickly to get out of Mary's way. "What's this?" Pete said again, taking a step toward the dance floor. Mary turned slowly on the ball of one foot, like a ballerina in a music box. She vibrated in perfect pitch to the music, but she hardly moved at all. Just fingers, hips, lips, and a smile that was both beatific and altogether nasty. As the music reached a crescendo, she reached down with one slender hand and tugged the hem of her dress up by a single inch. That was all – just …one … inch. At that point, Mary looked like a sexual Tomorrowland.

The DJ, forgetting his trade, his home address, and his mother's maiden name, also forgot to mix in another song. The silence that followed was deafening. The only sound in the room was a soft mewing coming from deep inside Dancing Mary. She opened her eyes and blazed a look at her fellow workers. Then she walked off the dance floor and out the door, as if she had just departed a Viking ship, leaving behind a thoroughly exhausted crew.

On Monday morning, no one knew what to expect. Everyone came in early and waited for the arrival of Dancing Mary. But she seemed no different on Monday morning than she had been on Friday afternoon. The bun was in place. The shoes were sensible. The dress was more than respectable. She handled the calls in a most efficient way, and passed the messages without making very many mistakes. She also stared into space, waiting for a bus that hardly ever arrived. When she wasn't on the phone, she listened to the music-on-hold. Or at least that's what Jean, who worked in Accounting, said she thought Mary was doing.

It was impossible to tell with this one.

Sweet Release

Prizzi jammed his van into the first available spot in the rest area's parking lot and hobbled furiously toward the rest room in a state of exquisite pain. It was the fifth cup of coffee and the traffic moving at the speed of cement that had done him in. He moaned as he shuffled, crab-like, through the herd of people making their way toward the concession stand on New Jersey's Garden State Parkway.

He was sweating by the time he saw the sign for MEN and he let loose a little chuckle of glee, knowing that in a moment he would be releasing a stream of urine such as the world has never witnessed.

A moment before he made the turn around the ceramic wall where the row of urinals hung in a long, patient line, Prizzi heard the grunting. It sounded like pigs snorting at a trough. He nearly lost complete control when he made the turn and saw their backs, their gray hair sprouting from beneath the caps on their old heads, their trousers hitched high, their white belts, their white shoes. Prizzi sobbed quietly and began his Dance of Pain as he watched the old men grunt and grimace, trying their best to urinate. It was a sight that would have made any urologist in America put a great big deposit on a new BMW.

Unfortunately for Prizzi, he had reached the rest area just minutes after the arrival of an Atlantic City-bound bus. And now he found himself standing in line behind the owners of a dozen defective prostate glands. These senior citizens grunted and moaned while cajoling and tapping their flaccid penises. But they were getting nowhere fast.

Prizzi aimed his tortured, bent body toward the ten stalls on the other side of the ceramic wall. The battleship gray doors were closed and locked and the grunting and tapping rose from behind the partitions as well, filling the room with hopelessness. Prizzi cursed Atlantic City and every bus that had ever carried a senior citizen to that evil place. The Bus Company should catheterize them all before they give 'em their quarters and buffet coupons, Prizzi thought as he squeezed his thighs together.

"Did you see . . . that story . . . in . . . Modern Maturity this month?" one of the old men grunted at the older man who was grunting next to him.

"WASSAT?" the older man asked, screwing up his face and tapping a bit faster on his limp and uncooperative member.

"MODERN MATURITY?" the old man said.

"WASSAT?" the older man asked, cupping his left hand behind his left ear, while still tapping with his right index finger.

"MODERN . . . MATURITY!"

Prizzi hobbled over to the sink. He didn't care anymore. His entire universe had spiraled down into one single goal – sweet release. The pipes all run to the same place, he reasoned. What is a sink but a horizontal urinal? He hobbled and fumbled, got up on his toes, and leaned forward.

The sound that left Prizzi's grateful throat cut through the rest area like a foghorn. People waiting on long lines for their Burger King and TCBY Yogurt turned to look at each other. The sound was long and continuous, a grateful, peaceful sound, like a Benedictine chant.

Prizzi's mind began to clear after fifteen seconds or so. He was trying to be quick about his business, but there seemed to be no end to the stream leaving his wracked and tortured body. And once begun, this is a process nearly impossible to stop, as any living human being well knows. Prizzi began to think back on certain cups of coffee that he had consumed last week and specific beers that he had guzzled at last January's Super Bowl party. He was feeling like a urological "dig" of sorts. His entire liquid history seemed to be flowing from him and into the white, porcelain sink. "Ahhhhhhhhhh."

Now, as fate would have it, the moment Prizzi began to pee into the sink, two things happened. First, the tap line of old prostate glands decided that enough was enough. They heaved a collective sigh of resignation, as old men so often will. There followed an almost military raising of zippers. They looked at each other, shrugged, and shuffled out in a line toward the waiting bus. What can you do? It's not easy getting old, eh?

As they passed Prizzi, they each shot him a look of utter disgust. "You should be ashamed of yourself, sonny!" the Modern Maturity man chastised while wagging a gnarled index finger at Prizzi. "Didn't your mother teach you better than that?"

Prizzi pressed his right cheek into the cool mirror and moaned. His eyes were closed; he didn't care about the old men anymore. They no longer meant a thing to him. "Die soon," he mumbled toward the line of codgers heading for the bus.

Now, the second thing that fate had in store for Prizzi that sunny morning occurred just as the last old man cleared the swinging door. Two New Jersey State Troopers scurried in to use the now vacant urinals. To Prizzi, these men looked like they were constructed from steroids and Lego blocks. Both cops were in nearly as much distress as Prizzi had been moments earlier. They scooted past the Living Stream, did a very police-like double take, and immediately went back on duty. Prizzi, incapable at this point of stopping, or even slowing, the flow, stared in horror at the two lawmen.

A rush of adrenaline surged through the cops, putting a temporary "cork" in their appendages. They grasped what Prizzi was doing, and then they grasped Prizzi. "Put your hands up on the wall," one of the cops shouted out of habit, not stopping to consider the consequences of his command. Prizzi, in a state of horror, shock, and embarrassment, did as he was told. This, of course, had the same result one would expect if one happened to let go of an active fire hose, and it's important to note here that a ceramic backsplash is aptly named for the function it serves. The troopers twisted their faces in disgust, looked down on their uniforms, and then they slapped the cuffs on Prizzi.

Which left them with one remaining problem, of course.

After some time, they finally were able to get Prizzi into the back seat of their squad car. They headed out into the lazy river of traffic on New Jersey's Garden State Parkway. They hadn't gone a quarter-mile when the traffic came to a standstill. As the troopers' adrenaline rush subsided, they suddenly realized with notable discomfort that they had never completed the task that had sent them to the rest room in the first place. They immediately began to rock and squirm in their seats. Prizzi glanced at the driver's eyes in the rear view mirror and gave him a sympathetic smile. They sat like this for another few moments. The traffic was nailed to the earth. Prizzi caught the driver's eye again and gave him that knowing and sympathetic smile. The cop blinked twice, shook his head quickly from side to side to clear his now foggy brain, and then hit the siren. He spun the squad car onto the median strip and made a beeline back to the rest area at 100 miles per hour on the grass.

The first thing they did when they slouched back from the men's room was to release Prizzi and send him scurrying for his van. There is a brotherhood among those who drink coffee and drive the highways of our fair land – a particular understanding that there are things in this life that take precedence over all other matters.

When you gotta go, you gotta go.

In All Honesty

Percy had been in the wholesale end of the business for as long as he'd been working for a living. He inherited the whole shebang from his father, and he would have been out of his mind to try something different because you can make a lot of money in the wholesale end of the business, if you're honest – which Percy was.

He'd go out into the field with any contractor that bought from him because Percy knew that every contractor in America has the potential to latch onto a big job. All you had to do was be honest, polite, and always on the alert for an opportunity to solve someone's problem. And that's why Percy happened to be down at the nursing home with Klaus the Contractor.

The problem at the nursing home was that some of the rooms were cozy warm, while others were a bit chilly. Since elderly people are very sensitive to changes in temperature, the folks in charge of the nursing home had called Klaus the Contractor, who had called Percy. Now, all they had to do was be methodical, and figure out what was wrong with the heating system.

They had spent a half hour in the basement, looking over the boilers, which (unfortunately) seemed fine. Now, they were upstairs, going from room to room, checking the air and water temperature at the convectors with a thermometer. Percy and Klaus wondered if the problem was related to flow balance, or air balance, or any of a few dozen other possible causes. They were being very polite to everyone they met along the way, not wanting to disturb the routine of the town's senior citizens.

When they got to the third floor, they decided to begin with the room at the end of the hall and work their way back toward the elevator. Percy tapped on the wide door and smiled at the two elderly women who shared the room. "Hello, ladies," he said. "May we come in?"

Irene, who was closest to the convector, turned her wheelchair toward the two men. She put on a pair of eyeglasses with thick lenses and squinted at Percy and Klaus. She wore a faded pink housedress. Her hair looked like month-old cotton candy. She smiled a toothless grin at Percy, the way old people do, and beckoned him in. Irene's roommate, Bernice, sat in a second wheelchair, but closer to the door than to the convector. She held an old pocketbook in front of her, like a mug-shot nameplate. Must be full of money, Percy thought, but he didn't say that. That would have been impolite.

Irene gestured for Percy to come closer, which he did. She continued to smile in that toothless way of the ancient and she offered him a thin hand, which collapsed in his like a pouch filled with twigs. "What's your name, son?" she asked softly.

"My name is Percy," Percy said, a bit too loudly, as most relatively young people will do when speaking to the elderly. He gave her his warmest and most polite smile. "And what's your name, mother?"

"My name is Irene," she whispered. "And that's Bernice." She pointed a bony finger at her roommate.

"I'm so pleased to meet you both," Percy exclaimed. "We're with the heating company and we're here to check on your heater." He cranked up the volume on certain key words, as if he were outlining the meaning of their visit so that there could be no mistaking their mission. "We want you both to be as comfortable as possible and we will be no trouble at all. We'll just be a few minutes."

Irene kept smiling at Percy, the way a mother might smile at a long-lost child. She touched his arm lightly, and then she said, "In all honesty, I think you have a sissy name."

To which Percy had no immediate response, other than to let his jaw drop open by about an inch.

"It's true!" Irene said with an emphatic nod of her wrinkled head. "Don't you think he has a sissy name, Bernice?" Bernice immediately nodded in total agreement.

"Sounds like the name of a really pantywaist," Bernice observed while working her gums. "There was a Percy in my grade school. The older boys used to beat the stuffing out of him. He was a regular jellyfish."

"Your parents must have been very prissy people," Irene added with the brutal honesty of the elderly. Percy stared at her, not knowing what to say. "But it's true!" she said, letting her thoughts spill unfiltered from her brain to her lips, as people who are near the Great Finish Line of Life are wont to do.

"Your father must have been a real milksop," Bernice offered from her chair. "Who names a boy Percy?"

"My father's name was also Percy," Percy said, trying to maintain his composure. "It's a good name, passed down through the family for generations."

Bernice shook her head with a sad finality. "The fruit doesn't fall far from the tree," she said.

"Hasn't anyone ever given you a nickname?" Irene wondered aloud from her seat near the convector. "Seems to me someone would have thought of a nickname for you at some point in your life."

To which Percy had no immediate reply, so Irene just barged on in the way that those who can hear the angels singing so often will. "Yes, a nickname. Like Skippy. Or Stumpy!" she said, seeming to favor Stumpy over Skippy.

"Or how about Porky?" Bernice offered from her side of the room. "I think Porky suits him just fine. Don't you think so, Irene?"

"I beg your pardon," Percy sputtered, trying not to sound indignant and prissy, but not really able to help it either.

"Well, it's true," Bernice shot back. "Porky suits you. You're a real lard ass, you know. You ever think about pushing back from the table once in a while, Porkster?"

"It's true," Irene agreed. "People need to hear the truth, you know. The truth shall set you free, Stumpy."

"No, Irene," Bernice insisted. "I like Porky."

"Oh, all right, then," Irene gave in. "Porky, it is." And with that, she rolled her chair toward Percy and tried to pinch his butt. "You should lose some tonnage, buster!" she shouted.

Now, truth be told, any of those nicknames would have suited Percy just fine, and that was the thing that had Klaus the Contractor giggling like a schoolboy. This, of course, just made Percy even more upset. "Klaus," he hissed. "Let's get this convector checked, and then let's get the heck out of here."

Klaus couldn't stop laughing. "Okay . . . Porky!" he was finally able to sputter between giggles.

"What did you say your name was?" Irene asked, directing her attention toward Klaus for the first time.

"I'm Klaus," he said.

"Klaus? Klaus? Are you some sort of Nazi?" Bernice asked, which started Percy laughing and gagging.

Once he was able to catch his breath, Percy asked the two old hags if they had a nickname for Klaus.

"Well, Porky," Bernice said, staring pensively at Klaus. "I don't think he needs a nickname. Klaus is a fine Nazi name. It suits him."

Percy and Klaus looked at each other and then, still chuckling, nodded in unspoken agreement. As the two fishwives continued their verbal castration, the men strolled over to the convector. They removed the cover, shut the valves on both sides of the coil, snapped off the handles, bent the valve stems, and crushed the element's fins.

"That'll do 'er!" Klaus said.

"All fixed," Percy agreed. "Have a nice day, ladies," he added, a bit louder than necessary on his way to the next room, where Klaus was about to bend another couple of valve stems – shortly after being nicknamed Adolph by two very Irish, and brutally honest, old crones.

What Curiosity Did to Katz

The bags beneath Katz's eyes looked like overripe plums as he rooted through the papers on top of Andy's desk with his stubby index finger. He figured that if he looked often enough, something incriminating was bound to turn up.

"Can I help you with something, Mr. Katz?" Andy asked in a clipped voice as he came through the door. Katz jumped like he has had just been hit with a cattle prod. He turned toward the door. Katz's overstuffed face is the color of rare roast beef. "Oh, Andy!" he said with a nervous laugh. "I was just looking for an order I must have misplaced."

"Uh huh," Andy said, standing in the doorway. "Any particular order, Mr. Katz? Maybe I can help, you know?" Katz stared at Andy, who is as big as a barrel of wire, and about as tough.

"Oh, no! It's all right," Katz sputtered. "I'm sure you have enough to do, Andy. I'll just look someplace else." He nudged his belly past Andy as though he were pushing a shopping cart with one loose wheel. "I'll just look out here someplace."

"You're sure I can't help you?" Andy said, grabbing a fistful of papers from his desk. "I mean, I'll be happy to go through all of this with you if it will help." But Katz had already lumbered around the corner and was gone – for now.

"Katz going through your stuff again?" Mike asked from the doorway. Andy looked up and smiled. Mike was Andy's best truck driver, as well as his best friend and next-door neighbor out on Long Island. They carpooled to work each morning in the pre-dawn gloom. They lived way out there in the boondocks because that was the only place they could afford to buy homes, considering what Katz paid them.

"Yeah," Andy said. "He's pretty nosy, ain't he?"

"Well, it is his company," Mike said. "I suppose he can look anywhere he wants."

"I just wish he'd stay the hell away from my desk," Andy said. "He gets everything all mixed up, you know?"

"He thinks you're stealing from him," Mike said. "How long have I been saying that? I mean, you're the shipping clerk, right? You're sending eight trucks out to make deliveries every day. Let's face it, it's not that hard to steal from a plumbing-and-heating wholesaler and Katz knows it. Besides, all the contractors really like you, Andy, and so do the drivers. Katz figures you're a natural to be ripping him off."

"I never took a stinkin' thing from him in the three years I've had this job," Andy said in annoyance.

"I know that, and you know that, but that doesn't mean that Katz knows that. He's never gonna trust you; you're too ripe for suspicion. He's never gonna quit checking up on you, Andy."

"I'd like to put a mousetrap under these," Andy said, pushing the papers into an uneven stack. "Let him find that one morning. Serve him right for thinking I'm a thief."

"He never actually accuses you of stealing, does he?" Mike asked as Andy handed him his route papers for the day.

"Nah," Andy said. "It's just the way he's always poking around in my stuff."

"It's his place," Mike said.

"I know, I know," Andy said. "So you've told me. Twice. Now get going and I'll see you later." Mike headed out to the loading dock while Andy sat and stewed.

The next morning it was Andy's turn to drive. He picked up Mike at his house as the moon was sinking toward the horizon. An hour later, they were on the service road of the Long Island Expressway, trying to avoid the heavy bulk of the rush-hour traffic. "Pull over," Mike said.

"Why?"

"Just pull over. Right over there."

"You have to take a leak or something?" Andy asked.

"No, I have to take a picture," Mike said. "C'mon, get out." Mike pulled a Polaroid camera from a paper grocery bag and hopped from the car. Andy followed, not sure what the heck his friend was up to, but willing to play along. "Stand over there," Mike said, holding the Polaroid up to his eye. "Move over to the right just a bit. That's it. This is gonna be so cool!" Andy turned and saw the house

Mike had him posing in front of. It was as big as a county courthouse.

"Who the heck lives here?" Andy asked.

"It doesn't matter," Mike said. "Just look happy."

"What's this picture for?" Andy asked.

"It's for your desk," Mike said, looking through the eyepiece. "A beautiful picture of the shipping clerk standing in front of his home in the country," Mike said. "Katz ever been to your house?"

"No," Andy admitted. "I don't think he'd come even if I ever invited him."

"Then from now on, this is your house, pal. Give us a big smile."

Which Andy did.

When Katz flipped over the photo on Andy's desk he immediately felt the dollars draining from his bank account. His worst fear had come true. "Something I can help you with, Mr. Katz?" Andy asked from the doorway. Katz jumped as if Andy had just poured a barrel of iced Gatorade over his head.

"Oh, Andy!" he said nervously. "I was looking for another missing order and . . . and, well, I happened to notice this photograph here on your desk." Andy came up next to Katz and glanced at the Polaroid shot.

"Uh huh," Andy said.

"I'm curious. Is this your house, Andy?"

Andy smiled proudly. "Yeah, what do you think, Mr. Katz? That's the best we could do in our price range, you know? There are some good buys if you move far enough out on Long Island. You ever been out my way, Mr. Katz? It's pretty nice out there." Katz stared at the photo thinking that Andy's house was at least as big as a Russian war memorial. He struggled to get a handle on his breathing. "Yeah," Andy continued, taking the photo from Katz's sweaty hand and shoving it deep into the pocket of his denim work shirt. "We're thinking about moving up to something a bit more spacious in a few years, you know? That is, providing things keep going as well as they've been going. Time will tell, I suppose. Time will tell."

A dozen houseflies could have made it safely in and out of Katz's mouth. Andy sat down and started straightening papers on his desk. "Let's see if I can help you find that missing order. What's the name?" Katz wasn't listening. He turned slowly and slogged from the office as though he were carrying three scuba tanks and wearing flippers.

Andy was trying to contain his laughter and get his pulse back into double digits when Mike peeked his leprechaun's face around the corner. "Did it work?" Mike asked.

"Better than the mousetrap would have," Andy said with an evil grin.

"Tonight," Mike said, "we're stopping by the marina on our way home. I want to get a shot of you standing next to your new yacht. Here, you'll be wearing this." Mike slipped a navy blue captain's cap with lots of gold embroidery from the paper grocery bag. "Ahoy, matey!" he giggled.

Katz sat on his wide leather chair at his polished mahogany desk. His eyes bulged like a trout's, his mouth gulped air, his body trembled. He didn't know what to do next. He had no idea what it took to buy such a place way out there on Long Island. Katz had never even been on Long Island. To Katz, Long Island was a place where the workers lived. To Katz, the civilized world ended at the East River. But this house!

Katz would have fired Andy on the spot if only he knew more about the price of housing way out there on Long Island. He needed more evidence. He had to have more evidence. Maybe he would call his broker. He needed evidence. He didn't want to have a problem with the Labor Board. Maybe he would call his lawyer. You can't just fire a guy without just cause, right? He needed more evidence, and he'd get more evidence. For sure.

The next morning, Katz looked cautiously over his shoulder. Good. The coast was clear. He gingerly touched the photograph on Andy's desk as if it were about to detonate. He flipped it over and stared with eyes as big as water balloons at Captain Andy's yacht, which was about half the size of the Titanic.

"SOMETHING I CAN HELP YOU WITH, MR. KATZ?" Andy shouted from the doorway.

The coroner said Katz probably never knew what hit him.

NYPD Flu

Nate wasn't new on the job; he had 15 tough years behind him, but with the kids being so young and all, retirement looked about as far away as the finish line of the Moscow Marathon.

This was a new precinct for him. They had put him here when they made him a captain not long ago. He had been sitting at his desk in Queens, doing his job, when the call came in. "Congratulations, Nate, you made captain," the man had said. Nate smiled, cleaned out his desk, picked up his coat, said good-bye to the crew he had been in charge of for the past few years, and reported to his new duty. When you're promoted in the New York City Police Department, it's as if the work you were doing no longer existed. You just stop, get up, and move on.

Nate reported to a precinct that most New York City cops think of as being one step below purgatory. It was one of those special places on the planet where, if you sit still for a half hour, you can hear the sharp crack of gunfire. "Tough break," one of his new sergeants commented right after they shook hands for the first time.

"You gotta start someplace," Nate said, giving the situation a philosophical shrug of his beefy shoulders.

Rising through the ranks of the NYPD is a lot like going through school. Just when you get used to being a senior, they make you a freshman again. So Nate found himself back on the bottom of the totem pole at a place near the sea.

His new precinct house stood a few blocks from the steel-gray Atlantic. On winter days, the wind battered the building like a blitzkrieg, digging with icy efficiency into thousands of uncaulked cracks and crevices that scarred the face of the turn-of-the-century building. The people forced to do time here had only one defense against the unrelenting wind and frigid temperatures. That defense was an ancient one-pipe-steam heating system that coughed and grumbled all day long and on into the night like a nasty old man.

Nate wasn't on the job more than two nights when he called his neighbor, Mike, who happened to be a heating contractor. "This radiator in my office is driving me nuts," he said. "It pumps out more heat than Madonna. It's making me nauseous."

"What type of heating system do they have there?" Mike asked.

"How the hell do I know? I'm a cop; you're supposed to be the heating expert."

"Well, what does the radiator look like?" Mike asked.

"It's one of those huge iron things. You know, it's got these wide bars like a jail cell? It takes up the whole space in front of the window."

"Sounds like steam. How many pipes are attached to the radiator?" Mike asked.

"One. It's down near the bottom."

"And is there an air vent on the other side?"

"What's an air vent?" Nate asked.

"It's a little silver thing. It might look like a bullet. Or it could be round, like a small can of shoe polish."

"Oh, you mean the faucet! Yeah, it's got one of those."

"Uh, what do you mean by faucet, Nate?"

"The silver thing. I get a bucketful of dirty water out of it every shift. The Day Captain showed me how to catch the water before it hits the floor or the walls. You have to angle the bucket a certain way. And we use a piece of cardboard to direct the spray."

"I see," Mike said, recognizing a familiar problem. "Do you have the valve on the other side of the radiator closed part way?"

"You bet I do!" Nate laughed. "That's the only way we can keep from roasting to death."

"You can't throttle that valve, Nate," Mike said. "You have a one-pipe-steam system. That valve is for service only. You have to keep it fully open or fully closed."

"Oh," he said. "Who knew? So you're trying to tell me I have a choice between freezing and roasting?"

"Maybe not," Mike said. "Did you call Building Maintenance?"

"Yeah, but I figured I could get a faster answer from you," he said. "Those Building Maintenance guys work in a different time zone. Isn't there something I can do while I'm waiting for them to shine?"

"Well, this is what I think's going on," Mike said, trying to explain it in a way that would make the most sense to Nate. "The steam and the condensate have to share the same space on the inside of that valve. If you throttle the valve, the condensate can't get out. It builds up in the radiator, and squirts out the air vent."

"What's condenstate?"

"Oh, sorry. Condensate is water."

"Why didn't you just say that?"

"Because we have our own special language in the heating business, Nate. It's sort of like cop talk, you know? For instance, how come you guys say 'pinch a loaf' instead of defecate?"

"Point well taken," Nate said. "So what am I supposed to do about this here condenstate?"

"It's condensate."

"Whatever."

"Okay, I want you to try something tonight. First, open that valve all the way. Then, get yourself three of the biggest cops you can find and have them try to pitch the radiator back toward that inlet valve. Once you get the radiator up, stick a block of wood under the end that you're lifting. That should help the condensate get out. My guess is the radiator's probably sagged over the years, and that's adding to the problem. It's all pretty common."

Nate paused for a long moment. "I think I'll wait for Building Maintenance to shine," he said. "What you're proposing sounds like a double hernia to me."

"Your choice."

The guy from Building Maintenance showed up a week later. He gave Nate the follow advice: This is a steam system.

It's supposed to act this way.

It's been acting this way since long before you were born.

If you're hot, open the friggin' window.

That's what everybody else does.

So Nate did as he was advised. He employed the ol' Double-Hung Zone Valve Method of Temperature Regulation, as so many millions do each and every day in America's older cities. New Yorkers have been doing this for so long, they've actually come to believe that this is normal. Imagine that.

"How's it going?" Mike asked the next time he saw Nate.

"I'm dying," Nate croaked as he wiped mucous from his nose. "I sit with my back to that hot hunk of iron and the open window. I'm roasting from my gunbelt down, and freezing from my nipples up. I can't seem to get the temperature right, and the condenstate is spitting all over the room. The wind's knocking all my papers on the floor. The pipes are banging like a Harlem boom box, and I can't leave the office for ten minutes because I'm in charge. I tell ya, this promotion's gonna kill me." He swabbed at his wet nose, and sneezed.

"Do you want me to stop by and look at it?" Mike asked. "I mean, I don't know what I can do, but maybe I'll spot something the Building Maintenance guy missed."

"That shouldn't be difficult," Nate said. "The Building Maintenance guy has been known to miss the whole borough from time to time."

Mike planned to stop by; he really did. But before the week was out, Nate developed double pneumonia. They made him work one last night shift, sick as he was, and then they gave him 20 days off to recover.

When he returned to work, they reassigned him to another precinct.

Nate smiled, cleaned out his desk, picked up his coat, said good-bye to the crew he had been in charge of for the past few weeks, and reported to his new duty.

The new captain should be wiping his nose right about now.

Smokey Johnson's God-Given Right

Smokey Johnson's breath could drive ticks off a badger, but he wasn't aware of this, having lost his sense of smell to the god Tobacco at a very young age. When he paid a visit to the supply house, the countermen would scurry off as quickly as possible, preferring the odor of sewer cleaner to the open-grave stench that wafted from Smokey Johnson's lungs.

"You could use that guy's breath to clean your oven," Frankie the Counterman said to Jimmy, who worked in the back.

"Tell me about it!" Jimmy said, holding his nose in recalled horror.

"Anybody back there?" Smokey Johnson shouted from the front. He cuffed his hands around his mouth and sent the words down the aisle like nuclear warheads. Frankie the Counterman looked at Jimmy and said, "Speak of the devil. You wanna wait on him today? It will be good for some credit toward your sainthood."

"No way!" Jimmy said, scurrying up an aisle. "I'm gonna go put my head in the toilet instead. It smells pretty good by comparison, ya know?" Frankie the Counterman shook his head in resignation and headed for the front.

Smokey Johnson was, of course, smoking when Frankie the Counterman approached him. "How ya doing, Smokey?" Frankie the Counterman said.

"Fine, Frankie!" Smokey said, pushing the "F" sound into Frankie the Counterman's face. "Just fine!" Frankie the Counterman gagged and turned his head, trying to avoid the onslaught of more "F" words, which he knew were sure to follow. "Life's full of fun. Just full of fun! Can you find me some flanges, Frankie? Four flanges should do it? Four of those flat flanges."

"What size, Smokey?" Frankie the Counterman asked, taking another step backward down the aisle.

"Four-inch," Smokey exploded, sending a noxious cloud of Marlboro residue in Frankie the Counterman's direction. "The flat ones." Smokey sucked the smoke from his cigarette the way a pearl diver breaking the surface gobbles in oxygen, and then he lit another off the butt of the first. Smokey Johnson considered smoking to be his God-given right. He didn't much care what anyone else on the planet thought about that. He considered nicotine to be a food group. "If God didn't want me to smoke," he'd say through a hacking cough, "God wouldn't have planted so much tobacco."

"I'll go get the flanges," Frankie the Counterman said, itching to get out of Smokey Johnson's immediate vicinity as quickly as possible.

"Not so fast, Frankie!" Smokey cajoled, pushing those "F's" toward Frankie like a hot rancid breeze. "Ain't you got no time to socialize? I wanna tell you a story. C'mere."

Smokey leaned his elbows on the counter and stuck a pinkie in his hairy ear. He ratcheted the finger around a bit and blew smoke in Frankie the Counterman's direction. Smokey Johnson had hands like root vegetables, all gnarled from work and yellow from the countless cigarettes he had consumed in his lifetime. "I go see this woman, right?" Smokey Johnson said, examining a chunk of earwax while sliding into his story. "She wants a new boiler so I show up to give her a price, right?" Frankie the Counterman nodded, taking another step down the aisle. "C'mere, Frankie!" Smokey said, trying to reel him in with a circular motion of the smoldering Marlboro. "How ya gonna hear me from way over there?"

"I can hear you just fine," Frankie the Counterman said. "I got 20/20 hearing."

"Suit yourself," Smokey laughed, exhaling a thick cloud of smoke. "Anyway, this woman meets me at the door, right? I'm right on time and I got an appointment and all that, right?" Smokey waits for Frankie the Counterman to nod. "And I no sooner get the word Hello out of my mouth when she closes the storm door and tells me through the glass that she's already got the new boiler installed by somebody else! Now, I'm thinking this has got to be one fast contractor who did this job because this woman had just called me right outta the Yellow Pages yesterday, right?" Frankie the Counterman nodded catatonically, trying his best to hold his breath for as long as possible. "And now she's got the boiler job done already? I don't think so!" Smokey Johnson exploded in sarcastic laughter that nearly knocked Frankie the Counterman back into the fitting bins. "No, I think she's just a cheapskate, this one. Right? I mean why call me all the way out there and then send me away as soon as I say Hello?" Smokey took off his Marlboro baseball cap and scratched his head. "It just don't make sense, Frankie. And it ain't the first time that's happened to me in this town, I'll tell you that."

"Maybe it was something else that made her change her mind?" Frankie the Counterman suggested.

Smokey squinted hard though a haze of blue smoke, as though he was trying to see three miles past the horizon. "And what might that be?" Smokey asked, suspiciously.

"Oh, I don't know," Frankie the Counterman offered, trying to take as shallow a breath as possible. "Maybe she was allergic to smoke or something?"

"That's a bunch of crap!" Smokey said, pounding his fist on the counter. "That's the trouble with this country nowadays. I've got a God-given right to smoke. Since when are cigarettes against the law? I'm over eighteen, and it's my choice whether or not I wanna smoke, right?" Frankie the Counterman nodded quickly, holding his breath against the evil stench and backing up a bit more. "Nah, she's just a cheapskate. Probably got one of those fly-by-night handymen to do the job. That's what I think." Smokey was as stubborn as an old rusted bolt when it came to the subject of tobacco and his God-given right to use it as he saw fit. To Smokey Johnson, cigarettes were as necessary to life as platelets.

"I'm gonna get you your flanges now," Frankie the Counterman said, gasping and fleeing down the aisle.

"FOUR, FOUR-inch FLAT FLANGES!" Smokey shot back, sending the words after Frankie the Counterman like the Black Death.

While Smokey waited, he lit another Marlboro off the butt of the previous one. A well-dressed man walked in with a small boy. The man gave Smokey a nod, and waited his turn. The little boy, being a little boy, scrunched up his nose and said, "What's that smell, Daddy?" The well-dressed man, obviously embarrassed by the boy's question, leaned down and whispered something in the kid's ear. "But that man STINKS, Daddy!" the kid shouted, as kids will.

A small wave of stifled laughter rolled down the aisles from the warehouse. Smokey heard the laughter and scowled. "Hey, hurry up with them flanges, willya? I ain't got all day, right?"

"Daddy! That man is making my belly sick," the kid whined, holding his nose. The father looked like he'd rather be at a rock fight right about then. He gave Smokey Johnson a nervous smile. "He smells like dirty ashtrays!" the kid continued, as kids will.

"You oughta teach that kid some manners," Smokey said to the man. "You ain't in the trade. You got no business being in here in the first place. Why don't you just take your kid and get the hell outta here."

"I came in for a recommendation," the well-dressed man said. "I'm looking for a contractor who knows something about these new radiant heating systems. I'd like to have one installed in a home we're building."

Smokey Johnson suddenly did a complete turnaround in the Congeniality Department. "Oh," he said, "I can do that sort of work for you. Look no further." He took a step closer to the man and the boy. However, having just lit yet another Marlboro, Smokey Johnson's breath was now powerful enough to stop a tornado in its tracks. "Your search for a contractor is finally finished," he said to the well-dressed man. The "F" words splashed across the counter area like rotten chum. The man recoiled and gagged. The kid started to cry out, "Daddy, I think I'm going to throw up." The man took that as a real possibility because, truth be told, he was feeling about the same. He smiled weakly, removed a handkerchief from his pocket, covered his nose and mouth, and hurried out the door, pushing the kid ahead of him.

"More cheapskates," Smoky Johnson muttered through the blue Marlboro haze. "Nothing but cheapskates nowadays."

The Baptism of Henry Higby

Dwyer's wardrobe is a simple one. He wears, each day, the same red Perry Como sweater and a too short, navy blue tie with more grease stains than a McDonald's Dumpster. His shirt is a yellowed white, and his gray trousers are shiny at the seat and knees. On his smallish feet he wears brown penny loafers that are worn at the heels and scuffed. Dwyer is a tarantula disguised as Mr. Rogers.

Dwyer owns a successful mechanical contracting company. He sits at an ancient wooden desk in a small office near the back of a cinder-block building. His desk has more scars on it than a butcher block, and it's piled high with plans and specifications that change with the seasons like leaves on an old oak tree.

Salesmen of all ages wait to see Dwyer because he alone decides what equipment his company will purchase for their next project. And since Dwyer's company has been very successful of late, most salesmen have come to believe that his is the only campfire in the woods.

Sylvia the Secretary funnels the salesmen back to Dwyer, one at a time. While they wait for an audience, the salesmen either do job take-offs in the dirty plan room, or they read back issues of trade magazines while sitting on a Naugahyde couch and stealing glances at Sylvia's legs. Sylvia the Secretary smiles knowingly as she types letters on an old IBM Selectric and snaps chewing gum to the beat of the music wafting from the radio. Sylvia the Secretary likes salesmen, particularly the young ones.

Henry Higby is as young as you can get and still be considered legitimate in the business of construction. He has been assigned to call on plan-and-specification contractors by his boss at the manufacturers' rep agency. The boss has given Henry Higby this task because he believes plan-and-spec requires the least amount of selling skills. This part of the business is about having the lowest bid, the boss tells himself. Even a child can deliver a low bid. "Our job is to get specified," the boss explains to Henry. "Mel and Charlie call on the engineers. Mel and Charlie have more experience selling than you have. They'll get us specified; you just have to do the take-offs and deliver the price to the contractors."

"But it is my job to, like, sell, right?" Henry Higby says to the boss. "I, like, close the orders, right?"

Not wanting to pee in Henry Higby's punchbowl, the boss says, "You think of it that way if you like, Henry." The boss knows that Henry Higby is about as important to the process of plan-and-spec bidding as the US Postal Service, but he doesn't say that because he's a nice man. "Your job is to deliver our best price to the contractors, Henry."

"Yeah, I close the sale!" Henry Higby says with the enthusiasm that so often marks the young and the uninitiated.

When he first sets his rheumy eyes on Henry Higby, Dwyer sees not a salesman, but a fetus with shoes. He smacks his lips, thinking of all the money he is going to steal from young Henry Higby.

"You got a pencil?" Dwyer asks after offering Henry a limp handshake.

"Sure do!" Henry Higby says, aiming to please right from the start. He fumbles a No. 2 Ticonderoga from his plastic briefcase and offers it to Dwyer. "You need to borrow it?"

"No," Dwyer says, "I need you to sharpen that pencil, Henry." This message is too cryptic for Henry Higby's innocent mind to grasp, so he just smiles like a choirboy and waits. Dwyer looks at Henry Higby the way a hungry man would look at a thick pork chop. "I need you to sharpen your pencil," Dwyer continues, "because I need to get this job we're bidding. I want you to give me your best price right now – going in. I don't want to haggle with you later on, Henry. I want you to be my partner on this job because I honestly like you. You remind me so much of my dead son." This causes Henry Higby's blue eyes to grow as wide as plums. "Son, I want you to give me the price you would offer me if we already had the job. I want this price up front because it will help us get the job. A good partner – a good son – understands this. Are you willing to be a good partner, son?"

Henry Higby can't believe that a man of Dwyer's stature would talk to him this way. He stands a bit straighter and nods his head in delight. He knows that he was born to be in the sales business. "So you're looking for, like, a no-haggle price?" Henry Higby says, "And you want it, like, right now? Before you get the job?"

"That's right," Dwyer says. A small smile cracks across Dwyer's face like a thin sheet of ice breaking. "If you help me get this job, son, and if I get it, then it will be your job too. We're going to be partners." The ice cracks a bit further. "And I'll work this way with you on every job in the future because you remind me so much of my dead son." Dwyer wipes his rheumy eyes with his nicotine-stained right thumb. Dwyer, of course, has no family; he lives alone. No woman has ever considered dating Dwyer, let alone inviting him to her bed. But he really likes what the "son" thing does to the young ones.

"So we'll, like, win this job together!" Henry Higby sputters, finally understanding the significance of Dwyer's suggestion.

"That's right, son," Dwyer says. "But there's one other thing I need you to do for me."

"Name it!" Henry cries out.

"There are other contractors quoting this job as well, you know."

"I know!" Henry Higby shouts indignantly, not believing that anyone would dare challenge his new partner. "There's Crescent & Schmidt and Lipton & Ross and another one too, I think."

"Yes, there is another one." Dwyer says, staring deeply into Henry Higby's blue eyes. "It's Shotsky and Son, a truly despicable company."

"I don't know them that well, but . . ."

"Henry," Dwyer interrupts, "I need you to quote these other three contractors the regular way."

Henry Higby begins to understand. He nods his young head. "Like, I'm supposed to quote you low and them high, right?"

"That's right, son," Dwyer says. "Quote them just like you would quote me if we weren't partners."

"And I give you the buy price right now, right? And that, like, helps you get the job? And then you, like, give it to me?"

"That's right, son. You give me the bottom-line price that helps me get the job, and that job will be yours."

"Is this, uh, like . . . legal?" Henry Higby asks.

"Of course it is, son. Would I ever ask you to do something that wasn't right?"

"Uhh, I don't think so," Henry Higby says.

"Then you'll be my partner, son?" Dwyer asks, holding out his bony hand.

"You bet!" Henry Higby shouts, grabbing the hand and reveling in the knowledge that he does, indeed, have the makings of a bitchin' fine salesman. Wait until the boss finds out about this! Henry Higby thinks. He'll have me calling on specifying engineers in no time at all. Just like Mel and Charlie.

Henry Higby goes into an outer office, rolls out the thick blueprint, sticks the tip of his tongue out the side of his mouth, and digs in. When he sees how much of his company's equipment is specified he swoons. Mel and Charlie are really doing their job!

When he's through with the take-off, he calls his boss and tells him he's working on this huge job, and that it looks like it's in the bag. The boss asks Henry if he needs any help, and Henry says, "No, I have everything under control."

Henry Higby takes all the information home and works on his quote until 11 o'clock. "Are you going to bed?" his mother asks from the top of the basement stairs. "In a little while, Mom," Henry Higby shouts back. "I just have to finish this."

"Well, you need your sleep."

"I know, Mom," he answers, like the good son that he is. "I'll just be another few minutes." Henry moves to the bottom line, reaches for his calculator, and slashes the meat from the bone. "It's such a big job," he mutters to himself. "If Mr. Dwyer and I are going to get this one, I'd best go in really low."

The next morning, he calls Dwyer and gives him this rock-bottom price. "That's fine, son." Dwyer says. "I'll call you right after the bid opening."

Needless to say, Dwyer's company wins the job. Henry Higby doesn't wait for Dwyer's call; he goes to see him the very next morning. "Can I see him?" he asks Sylvia the Secretary.

"Sure!" she says with a wicked smile and a wink that Henry Higby doesn't fully understand. She points a red plastic fingernail down the hall, and then slowly crosses her legs. "You know where to find him, hon."

"We won!" Henry Higby shouts as he enters the room.

"Yes, I did," Dwyer says. "And now, it's time for you to really sharpen your pencil, Henry. Have a seat."

How Stephen Got Even

Butch had a silo for a stomach and the muscle tone of a bruised banana. He sat back in his swivel chair and rested his feet in the second drawer of his old wooden desk. He was trying like crazy to rush the customer off the phone because the coffee truck was pulling up the driveway and he didn't want to miss it. He hadn't eaten in an hour.

"Yeah, sure, I'll take care of that. Okay, okay, I gotta go. There's a fire in the wastepaper basket. I need this line free so I can call the fire department. No, it's okay, I'll do it myself." Butch hung up the phone, rotated his bulk in the chair like a howitzer on a pivot and pulled himself up. He headed for the door and the blare of the coffee truck's horn. He returned a few minutes later with a liter of Pepsi, a ham-and-egg hero, a wedge of apple pie and a pack of Virginia Slims. "You ain't hungry?" he asked Stephen who sat at the next desk. Stephen shook his head. "You're probably just too cheap to buy anything from Charlie," Butch said. "If we don't buy from Charlie, he'll stop comin' around, you know?" Stephen shrugged his shoulders. "You don't care, right?" Butch said through a mouthful of ham and egg and apple pie. Butch was a two-fisted eater. He attacked the sandwich and pie as though they were enemies, something to be conquered. "You don't care about Charlie, do you?"

He took a pull on the Pepsi, as though he was afraid it might evaporate. Stephen shrugged again.

Stephen worked for Butch. Together, they answered the phones that rang all day at the factory. They were the customer-service people. Butch had been there the longest, so Stephen worked for him. There was no other reason for Butch to be the boss; this was just the sort of company that rewarded longevity.

Butch finished his mid-morning meal and leaned back in his swivel chair. He stuffed his back into his desk drawer and lit a Virginia Slims cigarette. He took a deep drag, held the thin cigarette out to the length of his pudgy right arm, and flicked the ashes onto the carpet.

"Ahh, why do you have to do that?" Stephen said in disgust, looking at the ashes that were gathering like tiny gray caterpillars on the blue industrial carpeting.

"Don't worry about it," Butch said with a sneer, blowing smoke in Stephen's direction. "The porter will clean it all up tonight." The expression on Butch's face was the sort that takes its color from the dark side of the soul. Stephen stared at Butch's mustache. You could sweep out a bus terminal with that mustache, he thought. Right now, it was filled with bits of yellow egg and piecrust. Stephen said nothing. Butch rotated his round body forward and swept the crumbs from his half-acre of sport shirt onto the pile of ashes. "The porter needs something to do, right?"

The words hit Stephen like thrown bricks, but still, he said nothing. Stephen was the porter. He'd taken on the job as a part-time thing a few months back because he and his wife needed the money. He didn't make much answering the phones at the factory, and the cleaning money, such as it was, helped out. Stephen and his wife were trying to save for a house. Butch wasn't making it any easier.

Stephen picked up a call from a customer. Butch reached into his top desk drawer, took out his three-hole punch and opened it over the pile of ashes and crumbs. He mouthed the words, "The porter," to Stephen while pointing at the pile of litter. He let loose an evil little cackle. Stephen said nothing.

What Butch didn't realize, though, was that after five o'clock, Stephen had complete access to, and total power over, all of Butch's stuff. Stephen went about the business of emptying the wastepaper baskets, cleaning the ashtrays and toilets, and vacuuming the rugs, and then he went to work on Butch's stuff. And he did this every night. Oh, he didn't do everything every night, but he did enough to make it count.

Butch came in the next morning and frowned down at his plastic chair mat. It was shoved as far as it would go under his desk. "Hey, porter," Butch said to Stephen. "You pushed my chair mat under my desk."

"Oh, sorry," Stephen said. "I must have hit it with the vacuum when I was trying to clean up all those ashes and crumbs and little round pieces of paper that were lying there on the floor. Sorry."

Butch bent over with great exertion and clutched at the corner of the plastic mat. He hated bending over. The little plastic thorns on the bottom of the mat bit into his fat fingers like a nest of rats. "Yeow!" he shouted. "That's a sharp sonovabitch! Help me out here, willya?"

"Sorry," Stephen said. "I'm on the phone." He quickly picked up a call. Butch grunted and struggled with the mat for a few more minutes before he got it just where he wanted it. He sank exhausted into his swivel chair, which let out a mechanical groan. "Don't do that again!" he commanded. Stephen nodded to Butch while listening to the caller's question.

That evening, Stephen disconnected the clear plastic wire from Butch's telephone and let it fall back behind Butch's heavy wooden desk. The next morning when Butch picked up his phone to make a call he heard only silence. He turned the phone around and saw that the wire was missing. He let out a moan and trundled his chair back a few feet and off the edge of the plastic mat. He bent forward to look under his heavy wooden desk. He saw the wire lying there, way back near the baseboard. He groaned and grabbed the handset as if it were someone to strangle.

"Problem?" asked Stephen.

"Ahh, the friggin' cord fell outta the friggin' phone and now I gotta crawl under the friggin' desk to get it." Butch huffed in resignation and then smiled at Stephen like a crooked politician. "Do you think you can get it? Maybe help me out here?"

"Sorry, I'm on the phone," Stephen said, picking up the handset on the first ring.

So Butch got down on all fours and rooted under his desk like a huge hog at a trough. He tried to snake the thin wire up the back of the desk while grabbing it from the top of his desk with his other arm, which was a tad too short. The wire was as limp as overcooked linguine and this didn't make it any easier. "Help me!" Butch pleaded.

"Can't," Stephen said. "I'm on the phone."

It never occurred to Butch to disconnect the cord from the wall, plug it back into the phone, and let gravity do the rest. Butch's mechanical ability was strictly textbook. He kept trying to do the Indian Rope Trick with that phone wire, much to Stephen's amusement. Finally, Butch gave up and huffed and puffed the heavy desk away from the wall. He squeezed his bulk back there, grabbed the wire, and plugged it into the phone. Then he had to put everything back in its place. When he was through, the sweat marks went from his armpits to his waistband.

Stephen thought that was a pretty good one. He considered doing it again that night, but then he figured he'd best not press his luck. Instead, he stood back and gazed at Butch's stuff the way an artist might look at a partially completed canvas. His gaze drifted up toward the pine shelves that rose like the steps of a ladder over Butch's big wooden desk. They were loaded down with heavy binders that were filled with product catalogs. Stephen smiled to himself and set to work opening each binder and freeing the product literature from the chromed steel rods, but leaving it all in the binders. He then gingerly slid each binder to the very edge of the shelves.

The next morning, Butch arrived at exactly 9:00 AM. He huffed over to his desk and set down his jumbo Dunkin' Donut coffee in its paper container. Next to this, he placed his six Bavarian creme donuts and his lunch, which consisted of a meatball parmesan hero, a small mushroom pizza, a quart of lentil soup, and an aluminum pan filled to overflowing with stuffed cabbages. He sank into his swivel chair, lit a Virginia Slims, flicked some ashes on the floor, glared at Stephen defiantly, and waited for the phone to ring.

Which it did.

The customer had a question about a pump. This information happened to be in a four-inch-thick binder on the first shelf. Butch didn't bother rising from his swivel chair. He just leaned back, in defiance of gravity, and reached over his head for the heavy binder. He slid it off the shelf and watched in amazement as five pounds of glossy product literature dropped with a sickening Thump! onto his breakfast, lunch, and testicles. The damage, as you can imagine, was quite extensive.

"Don't worry," Stephen whispered from the quiet of his corner. "The porter will clean it all up . . . tonight."

A Matter of Opinion

Lloyd carried a blank stare like a lunch pail to his first day of work at Mickey's Plumbing & Heating. He immediately pressed himself into a corner of the shop and waited for Mickey to tell him what he should do next. Lloyd has never been inspired to express himself, and that's exactly why Mickey hired him. Mickey hires only people who take direction well – people who will gladly fall on hand grenades, should Mickey command them to do so. Mickey likes to be able to turn to an employee and say, "Ay! Take this bucket, get your butt down in that cesspool and start bailing." Any employee of Mickey's would jump right in that cesspool and scoop poop. This is because Mickey hires only people who have not yet been inspired to express an opinion.

Mickey raced into Lloyd's corner that first morning like the heavyweight champ going after the bum of the week. He didn't waste any time laying out the ground rules. "How old are you right now, kid?" he asked, poking Lloyd in the chest with a thick finger. "Right now." He poked him again.

Lloyd chewed on his fingernail. "Uh, twenty?" he said, but not sounding at all positive.

"Don't bite your fingernails!" Mickey shouted, slapping Lloyd's hand away from his mouth. "Didn't they teach you that in vocational school? Worse thing you can do in the plumbing business is to bite your fingernails, kid. I don't need any employee who's gonna be calling in sick half the time with the Hershey Squirts. You understand what I'm saying to you, kid?" Mickey stuck his face right in Lloyd's face – got in real close. Uppercut-close. Lloyd nodded furiously. "Good!" Mickey shouted, backing off a bit, but not so far that he couldn't still land a left hook, had he felt like landing a left hook.

"Now let me explain something to you," Mickey pressed on. "You're twenty, right?" After a safe pause, Lloyd again nodded, even more furiously. "Okay, I don't want to hear any opinions from you for the next ten years. You got that?" Lloyd hesitated, and then nodded again. "Good," Mickey said. "You're not allowed to have an opinion until you're thirty years old. That's the rule around here. You gotta eat a lotta spaghetti before you can mouth off around here. You understand?" Lloyd nodded again. "Good," Mickey said. "You watch baseball, kid?" Lloyd thought for a moment, and then slowly nodded. "Wadda you think of the Cubs?" Lloyd smiled a silly grin, and then shrugged his shoulders. "That's what I like to see!" Mickey said, cuffing Lloyd lightly on the chin. "You'll do just fine here, kid. But don't bite your fingernails! You understand?" He reached out and smacked Lloyd's hand again. "Stay off the bacteria, okay?" Lloyd let his head rock up and down. "Good!" Mickey said.

Mickey went back to his office and continued his pursuit of his new secretary, Chlamydia. Like Lloyd, Chlamydia was twenty years old and newly hired. She was built like a Ferrari, and from what Mickey could tell, she was just smart enough to answer the telephone.

Chlamydia's mother, who was only sixteen years older than Chlamydia herself, had picked her daughter's name from a Planned Parenthood brochure. She thought it was the most beautiful name in the world.

Chlamydia represented the one exception to Mickey's No-Opinion-Whilst- Under-Thirty Rule. She was the one person in the company Mickey hoped would have an opinion, and he knew exactly what that opinion should be. She should be of the opinion that Mickey was more desirable than Tom Cruise. However, and unfortunately for Mickey, Chlamydia had not been inspired to come up with an opinion of her own on anything so far in her young life.

"How do you like my new tie?" Mickey asked Chlamydia. She smiled and shrugged, crossed her long legs and smiled again. Finally, she just shrugged. "I don't know," she said, and smiled once more, allowing Mickey to marinate in sexual desire. Then she added, "I don't buy ties, so I don't know what to think." She smiled again, and shrugged.

"You like these slacks?" Mickey snapped, moving a step closer and pushing his crotch toward her.

Chlamydia stared real hard at Mickey's slacks. "I don't know," she said and shrugged.

Mickey gulped and asked, "You like dinners in fancy restaurants? You know, champagne?" Chlamydia shrugged and giggled. "I don't know," she said. "I go to Taco Bell most of the time."

"How about ski trips to Vermont? You like that? Weekends by the fireplace?"

"Vermont? Is that in upstate New York?" she asked.

"Yeah. Pretty close anyway. I could take you there," Mickey said. "You wanna go there with me?"

"I was going to go to the beach this summer," Chlamydia said. "Get a tan."

Mickey tried a different tack. "You like diamonds, don't you?" he asked. "Girls like you always like diamonds." She shrugged again. "I don't have any," she said.

"That's hard to believe!" Mickey answered, going wide-eyed. "You want me to buy you some? Huh?" He propped his big butt on the edge of her desk. She could smell his Jade East cologne. She didn't know if she liked Jade East cologne.

She was still mulling over the diamond thing, trying to figure out what Mickey meant by it when young Lloyd crept into the office. He had been looking for the keys to his truck for the past ten minutes, but with no success. He'd finally worked up the courage to ask Mickey for some advice on what he should do next. But when he raised his eyes from the floor and saw Chlamydia for the first time, the synapses that connected his brain to his legs stopped transmitting. His gaze met hers like metal drawn to a magnet. "Hi," she cooed, looking right through Mickey. Lloyd said nothing. He just stood there with his mouth open. "Hi!" Chlamydia repeated, letting her sweet white heat reach out toward Lloyd. Lloyd stood up straight, his eyes glazed over. Mickey turned toward his newfound rival and began to growl. "What can I do for you?" he spat. Chlamydia giggled at Lloyd. Her giggle sounded like wind chimes.

"Uh, keys?" Lloyd stammered, spitting on his shoes.

"GET OUTTA HERE!" Mickey shrieked as he jumped from Chlamydia's desk. Lloyd nearly passed himself running for the door. Mickey bounded after him and slammed the door.

"That guy needs a check-up from the neck up," Mickey said, breathing heavily and turning his full attention back toward Chlamydia. "He's a real moron." He sauntered back over to her desk.

"Well, I think he's cute," she said.

"You think?" Mickey sputtered. The words had left his mouth before his brain had a chance to grab hold of them. "You ain't allowed to have an opinion around here until you're thirty!" The way her eyes narrowed made him instantly sorry he had said that.

"I don't think that's very nice," Chlamydia said. "And I don't think you were very nice to that young guy."

"Ahh, forget about it, willya? Can't we get back to us?" Mickey pleaded, looking longingly again at her long legs.

"And I don't think you should be telling me what to think," Chlamydia said. "I can have an opinion of my own if I want one. I don't have to be thirty. I can have one now if I want one." She pouted and crossed those legs again. Those legs! "In fact, I can have all the opinions I want. If I want, I mean. I don't think you should tell me what to think."

"You don't think?" Mickey stammered.

"I don't," she said and she slouched in her seat. Mickey just stared at her. Chlamydia's silky legs and her defiant words had lined up on opposite sides of Mickey's brain and raced at each other, the collision being awful. He grabbed his temples and moaned softly. What to do? What to do? Those legs! These words!

And it was at that exact moment that Lloyd chose to burst into Mickey's office. "THE CUBS SUCK!" Lloyd shouted.

Chlamydia giggled, and sent some more blazing white heat Lloyd's way.

By The Book

The old guy was dead, of that there could be no doubt. The undertaker had carted away his frail remains earlier that morning. Eddie had gotten the call right afterwards. He figured the next call would be from the lawyers, but those calls weren't going to be for Eddie. The bosses took the lawyer calls. Eddie didn't even want to think about those calls. He just wanted to get in his truck with Richie and go to the job. He wanted to get there before anything changed. Maybe he and Richie would be able to figure out what had happened.

"Scalded to death?" Richie said, shivering a bit at the thought.

"That's what I hear," Eddie said as they merged onto the highway. "The nurse wheeled the old fella into the shower and turned the spray on him. The water was hot enough to stop his heart."

"Man," Richie said.

"Yeah, from what I hear, she hit him right in the family jewels."

Richie cringed and snugged his legs a bit closer together. "But where do we come in?" he asked.

"We were the last ones on the job. Remember? We changed that domestic hot-water recirculation pump? They had an iron one that rotted out. We put in a bronze one? Remember?"

"I'm not sure," Richie said. "Was that the place with the roaches?"

"Nah, that's the other nursing home. This is the one with the furniture all piled up inside the boiler room. The superintendent called me this morning to let us in on what happened. He's a good guy."

"Oh yeah, I remember that place," Richie said. "They had all the old wheelchair parts and whatnot in the boiler room, right?"

"One and the same," Eddie said.

"So are they blaming us for the old guy's death?" Richie asked.

"Who knows? I guess they're blaming anyone who's been on the job during the past fifty years. At least until they figure out what happened. Anyway, that's up to the bosses and the lawyers. We're just gonna poke around a bit in the boiler room to see if there's anything weird going on."

They drove the rest of the way in silence, thinking about what it must feel like to be launched into the next world by a hand-held shower spray. When they got to the job they went right to the boiler room. They didn't stop and ask permission; they just went. Guys in work uniforms never need permission to go to the boiler room – even when it's a potential crime scene. At least that's the way Eddie and Richie saw things. Eddie and Richie were particularly good at walking around a job as if they owned the place.

Richie grabbed hold of the "tempered" water line and winced. "Man, that's hot!" he said. "Gotta be 180 degrees." Richie prided himself on being able to tell temperature with his bare hands. As far as he was concerned, there wasn't a thermometer made that was more accurate than his callused palms.

"Let's check to make sure," Eddie said, taking a digital thermometer from his toolbox.

"You doubt me?" Richie asked.

"Nah," Eddie said, "but this one's gotta be official, you know?" He took the temperature at a slop sink in a utility closet about twenty feet down the hall. "You're wrong, Richie," Eddie said with a sly grin. "It's only 178 degrees."

"You're gonna pick nits over two stinking degrees?" Richie asked. "Water can take a two-degree drop in twenty feet, right?" Eddie smiled again and shrugged. He was as proud of those hands as his partner was. They walked back to the boiler room and looked around, trying to find the heating equipment among the furniture.

After a while, Richie pointed at the mixing valve. "Isn't that supposed to be one of those fail-safe models?" he asked. Eddie took a look at it and nodded. "It looks like that might be the problem," he said. "Evidently, she didn't fail safe. That thing's not supposed to let water hotter than one-fifteen out of this boiler room. I suppose that's what killed the old guy."

"But don't they have another shower valve upstairs?" Richie asked.

"I think they use pressure-balanced valves up there," Eddie said. "That's what you find in most of these places. This one's supposed to take care of the temperature." He pointed at the master-mixing valve. "And the one upstairs takes over when somebody flushes a toilet." He touched the pipe again and winced. "I know they sometimes leave all those shower valves set and just use the knob that goes to the shower spray. This master-mixing valve could have been broken for days. The pressure-balancer was probably protecting the old folks all the while."

"But when the pressure-balanced valve failed . . ." Richie added.

"Exactly," Eddie said. "Then they had no protection at all. But that doesn't explain why this one's doing what it's doing." He pointed at the master-mixing valve. "I'm gonna make a call." He took a cell phone out of his coat pocket and dialed the manufacturers' rep that handles the master-mixing valves. "Customer Service, please," he said to the operator. She passed him along to Tommy. Tommy had been with the company for eighteen months and had read all of the catalogs. He believed he knew more about the products he sold than any contractor alive. He'd been at it for a year and a half!

"This is Tommy. How may I help you?" Tommy said.

"Yeah, Tommy. This is Eddie from Ace Contracting and I'm standing in the basement of this nursing home where one of your fail-safe master-mixing valves just parboiled an old-timer. You wanna tell me how that could have happened, buddy?"

Tommy got flustered, but quickly recovered his professional composure. This, after all, was just a wrench jockey on the phone, right? "Which of our valves are you referring to, sir?" Tommy asked in a most professional manner. Eddie gave him the model number and serial number. "Please hold," Tommy said, and he reached for his product catalog. He paged through the thick binder and found the specifications for the valve in question. Finally, assured in his position, he picked up the phone and said, "That's a fail-safe valve, sir."

"Well, this time, Tommy Boy, she didn't live up to her billing."

Tommy looked again at the specifications. "No, I'm sorry, sir" he said. "That valve is fail-safe under any circumstances. I'm looking right at the specs. They're very, very explicit. Here, let me read it to you. If either the hot water or the cold water should fail, the internal shuttle will move instantly into a safe position, stopping the flow of water to the mix port of the valve, thus protecting people from scalds or chills."

"Tommy Boy?" Eddie whispered into the phone.

"Yes, sir?"

"We got a dead old-timer here. He can't read your specification, pal. My partner has magical hands that can read temperature. Those hands say the water leaving your valve is hotter than McDonald's coffee. We confirmed this with an actual thermometer. How 'bout that?"

"Please hold," Tommy said. He read the specifications again, just to be sure. Then he took a deep breath and picked up the phone once more. "This is not possible, sir," he insisted. "You people must be doing something wrong there on the job. The specifications clearly state that what you're claiming is not possible." He followed the words in his thick book with his index finger and read them slowly into the phone. "If either the hot water or the cold water should fail, the internal shuttle will move instantly into a safe position, stopping the flow of water to the mix port of the valve, thus protecting people from scalds or chills."

"Tommy?" Eddie said.

"Yes, sir?"

"Would you like to come down here to the job? I'll put your thick skull in this slop sink, and then you can feel for yourself how hot the water is."

"I'm sorry, sir, but I'm not permitted to leave the office," Tommy said, shaking a bit over the disrespect in Eddie's voice. "I'm customer service."

"Your valve failed, Desk Boy," Eddie replied. "The old duffer's dead and the water is hotter than Bill Clinton's libido."

"I don't have to take this abuse from a mechanic," Tommy sputtered into the phone. He hung up and looked toward his boss's office to make sure no one had heard him. He looked down at his shaking hands, and once again checked the specifications in his big, thick book. He wanted to make sure he was right. And sure enough, what Eddie had described couldn't possibly have happened.

It said so right there in the book.

Right there in black and white.

The Importance of Being Punctual

Ravitz looked at his Rolex and pounded the steering wheel with the heel of his right hand. He punched the Seek button on his radio, desperately searching for traffic reports. He had two hours to go just two more miles, and he was beginning to get really nervous. He crept a bit closer to the car in front of him and stopped abruptly when he saw the angry eyes glaring at him in the rear view mirror. He let the other driver pull up a few inches before he moved again. "Damn!" he muttered to himself. "I can't be late."

Ravitz was never late. His mother, bless her soul, used to brag about how Ravitz arrived in this world three weeks early. "He just hates to be late," she used to tell her neighbors. "My son is always early. He's never missed an appointment in his business, you know. People know him for that. He's very punctual."

When Mrs. Ravitz died, Ravitz was at the funeral home six hours before the burial. "You never know with the traffic in this city," he explained to the funeral director. "You think we should leave earlier for the cemetery? I mean, how long do they keep the hole open?" Mrs. Ravitz would have been so proud of her boy.

Ravitz looked at his watch again. He now had one hour and fifty-five minutes to go less than two miles. His stomach was churning. He chewed another TUMS and looked around for a way out. The woman in the car next to Ravitz smiled and waved him ahead of her so that he was now in the lane that wasn't closed. He gave her a pained look, but no Thank You wave. Ravitz had no time for such pleasantries. In the closed lane he saw that there was one guy sweeping and five guys watching. Ravitz rolled down the passenger-side window and shouted, "These are my tax dollars at work? You're a bunch of bums!" The sweeper flipped Ravitz the bird. One of the watchers launched a big phlegm-wad that landed with a satisfying Splat! on the BMW's trunk. "I hate this city," Ravitz mumbled as the traffic lightened up. He pressed the accelerator and got as close as he could to the guy in front of him. "Can't be late," he said. "Can't!"

Before he had left his office that day, Ravitz said to his secretary, Helen, "Not everyone's on time like me, you know."

"I know," Helen said, "I know."

"In fact, I'm better than on time. I'm always early! You know there's a name for someone who is always early," Ravitz said, puffing out his chest.

"Premature ejaculator?" Helen asked.

"NO!" Ravitz shouted. "PUNCTUAL! The word is punctual. And that's what I am. I'm punctual. Never ever late! Never!"

"That's nice," Helen said. "Well, you'll have to excuse me, Mr. Ravitz. I'd like to be punctual with this typing." She turned back to her work and Ravitz crashed out the front door, crammed himself into his BMW, and aimed it toward Manhattan.

He made it to the correct street with an hour to spare, but he didn't feel any more relaxed because he still had to park his BMW. He had passed three parking lots within a five-minute walk of his appointment, but Ravitz did not like to leave his car in a New York City parking lot because you needed a home equity loan to get it back. Ravitz was also frugal, you see. He figured the parking lot would be the absolute last option, and used only if he couldn't get a spot at a parking meter – which in New York requires the timing of Mario Andretti and an extreme amount of luck. He circled the block, cursing quietly, and watching the pedestrians to see if any of them reached into a pocket for car keys. That was the big giveaway in New York City. If you waited for a pedestrian to actually touch a door handle it was too late – the driver behind you would get the spot. No, you had to catch a key-fiddler on his way down the block and then stalk him like a serial killer. This, of course, caused every stinking driver in your wake to lean on the horn, but it was every man for himself in the Big Apple.

Ravitz spotted a young guy in a navy pea coat and jeans. He was swinging a ring of keys on a lanyard. Ravitz slowed and followed the guy until he stopped by an old green Chevy Impala and stuck a key in the door. The driver behind Ravitz leaned on her horn, but Ravitz just squeezed closer to the Impala and waved her around with tremendous annoyance. The kid in the pea coat smiled at Ravitz and walked over to check out the parking meter. He then strolled over to Ravitz's BMW and signaled for him to lower his window, which Ravitz, now nearly losing his mind with fear that he would be late for his appointment, did.

"You want this spot?" the kid in the pea coat asked.

"Yes. Now will you please move?" Ravitz hissed through clenched teeth. "I'm going to be late for my appointment."

"There's an hour left on the meter," the kid in the pea coat said.

"That's not my problem," Ravitz said, waving another angry driver around his BMW. "Will you please just move?"

"It costs fifty cents for fifteen minutes at this meter, you know. I have two bucks invested in this meter. Give me two bucks and I'll move," the kid said.

"But you were on your way out!" Ravitz sputtered. "Why should I pay you for the time that's left on a New York City parking meter?"

"Because you want my spot," the kid explained.

At this point the Punctual Ravitz checked to the Frugal Ravitz who could not see the justice in this situation. "This is not like some condominium you can put up for sale!" Frugal Ravitz shouted. "It's a parking spot owned by the City of New York! Just get the hell out of my way."

"You don't think there's a value to this spot?" the kid said, incredulously. "Watch." He stepped out into the street and shouted, "Yo! Who needs a spot? Anybody need a spot?" He waved at the old green Chevy and three drivers pulled in behind Ravitz and waved furiously from their windows. The kid in the pea coat walked back to Ravitz, who was staring a hole in his Rolex and banging on his steering wheel. "Still think there's no value to my piece of New York City real estate, big shot?"

"All right!" shouted Ravitz. "I'll pay the two dollars. Just get the hell out of my way!" He unhooked his seat belt and fumbled for his wallet.

"Whoa, Mr. Bavarian Motor Works," the kid said. "Now that we have a few more bidders, I don't see how I could possibly let this spot go for less than twenty bucks."

Frugal Ravitz stepped up. "Twenty bucks! You're out of your mind. I could put my car in a private garage for twenty-five, you thief!"

"And you'd be spending five more bucks than you have to, Mr. Young Urban Professional," the kid said. The drivers behind Ravitz blew their horns and made How About It? gestures. Ravitz looked in his rear view and cursed his competitors. "Your choice, Mr. Rolex," the kid in the pea coat said.

The Frugal Ravitz gave it one more shot. "Look," he said. "We've been arguing here for, what, five minutes? The time on your meter has run down. How about if I give you nineteen bucks instead of twenty?"

And that's when one of New York City's Finest walked up behind the BMW. The cop slapped a meaty palm on the roof of the BMW and said, "Move it, fella."

Ravitz looked at the cop the way rich folks always will. "Officer!" he proclaimed. "This miscreant is trying to sell me his parking spot. I want him arrested!" At that, the kid in the pea coat took two quarters from his pocket, inserted them into the parking meter, flipped Ravitz the bird, and walked away.

"Move it!" the cop said to Ravitz. "You're blocking traffic."

"I want that man arrested!" Ravitz screamed, pointing at the pea coat that was now blending into a sea of people. "Do your duty. I pay your salary, you know!"

The cop looked at Ravitz with new interest. "Step out of the vehicle, sir," he said, moving back a few feet and placing his hand over his nine-millimeter. "And keep your hands where I can see 'em. Move!"

The phone on Helen's desk rang. She picked it up on the first ring because she likes to be punctual. "I've been waiting an hour for Ravitz to show up for our appointment," the caller said. "He never came and he never called. When you see him, tell him I'm giving the job to Schmegel. Schmegel is never late for an appointment. He's punctual. You tell Ravitz that my time is just at valuable as his."

He hung up. Helen stared at the telephone for a moment. Then she shrugged and went back to her typing.

Billy Youngman's State of Mind

Billy Youngman hated his name. He would have preferred "Bill," but his father was already "Bill" and so Billy had to be "Billy" to avoid confusion, both within the company, as well as within the family. Bill, you see, was not only Billy's father, but also his boss in the family's heating business.

Youngman, he couldn't do much about. That was his family name and he was stuck with it. His only option was to grow older when he would just be Youngman rather than the implied Young man.

That, in a nutshell, was Billy's problem. Everyone thought of him as a kid and this name of his certainly wasn't helping. He worked doubly hard to look older. He had grown a mustache at the earliest possible age, but it came in blonde and downy, like the feathers on a baby chick. People would smile and say, "Look! Little Billy's trying to raise some peach fuzz on his face. Isn't that sweet?" Billy hated it when they told him he looked sweet. He didn't want to look sweet. He wanted to look old and believable.

He had gotten a tattoo, thinking that would make him look more grown-up. He was 18 years old at the time, just legal enough to make the decision. He told Meatball, the tattoo guy with the beer belly, to give him a big blue monkey wrench on his left forearm so that everyone would see it as he worked. He told Meatball to put the word "Experienced!" right over the wrench. He wanted to make sure that everyone that looked at it as he worked would know that they were watching a man and not a boy.

Unfortunately, however, Meatball had a bit of a spelling problem and the word on Billy Youngman's forearm now read "Expeeriensed!" which meant that Billy had to wear long-sleeved shirts all the time. When Bill Youngman saw his son's brand-new tattoo he just shook his head and rolled his eyes. Billy hated when his father did that. It made Billy feel like a little kid.

The bright side was that Billy loved his work. Heating had been a part of his life for as long as he could remember, and at 25 years old, he was really good at it. He had gotten a lot of "expeeriense" since the tattoo incident and Bill trusted his son on just about any problem job there was. He'd send Billy out on calls all over town. "I'm sending you my best man," he'd tell the customer over the phone, and then he'd hand the call to Billy. More often than not, Billy would return to the shop with a scowl on his face.

"What's wrong?" Bill would ask.

"Nothing," Billy would sulk.

"They question your age again, son?" Bill would ask, laying a hand on his son's slight shoulder. Billy would nod slowly and sigh. "You'll be looking older soon enough, Billy," Bill would say with a laugh. "Enjoy it while you can." But the older man's words didn't make the younger man feel any better.

One night, a pretty cashier carded Billy when he tried to buy a ticket for an R-rated movie. His friends laughed until they nearly fell over. Billy sulked for the rest of the night. Age, and the respect it brought, couldn't come soon enough as far as Billy was concerned.

Not long after the incident at the movies, Bill sent Billy out to look at a problem with an old steam-heating system. It was over on the other side of town. There was no one more qualified than Billy to look at this one, and everyone knew that was true. Billy had made it his business to study steam heat. He had devoured every book he could find in the library on the subject. He had scoured used bookstores for turn-of-the-century engineering texts, and he had stayed up late at night reading them all. He had even taken some seminars on the subject of steam heating. You could safely say that the lad was consumed by this antique technology. He knew that steam heat was a subject that scared the hell out of most heating contractors, and he saw this as a way to gain the respect of his elders. "Some day, they'll all be coming to me for advice," he had told Bill. "You'll see."

"Yep," Bill had chuckled. "You'll definitely be the guy with the . . . experience, Billy!" And Billy had glared at his father, and then tugged at the cuff of his long sleeve shirt. "Go get 'em, son," Bill said as Billy headed out the door.

Billy walked up the brick driveway and took in the glory of the old house before him. "I'll bet it has a two-pipe Vapor system," he mumbled to himself. "Maybe a VECO or a Broomell. I hope it's a Broomell. I love those." He tapped on the door and Mrs. Archimedes opened it a few moments later. She smiled at Billy. Mrs. Archimedes looks like everyone's grandma.

"Hello. I'm from Youngman heating," Billy said. "I understand you're having a problem with your steam system."

"Why, yes I am. Will you people be sending a mechanic to look at it?" Mrs. Archimedes very politely asked.

"I am the mechanic," Billy said.

Mrs. Archimedes squinted at Billy through her trifocals and smiled again in a motherly way. "But I was hoping for someone older," she said. "Doesn't your company have anyone who is older?" Billy choked back the words that were coming up from deep inside him like hot vomit. "You don't seem quite dry behind the ears to me," she said. "This is an old house. It calls for an older person. An older man." Billy gave her a look that could have set her flowered housedress on fire. "But please don't take that the wrong way," Mrs. Archimedes said. "I don't mean it in a bad way. It's just that I would prefer a more seasoned mechanic. Someone who is older. Someone who can understand an older system such as the one in this house. That's all."

"I'm fifty-six years old," Billy blurted. He wasn't sure where the words had come from. They just sort of popped out. "I'll be fifty-seven years old next month. I've been married to the same woman – Martha is her name – for thirty-five years. We live in a house just like this one and it has a similar steam heating system. I'm an expert. I'm fifty-eight years old. I'll be fifty-nine next week."

The old woman cupped a hand behind her right ear and took a step closer to Billy. "How old did you say you were?" she said. "You don't look a day over fifteen."

"I'm fifty-nine years old," Billy said, stepping across the threshold. "Which way to the basement?"

"But you look so . . . young!" Mrs. Archimedes said as Billy walked right past her.

"It's the uniform," Billy said, looking around for the basement door. "It makes us all look a lot younger than we really are. But thanks for the compliment. I also keep in shape by walking the mall every night with my grandchildren. Eight miles a night! I also take Geritol. I have an AARP card if you'd like to see it." Billy reached for his wallet and started to fumble through it while walking further into the old house. "I get free coffee refills at McDonald's. Where did you say the basement door was?"

Mrs. Archimedes pointed down the hall. "It's, ah, in the kitchen," she said. "Right over there." She watched as he walked away. "How old did you say?"

"Sixty next month," Billy answered as he headed down the stairs to solve her steam heating problems once and for all. "It's the uniform," he shouted up at her. "And the Geritol. I swear by the Geritol."

"And you know what to do with my old steam system?" Mrs. Archimedes called from the top of the stairs.

"Yep!" Billy Youngman shouted back. "I'm very experienced. I've been doing this since I was just a young pup!"

The Guerrilla Fleet

Johnny's problem screamed at him from the Yellow Pages. It was a full-page problem and it had Butz's smiling face all over it. Butz had one of those cartoon balloons coming out of his mouth. "When plumbing and heating problems make you nuts, call Butz!" it read for the entire town to see. Below the color picture of Butz was a drawing of a radio tower with lightning bolts coming out of it. "Our fleet of radio-dispatched trucks is always ready to serve!" shouted the caption. And then, right below that, "Why bother with small-time operators? Butz has the biggest fleet on the street!"

Johnny had but one truck. That, he figured, was his biggest handicap. The only radio he had in his truck played AM and FM. Besides, even if he had a two-way radio he still didn't have anyone in his office that could call him. Hell, he didn't even have an office; he worked out of his garage. Johnny was the small-time operator that Butz referred to. All Johnny had going for himself was his willingness to work hard and his cell phone. People could get him pretty easily by dialing his "800" number. And he had voice mail. Even if he was under somebody's sink he still answered his phone. But he only had the one truck and that was a problem. Butz looked so much bigger and important, both in the Yellow Pages and out on the street. Butz was bigger! There was no getting around that. Butz had been around a lot longer too. Tough to beat.

Johnny scowled at Butz's ad. "Our fleet of radio-dispatched trucks is ready to serve!" The words ate at Johnny like acid. Butz had lined up his trucks in his big parking lot for the Yellow Pages ad. He had taken a photograph of them from the roof of his big building. The trucks seemed to go on forever, like the way you look when you see yourself in one of those dressing room mirrors. The line of Butz's trucks stretched all the way to the edge of the yellow page. Johnny counted them. There were 26 of them in all, one for every year of Johnny's young life. But one customer needs only one truck, Johnny thought. Someone calls Butz and Butz sends one truck, right? No customer needs a whole fleet of trucks, do they?

And that's when he got the idea for the guerrilla fleet. Little guys can beat big guys – if the little guys are shrewd enough. Right?

The first thing Johnny did was to go see Mr. Hecker, the radio guy. Everyone in town knew Mr. Hecker because he had screwed up their TV reception at one point or another. Mr. Hecker had single-handedly convinced more citizens of the town of the importance of cable TV than any cable TV salesperson. Mr. Hecker was ancient and spent most of his days and nights talking to other ham radio enthusiasts from all over the planet. Mr. Hecker was also hard of hearing and he screamed a lot. He had an antenna on his roof that could tune in Neptune.

"Mr. Hecker," Johnny shouted. "You got an old antenna I could have?"

"Old Aunt Henna?" Mr. Hecker shouted back. "From Berlin? I talked with her last week, I think."

"No, no. Antenna." Johnny pointed up toward the roof. "You got an old one you don't need?"

Well, they went around and around like that for a while before Mr. Hecker finally figured it out. And since he thought Johnny was a nice boy, he gave him an old antenna that he used to use on his car when he still owned a car. The thing was about 20 feet long and just perfect. Johnny screwed it to the side of his van. It made it look like it he could take a radio-dispatched call from Pluto. When he drove the van over to see Sal at the sign shop, the antenna waggled like a reed in a high wind.

"You sell those radio tower decals with the lightning bolts?" Johnny asked Sal.

"We sell everything that looks like a sign," Sal said.

"Good. I'll take four of them. And do you have those stickers that work like Colorforms?" Johnny asked Sal. "You know, the kind you can change whenever you want?"

"You bet," Sal said. "In any of twelve gorgeous colors. What are you interested in?"

"Numbers," Johnny said with a sly smile. "Four sets of numbers from zero to nine, each about a foot high. Also give me four big plastic signs that read, TRUCK NUMBER. Can you do that?"

"Piece of cake," Sal said, and got to work.

When Johnny got back to his driveway he stuck TRUCK NUMBER 26 on the rear door of his truck. He stood back and looked at it. "Cool," he mumbled. He then walked around to the right side of the truck and assembled TRUCK NUMBER 52 on the door. He backed up a bit and checked it out. "Not bad," he said. On the left side, he plastered TRUCK NUMBER 17 right there on the driver's door. And then on the front, right below the windshield, he posted TRUCK NUMBER 96. "That oughta do it!" he whispered to himself.

He drove out of his driveway and just started cruising around town. He stopped at as many red lights as he could. Johnny figured that no matter where folks were driving, they could only see one side of his truck at any given moment. He planned to change the numbers daily. He figured that this would drive Butz nuts.

It did.

"I wanna know every time one of our guys see another one of this new guy's trucks," Butz told the dispatcher. "It must be one of those stinking consolidators! How many trucks do those bums have on the street now?"

The dispatcher checked his notes. "Fred radioed in a half-hour ago to say he spotted TRUCK NUMBER 107 on Montgomery Avenue."

Butz moaned. "I knew I should have sold out when I still had a chance," he said. "Now what am I gonna do? This outfit is gonna kill us! They have four times as many trucks as we do, and they're growing every day!"

Business was picking up nicely for Johnny. His cell phone was ringing nonstop and he was even thinking about maybe putting on an employee or two. He'd have to get another truck, of course, and that would bring the number of virtual trucks in his fleet up to 200 or so. He'd have to remember to order four more 2s from Sal the next time he went by his place.

And from what Johnny had seen so far, one customer still only needed one truck. And he was more than capable of providing that one truck.

Johnny went back to see Sal a few days later. "Got any 2s, he asked."

"Of course," Sal said.

"And can you make me four more signs?" Johnny asked.

"Sure," Sal said. "What do you want this time?"

"Have them read NONE OF OUR EMPLOYEES HAVE BEEN ARRESTED FOR SELLING DRUGS OR SEXUAL MISCONDUCT!"

"What color you want 'em?" Sal asked.

"Red," Johnny said. "Bright red."

This, needless to say, forced Butz to run ads in the local newspaper explaining that none of his employees had been arrested recently for selling drugs and/or sexual misconduct either. Butz's ads, however, made people wonder why Butz was doing this in the first place. Could there be some truth to the rumors that were flying around town? Hmmm.

Anyway, why take a chance? Better to give the business to Johnny. Besides, Johnny's got a bigger fleet of trucks, doesn't he? His trucks are everywhere. Radio-dispatched, too!

"You back again?" Sal asked Johnny a few days later.

"Yep," Johnny chuckled

"What's it gonna be this time?" Sal asked.

"Sal, I'd like you to make me four signs that read, ALL OUR EMPLOYEES WEAR BELTS!"

"What color you want?"

"Do you have a nice flesh tone?" Johnny asked.

The Apprentice

Nathan got these Christmas-morning eyes whenever he entered an empty boiler room. The potential of the place made him almost dizzy. He knew that he and Mark would soon move the most wonderful equipment into that empty room and use it to work mechanical magic. They'd put pipes to boilers, and valves, and radiation, and the result would be a heating system that was worthy of being on display in the main room of a museum. And even if no one else recognized their art, as such, it didn't much matter to Nathan. He and Mark would know the work was worthy – and that would be good enough for both of them.

Mark, who was a few decades older than Nathan, was a charter member of the Close-Cover-Before-Striking School of Heating. Mark viewed every job as a journey, with perfection as the only possible destination. He took no shortcuts. He spared no expense. Mediocrity was not an option for Mark. He wouldn't take on a job unless he could do it the right way, and that is what he had been teaching Nathan. "Buying cheap tools to save money is like stopping the clock to save time, Nathan," he'd tell his apprentice. "A professional is defined by his tools, and by what he does with them. Always remember that." Nathan looked at Mark with adoring eyes, and nodded in understanding.

Because of the way they saw the world, Mark and Nathan did mostly high-end work because the folks desiring those homes were the folks who could best afford their services. Mark and Nathan loved the challenge of the really big homes and they reveled in delivering systems that were nearly invisible. "People should feel what we do, Nathan, not see it," Mark explained. "A professional heating contractor is in the business of delivering the sensation of touch." And then Mark would lay his big hands on Nathan's shoulders and look hard into his apprentice's eyes. "Do you understand what I mean?" And Nathan would nod and smile.

On their last job, they had installed a radiant heating system with many zones. Each zone had a temperature sensor in the wall. The sensor was no bigger than the head of a 10-penny nail. They had the decorators put a thin coat of paint over each sensor to hide it from view. When you entered that house, you saw no heating equipment whatsoever. But you could feel the results of what Mark and Nathan had done. It didn't matter if anyone else recognized their skills. They knew.

Today, they were working in the home of James Buckland. This was their biggest job ever. James Buckland was about ten years younger than Mark. He had made his fortune in the stock market and he liked to live lavishly. He had a number of homes and this one was to be just another of the many vacation "cottages" that he would visit for a few days each year. Mark had designed an incredible system for the new home and had spent a good deal of time explaining it all to James Buckland's architect. When the plans were approved, the architect called Mark and said, "Mr. Buckland is very fussy, you know. He may want to stop by the site and watch you work. He may even have some questions for you as the job goes along."

"That would be fine with us," Mark said. "Maybe we'll put him to work!"

"Please!" the architect begged. "Don't even joke about that. The last thing I want to do is offend this client. He's much too important to me."

"Hey, there's nothing wrong with hard work," Mark said, a smile in his voice.

"You may feel that way," the architect replied. "But I'm not so sure how Mr. Buckland feels about it. He invests. He doesn't get his hands dirty like you two do."

Mark had smiled at that. They did get pretty dirty when they worked. There's no getting around the dirt.

Nathan was handing Mark the flux when James Buckland appeared in the doorway of the boiler room. "Hi, fellas," he said. "Everything going all right?"

"We're right on schedule," Mark said, not looking up from his work.

Mr. Buckland was quiet for a while, but they could feel his presence like a dog's hot breath. "What's that you're smearing on the pipe?" James Buckland asked, moving closer to where Mark and Nathan were working.

"It's flux," Nathan said. "It helps the solder run between the pipe and the fitting. You can't make a proper joint without it."

"I see," James Buckland said, leaning in to get a closer look.

"Careful, sir," Mark said. "You don't want to get too close. You're liable to get hurt."

"Can I try it?" James Buckland asked.

"Try what?" Mark said.

"Can I put some flux on the next joint?" James Buckland said, pointing at the pipe.

"Why would you want to do that?" Mark asked.

"Because it seems like fun!" James Buckland replied, looking Mark square in the eye. "It is fun, isn't it?" he repeated, this time to Nathan. Nathan nodded and smiled. "You two are having . . . fun!"

Nathan nodded again, and laughed. Mark laughed too.

"That's why I want to try it!" James Buckland said.

Mark handed the brush to the rich man. He showed him how to put the flux on the cleaned fitting.

"Can I hold the torch?" James Buckland asked when he was done. Mark looked at Nathan and then back at James Buckland. "Please?" James Buckland pleaded. "I've always wanted to do this."

"Oh, what the heck," Mark said and handed the torch to the wealthy man and showed him how to hold it on the fitting. Then he handed him the spool of solder and showed him how to make a good joint. James Buckland was getting that Christmas-morning look in his eyes, just like Nathan. "You like this, don't you?" Mark asked quietly.

James Buckland had the tip of his tongue sticking out of the side of his mouth as he soldered. He nodded and let loose a childlike giggle. "Yeah, I like this a lot!" he said. "I never get to do cool stuff like this."

"Like soldering?" Nathan asked.

"Like building," James Buckland said softly. "I have never built anything in my life. I invest. I sit in boardrooms. I go to meetings. I have more money than I can possibly spend, but I have never built anything." He was quiet for a long moment. And then he handed the torch back to Mark and stood up. "Thank you for letting me try that," he said wistfully.

Mark looked at Nathan and they both understood what had to be done. "Would you like to make some more joints?" Mark asked, handing the torch back to Mr. Buckland.

"May I?" the rich man asked, as excited as a kid at a County Fair.

"Tell you what," Mark said. "Why don't you go upstairs and find yourself some old clothes. You do have old clothes somewhere, don't you?"

"I must!" Mr. Buckland shot back.

"Well, go get 'em," Mark commanded. "We've got some work to do here." And the billionaire shot up the stairs.

They finished the job later that month. James Buckland worked side by side with Mark and Nathan every day. When they were done, James Buckland asked Mark if he could become his apprentice and learn more about this trade that so fascinated him. He had learned, by touching flame to metal, that there is a lot more to life than money. For the first time in his life, he was able to stand back at the end of the day, look at something that he had built with his own two hands, and quietly say, "I did that."

And this gave him tremendous satisfaction.

When the house was finished, James Buckland approached Mark with an interesting offer. He would like to apprentice to the master, but he realized that the knowledge in Mark's head was very valuable. "I'll pay you $500,000 if you will allow me to apprentice to you for one year," James Buckland proposed.

Mark considered the offer for approximately five seconds, and then agreed to give some mechanical meaning to the rich man's life.

He put Nathan in charge of the new apprentice for the first six months, of course. That was only proper.

And they all lived happily ever after.

Quinn Lends a Helping Hand

In Quinn's mind, everything was orderly, except when it wasn't – like nuclear fission. There were those who should be doing heating work, and there were others who shouldn't. When there was a violation of this maxim, Quinn became somewhat unstable, and then there was no telling what he might do.

On this particular day, he clenched a cigar between his teeth the way a bulldog might hold a hunk of rawhide. He scowled at the road ahead and thought about how slow business had been lately. Quinn needed a job. A big one would be great, but a small one would do. Any job would do at this point, but what stood in his way were the damn handymen. This town was crawling with handymen. They were like vermin. They'd take on any job for hardly any money, and Quinn was finding it nearly impossible to compete with them. The public didn't see much difference between Quinn and the handymen, and that troubled Quinn deeply, but he didn't know what to do about it.

He had put together a price for a radiant heat job one day. It wasn't a huge job, but it was worth bidding. He worked with a local wholesaler on the pricing. Quinn had looked at his bill of material for this job. It wasn't going to go cheap. The list of numbers ran down the page like snot off a kid's nose. He also had pages of computer-generated engineering that the local rep had come up with. Quinn didn't completely understand all those formulas and computations. To him, they looked like what worms do under flat rocks, but he thought the whole package was pretty impressive nevertheless.

He showed it to the homeowners on a Wednesday. They said they would get back to him, but they never did. On this particular day, Quinn drove by the job to follow up, and got sick to his stomach when he saw Handy Randy's truck parked in the driveway. Handy Randy was laying radiant heat tubing on the ground, standing up every now and then to look it over, and then bending over again to attach some more. "You got this job?" Quinn asked.

"Uh huh," Handy Randy said. "If you're here to see the owners, I'm afraid you're out of luck. They went on vacation because the wife can't take the dust and the noise. They said they'd be back when I'm done."

"So you're doing the heating?" Quinn asked, looking at the tubing.

"Yep," Handy Randy said, gesturing at the footings he had dug the previous week and smiling at Quinn. "I'm doing it all. They wanted radiant heat because they saw it on TV and that's what I'm doing today. I saw it on TV too. I'm installing the tubing, and the concrete's going down tomorrow. Then I'm gonna start framing." He touched the tubing with the toe of his shoe. "It's really not that hard to do. I saw it on the TV."

"Do you have a license for this?" Quinn asked.

"I don't think I need a special license for this," Handy Randy answered. "I mean, I have my home-improvement license, if that's what you mean. And what's the big deal? All I'm doing is laying some tubing on the ground. It's not rocket science. You ever do this sort of work?"

"Have I ever done this?" Quinn said incredulously. "This is all I do – when I can get the work."

"Yeah," Handy Randy said. "I know what you mean, man. Things have been pretty slow lately, huh?" Quinn stared at Handy Randy and nodded very slowly, like a fuse burning. "Hey, as long as you know about this stuff," Handy Randy continued, "maybe you'd be able to tell me how I can attach the ends of the tubing to those manifold thingies over there. Some ends are longer than others, and I'm not sure what to do."

"Didn't they show that part on the TV?" Quinn asked.

"Not that I remember," Handy Randy said, scratching his neck. "I may have been up getting a beer or something." He lightly kicked the tubing. "I'm not sure if this stuff stretches," he said. "I heard that it grows when you heat it, but I can't figure out how to heat it without putting the water inside of it. And I can't get the water inside of it until I hook it up to the manifold thingies." Handy Randy gave Quinn a boyish grin. "Any ideas?"

"You looking for a consultation?" Quinn asked, looking hard at Handy Randy. "Is that what you want, son? A consultation?"

"Gosh, I don't know if I'd call it that. I mean 'consultation' sounds like something I'd have to pay you for, ya know? I don't have that kind of money in this job. I had to come in pretty cheap to get it in the first place. Nah,

I just thought you might have a bit of friendly advice for me. You know? From one contractor to another?" Handy Randy winked at Quinn and gave him a conspiratorial grin. "Professional to professional? You know?"

The combination of the grin and the galling question was causing Quinn to approach critical mass. Quinn considered his options. He could grab hold of the end of the 700-foot length of radiant tubing that Handy Randy had attached to the ground with tent pegs. Quinn figured he could run down the street with the tubing and explain to Handy Randy that this is how you stretch PEX tubing. He also considered advising Handy Randy to heat the PEX tubing with a propane torch until it took on the consistency of taffy.

But then he came up with a much better idea. He smiled at Handy Randy in a most benevolent and understanding way. "It's advice that you're after, son?" he asked and Handy Randy smiled back and nodded. "And the homeowners are away, right?" Handy Randy's smiled widened and he nodded some more. "Then advice I shall give you," Quinn concluded. "And no one will be any the wiser." Quinn looked around, and then leaned in to whisper in Handy Randy's ear, "But you have to make me a promise, my friend."

"What's that?" Handy Randy whispered back.

"You must pass the knowledge I am about to bestow upon you to other professionals such as yourself."

"You mean to other handymen?" Handy Randy whispered.

"Exactly!" Quinn whispered back. "And it will be in this way that our great industry will move forward. We must pass the torch to the next generation."

"You're a good man!" Handy Randy shouted with delight, and obvious relief. He was in way over his head on this job, and he knew it. "I honestly wasn't sure what I was going to do once I got all this tubing down," he admitted.

"No problem," Quinn said solemnly, backing away from Handy Randy. "Now, let's roll up our sleeves and get to work, son." He grasped Handy Randy by the shoulders and gave him a shake and a smile. Handy Randy smiled back, and gave Quinn the thumbs-up sign.

Quinn spent the rest of the afternoon showing Handy Randy how to splice PEX tubing by using automotive hose clamps. "All you have to do, Randy me boy, is to make sure that you don't tighten those clamps too much. The concrete's gonna hold it all together so don't fret. You don't want things rubbing." Handy Randy nodded, and did as he was told. "And we'll have to get some longer runs of tubing. I'm not sure that 700 feet is long enough for an extension this size. I think we'd better make it a thousand feet, my friend. Throw another splice in there and bury it in the concrete. And make sure you set that tubing on one-inch centers. Otherwise, there might not be enough heat on the coldest day of the year. And can you make those bends a bit tighter, son? You're not crimping the PEX enough at the ends." Handy Randy stepped on a random turn to make sure the bend was as tight as a closed matchbook. "That's the way to do it, Randy me boy! Bend that sucker tight around those turns. The tighter the turn, the faster the water. The faster the water, the better the heat. It's just like a ride at the amusement park, son. The water's gotta whip around those corners!"

"Man!" Handy Randy exclaimed. "You really know your stuff." He gave Quinn a huge smile, which Quinn immediately returned. "Just tell all your buddies about what you've learned today, son," Quinn said. "Remember, that's how we're going to move this industry forward. Professionals helping professionals, right? I don't mind helping you out because business is pretty slow right now."

"Will you be able to stop by tomorrow?" Handy Randy asked. "That's when I'm going to be pouring the concrete."

"Wouldn't miss it for the world!" Quinn said. "In fact, tell you what. I'll bring over a special additive that will make the concrete run more easily around the tubes."

"Does the additive cost a lot?" Handy Randy asked. "I mean, I don't have that much money in this job, you know."

Quinn put his arm around Handy Randy's shoulder. "Son, I'm gonna give you the additive for free. It's my contribution to your education. We'll just pour it into the concrete while it's still nice and wet and goopy. The additive's on me, son."

"What a great guy you are!"

"Think nothing of it," Quinn said.

On his way home that night, Quinn stopped by the supply house and picked up seven gallons of hydrochloric acid and some empty plastic jugs.

Bill's Retirement Plan

He sat at the end of his couch in his living room and listened to a silence that was heavy enough to hold in the palm of your hand. Since he had retired, his days had blended together like smoke. He stood and walked to the front door of his little house. He opened it, and looked out past the small lawn and the broken sidewalk, and out into the street where a woman with a small child tucked safely away in a car seat was driving by. He watched them until they disappeared around the corner, and then he closed the door and sat again on his couch, this time at the opposite end. He tugged at a loose thread in the upholstery. Time passed and he stood. He looked around for his daily newspaper, which he had already read three times that day. He found it, and opened it, and idly turned the pages. He thought of work and he looked at his watch. They'd be at lunch now, he realized. Some would be going to the deli; others brought their lunch and they'll stay inside for the entire hour, he thought. They won't go out. "They'll all be back in a half hour," he said aloud, cracking the silence like an egg and startling himself. He realized he hadn't used his voice in nearly 18 hours. He looked around the empty house, turned the pages of his newspaper, got up, walked to the door, opened it, and looked out. No one drove by.

He paid a visit to the office that afternoon, as he had every afternoon for the past month. He walked in, smiled, and watched them as they worked. They were happy to see him, of course. They were always happy to see him. He brought donuts, day-old, but still good. He got the donuts for half price at the day-old bakery. Everyone thought the donuts were perfect for the afternoon coffee break. Everyone was happy to see him.

"Bill! You're going to make us all fat!" Millie squealed with delight when she saw the day-old donuts. Millie weighed more than a Chevy Blazer, but didn't think of herself in that way. "Come and sit," she said, daintily patting the chair across from her desk. He did. "What's new?" she asked, giving him a smile that came up from her stomach.

"Since yesterday afternoon?" Bill asked. Millie nodded and smiled. "Not much!" he admitted. "You watch ER last night? It was a rerun, but it was a good one."

"I thaw that one!" she mumbled through a mouthful of donut. "It wuf good, wuffn't it?" He smiled and nodded.

"I watched Judge Judy this morning," Bill said. "She had a couple of good cases. I never knew that show was on when I used to work. She had a case about a guy who let his dog crap on the neighbor's lawn. The guy said the family that used to live there never minded, so why should this new guy mind? They called it 'The Case of the Squatter's Rights.' Ain't that something? Squatter's rights! Get it?" Millie smiled and nodded. Bill chuckled and shook his head.

"I'm gonna get some more coffee. You want?" she asked. He smiled and nodded, and she waddled off to the coffeepot. While she was away her phone rang. He picked it up and said, "Hello!" The customer was happy to hear Bill's voice. "I thought you had retired," the customer said. "I'm visiting," Bill answered. The guy gave Bill an order. Bill thanked the guy, grabbed an order form, and wrote it up – just as he had done for so many years. Millie returned with their coffee. "I got an order for you," Bill said. She smiled and nodded. The phone rang again and he grabbed it before she could. "Drink your coffee," he said, covering the mouthpiece. "Have another donut." He pointed at the box, smiled, and took another order.

The boss came by for a donut. "Hey, Bill! Good to see you again! What's new?"

"Since yesterday afternoon? Not much. You watch ER last night?"

"Nope, went to bed early," the boss said, picking up a donut that was thick with powered sugar.

"It was a good one," Bill said. The boss smiled and nodded and then went about his business.

The phone rang again and Bill lunged for it. Millie didn't mind this one bit, of course. She scarfed down another donut. Bill took the order and wrote it up. He did this until 5:00 PM, as he had been doing every afternoon since the day he wandered back to his job. That had happened six months after his retirement party. The only difference between his pre- and post-retirement time was that Bill now worked much harder, and for free. This endeared him to everyone, of course. It especially endeared him to his old boss.

One Wednesday morning, several months later, Bill woke and decided he didn't want to watch Judge Judy that day. He searched his driveway at daybreak and found his newspaper. He carried it inside and read it on the white, Formica table in the thick, heavy silence of his small kitchen. And then he drove to his old job and waited out front. His old friends were surprised to see him so early in the morning, but they welcomed him nevertheless. "I'll get the donuts during the lunch hour," he told Millie. She smiled and nodded.

The phones were slow that day so Bill wandered out to the warehouse and spent some time hanging around Jerry's desk. Jerry was the warehouse manager. "You see NYPD Blue last night?" Bill asked. Jerry smiled and nodded. "Good one, eh? I love that Sipowitz! He's some guy, ain't he?" Jerry nodded and went about his paperwork. "Anything I can do for you, Jerry?" Bill asked.

Jerry looked up. "You can sweep the floor if you want," he said, which Bill willingly did.

Bill had retired from this company after 39 years of dedicated service. He had retired because he could no longer stand his fellow employees. He hated every stinking one of them and he never wanted to see them again. They grudgingly threw a retirement party for him at a local tavern, and he grudgingly attended. He left that party, vowing never to return.

But then came Judge Judy and all those silly small-claims trials where people said the stupidest things. How much of that could one man take? And those people on General Hospital! They got to him big time after a few months. What the heck does this have to do with a hospital? he thought. Enough already! Gilligan's Island on Nickelodeon was okay for a few weeks. So was The Brady Bunch. But there's a limit to how many reruns one retired man can watch in one lifetime, and Bill had had his fill.

He had never had a hobby, and he figured retirement was no time to start looking for one. Hobbies were for people who didn't have anything better to do with their time, right? He would have traveled, but where the heck would he go that was any better than where he already was? Besides, when you figured out how much per hour those motels charge you just to sleep, well, it's enough to give a man an ulcer. So he went back to visit the people he couldn't stand, and, to his surprise, he found they weren't so bad after all. Since he had retired he was no longer a threat to some of them and a pain in the ass to the rest of them. They tolerated him during that first afternoon when he visited. They remembered the few good times they had had and they sensed his loneliness. Someone (he forgot who exactly) told him to come back again whenever he felt like it. So he did. He went back the following week, and again, they were all very happy to see him. He, to his astonishment, was also happy to see them.

Two days later he started to bring in the day-old donuts. They really liked the donuts. He thought about this as he followed the rhythm of the broom across the warehouse floor – aisle after aisle after aisle after aisle. "Man's gotta have something to do," he said softly to the stock on the shelves. "Can't just wake up every morning and have nothing to do. It ain't right. It just ain't right."

The boss came out and mentioned they would be taking inventory on Saturday and that Bill was welcome to stop by, should he feel like it. He did, of course. He spent 50 hours at the old place that week.

The next week he added up his time and found he had spent 45 hours visiting his old job. He had answered the phones, taken orders, swept up, and generally helped out wherever he could. He had collected no paycheck, received no benefits, and he had spent $9.45 on day-old donuts that week.

When summer arrived, hot and hazy, he took no vacation from his daily visits. After all, why would a retired man ever want to take a vacation? When you're retired . . . every day is a vacation.

Isn't it?

Katsu for you!

Phil was flopping around on the mat the way a barracuda does when it realizes it is no longer in the sea. He let out a yelp a hound would have been proud to claim, and he hugged his sore shin with both arms. Sensei Nakabiashi, the karate instructor, came strolling over.

"Where does it hurt?" he asked. Phil grimaced and nodded toward his right shin. Phil's shin had just been assaulted by the rock-hard side of Augie's foot. The two men did things like this to each other several times a week. They're good friends, mind you, but they do like to beat the snot out of each other several times a week. Karate people are like that.

"Does it hurt right here?" Sensei Nakabiashi asked, gently touching Phil's wounded right shin. Phil clenched his jaw and nodded fast and furiously.

"Oh, it hurts like hell," he said, gasping for breath.

"I'll be right back," Sensei Nakabiashi said. Phil continued to wriggle in agony, but Sensei Nakabiashi didn't go far. He just walked to a shelf along the wall, reached up, and grabbed a two-foot length of split bamboo wrapped in duct tape. "Give me your left shin," Sensei Nakabiashi said, returning to Phil. Phil stretched his left leg out toward Sensei Nakabiashi, anticipating some sort of magical treatment. And that's exactly what he was about to receive. Sensei Nakabiashi took that short piece of bamboo and immediately set about beating the crap out of Phil's left shin. And all the while he was doing this, he was shrieking like Bruce Lee in a bad Martial Arts movie.

Phil's eyes bulged out of his head like cue balls. He tried to squirm away, but Sensei Nakabiashi was as tenacious as a pit bull. He just kept whaling away with that hunk of bamboo as Phil, not believing what was happening, half-yelped and half-laughed at the absurdity of it all.

Finally, Sensei Nakabiashi stopped flailing the bamboo. He stood back and smiled with great satisfaction. "How does your right leg feel now?" he asked.

Phil, who was now clutching what moments before had been his good leg, looked up and said, "Huh?"

"The first leg," Sensei Nakabiashi said. "The right one. The one you were complaining about. The one Augie kicked. How does it feel now?"

"It feels a lot better than the one you just went to town on," Phil admitted, still stroking his sore left leg.

"That's katsu!" Sensei Nakabiashi exclaimed. "It's the best way there is to forget your pain, and it works every time! This is the way I learned karate in Japan. Good stuff, eh? Right leg feels better, doesn't it?" Phil nodded. "Katsu!" Nakabiashi shouted.

Phil hobbled to the edge of the mat and sat down. Sensei Nakabiashi appraised each member of the class to see if the lesson had sunk in. One white-belted newcomer stared at Sensei Nakabiashi as if he were the Grim Reaper.

Sensei Nakabiashi walked over to him, lifted him up, spun him around, and smacked him several times on the back. "Yeow!" the white belt bleated.

"How does that feel?" Sensei Nakabiashi asked.

"It hurts like hell, Sensei," the white belt complained.

"Here, I'll fix it," Sensei Nakabiashi said with a smile. And then he whipped the kid through the air as though he were a matador's cape.

"Whoa!" the white belt shouted as he crashed to the mat. Sensei Nakabiashi was on him like soy sauce on rice. He grabbed the white belt's bare left foot and smacked its bottom several times with his oaken palm.

"Yikes!" the white belt shrieked.

"How does your back feel now?" Sensei Nakabiashi asked.

The white belt looked confused for a moment as he rubbed his sore left foot, but then he smiled and said, "My back feels fine, Sensei. Just fine. Compared to my foot, I mean."

"That's katsu!" Sensei Nakabiashi shouted at the class. "It's the Japanese way of letting you know things could always get worse for you. It's a good way to remember that you should always keep your present troubles in perspective."

Everyone in the class nodded. They had learned a lesson in life.

Phil was waiting for his stuff at the supply house counter the next morning. As he sipped his coffee he listened to Al, one of his many competitors, bitch and moan about this problem steam job. Al was the King of Complainers and he never shut up.

"I'm tellin' ya, it's the boiler job from hell, Phil," Al whined. "It won't heat all the rooms. The pipes are banging. The water's squirting from every orifice, and the people are saying they never had these problems before they met me. I don't know what the hell I'm gonna do next. This one's hopeless. It couldn't possibly get any worse."

"How much do the people owe you?" Phil asked.

"Fifty-three hundred bucks," Al said, feeling terribly sorry for himself.

"You ever hear of katsu?" Phil asked.

"No, can't say as I have," Al said. "That some sort of boiler treatment?"

"Nah, it's better than a boiler treatment," Phil said with a laugh. "It's a head treatment. Katsu is a way of making your present troubles vanish."

"Hey, where do I sign up?" Al chuckled. "Things can't possibly get worse than they are right now."

"That's what you think," Phil said.

"Huh?"

"Okay," Phil pressed on. "It sounds like that system of yours is dirty, so here's what I want you to do. Go back to that job this afternoon and pour two gallons of chlorine bleach and two gallons of ammonia into the boiler."

"Huh?" Al said again. "Chlorine and ammonia? You sure that's the right thing to do here, Phil?"

"Sure I'm sure!" Phil chuckled. "Chlorine bleach and ammonia are cleaning agents, right? Either one will work beautifully, so when used together, they should work twice as fast!"

"Uhhh, I'm not so sure," Al said cautiously.

"Well, I guarantee they'll make you forget your present worries," Phil shot back.

"But won't the chemical fumes from the chlorine and the ammonia drive everyone from the house?" Al asked.

"Nah, the chemical fumes from the chlorine and the ammonia will kill everyone in the house!" Phil explained. "And that should make your current worries seem like trifles! Just think about how you're gonna feel when those lawyers are ripping the bones from your business. That's gonna hurt!"

"Uh. I don't know about this," Al sputtered.

"You want your current worries to vanish, don't you?" Phil asked in a most sincere way.

"Uh. I'm not so sure."

"Hey, don't turn chicken on me now, Al. Here, listen to me. This is a very important part of the treatment. Before you use the bleach and the ammonia, I want you to install a case of Orville Redenbacher microwave popcorn in their flue pipe and then start the boiler. Make sure you get out of the way in a big hurry, though."

"This is katsu?" Al asked.

"Yep," Phil said. "What do you think?"

"I think the problem I'm having right now looks pretty manageable," Al said.

"See? It works!" Phil said. And then he gave Al a slap on his back with a hand that was as hard as a steam iron.

"Yeow!"

Partners

She sat on the couch and cried as he sat across from her in his easy chair and watched and waited. He wasn't sure what to say, or whether he should say anything at all. He should have been at work, but business was slower than ever and that had a lot to do with her tears. The bills were more than their income, and they'd been like that for some time. He was trying his best, but that didn't seem to make much of a difference. And what more could a man do than to try his best?

He was too far away to touch her and not sure if he should move any closer right now. She had her moments, as did he. He knew that. He hoped that this moment would pass before long. She was sobbing words that were hitting him like thrown bricks. He knew she didn't mean them – that she was just frustrated and tired and afraid– but the words hurt, nonetheless.

He did the physical work and she kept the books. They had gone into this thing with such hope. It was to be their ticket to ride. They'd be on their own, at long last, and they'd be in charge of their destiny. No boss would ever again tell them how much money they could or couldn't make. He'd be able to do what he loved, and she would manage their money and take care of all the tedious business details that he had absolutely no interest in. They would never again have to take any crap from anyone. They would work only for nice people who paid their bills on time. If someone tried to give them a hard time, they'd just walk away. There was plenty of work out there, and there was no reason to take abuse. And as their business grew and prospered, they would hire young helpers and teach them the right way and treat them really well because he and she would never forget what it was like to be treated poorly. And that's how it was going to be. And it all seemed so simple.

He was really good at what he did. He was a quick learner and he was both neat and thorough. He gave what most customers considered to be "a good deal." He wasn't the cheapest guy in town, but neither was he the most expensive. He had found a comfortable place somewhere in the middle, and they had done all right at first. He especially liked the physical part. He was born to do this sort of work. He was happiest when he had the tools in his hands.

She was methodical and she liked to work with the numbers. She hadn't gone past high school but she had this knack for the numbers. The numbers were orderly and you could believe in them. They told a story. They never lied. You could trust the numbers. What she didn't like, though, was when too many things came at her all at the same time. She wanted her life to be orderly, and she preferred to take things one step at a time. She never liked chaos, even though she knew that business could often be chaotic. She did her best to cope when those times rolled around. But she never liked it one bit.

He, on the other hand, never seemed to do just one thing at a time. He always had more than one job going, and that usually frustrated her, although she never said this out loud. She had a tough time keeping track of what material went with which job, for instance. He had never been any good at keeping records. He liked to do the physical work, but he couldn't be bothered with the paperwork. He was the sort of guy who couldn't sit still for long. He'd switch the channels all the time when they were watching the TV. This annoyed her, but she didn't say anything to him about it. They were spinning at different RPMs, but she loved him. And he loved her.

When they had worked for the other company, they would go on dates and he would talk about how much good work he would do and all the money they would make once they were married and out on their own. She would dream of the things they would buy with that money, and how they would have kids and how the kids might someday join them in the family business, and how well they'd all do. It all seemed so simple and they were filled with hope.

So they were married. They quit that company and started this business and they did pretty well at first. The kids followed before long, and, lately, they were sucking her attention away from him and from the business, and he resented that, although he was ashamed to mention these feelings to anyone. He just held them inside like hot coals.

She continued to try to be as methodical as ever, giving her time to the kids, and to the bookkeeping, and to the paying of bills that, more and more, were way past due. And too much was happening all at the same time. And it was getting scary because there wasn't enough work coming in anymore, and something was terribly wrong and she didn't know what to do about it. The supply house had called that morning and said that they were putting her on C.O.D., and she was embarrassed by that, and ashamed. And then he walked through the door. And he didn't know what to say to her about this.

So he sat in his chair and he watched as she cried into the throw pillow and said things to him that a wife should not say to her husband. And while he listened to his partner sob, he wondered if he had made the right decisions in his life.

And she, in her sobbing, wondered if he would walk the few feet to where she was lying, and just hold her for a moment. But he was waiting for that moment to pass – just hoping that it would soon run its course and pass.

And then it began to rain softly. So they listened alone to the sound of the rain.

And neither partner knew what to do next.